SECRET PLACE
OF THUNDER

CHENEY DUVALL, M.D.
5

Lynn Morris & Gilbert Morris
Secret Place of Thunder

BETHANY HOUSE PUBLISHERS
MINNEAPOLIS, MINNESOTA 55438

Published by Bethany House Publishers
A Ministry of Bethany Fellowship, Inc.
11300 Hampshire Avenue South
Minneapolis, Minnesota 55438

Printed in the United States of America.

Library of Congress Cataloging-in-Publication Data

Morris, Lynn.
    Secret place of thunder/ Lynn Morris and Gilbert Morris.
      p.   cm. — (Cheney Duvall, M.D., ; #5)
    ISBN 1–55661–426–8
    1. Duvall, Cheney (Fictitious character)—Fiction. I. Morris, Gilbert. II. Title.
III. Series: Morris, Lynn. Cheney Duvall, M.D. ; 5.
PS3563.O874435S4   1996
813'.54—dc20
                                       96–45784
                                          CIP

IN LOVING MEMORY

Great-aunt Geraldine, who laughed with me;
Great-aunt Goldie, who took care of me;
Grandmother Jewel, who loved me no matter what;
and
Grandmother Margucrite,
who made me fried squash blossoms.

I miss you.

Thou calledst in trouble,
And I delivered thee;
I answered thee
In the Secret Place of Thunder . . .

Psalm 81:7

Contents

PART FIVE ▪ THE CONGREGATION OF THE MIGHTY

PROLOGUE

The Seventeenth of January, 1867
La Maison des Chattes Bleues
Louisiana

Mr. and Mrs. Richard Duvall
Duvall Court
New York

Dearest Irene and Richard,

Where is Cheney? Truly, I thought she would be here by now. Am I to understand that she is still flitting about in Charleston? It is most important that she come with all speed, because the servants and share-croppers are still taking ill with this mysterious malady, and it is really quite tiresome and upsets the entire household. Once I was unable to get the Amethyst Room aired for an entire week! Also, Elyse keeps fussing on that something is wrong with some of the crop, although how she thinks Cheney can remedy that is beyond me. And truly, those vaudou upset all of my schedules, and besides that they frighten some people. Elyse is frightened, but I am not. When do you think Cheney will arrive?

Your loving Tante Marye

Darling Irene and Richard,

Don't pay any attention to what she said because I am not frightened by the vaudou, although Marye hides whenever they come, especially at night because that is upsetting. However, some of the indigo plants are sickening and I cannot for the life of me understand it, and besides that some of the sharecroppers are sick, and I do think Cheney could help with that, of course. Can you write her and ask her to hurry, please? Thank you, and we love you both very much.

Your loving Tante Elyse

A MISCHIEVOUS

· PART · ONE ·

DEVICE

For they intended evil against thee:
They imagined
a mischievous device,
Which they are not able to perform.

Psalm 21:11

1

La Maison des Chattes Bleues on Bayou du Chêne

"Ghosts . . ."

Cheney Duvall whispered the word. Behind her Shiloh Irons was stretched out on the deck of the flatboat, his back up against one of Cheney's great trunks, his long legs crossed, and his wide-brimmed gray hat pulled down over his face. He stirred slightly but did not look up.

In a low, tense voice Cheney called, "Octave, *haltez le bateau! Attention!*"

Though she had spoken in French, Shiloh stirred and looked up. Cheney was a stark figure outlined in the harsh circle of light cast by the kerosene lamps hung at the corners of the prow. She stood at the side, grasping the rope rail tightly, her back stiff. Shiloh could see nothing beyond the white glare of the lamps. Octave, the boatman, steadily poled the flatboat, ignoring Cheney's command to stop. With a muttered exclamation Cheney hurried to the prow and turned out both of the lanterns, then turned back to look off the starboard side.

Shiloh got to his feet and hurried to her, blinking quickly, his eyes struggling to adjust to the sudden muddy darkness.

Wordlessly she pointed.

Looming up close beside the boat was a burned-out hulk of a great stern-wheeler. In the bayou blackness the riverboat was a sad but eerie sight. Listing slightly, forever moored on a sandbar, the skeleton retained a semblance of its former grandeur but with the air of a sepulcher, its grave clothes long, ghostly tatters of Spanish moss. It looked like a huge, shambling tomb, and its gray outlines resembled a hundred black eyes and rotting teeth.

"What is it, Shiloh?" Cheney asked even more quietly than before. He barely heard her.

"It's nothing to be afraid of, Doc," he whispered back, and he touched her arm reassuringly. "It's just a wreck—"

"No," she interrupted in a hiss. "*That!*" Her long white finger jabbed toward the hulk again.

Shiloh obediently looked up and saw it—or them.

Flickering, phosphorescent green lights, two of them high on an upper deck, one below, almost on the level of the bayou mud, danced up and down. Through the square blackness of a porthole he saw a tatter of white fluttering, then it disappeared; then it appeared about forty feet down in another porthole and disappeared. The foul green lights went out all at once. Then one appeared up top, brightened for a brief moment, then slowly began to fade. Again white flutters showed through the portholes.

Cheney swallowed hard and murmured, "What in the world is it?"

Shiloh shrugged. "Ghosts."

Cheney almost made a heated retort, but she was mesmerized by the frightening sight and remained silent. Shiloh kept searching the hulk through narrowed eyes, his tense stance belying his careless tone.

"Some t'ings worse dan ghosts, mam'selle."

Cheney and Shiloh had completely forgotten about Octave. Now they turned to the boatman, who was poling them up Bayou du Chêne as fast as he could, his eyes searching resolutely ahead. He was small, but wiry and strong. The tendons in his arms stood out in thick cords as he pushed the square flatboat along the bayou.

"Wh-what? What did you say, Octave?" Cheney asked in a rather high voice. Then she smiled weakly. "What could be worse than ghosts in a burned-out hulk deep in the bayou in the middle of the night?"

Octave poled the boat, his jaw set, and made no answer.

Cheney turned back to stare at the riverboat. They were passing the bow, and soon a turn in the bayou would hide the haglike sight from them. As they passed, both she and Shiloh unconsciously turned their bodies to watch it, until they were both facing backward. Neither of them felt comfortable with the immense skeleton, with its ghosts and phantom lights, behind them.

Octave shifted his frozen gaze first to Cheney's face, then to Shiloh's, and finally answered Cheney's question.

"*Vaudou.*"

★　★　★　★

Two hours up the Mississippi River from New Orleans was Bayou

16

du Chêne—"bayou of the oak"—and two hours more down Bayou du Chêne was La Maison des Chattes Bleues. Along the great river were rolling farmlands, thick woods of cypress, magnolia, and cottonwood, and dozens of tributaries, large and small, lazily winding into and out of the wide muddy expanse.

But Bayou du Chêne drifted south through a wild and alien country. Junglelike swamps often melted into the bayou, where the earth seemed unable to make up her mind whether to be land or water, and finally melted into a combination that was both and neither. Great cypresses crowded around the flatboat, their mourning shawls of lacy gray Spanish moss sometimes brushing down to the still surface of the secret streams. Cheney wondered how Octave knew where the course of the bayou actually lay. She glanced at him and saw that his pole still measured about four feet into the brackish water when he pushed. But when he lifted it up, fully two feet of the end was dribbling black ooze. Cypress knees formed ramparts of the huge trees, some as tall as three feet, some small and dangerously pointed. The knees rose everywhere around them, and again Cheney wondered how Octave managed to miss them.

Suddenly the land rose again, and the sides of the boat almost touched either bank. Willow trees grew lopsidedly, their soft sad fingers brushing Cheney's face, and nervously she swatted them away. Shiloh still stood beside her, and he tried to reach up and hold the green curtains aside as the boat made its way slowly. Farther along, the width of the bayou increased somewhat, but the great trees on either side almost formed a tunnel. Owls hooted eerie warnings, immense bullfrogs bellowed, small scrabblings sounded in the branches of the trees close overhead. Furtive splashings were the only water sounds the "sleeping water" of the bayou made. Once they heard a loud splash, and once Cheney thought she saw a log with eyes. The log suddenly glided past the boat, causing Cheney to start and take a deep breath. She knew, of course, that the Louisiana bayous were teeming with alligators, but she hadn't been prepared for her first casual meeting.

At last the bayou forked into two branches, the mouth of these tiny tributaries forming a small lagoon. On the rising bank on the left Cheney and Shiloh could see occasional soft points of light far off. Les Chattes Bleues was still awake, and the thought of the warm glow of candles in windows made them both feel relieved.

Expertly Octave poled the boat straight to a good-sized cypress dock with a gazebo behind it. The land rose up to a gentle slope, heavily wooded, but Shiloh's night-eyes could pick up a wide avenue between great trees, and the occasional candle-glimmer far off at the end of the way.

Cheney and Octave spoke together in low voices, Octave in short, curt sentences, and Cheney in hesitant French phrases. Octave was an Acadian, a descendant of those sturdy Frenchmen who had fled France in the 1500s because of religious persecution and had finally settled in Nova Scotia. In the bewildering twists and turns of the Seven Years' War, England had expelled the Acadians from Canada in 1755, and the Spanish government in Louisiana had offered them a home. By 1763 they had begun to found settlements deep in the swamps to the south and west of New Orleans. The Acadians were a proud, passionate people, and they had stubbornly formed their own closed society, adhering to their culture, traditions, and language. Although Octave spoke French, it was almost a different language from Cheney's classical Parisian French; she learned later that the Acadians still spoke a version of sixteenth-century provincial French.

"Octave said we can go on up to the house," Cheney said at Shiloh's elbow. "He'll secure the boat and bring the luggage."

Shiloh jumped onto the dock, which was blessedly fixed, and held out his arms for Cheney. He grasped her firmly around the waist, conscious that his hands could almost span it, and set her down as lightly as a butterfly. Her face was averted, her hat shadowing her features, and he wondered if she was blushing. She always did when he touched her, no matter how casually.

"Are you sure that's what he said, Doc?" he teased as he took one of the kerosene lanterns in one hand and offered the other arm to Cheney. "Sounded to me like you two weren't exactly meeting in the middle, if you get my meaning."

She clasped his arm close. "No, I'm not completely certain what he said. Either he is bringing the luggage, which is *le bagage*, or he is going to take a bath, which is *se baigner*. I chose to believe he was saying he'd bring up my trunks," she finished primly.

Shiloh laughed. "I choose to believe it, too. 'Specially since that means I don't have to haul 'em like I already have all over creation." Cheney's trunks—by quantity, girth, and heft—were legendary.

Cheney pinched his arm but said nothing. They walked through the open gazebo and started up the rise. Soon they were in a wide bower, with great live oak trees towering above their heads like the eaves of a great cathedral. No breeze stirred them in the heavy Louisiana night. Though it was February, the air was warm, and Cheney and Shiloh could feel its moistness. Their footsteps crunched along the broad way, and Shiloh lowered the lamp so he could see the surface. Bleached white shells formed the pathway.

It was a long way to the house, perhaps half a mile. Though two rows of windows on the first and second floors flickered with candlelight, the outlines of the house were indistinct until Cheney and Shiloh were quite close. When Shiloh could see the house clearly he was a little surprised; he had vaguely been expecting turrets and battlements and gray stone walls, something Gothic, something a lord would have built in eighteenth-century France on a high hill overlooking the sea.

But by the time Cheney's great-grandfather, Augustin-Caron-Philippe de Cheyne, fourth son of the sixth Vicomte de Cheyne, had turned thirty in the year 1801, he had not been tempted by castles and lords. He had built a sturdy, serviceable, practical Creole house on his 3,500-acre indigo plantation. It was a big house, but not grand.

Built entirely of cypress, La Maison des Chattes Bleues was constructed in the eminently sensible West Indies plantation style, with wide galleries all around the first and second floors, a high peaked roof, asymmetrical chimneys, and triple dormers. The added Creole flair was integrated by the use of interior chimneys, large columns on the lower story, and colonnettes on the upper floor. The house was, of course, raised so that the erratic water table and flood waters of the delta country could not invade.

Shiloh studied the house and decided it looked inviting and warm, even in the night. "Now tell me the name of this place again," he prodded Cheney.

"La Maison des Chattes Bleues," Cheney answered.

"And that means 'the house of the blue cats.'"

"Yes."

Shiloh was silent for a few moments, and Cheney watched him defiantly. Finally he drawled, "Well, I can see why y'all always say it in French. I guess I don't need to call your great-aunts' place a blue cat house."

"Shiloh!"

"Well, didn't you just say that's what it is?" he said innocently.

"No! I mean, yes! I mean—that's what the—but it's ... it's ..."

Cheney knew she was sputtering. "It's not named after—because of—my aunts! It's—"

"Your great-aunts," Shiloh said helpfully.

"It's because of the dogs!" Cheney almost shouted.

"Oh, I see," Shiloh said with exaggerated patience. "Yes, Doc. It's named 'The Blue Cat House' because of the dogs. I was going to guess that. Really."

"Oh, for heaven's sake!" Cheney said, and then she laughed. "You'll see when you meet the dogs, and in the meantime learn to say it in French, Mr. Irons! And you really are the most infuriating man I've ever met!"

"I know, you told me 'bout a million times. But you like me, anyway."

She looked up at him. In spite of his teasing tone, his face was grave, and he was staring hard at her. "Yes," she said softly, "I do."

He seemed satisfied, and they walked to the house in companionable silence. Their footsteps echoed hollowly on the steps and across the wide gallery, and the knocker on the door clicked brassily in the quiet. Though the night sounded with a thousand crickets and cicadas, and bullfrogs called continuously near and far, still the darkness seemed to envelop them in a heavy veil of quiet.

The air is heavier, and it mutes the sounds, Cheney thought, breathing deeply. Southern Louisiana nights always smelled of rich wet earth and growing things. *I'd forgotten . . .* It had been twelve years since she'd visited her great-aunts.

The door opened on silent hinges. A tall, slender Negro man stood holding a candelabra, the twelve candles flickering weirdly in the air stirred by the open door. He stepped aside and bowed. "*Mademoiselle* Duvall, please come in," he intoned in a deep, rich voice, the formality of his address matching his black suit, white shirt, and black tie.

"*Bonsoir*, Monroe," Cheney said, matching his formal tone. "May I present my friend and medical assistant, Mr. Shiloh Irons. Shiloh, this is Monroe."

"Pleased to meet you, Monroe."

"*Monsieur*, it is my pleasure. I will take you to your great-aunts, *Mademoiselle* Duvall, they are expecting you. And your luggage?"

"The boatman said he'll bring it up," Cheney replied, "but I'd appreciate it if you'd see to it, Monroe."

"Very well, *mademoiselle*. They are upstairs in the parlor."

Shiloh was looking around the room with interest. The first floor seemed to be a series of open parlors on the left-hand side, and the right-hand side of the house was a single great formal dining room. A massive table and chairs were centered on what was actually the right half of the house, with six white pillars in a row serving in place of a wall. At Monroe's words, Shiloh looked for stairs but saw none, and to his surprise the butler and Cheney turned to go back out the front door.

"Sir?" Monroe said politely, holding the door open.

Shiloh followed obediently and saw that outside staircases on each end of the house, shielded by louvered screens, went up to the second floor. Monroe led them upstairs and to one of many doors lining the gallery. Shiloh reflected that each room must have an outside entrance and wondered if there even was an inside staircase.

"*Mademoiselle* Cheney and *Monsieur* Irons," Monroe said to the room, then stepped aside for Cheney and Shiloh to enter.

Cheney stopped abruptly and Shiloh bumped into her. "Mother! Father! You're already here!"

She ran into the room.

Richard Duvall jumped out of his chair, his arms wide, and Cheney threw herself into them. He lifted her up in a bear hug. "Cheney, dear! I've missed you terribly!"

"I've missed you too, Father," she whispered against his neck.

Shiloh shifted awkwardly from one foot to the other. Richard Duvall hurried forward, one arm around Cheney's waist and the other extended to Shiloh. Shiloh noted that Richard barely limped, though a silver-headed malacca cane was propped against his armchair. Richard was tall, although not quite as tall as Shiloh's six-foot-four, with thick silver hair and steady gray eyes.

"Shiloh, so good to see you. Thank you for taking care of Cheney and bringing her to us safely."

"My pleasure, as always, sir."

"Hmm! Maybe I took care of him and brought him safely, Father!" Cheney teased.

"Doubt it," Richard Duvall grumbled. "Here, Cheney, let Shiloh see the ladies. Rude of me to jump up and dance around right in front of them. Here's Irene, Shiloh."

Cheney's mother, a glimmer of flowing satin in the soft candlelight, rose, kissed Cheney, then took Shiloh's hand. To his great pleasure, she pulled him slightly, causing him to bend over so she could kiss his cheek. Irene Duvall was small, with fair skin. Her hair was a rich auburn glow with a single white streak at the right temple, and she had a beauty mark, which Cheney had inherited, high on her left cheekbone. "Hello, Shiloh. It's so very good to see you again. Please, let me introduce you. This is my aunt, Marye-Rosarita de Cheyne Edwards. Tante Marye, may I present to you Mr. Shiloh Irons, Cheney's medical assistant and a good friend of our family."

A thin, gaunt woman with bright white hair sat stiffly erect in a horsehair armchair. Her eyes were faded blue and glittered as she looked Shiloh up and down. Finally she extended a paper-white hand. Shiloh pressed her cool hand to his lips briefly and murmured, "It's a very great honor to meet you, Mrs. Edwards. Thank you so much for graciously inviting me into your home."

The sharp blue eyes softened, and Tante Marye nodded with approval. "I'm very pleased to meet you, Mr. Irons, and you are most welcome here at La Maison des Chattes Bleues."

Gently Irene led Shiloh to the next armchair, and a lovely little woman bounced up, her dark eyes dancing like a young girl's. "I'm Tante Elyse, Mr. Irons. May I call you Shiloh, too? And oh! You are so very handsome!" She was short and curvaceous, almost plump, and to Shiloh's surprise she was olive-skinned. Her face was unlined, her expression bright and youthful, and her black hair had no trace of gray. If he had not known she was Cheney's great-aunt, Shiloh never would have guessed that this woman was—must be—almost sixty years old.

"This is my aunt, Querida Elyse de Cheyne Buckingham. Tante Elyse, it is my pleasure to present to you our friend Mr. Shiloh Irons." Irene smiled indulgently as Shiloh took Tante Elyse's hand and kissed it. It was rough and work-worn, as contrasted with Tante Marye's soft parchment fingers.

He looked back up and grinned devilishly. "It's a very great honor to meet you, Mrs. Buckingham, and thank you for the compliment. I would be very pleased if you would call me Shiloh."

"And you must call me Tante Elyse," she said, smiling.

"That's quite forward, Elyse," Marye grumped. "I can't believe you're making a scene already."

"But he is so handsome, is he not, Marye?" Elyse said, still clinging to Shiloh's hand and searching his features with evident pleasure. "And so tall! And such wide shoulders! Cheney, dear, aren't all the ladies madly in love with him?"

"I grew weary of that subject long ago, Tante Elyse," Cheney warned as she kissed her aunts. "And don't encourage him. He's quite intolerable already. Victoria! I'm so happy to see you! I can't believe you decided to come, but I'm glad you did."

Victoria Elizabeth Steen de Lancie rose gracefully to embrace Cheney and offer her hand to Shiloh. Cheney's friend was a small-boned woman, delicate and languid, her silvery blond hair shimmering in the muted glow of the room. "Hello, Mr. Irons. Oh, Cheney, I'm glad to see you! I've missed you so much. And New York is so tiresome this time of year, and your parents were kind enough to invite me to accompany them, and I did want to see you again. Your great-aunts have been gracious enough to make me very welcome, despite the fact that I'm an uninvited guest."

"Nonsense," Tante Marye intoned. "Any friend of the Duvalls is always welcome to Les Chattes Bleues, and that includes you, Mr. Irons. Please, everyone be seated. Cheney, don't sit on that chair. It is entirely too scratchy and you will fidget. Mr. Irons, perhaps that divan will accommodate you comfortably."

"Perhaps they can sit wherever they'd like," Elyse said faintly.

Tante Marye ignored her. "I know you and Mr. Irons are tired, Cheney, but I've directed Monroe to bring up a light supper for you and tea for us. We can visit for a while, and then I know you'd like to retire for the evening."

Wearily Cheney removed her gloves and sat down in the green velvet armchair as Tante Marye had directed. "I'm tired, I'm travel-stained, and I'm too warm! I can't believe it's so warm, and I'm wearing these heavy woolens!" Cheney's traveling dress was a simple chocolate brown skirt with a matching Zouave jacket with gold braid. She had worn a wool mantle in Charleston, which was still in the grip of an icy winter, but even without outerwear Cheney had found her winter clothing too heavy as soon as they reached New Orleans. "And I have six trunks, all full of winter clothes," she groaned.

"Sounds like a visit to a dressmaker in New Orleans to me," Richard sighed. "Or to several of them."

Irene looked amused. "I brought some of your summer clothing, Cheney dear, but naturally I couldn't bring enough. We shall certainly

23

be obliged to buy some light dresses, as it seems that spring has already come upon us here."

"And I deliberately did not bring enough summer clothes," Victoria added with satisfaction. "I need a new summer wardrobe anyway, and I know of a quite satisfactory dressmaker in New Orleans. I'm certain, Mrs. Duvall, that she will be happy to oblige you and Cheney."

"Well, that takes care of our most important concerns," Richard said under his breath.

"It certainly does not, Richard," Marye said with spirit. "What about this illness that everyone at Les Chattes Bleues is coming down with?"

"And what about my indigo?" Elyse demanded.

"Don't worry, *mes tantes,*" Irene said soothingly. "Richard and Cheney and Shiloh will take care of all of this. Now, Cheney looks exhausted and even Shiloh looks tired. Suppose that just tonight we let Shiloh and Cheney tell us about Charleston and their trip?"

"Before I do—have the horses arrived? Are they all right?" Cheney asked anxiously. A friend of Cheney and Shiloh, Allan Blue, had escorted their horses, Sock and Stocking, to New Orleans from Charleston on a freighter.

"Oh yes, Cheney, Mr. Blue delivered them three days ago," Tante Elyse answered quickly. "Such wonderful horses! So gentle, but energetic . . . especially when one has grapes on one's person, they are quite insistent . . ."

Shiloh nodded wryly. "Yes, we should attach warnings to their bridles. They'll knock you winding if you have a single grape anywhere. So Captain Blue treated them all right?"

"He's a captain?" Tante Elyse said in surprise. "He didn't tell me that. But, yes, the horses looked marvelous, exquisitely groomed, and they had obviously been exercised regularly. But I didn't have time to ask Mr. Blue many questions, as he was in a great hurry to get back to New York and had booked on a freighter the same night he arrived! He didn't even stay for a meal."

"He was terribly anxious to see his wife and children again," Cheney said with satisfaction.

Victoria looked bored and said in a ho-hum voice, "And that is one reason why I came to New Orleans. Since Mr. Blue has finally regained his senses, I knew he would be begging to help Jane Anne at the orphanage. I'm certain they won't need me for a while."

"Oh, how is the orphanage, Victoria?" Cheney asked eagerly. Victoria was the patroness of the Behring Memorial Orphanage in Manhattan.

"It's doing wonderfully well," Victoria replied with satisfaction. "When I left Jane Anne had just gotten a brand-new baby, a beautiful little girl . . . left on the steps of St. Patrick's. . . ." Her voice trailed off, and her cornflower blue eyes looked into the distance with unmistakable sadness.

Cheney was surprised; Victoria de Lancie had come to her last year to request an abortion. But when Cheney examined her, she found that Victoria had a number of ovarian cysts, which required surgery. Victoria would never bear children. But even after Victoria had become a Christian, Cheney somehow thought that her friend wasn't interested in children, mainly because she hadn't seemed too interested in marrying again. Now, however, Cheney could see that Victoria was certainly touched by the thought of the newborn baby, and she wondered how much Victoria had changed in the last few months.

"I . . . I know that the new baby has found the best home possible," Cheney said hesitantly. "God must have watched over her very carefully."

Victoria was still lost in her thoughts, her eyes searching an unknown vision. Shiloh thought, *Mrs. de Lancie doesn't look like herself. She's usually so . . . cool and composed . . . and sharp. . . . Wonder if this has something to do with Devlin Buchanan? She seemed awfully upset when he left Manhattan and took off back to England. . . .*

With a quick, shrewd glance at Victoria's wistful face, Irene smoothly said, "Please, Cheney, I'm so anxious to know about Charleston! How was your visit? Your letters were rather vague about everything except about straightening out the misunderstanding with Mr. Alexander Dallas."

Cheney glanced a warning at Shiloh and said hurriedly, "Oh, it was a good visit, Mother. Charleston is a lovely city. And I got to know one of the city's most well-respected physicians and tour his hospital, which I enjoyed very much. And, of course, it was quite interesting making the acquaintance of General Nathan Bedford Forrest."

"I've always wished I could meet him," Richard declared. "He was a fascinating opponent, I must say. But, Cheney, I never understood why, exactly, he was in Charleston."

"He . . . he has a brother there, Father. He was . . . um . . . visiting

25

him, you see," Cheney replied with some difficulty, dropping her eyes. Cheney had become embroiled in quite a tangle with General Forrest and his brother, Shadrach Forrest. Once she and Rissy had been in grave danger, but she surely didn't want her parents to know about that.

"Oh yes," Shiloh drawled, his blue eyes sparking with mischief. "General Forrest and his brother became good friends with the Doc. She got to know so many people in town . . . like a judge, and some of the provost marshals, and—"

"You really should talk to Shiloh about his war experiences with General Forrest, Father," Cheney interrupted with desperation, her sea-green eyes turning a poisonous shade as she glared at Shiloh. "He does enjoy talking so much, I'm sure he can tell you everything. Probably more than you really care to hear."

Irene sighed and shook her head slightly; she knew very well what these signals and glances between Cheney and Shiloh were all about. Cheney had, as usual, gotten into some kind of danger in Charleston, and she didn't want to tell her parents about it, and Shiloh was teasing her unmercifully. Richard merely looked confused, his honest gray eyes going back and forth from Cheney's frown to Shiloh's lazy grin.

"I'm really very tired," Cheney said, theatrically biting back a yawn. "And there's something else I wanted to talk about."

"What's that, Cheney?" Irene asked.

Cheney looked around at everyone, her eyes finally resting on her father's face. "We saw something . . . odd, something . . . frightening tonight. On the way down the bayou. And Octave, our boatman, said it was the *vaudou*. What is that, Father? What is the *vaudou*?"

Richard's eyes went to Tante Marye, who sat up even more stiffly in her chair. "I don't want to discuss them right now, Cheney," she said harshly. "Some things are not meant to be talked about in the dark of night."

"You're afraid, Marye." Elyse's voice was soft and full of pity.

Marye's eyes narrowed. "Yes. I'm afraid. And I think that soon all of us will be."

2

DE CHEYNE LEGACY

Tante Marye kept the remainder of the conversation resolutely light, so everyone had tea while Cheney and Shiloh ate a light supper of fruit and cheese, and no one mentioned the ominous *vaudou* again. Shiloh was disappointed, for he was very curious; he also had to admit to himself that he felt a strange sense of foreboding, almost of dread, much the same as he had experienced when he saw the burned-out riverboat. It was not fear—he didn't actually feel that he and Cheney were in physical danger—but yet something about the eeriness of the scene in the bayou and the dread in Tante Marye's voice when she spoke the mysterious French word made Shiloh's senses come to full alert. He was a naturally intuitive man, and sometimes he felt things, saw things, knew things about other people with a certainty that was almost uncanny. He felt an aura of menace, of peril, in the dark depths of Bayou du Chêne and surrounding La Maison des Chattes Bleues.

He was tired, however, and he dismissed all such oppressive thoughts. About midnight Tante Marye announced that Cheney and Shiloh should retire, so the party broke up with plans for everyone to meet at a late breakfast. Monroe solemnly announced that he would escort Shiloh to his *garçonniere*. Shiloh had no earthly idea what this was, but he wearily followed the butler back outside, downstairs, and down a path through a garden. To his delight, he found that a *garçonniere* was a little house, constructed especially for the sons of the household or gentlemen visitors.

His *garçonniere* was octagonal-shaped, with two stories. The lower story was a pleasant study with a marble fireplace, two oversized leather armchairs studded with silver tacks, a sturdy cherry desk, and a glass-fronted bookcase with a pleasing assortment of books.

A steeply spiraled staircase wound upstairs, and Shiloh was especially glad to find a grand half-tester bed invitingly turned down to reveal fresh white linens. He didn't care that the bed was made of the finest rosewood, exquisitely hand-carved by the famous New Orleans craftsman Prudent Mallard. He was, however, glad to see that it was unusually long. He only had time to wonder if the de Cheyne men were tall before he fell into a heavy, dreamless sleep.

The following morning he heard small sounds downstairs and he came fully awake at once. He was about to jump out of bed when a voice called softly, "Good morning, Mr. Irons. Here are coffee and fruit. Breakfast will be served in an hour."

"Thank you . . . um . . . whoever," he called back, struggling to get dressed quickly.

A whisper of a giggle drifted upstairs, and he barely heard the voice say, "I'm Chloe, sir."

Shiloh frowned as he pulled on the same clothes he'd worn last night and decided not to attempt his boots. Barefooted, he hurried down the stairs, reflecting that Creole society must indeed be very different from New York society. In New York, among the Duvalls' set, gentlemen were waited upon by menservants. Shiloh shrugged; he could not imagine any impropriety allowed in the services of Marye-Rosarita de Cheyne Edwards' household.

A young girl stood by the tea table, dressed in a simple black dress with a clean white apron. She wore a *tignon*, a headdress traditionally worn by free women of color in New Orleans. The *tignon* was a brightly colored Madras handkerchief, or two or three handkerchiefs of contrasting colors, wound cleverly about the head. Large gold hoops hung from her pierced ears.

Chloe, Monroe's youngest daughter, was just sixteen. Both Monroe and his wife, Molly, were mulattos; Chloe looked more white than either of them. She had delicate tan skin, smooth dark hair, a small nose, and a cupid's-bow mouth. Her eyes were modestly downcast, but she furtively watched Shiloh as he came down the staircase.

"You don't have to stay and wait on me, Chloe," he said casually. "Thank you for bringing this, though." A tray with a silver coffee service and a bowl of apples and grapes was on the tea table between the armchairs.

"Mr. Irons, if you will give me your clothes, I'll see to it that they're cleaned and pressed." She gave him the briefest of glances and the slyest of smiles.

Warily Shiloh replied, "Thank you, but that's not necessary. I'll see to them myself. You may go now." He wanted no part of this young girl's flirting.

Her full lower lip pouted a little. "Yes, sir," she said obediently and breezed out the door.

Shiloh forgot her as soon as she was out of sight. Women of all shapes, sizes, ages, and intentions had flirted with him since he was sixteen years old. Shiloh liked women, and they could see it in him, and they instinctively liked and trusted him. Also, he was extraordinarily fine-looking, with his shiny golden hair, clear blue eyes, straight thin nose, even white teeth, and lean, muscular body. He was aware, of course, that he was a good-looking man—it would be stupid to try to pretend he didn't realize it—but it was of little import to him, as he knew that it was simply a legacy of his parents, whoever they were. Shiloh was an orphan and had never known his mother and father.

The coffee was thick and strong and was laced with chicory. Shiloh gulped down two cups, demolished an apple and all the grapes, and hurried back upstairs. In the modest armoire he found his shirts neatly hung up and his breeches folded. He chose a simple tan muslin shirt and denim jeans. His Western boots were muddy and travel-stained, so he wore his cavalry knee boots.

He followed the curving path through the lovely garden back up to the front door of the house. Unsure of the etiquette involved, he decided to knock, but through the open window he heard Cheney call, "Shiloh! Come on in, silly, so Monroe won't have to come fetch you!"

"Cheney, behave yourself," he heard Tante Marye say sternly. "Ladies do not call out of windows to gentlemen."

"Yes, ma'am," Cheney was saying meekly as Shiloh came into the dining room.

"I should think that Cheney could call out to Shiloh in such a situation, Marye, as he wouldn't presume to enter the house without instruction," Elyse said thoughtfully.

As usual, Tante Marye acted as if Elyse had not spoken. "Mr. Irons, please make yourself as comfortable here as if you were in your own home. Certainly it is not necessary to knock each time you wish to come into the house. We have the *garçonnieres* to lend privacy and comfortable accommodation, but their removal from the main house should not discomfit you."

"My *garçonniere* is marvelous, Mrs. Edwards," Shiloh said warmly. "And now that I understand the rules, no one will have to call out instructions to me and get into trouble." He winked at Cheney, and even Tante Marye's eyes twinkled.

The formal dining room was immense, as it was fully half the house. Six white pillars stood in a row to the side of the front entrance. The floor was a chessboard of black-and-white Italian marble tiles. Everyone was gathered at one end of an immense Empire mahogany table that could seat at least thirty people. The chairs were Louis XVI, with cane backs and seats for coolness, and extra chairs were lined against a far wall. The room was light and airy with many tall windows, and all of the white shutters were opened to the morning.

Since it was ten-thirty, they did not have a breakfast buffet on the sideboard but a combination of breakfast and lunch served by Monroe and his wife, Molly. Richard was seated at the head of the table, with Tante Marye on his left and Tante Elyse on his right. Irene sat by Elyse, and Cheney and Victoria were seated by Marye. Shiloh took his seat by Irene, and immediately a plate was placed in front of him. It was filled with honeyed strawberries, biscuits, butter, sliced ham, and an egg cup holding a large brown egg, which Shiloh eyed warily.

Richard said grace and everyone began to eat hungrily. The food was delicious, and Monroe and Molly unobtrusively offered replenishment whenever anyone finished any item on the plate.

"Now, then, Cheney, please tell us what happened to you two last night on the bayou," Richard said firmly. "We'll explain to you about the problems Marye and Elyse have here, but I'm very curious about this."

Cheney's voice dropped to a low, tense tone. "It must have been a terrible accident. There is a wrecked riverboat on Bayou du Chêne north of here. It's—it was burned, and some of it was blackened . . . but you could still see the paddle wheel, and the outside of the frame was still a deadly white blur. It was covered with Spanish moss, long trailing tatters of it. . . ." Cheney shivered slightly and looked gravely at her father. "But even worse, when we came by it last night—it—there were—" She glanced at Shiloh, who nodded warmly at her, and she went on, "There were ghostly white . . . things floating around on it, Father. Several of them, on all the decks. They just . . . flitted through it, so you could see them clearly one moment, and the next you were straining your eyes and thinking you were imagining things, but then you'd see them again, in another place . . . and the lights. Just glowing, really, a putrid green hue, and they floated, too, and came on and went out, and then came on again. . . ."

Everyone looked startled. Irene turned pale, and Tante Marye's thin lips were compressed even tighter.

"How very odd," Richard said quietly. "Shiloh, did you see or notice anything else?"

"No, sir," he replied. "It was very odd, and I can't explain it."

Richard chewed thoughtfully for long moments, his eyes staring into the distance. "We came downriver, you see, and entered Bayou du Chêne from the north, so we didn't pass this hulk."

Elyse murmured, "Oh, it's awful, it was a horrible accident. It happened three years ago. Because the bayou had shifted, you see, the *Creole Princess* ran aground. But there was a terrible explosion and fire, and eighty-one people died."

"Oh, Elyse, tell it correctly," Marye said with exasperation.

"I thought I did," Elyse said with wide doe eyes.

Marye grimaced and turned to Richard. "All our troubles began because Bayou du Chêne has shifted its course, you see. It cut the new channel over there"—she pointed north—"about five years ago and isolated that accursed triangle of land. Meanwhile the water levels shifted very slowly, until the *Creole Princess* grounded that terrible night. But still, they think that the explosion and fire happened first, because no one survived. It would seem that if they had grounded first . . ." She made an expressive Gallic gesture with her upturned hand.

"They could've just gotten off the boat," Richard finished.

"Perhaps, if they'd climbed the bank," Elyse said in a low tone of dread. "But that sandbar—it's quicksand, you see, and . . . and . . . twelve people were never found. . . ."

"Horrible," Irene shuddered.

"Lovely breakfast conversation," Victoria remarked coolly.

"Perhaps I'd better talk to Shiloh in private later," Richard said with concern.

"Yes, do," Tante Marye said with finality.

"Marye, that's silly," Elyse said indignantly. "We're all here, and it's all part of our troubles, you know."

Now Tante Marye seemed uneasy and unsure of herself. "But Mrs. de Lancie and Irene don't have to deal with all of this unpleasantness, do they?"

"You just don't want to deal with it, Marye dear," Elyse said comfortably. "And that's quite all right. Richard and Shiloh can come with me to see Gowan."

Shiloh looked mystified, and Tante Marye rolled her eyes and explained, "Gowan Ford is our overseer and also our largest sharecropper. He knows everything about everyone. Mr. Ford will be able to talk to you about Les Chattes Bleues in a coherent manner," she finished with heavy meaning and a glance at her sister.

Elyse smiled vaguely and asked, "What are you ladies going to do today?"

"I'm going to stay with Tante Marye and help air the Blue Room linens," Irene announced. "She's promised me some of her mother's beautiful handkerchiefs with the Spanish lace if I help."

Victoria was smiling, but Cheney secretly thought she looked rather wan and pale as she said, "I'm going to go hide somewhere in these magnificent gardens and paint. It's so cool and pleasant, and I'm certain I can hide so well that no one will be able to find me and see my hideous paintings. I only allow Zhou-Zhou to go with me, because she is so silly she thinks they are marvelous paintings, and tells me so quite often." Victoria Elizabeth Steen de Lancie rarely went anywhere without her maid, especially if it meant that Victoria's hair might get mussed or her shoes might get dusty.

"I'm coming with you," Cheney said. "We have so much to catch up on. You can paint, and I won't watch."

"Fine." Victoria nodded. "Just so you don't look. I should be so embarrassed if anyone actually saw a painting of mine."

"I'm certain they're wonderful," Cheney argued, "because you wouldn't do it if you weren't accomplished at it."

"Perhaps I'll let you see one," Victoria said languidly, "just so I can prove you wrong."

Cheney turned to Tante Marye. "But didn't you say last night that someone was sick? Should I see them today?"

"None of the house servants are sick—right now. They weren't yesterday, anyway, dear," Tante Marye answered in an ominous tone. "But Gowan will know if any of the sharecroppers have gotten ill again."

"Then I'll go with Tante Elyse and Father and Shiloh first, and find you later, Victoria," Cheney decided. "And I am looking forward to seeing Mr. Ford again."

"He's looking forward to seeing you, too, Cheney," Elyse said, smiling happily. "You always were a great favorite of his, you know. Especially after you asked him to marry you."

"What!" Shiloh exclaimed.

"Tante Elyse!" Cheney said, blushing hotly.

"She was seven years old at the time, and Gowan was about thirty," Tante Elyse said mischievously. "But then again, Gowan never did marry. . . ."

"Broke his heart, huh, Doc?" Shiloh teased. "For shame!"

Cheney, regaining her poise, sniffed. "But no, he refused to marry me, you see, so he's the one who broke my heart. And I was so terribly in love with him at the time."

"I gotta meet this man and figure this out," Shiloh mumbled.

Irene raised an eyebrow delicately, but she saw that no one else had heard Shiloh's mumblings, so she said lightly, "Naturally we didn't give Cheney permission to marry Mr. Ford. But I certainly understood why she fell in love with him. He always reminded me of Richard. Why, I was halfway in love with him myself!" she declared with a sly glance at her husband.

"Well, if you all will excuse me," Richard said, pretending to rise, "I must go and challenge Gowan Ford to a duel."

Everyone laughed, but Shiloh noticed that Tante Elyse looked thoughtful and even rather sad.

★　★　★　★

As Cheney, Shiloh, and Tante Elyse walked to Gowan Ford's cottage, Shiloh asked courteously, "Tante Elyse, I would very much like to know some of the history of this place. The Doc's told me a little, but not much."

"You truly would?" Elyse asked, her brown eyes shining. "You're not just being polite?"

"He's not that polite, Tante Elyse," Cheney teased. "If he asked, he must really want to know."

"I do," Shiloh said solemnly.

As Tante Elyse began telling the legacy of the de Cheyne family, Cheney thought, *I know I've heard it at least a dozen times, but I never get tired of it. . . . It seems I hear something new each time Mother or Tante Elyse or Tante Marye tells the story. . . .*

The de Cheyne family were the *seigneurs* of a rich champagne fief in Varennes, awarded in 1589 to Henri Philippe de Cheyne by his third cousin, Henry IV, the first Bourbon King of France. Two hundred years later, the sixth Vicomte de Cheyne ruled his rich fiefdom, his serfs, his wife, his mistresses, and his sons in much the same way: with careless indifference as long as he was unquestioningly obeyed, with sternness when he was questioned, with cruelty when necessary. His eldest son would inherit the title, the lands, and his father's disposition. The two younger sons were wild, careless, and completely dissipated by the time they were eighteen years old.

But the youngest Vicomte de Cheyne was different.

Augustin-Caron-Philippe de Cheyne loved his mother dearly and pitied her greatly, for his father was cruel to her. The one time he had tried to defend her to his father, he had been savagely dressed down in front of her, and then the vicomte had railed at her for days. Augustin never openly defied his father again.

He met Lausanne-Heloise-Jacqueline Bayard when he was seven and she was three. She was the daughter of the governess who served the Nicoise family, wealthy merchants who lived in nearby Valmy. The governess was said on the one hand to be a widow, and on the other hand never to have been married. But Augustin de Cheyne didn't care, and by the time he was sixteen knew that he would marry Lausanne Bayard. They married in 1790, when he was nineteen and she only fifteen.

Though the Bastille had fallen in that hot summer of 1789, and Paris had become a city besieged, Augustin-Caron-Philippe de Cheyne, a young noble of the Second Estate, an accursed *aristo* of the *ancien régime*, barely took note. His father practically lived in Paris, his brothers took no note of him, his mother had died the year before, and Lausanne Bayard filled his thoughts and his heart.

But when Augustin became a husband in 1790, and a father in 1791, the Revolution suddenly became real to him, a tangible danger, a physical threat to him, to his wife, and his infant son.

His father and brothers scarcely noted when Augustin announced that he was moving his family to Cap Français in Saint-Domingue. His father owned a small sugarcane plantation there, and Augustin requested that he be given this as part of his inheritance. His father acceded to his request with great relief. Augustin's three brothers constantly nagged the vicomte for more and more riches, and the plantation Augustin asked for was a modest portion, indeed. Augustin,

Lausanne, and Maxime-Louis-Augustin de Cheyne moved to their new plantation.

The next year, 1792, France imploded and the Reign of Terror began. Augustin's father and his three brothers all met Madame Guillotine in that terrible summer of blood. Augustin did not even hear of their executions until September.

In peaceful, tropical Cap Français, the news seemed alien, inexplicable, and even as he grieved, Augustin was grateful for his family's salvation. It was a week before he realized that now, instead of holding a courtesy title, he was the seventh Vicomte de Cheyne. As far as France was concerned, of course, this was irrelevant at best and criminal at worst, and Augustin tried to put away all sorrow for his lovely home in Varennes and his lost heritage.

But this interval of peace for the surviving de Cheyne family was not to last long. The slaves in Saint-Domingue had never, and would never, bow to the yoke. In the bloody revolt of 1791 they had risen up and killed their white masters. In 1793 they burned Cap Français and massacred thousands of colonists.

Augustin de Cheyne and his family barely escaped with their lives and fled to America. Because it was at least half French, and Augustin was desperate for any touch of home, he landed in New Orleans, Louisiana.

But desperate white colonists were not the only import from Saint-Domingue. Negro slaves had been imported from that dark island and would continue to be until all slave traffic was finally, forever, stopped. A great many of the Negroes in New Orleans were from Saint-Domingue. When they came, they brought their religion with them, and it was voodoo.

★　★　★　★

Tante Elyse finished telling the story to Shiloh as they walked through the magnificent gardens toward Gowan Ford's house. Behind them Cheney and her father walked, talking together in low voices.

"So it's a religion," Shiloh said thoughtfully, taking short, slow strides to accommodate the tiny woman on his arm. "But what does all this have to do with you and your sister and this plantation?"

"I don't know," Elyse replied innocently.

Shiloh hid his smile. Tante Elyse might not be the sharpest woman in the world, but she was certainly truthful.

They passed through manicured gardens, set off into neat squares, each with different varieties of flowers. Once they passed twin gardens on each side of the path with elaborate six-foot fountains centered in the square. The two fountains were mirror images of three dolphins facing one another, the topmost dolphin spouting a stream of water toward the mild blue morning sky. Some of the gardens were lined by neat white picket fencing, some of them were bordered by shrubs, some were formed by lining the squares with the same shells that formed the great walk in the front of Les Chattes Bleues.

The wide walk narrowed to a footpath through what at first seemed to be a garden, untended and run wild. Then, as Shiloh's eyes adjusted to the wildness, he could see a certain order, a certain deliberation, although it was altogether unrestrained. The path wandered and curved, and side paths came in and out, forming odd corners. Here and there he caught glimpses of groups of large rocks, carefully arranged to fit with the flowers surrounding them, but with a pleasing randomness. "Now this is a great garden," he murmured. He liked the exuberance of it, compared to the precise geometric presentation of the formal gardens.

Tante Elyse beamed. "I call it my Serendipity Garden. Marye hates it. She calls it The Untidy Acre. But it doesn't matter, because Marye never comes outside anyway."

"Never?"

Elyse shrugged carelessly. "I'm so glad you like this garden best! Men do, I think. Except for the Japanese garden, which has a sort of quietness that men seem to like. But I haven't finished it yet, and Gowan does complain so about trying to keep up the pool. He says that this whole state is knee-deep in water, and I have to go and have a pool in one of the few places where there isn't any. To say nothing of how much he hated trying to buy the rocks. Said he felt like a pure fool, buying rocks. Did you know there are no rocks in the southern part of Louisiana? So it seems to me that bringing in decorative rocks, to be seen and enjoyed in a Japanese garden, can only be good for the soul. . . ."

As this gentle tirade went on, Shiloh reflected that Gowan Ford must be a patient and long-suffering man.

They rounded a corner in the path, and two immense black dogs bounded up the path toward them, their black mouths wide open, their teeth dripping. But they made no sound. Shiloh stopped dead in his tracks, then instinctively tried to step in front of Elyse; but she started running like a young girl. Then she dropped to her knees on the path and held out her arms.

"Riff! Raff! Come here, boys! Oh, I've missed you!"

The two dogs, still without making a sound, began to bound in silly circles around the kneeling woman, pawing her, licking her face, almost knocking her down in their joy. Elyse petted them, shook their paws, and rubbed their ears, all the while talking the most inane nonsense Shiloh had ever heard.

Cheney and Richard, smiling indulgently, moved up close to him. "Are these the famous blue cats?" Shiloh teased.

Elyse looked around and said, "Oh no, Shiloh dear, these are dogs."

Everyone burst into laughter, but Elyse paid them no mind. She had made a grave error in turning around, however, as it put her off her center of gravity; Riff brushed against her in a bound, and Elyse sat down hard on the path.

Shiloh rushed toward her, and suddenly Riff and Raff turned into snarling monsters. So quickly their movements could barely be seen, they stepped in front of Elyse, their teeth bared, growling low in their throats, their powerful hindquarters quivering for a spring.

Shiloh stopped dead, dropped his eyes, and didn't move.

Elyse, who had almost had her breath knocked out of her, managed to recover somewhat. "Riff, Raff," she said softly, "it's all right, really. This is Shiloh, and he's a friend."

Shiloh was amazed at the response in what had been only moments before two vicious killer dogs. Immediately they became overgrown puppies, their tails wagging, their eyes bright, hackles down and smooth. They looked up at him apologetically but didn't approach him.

Slowly Shiloh put out one hand and said in a low, friendly voice, "C'mere, you thugs." They bounded toward him and he petted them both with rough affection.

Richard and Cheney hurried to Elyse, who was still sitting comically on the ground, watching Shiloh and the dogs. "Are you all right, Tante Elyse?" Cheney said anxiously as they helped her up.

"Oh, of course," she replied calmly, making dusting motions at her knees. "Riff and Raff always knock me down. Marye gets mad at me because I get my clothes so dirty, but I can't imagine why. After all, Molly does the laundry and she never complains. Besides, Molly likes

Riff and Raff." Her attempts at dusting off did no good, of course, on the rich, thick delta dirt, and she had two round dirt-prints on the knees of her white apron. Her posterior also had an earth impression. Unselfconsciously she dusted behind her, but it did little good either. At least it was not quite so noticeable, as her skirt was dark gray.

"I've never seen attack dogs respond to such a kindly command," Shiloh commented. "Normally when they're upset you have to shout at them."

"Oh, these aren't attack dogs," Elyse said affectionately, moving again to caress the dogs. "They're just good dogs, and they take care of me. But they mind, you see. They listen to me, and understand me, and do whatever I say."

"They're beautiful dogs, Tante Elyse," Shiloh said in a kindly tone. "But what are they? I've never seen this breed before."

"They're Catahoula Leopard dogs. Most people call them Catahoula Curs," Elyse said proudly, taking Shiloh's arm again and starting back down the path. The dogs ran back and forth and all around Shiloh and Elyse and Richard and Cheney. "The Catahoula Indians bred them from Spanish war dogs and the red wolf. This particular strain—blue-black, white blaze on the chest, black mouth, and blue eyes—was developed by my father."

Riff and Raff were muscular dogs, but lean. They had broad, well-rounded heads, well-defined cheeks, and powerful jaws that looked as if they could do a great deal of damage. With their long bodies and hocks well let down, they did move in a manner that was rather feline.

"Hmm . . . I bet I can guess how this place got its name now," Shiloh said, smiling down at Elyse. "A little girl keeps hearing them called 'Catahoula Curs,' and their coat is so black it looks bluish in the sun, and with those blue eyes . . ."

Elyse looked delighted. "I can't believe it! You're the first person who's ever guessed. And yes, it was I who kept calling them 'the blue cats' when I was little." She sighed and looked up at Shiloh through her long thick lashes. "What a wonderful man! So handsome, and smart, too!"

"Tante Elyse, stop flirting with him," Cheney said grumpily from behind them. "I told you, he's so conceited already."

"No, I'm not," Shiloh grinned. "I'm a pretty humble guy."

"Modest of you to say so," Cheney retorted.

"I know."

"I give up," Cheney grumbled.

"I wouldn't do that if I were you, dear," Elyse said with an innocent air.

Richard Duvall began to chuckle, but Cheney pinched his arm and changed the subject. The four of them continued down the garden path accompanied by "the blue cats."

3

PERCEPTIONS

Gowan Ford's house was cypress—called "wood eternal" in Louisiana—and two stories, but was much smaller than Les Chattes Bleues. It was modeled after the logical West Indies/Creole fashion. Raised on the inevitable pilings, the pretty house had the ever-present wide galleries on both stories. As Shiloh, Tante Elyse, Cheney, and Richard came out of the wilderness of the Serendipity Garden, they could see Mr. Ford sitting on the gallery waiting for them. Elyse waved and called out, "Hullo, Gowan! Here we are!"

Cheney thought with amusement, *Tante Marye would be positively scandalized, but then again I do think that's precisely why Tante Elyse does these things.* The dogs bounded up onto the gallery, and Gowan Ford rose slowly from his planter's chair to greet them.

"Hello again, Gowan," Elyse said agreeably. "Here's Cheney and Richard. And this is Shiloh Irons. Shiloh, this is Gowan Ford."

Richard missed a step as he walked up onto the porch, but he recovered quickly. Shiloh looked at him and saw that his face was frozen into a startled expression. Then Shiloh saw Cheney; she had stopped dead, one foot on a stair, her face riveted on Gowan Ford's, her eyes dark dull green with shock. Bewildered, Shiloh followed her gaze to Gowan Ford.

He was about fifty-five, six feet tall, with thick black wavy hair and silver streaks at the temples. Dressed in a simple white shirt, gray waistcoat, gray breeches, and knee boots, he looked exactly like the overseer of a large plantation who has just come in for lunch. Ford was lean and slightly stoop-shouldered, with a strong jaw and prominent nose.

But Shiloh saw first the empty right sleeve, the patch over his right eye, and the ropy scars on the right side of his face.

"Elyse, you didn't tell them, did you?" Ford growled in a deep baritone.

"Hmm . . . wha—Tell who what?" Elyse said, obviously lost. She was looking quizzically up at him and took no note of Richard's and Cheney's discomfort.

Ford shook his head and a grim smile turned his mouth crooked. "Elyse, I swear the Good Lord does watch over you," he muttered, then moved slowly to Richard, his hand outstretched. "Colonel Duvall, it's a great pleasure to see you again."

Richard shook his hand and murmured, "It's good to see you again, Mr. Ford."

With quiet grace Ford moved toward Cheney, who was still frozen midway on the stairs. Very slowly he extended his left hand and spoke softly, as if he were coaxing a small, frightened animal. "Miss Cheney, I know I could give a person nightmares, but I tell you it's surely me. Elyse ought to have warned you."

"Oh, Mr. Ford . . . I . . . I'm so sorry! How unforgivably rude of me!" Cheney said. She hurried up the stairs to grasp his hand in both of hers. "And of course you're not frightening, or . . . or . . . anything like that! You—it was just such a shock!"

"Ohhh," Elyse moaned, her eyes wide. "I forgot. Gowan went away to fight in the Late Unpleasantness and got shot."

"Thank you so much for telling us, Elyse," Richard said with mild irritation.

"But I just forgot, Richard," Elyse said in a small voice.

Privately Shiloh reflected that this was not a lack of perception on Tante Elyse's part. Instead, it reflected a true perception of Gowan Ford. Quite simply, Tante Elyse didn't see an empty sleeve and ugly scars and a lost eye—she just saw Gowan Ford. Shiloh liked Tante Elyse even more.

Cheney finally recovered and smiled brilliantly up at Ford. "It's just because she doesn't see you as any different from before, Mr. Ford. And I think you look dangerously handsome and daring with that eye patch. Would you consider marrying me now?"

Gowan Ford laughed, a deep pleasing baritone rumble. "Miss Cheney, it's going to take a man with more than one hand—maybe even more than two hands—to deal with a double handful like you!"

"That's the truth," Richard and Shiloh mumbled in unison.

Ford turned and held out his hand to Shiloh, who took care to shake hands with his left. "It's a pleasure to meet you, Mr. Irons. For the life of me I haven't been able to get Elyse to make sense about you, but you look capable of explaining yourself."

"Yes, sir, I generally can," Shiloh said with a grin. "It's a pleasure to meet you."

The little party sorted themselves out and decided to sit out on the gallery. Ford disappeared into the house, promising lemonade, while Shiloh and Richard seated themselves in the handsome mahogany planter's chairs and Cheney and Elyse sat on a bamboo loveseat piled with overstuffed pillows in bright floral chintz.

"Gowan made this loveseat, you know," Elyse said quietly. "I just never think about it, or notice it. I truly didn't think about telling you, Cheney, dear."

Cheney patted her hand. "It's quite all right, Tante Elyse. Believe me, I think that makes you a very special person."

Gowan Ford returned, balancing a heavy tray in his left hand. Deftly, by some sliding motion that was hard to see, he set it down on a table by the loveseat. "Would you serve, Elyse?" he asked.

"Certainly, Gowan," she answered and proceeded to drop shards of ice from a small wooden bucket into the tall glasses, then pour lemonade from a battered tin pitcher.

"I didn't know you went into the army, Mr. Ford," Richard said. "Elyse and Marye didn't tell me." His voice held the mildest of reproofs; he hadn't realized that Irene's aunts had been without Gowan Ford's protection during the war.

"I'm not surprised," Ford shrugged. "Elyse can handle this plantation just fine by herself. She doesn't need me, never has, she's just gotten used to me being around."

"True," Tante Elyse agreed as she handed out tall frosty glasses of lemonade.

"Elyse!" Richard said sternly.

She turned wide dark eyes to him. "Well, it is true! And you, Richard, you felt that it was your duty to go off to the war and leave Irene, didn't you? How did she fare without you?"

The sudden surprise on Richard Duvall's face was comical, and Cheney stifled a giggle.

Shiloh said easily, "These de Cheyne ladies do seem to make it fine on their own. Good thing for us they get used to having us around." His Caribbean blue eyes were trained right on Dr. Cheney Duvall, and she blushed and looked down into her glass of lemonade.

"And I don't want you men to start talking about the war because we'll be here all day and all night," Elyse said firmly. "I want to talk about Les Chattes Bleues. Tell them, Gowan."

"Tell them what, Elyse? The whole history of this place starting in 1792? Haven't you told them anything?"

"Yes," she answered with spirit, "I told them the history of the de Cheynes up until 1792."

Gowan Ford took a long swallow of lemonade and said dryly, "Well, that's sure some lot of useful information, isn't it, Mr. Irons?"

Shiloh grinned. "Actually, I did find it interesting, and it did—eventually—lead into the *vaudou*. Suppose you pick it up there."

Ford's single glittering dark eye narrowed. "The *vaudou*," he spat. "Those people ought to be declared criminals. But"—he shrugged one shoulder—" 'Vengeance is mine, saith the Lord.' I hope I'm not here when He gets around to it with that bunch, and they're going to wish they were somewhere, anywhere else, I think.

"It all started—here at Les Chattes Bleues, anyway—when Bayou du Chêne cut that course over there." He pointed northwest.

"Where the lagoon and landing are now used to be just a wide place in the bayou, and it looped on up and around about a mile farther north and finally meandered back to the river. But we had a flood in '61, and when it went back down, a big piece of Les Chattes Bleues had just sunk, and the bayou cut a new course around to the west. It isolated a triangular shape of land."

"Yes, it's quite noticeable," Cheney said thoughtfully. "On the other side of the lagoon, yes? A high rise with those huge oak trees crowning it?"

"That's right, Miss Cheney." Gowan nodded. He made a careless gesture, and the ice in his glass of lemonade clinked loudly. "On the night of December eighteenth of last year, I saw a fire on that rise. A big fire. I hurried across and those accursed *vaudou* were dancing around a big bonfire, and—" He glanced cautiously at Cheney and Elyse before continuing. "Well, they were there. I spoke to that woman, Dédé, who calls herself the *mambo*. She told me that this was 'spirit' ground, and the *loa*—that's the spirits of the dead—told her that she and the *vaudou* had a right to be there. She also informed me that the whole of Les Chattes Bleues was on 'spirit ground,' and that the *loa* would have it back from the unbelievers who thought they owned it. That these spirits had already started setting apart the land when they water-enclosed that triangle. That was the gist of it, anyway."

He took another long drink. Everyone else sat in stony silence. Richard was appalled; Cheney was stunned; Shiloh was worried. Elyse sighed softly and toyed with a corner of her apron.

"All right," Richard said, frowning. "Tell me about the people who've been sick."

Obediently Ford responded in a reporting tone. "First Diana Court, one of the sharecroppers, got sick. She was sick for three days, and then she was fine. Next was one of the other sharecroppers' children, Leah, her name is, and then her mother and father and both sisters and one brother all got sick in the course of one day. The children stayed sick for a week, but the adults got better in three days. Then one of the oldest women on the plantation, a lady named Dolly, got sick, and she almost died. Finally, after a week, she got better, but she hasn't quite regained her strength. She just came down with it two weeks ago, and that was the last one."

Immediately Cheney started asking rapid-fire questions. "What were their symptoms? Were they all similar? Did they—"

"Cheney, darling," Richard said gently but firmly, "first I want to get the whole picture from Mr. Ford. Then we'll sort out the specifics. Don't start looking at just the details first, or you'll have a good chance of missing the main problem and also its solution."

Cheney looked rebellious for only a moment and then smiled. "Yes, Colonel Duvall. I'll defer to you since you're the strategist and tactician." Richard had been an adviser to General Ulysses S. Grant in the war, and he had been a good one.

Richard smiled at her, then turned back to Gowan Ford. "What about the crop? The indigo plants?"

Ford considered for long moments, studying the verdant view of the garden. "I can't say yet that the problem with the plants is connected, Colonel Duvall. We just don't know what's wrong with them."

"It's inexplicable, right?" Richard said quietly.

"Yes, for now."

"And so is this illness?"

"To me it is."

"And both of these problems began after the *vaudou* started meeting over at the rise?"

"Yes."

Shiloh, Richard, and Gowan Ford all frowned darkly. "Too many coincidences in too short a time," Richard muttered. "Bound to be all the same problem."

"But ... wait ... you mean that these people, these *vaudou*, are actually harming the sharecroppers?" Cheney asked, stunned. "And sabotaging the crops?"

"I'm going to go on that assumption," Richard said with quiet determination, "and I'm going to pray that it's wrong."

★   ★   ★   ★

With directions from Monroe, who always seemed to know where everyone was at any given moment of the day or night, Cheney found Victoria up by the bayou, close to the lagoon landing. A thick wood of cypresses, cottonwoods, magnolias, and weeping willows grew all along the bayou, which formed the north and west boundaries of the de Cheyne plantation. The vicomte had allowed the trees to remain, but the undergrowth was always cut back so that the barrier formed deep glades. Now, in the warm but weak sun of early spring, the woods were quite gloomy and dark. Ahead of her Cheney saw Victoria, her cream-colored morning dress a light blur moving slowly along the bank of the bayou. Cheney thought again that Victoria seemed distant and rather sad.

Finally Cheney caught up with her, and Victoria turned to smile and give her a quick hug. "Have you done all your unpleasant business, Cheney?" she asked lightly. "Being in this place, hearing about your blue blood, should remind you that you should be a lady of leisure."

"Sounds boring," Cheney said mischievously. "Besides, you're leisurely enough for the both of us. You aren't even applying yourself to that most genteel of ladylike occupations—painting muddy watercolors."

"I have decided that I dislike watercolors intensely," Victoria said with exasperation. "It is the most difficult medium. It takes half a day to gather your paints and supplies, half a day to clean up the mess, and two minutes to do a painting. It's the most tiresome pastime."

Cheney entwined her arm with Victoria's, and the two wandered along the bank of the bayou together. "Um, here is a novel concept for you to consider, Victoria. Why don't you do something you like, instead of something you despise?"

"Because I don't like anything."

"My, my, we are petulant this morning, Mrs. de Lancie," Cheney said with heavy humor. "Victoria, what on earth is the matter? Are you ill?"

Victoria sighed, then squeezed Cheney's arm lightly. "No, no, of course not. I'm never ill, and I find women who always think they are to be quite tiresome people. It's a most absurd convention these days, for women to pretend they are all frail and vaporish and lightheaded. 'Empty-headed,' I think, describes them more accurately."

"That sounds much better," Cheney teased. "Haughty and sarcastic as usual. But I'm not going to allow you to change the subject, Victoria. I'm not only your friend, I'm your physician. Is anything wrong? You do look rather pale and wan, I think."

Victoria looked unsure for a moment, chewing delicately on her bottom lip. Then her expression changed into languid, heavy-eyed boredom. "But my dearest Dr. Duvall, you know that white skin is so very fashionable these days. I must say, though, that after seeing these lovely, exotic Creole women—like your Tante Elyse—that I think we pale ghosts suffer in comparison."

Cheney relented; she knew that Victoria was not going to confide in her now. "Isn't it true!" she exclaimed. "It's odd that the standards of beauty are so different here. But so many of the families here have Spanish blood—like my great-aunts—that I suppose that rich olive-colored skin is recognized as being lovely."

"I'm unclear about that," Victoria said vaguely. "About the Spanish blood. I thought that your . . . um . . . great-grandfather, the vicomte, was married to a French woman?"

"His first wife was French," Cheney replied. "My great-grandmother. She bore him four sons; she died having the fourth son, my grandfather, Leopold Alexandre Severin de Cheyne. A year later the vicomte married a Spanish woman, Doña Isabella Maria Rosarita Querida de Galvez, who was Tante Marye's and Tante Elyse's mother."

"How terribly romantic and aristocratic!" Victoria announced. "But . . . hmm, that means that actually Tante Marye and Tante Elyse are really—how does one say it? Your half-grand-aunts? Grand-half-aunts?"

Cheney giggled. "It's much easier just to say Tante Marye and Tante Elyse. And aren't they so different? Tante Marye looks like my great-grandfather, Mother says, and Tante Elyse is like Doña Isabella. Instead of being the true Creole mix, one of them seems to be French and the other Spanish."

"And as I said, I must admit that the Creole women with that Spanish look are quite lovely." Victoria dropped her voice to a conspiratorial tone. "And what about the quadroons?"

Cheney looked bewildered. "Quadroons? What about them?"

Victoria's blue eyes widened with disbelief. "Oh, Cheney, surely you aren't that naive? You know about the quadroon balls, don't you? And about the quadroon and octoroon women who live in those little one-story white houses along Rampart Street?"

Cheney's cheeks flushed a deep pink and she said primly, "No, Victoria, I know nothing of the little one-story white houses along Rampart Street, and I don't want to know. And neither do you."

Victoria laughed, a light, careless sound that was pleasing for Cheney to hear after her friend's previous dismal disposition. "Oh, but that's the difference between me and you, Cheney, dear. You don't want to know these things, and I dearly love to know them."

"No, you don't," Cheney insisted. "You just love to talk about them to shock me."

"It's amazing to me that you, being a physician, are so easily shocked," Victoria teased. "I'll bet that if we stay here very long, Shiloh will be invited to attend one of the quadroon balls. Then we can get him to tell us all about it. White ladies are never allowed to attend, of course, as if any of us would if we should receive an invitation; but handsome young men of social stature are—"

"Victoria! Really! Shiloh will do no such thing!" Cheney finally exploded.

"Are you so sure?"

"Of course!"

"Hmm. Perhaps you don't know him as well as you think?"

Cheney narrowed her eyes to slits and stared at Victoria. "What are you implying, Victoria? Do you know of something stupid that Shiloh has done, or . . . or . . . is going to do? What is it?" Cheney was almost shouting.

Victoria immediately looked repentant; she had not anticipated such a passionate response from her careless teasing. Suddenly Cheney looked shocked herself, for she realized how angry she was, and how silly it was, and how embarrassing it was to be caught getting angry over Shiloh.

"*Malédiction!*" Cheney fumed. "Victoria, why are we having this ludicrous conversation? I have serious things to do and serious things to think about!"

"I'm sorry, Cheney dear," Victoria said softly. "I know I'm hard to deal with this morning. I was just talking stupid nonsense. Please don't be angry with me. You're the best friend I've ever had, and more than anything I want you to stay my friend."

Cheney stared at her for long moments, startled at this display of vulnerability from Victoria Elizabeth Steen de Lancie. It was not often that Victoria allowed herself to show her true emotions, and suddenly Cheney was a little ashamed of herself. "I can't quite piece together how and why I'm so upset, Victoria, and to tell the truth I feel rather silly. But of course I'm your friend, and I always will be."

Victoria listened anxiously to her, her lovely cornflower blue eyes searching Cheney's face. When Cheney finished, Victoria sighed again, then said gaily, "Tell me all the gossip about Charleston, and Rissy and how you let her get away from you. Really, Cheney, you must learn how to keep good servants. I have forbidden Zhou-Zhou to get married at least a dozen times," she finished with a sniff.

"Which tells you how seriously she considers it," Cheney laughed. "And I wouldn't dream of trying to keep Rissy and Luke Alexander from getting married. They are so happy, and I believe the Lord made them to be together."

Victoria gave Cheney a strange look. "Do you really believe that, Cheney?"

Cheney stared at her. "What? That Rissy and Luke should be married?"

"No, not exactly," Victoria said. She stopped, pulled her arm away from Cheney, and restlessly plucked a long wand of green from a willow tree. She was looking down, and her voice was slightly muffled. "I mean—do you think—that the Lord designs us to love, and to be married, to one specific person?"

Cheney had led Victoria to the Lord less than six months ago, and Victoria was a devout Christian. But, unlike Cheney, the Steen family were Christians in name only, and Victoria had never received a true grounding in the Bible and had never been taught the realities of a loving Father God and a personal Savior in His Son, Jesus Christ. In so many ways Victoria was like a child, still learning, and Cheney appreciated that Victoria asked her these questions.

But this particular one was rather difficult for Cheney to answer.

Victoria had married—an arranged match—a much older man when she was very young. Lionel Jann de Lancie had died in the war, but Victoria had told Cheney very little about her marriage and her husband. Cheney wasn't sure whether Victoria was going through some sort of delayed grieving process, or if she was wondering if Jann de Lancie was the only man she might ever love—or if it was something else entirely.

Finally Cheney answered in a gentle voice, "I think that when we surrender completely to the Lord and seek His counsel, He sets us in a place of peace, joy, and security in the knowledge of His will. I think this knowledge comes to us in all things—love and marriage included." Cheney hesitated, then moved to put her arm around Victoria's slim waist. "Victoria, are you thinking about getting married again?"

Glancing at Cheney's face for only a brief moment, Victoria murmured in a choking voice, "Cheney, I can't stop thinking about it . . . but it's no use. He doesn't—he can't—I don't think—"

With difficulty Cheney asked, "Do you mean that this man doesn't—isn't interested in you, Victoria?"

"I think he is," she whispered.

"But . . . please, Victoria, please tell me he's not married," Cheney moaned.

"No, he's not . . . married."

Cheney hugged her lightly and smiled. "Then, darling, he won't be able to resist you, if you sincerely believe that he's the man the Lord has for you."

Victoria Elizabeth Steen de Lancie—acknowledged New York beauty, darling of Polite Society, a worldly wise woman, an extremely wealthy woman—continued to stare down at the weeping willow branch in her white-gloved hands. Tears began to fall on the slender leaves, sliding down their smooth verdant surface to drop to the earth below.

4

INDIGO HORIZON

The night Cheney had arrived at Les Chattes Bleues, she had naturally been happy to see her parents again, as she had been in Charleston for over a month. But she was very glad, and secretly vastly relieved, that they had brought Nia Clarkson with them. Cheney did not exactly admit to herself that she needed a personal maid—much less a chaperone—but still, she was glad to see Nia.

The Clarkson family was inextricably intertwined with the Duvall family. Dally—she had no last name in those long-ago days in Georgia—had been Irene Cheney's slave and had come to New York with Irene when she married Richard Duvall. The Duvalls had soon manumitted her and offered her a position as their housekeeper. Dally married Big Jim Clarkson, who was the blacksmith at the small Duvall Iron Foundry. Dally and Big Jim had three daughters: Rissy, Tansy, and Nia, and one son, Demi-Jim. Rissy Clarkson was born exactly one month before Cheney Duvall, and the two had been lifelong companions. After Cheney graduated from medical school and began her journeys, Rissy accompanied her to Arkansas in 1866 and to Charleston the previous month, serving as Cheney's chaperone, personal maid, and best friend.

But in Charleston Rissy had met Luke Alexander, and the two had fallen deeply in love. Luke Alexander had wasted no time asking Rissy to marry him. So Rissy had stayed behind in Charleston, and Cheney came on to New Orleans.

As Cheney returned to Les Chattes Bleues after walking and talking with Victoria, she reflected, *Victoria seems so lonely . . . she isn't friends with Zhou-Zhou as I am—was—with Rissy. . . . I miss Rissy so much! I must try to make better friends with Nia . . . I just don't know her as well as I do Rissy and Tansy.*

Cheney liked Nia, certainly, but Nia was only eighteen years old, and with her high, soft, baby-girl voice and shy ways, she seemed even younger. Cheney smiled to herself; her mother worried about Cheney going all over the country unchaperoned—particularly in the company of Shiloh Irons. Cheney was not too concerned with such strictures of society. She had chosen to be a physician, and that already broke so many rules that the one about chaperonage for unmarried ladies seemed unimportant in comparison! But Cheney honored her parents' wishes, so she had always been respectably chaperoned by Rissy.

But Nia . . . will Nia want to pick up and go whenever I decide to . . . if I should decide to? Cheney worried. Then as a huge yawn overtook her she thought, *Maybe I'd better decide whether or not to take a nap this afternoon, instead of deciding my entire future right this minute. . . .*

She reached the louvered French door that led from the second-floor gallery into her bedroom. Cheney loved the bedrooms at Les Chattes Bleues. Each of them was called by the dominant color scheme of the room. The master bedroom, which Richard and Irene were occupying, was done in a deep, rich red; Tante Marye's room was the Blue Room; Tante Elyse's was the Rose Room; Victoria was in the Amethyst Room; and Cheney was in the Gold Room.

The Gold Room had an exquisite hand-crafted bed. Tante Marye had told her that the vicomte had imported the teak and mahogany wood from his plantation in Cap Français, but all of the beds had been made by the New Orleans craftsman Prudent Mallard. Each was done with a different West Indies motif. The bed in the Gold Room was a four-poster, and oversized. It was made of mahogany from Saint-Domingue, its headboard, footboard, and six-foot posts intricately carved with pineapples and palm fronds. The rich mahogany had a brilliant, burnished shine so deep that Cheney could almost see her reflection in it.

An immense armoire from Saint-Domingue dominated one wall. It was inlaid with panels of extremely rare "raisin" mahogany, which was some of the most beautiful wood Cheney had ever seen. But the interior was lined with cypress, and the drawers were made of the same. Cypress truly was the perfect wood for the unbelievable humidity of southern Louisiana. It discouraged mold and mildew, and bugs didn't like it, either.

Nia stood in front of the armoire, carefully smoothing talcum powder on newly ironed handkerchiefs, folding them precisely, and arranging them in one of the deep drawers. She looked up when Cheney came in, smiled sweetly, and said in her little-girl voice, "Hello, Miss Cheney. Mistuh Arns said to tell you that him and Mistuh Ford's gonna go all over the plantation, and he wants to know if you want to go with 'em." She folded the last of the handkerchiefs, dusted her hands in a businesslike manner, closed the armoire doors, and turned to face Cheney. "I say you ought to take a nap."

Cheney laughed as she removed her gloves and hat and seated herself at the small dressing table. "You know, Nia, I was just thinking that you're not much like Rissy, but I might have to revise that opinion. You're bossing me just as she always did!"

"Rissy and Mama says you need bossin'," Nia gravely replied. "An' I may not be as big as them, but I can boss as good as them." Rissy and Tansy both looked like their mother: big-boned, with long arms and legs and strong features. Nia, on the other hand, was tiny and delicate, with large liquid brown eyes. She had worked briefly for Cheney in Manhattan, at her office, and Cheney knew that although Nia seemed little and timid, she had the same wellspring of strength that her mother and her sisters had.

"And I can not mind you as well as I don't mind them," Cheney sassed. "Here, Nia, see if you can do something . . . my hair's coming down back here . . . I declare, it does seem to positively throw out hairpins, doesn't it?"

Nia picked up a silver comb and began poking and prodding at Cheney's hair. "Yes, Miss Cheney, your hair's hard to fix, because it's so thick. But it's about the most beautiful hair I've ever seen, 'cept maybe for Mrs. de Lancie's. Hers looks like silver, pure silver. But Zhou-Zhou says it's hard to fix, too, 'cause it's so fine. . . ."

"Yes, it is," Cheney agreed absently. "Where is Shiloh? Is he waiting for me?"

"Yes, ma'am. He's down in the dining room, I guess, or maybe in one of the parlors by now. Him and Mistuh Duvall and Mistuh Ford decided to have tea with Mrs. Edwards and Mrs. Buckingham."

Cheney frowned as she tried to decide what to do about the servants and sharecroppers who'd been sick. She wanted to see everyone on the plantation, take histories, and see if there might be some common thread in this mysterious illness that was affecting them. But Les Chattes Bleues was a big plantation. Cheney wondered how many people were on the plantation now, including servants, sharecroppers, and their families. Too many for her to see in one day, certainly.

"Miss Cheney?" Nia pushed a final hairpin securely into the thick French roll at the nape of Cheney's neck.

"Hmm? Did you say something, Nia?"

"Not yet. But I have something to ask you, Miss Cheney."

Cheney turned around to look up at Nia. Her heart-shaped face was troubled, and she was looking down, fidgeting with her apron. Cheney got up and went to an intricately carved rosewood chaise, sat down, and patted the damask expanse beside her. "Come here, Nia. Whatever it is can't be that bad. What's the matter?"

Nia moved slowly to perch on the very edge of the chaise. She sat up very straight, folded her hands, and looked across the room for long moments. Finally she sighed. "Miss Cheney, there's nothing at all wrong. But . . . there's something . . . something important . . . that I need to ask you, and I . . . I . . ."

Cheney put her arm around the girl's narrow shoulders and gave her a small hug. "Nia, we don't know each other too well, but you do know that I'm no ogre. Don't ever be afraid to ask me anything, or to tell me anything. I want us to be friends, and I would do anything I could to help you. Just as I know you'd do for me."

"Oh yes, Miss Cheney, I would!" Nia's dark eyes were enormous as she searched Cheney's face. "But . . . this is—" She stopped, took a deep breath, and launched into it. "Miss Cheney, I want to be a doctor. I want to work for you, be your maid, of course, and I promise I'll be a good one! I'll work real hard! But I want you to apprentice me so I can become a doctor."

Cheney was positively stunned. Of all the things she'd thought Nia wanted to ask her—for a night off, perhaps, or to go into New Orleans, maybe with Monroe and Molly's girls, or for a cast-off dress, or maybe for money—but this? Nia, little Nia, with her breathy voice and tiny little girl's hands? A *doctor*?

"I . . . I . . ." Now Cheney was obliged to take a deep breath and start all over again. "Nia, I'm so . . . surprised . . . by this that I can't quite think what to say. I . . . suppose I need a few moments to consider—"

"Will you let me tell you why I decided this and explain to you how important it is?" Nia now seemed determined and more grown-up somehow, now that she'd "waded in."

"Yes . . . yes, of course."

Nia jumped up and stood in front of Cheney, her hands folded in front of her. She looked exactly like a schoolchild about to recite. "Miss Cheney, you're a good lady, but I don't think you've thought much about somethin'. There ain't no—aren't any colored doctors. And there won't be any for a long, long time—not any who'll be able to go to a fine medical school like you did."

Listening to these simple words, Cheney felt positively loutish. *Of course there are no Negro doctors . . . they weren't even allowed to learn to read, in most states! And women . . . Negro women . . . not in a million years will there be a Negro woman accepted at the University of Pennsylvania, or any other accredited medical school, even the ones who have finally taken women. . . .*

"Miss Cheney, I already know what your first thoughts will be," Nia said with an unmistakable plea in her voice. "I know you don't approve of apprenticed doctors."

"Well, that was not exactly my first thought—but no, I don't," Cheney said firmly. "I think, in general, it's a terrible, flawed system. But . . . but . . ." she faltered, and asked with exasperation, "How did you decide this, Nia? And what made you decide to approach me with this?"

"Mistuh Arns," she replied quietly. "I talked to Mistuh Arns about it, back in New York last year. He told me to explain how I felt to you, and to make sure you could see that I don't really have no other way. . . . This is the only way I'll ever learn, don't you see, Miss Cheney? And I knew then—I wanted so bad to learn everything when I was working for you in your office. I tried so hard to learn!"

"You talked . . . to Shiloh, and he—you tell Shiloh your problems? What is it about that man—" With an effort Cheney directed her thoughts back to the problem at hand. "Oh, never mind about him! But . . . but, Nia, I thought you wanted to go work at Duvall Court with your mother, and have your new cottage, and everything. . . ." Cheney finished rather lamely.

Nia smiled. "I tried to be satisfied with that, Miss Cheney, because Rissy was your maid then, and I thought it was the right thing for me to do. But since Rissy's not with you anymore, and Miss Irene does worry so about you traipsin' all over the country with Mistuh Arns, I knew she'd like it if I asked to come to New Orleans and be your maid. And I thought then that the Lord was givin' me my heart's desire, that I been praying for. To learn to be a doctor." Tears welled up in her eyes and shimmered darkly there.

"Oh, blue skies!" Cheney blustered, starting to her feet and pacing restlessly. "Why am I making everyone cry today? All right, all right, Nia, I'll . . . I'll . . . teach you, and let you . . . do everything you want to do! But we'll talk about this being a doctor later!"

Nia flew to Cheney and threw her thin arms around her. "Oh, thank you, thank you, Miss Cheney! So can I come with you and Mistuh Arns now to see about the sick people?"

Cheney laughed and hugged Nia hard. "Nia, I hate to say it, but you do sound as excited about seeing sick people as I used to be—and still am, I guess! Yes, you can come with us. You might as well start right now, because you certainly have a lot of work to do!"

"Thank the Lord," Nia breathed, still hugging Cheney.

"Yes," Cheney agreed softly, "I do, always."

★　★　★　★

"Nia's coming with us," Cheney announced belligerently to Shiloh as she entered the downstairs parlor, "but I'll tell you right now, Nurse Irons, that I'm going to have her arrested if she starts calling herself a doctor!"

"Hi, Doc," Shiloh drawled as he lazily got to his feet. "Hi, Nia. Don't let her scare you, she's bluffing. In fact, I've been her nurse for two years come this April, and then I'm going to start calling myself Dr. Shiloh Irons."

"Shiloh, you'll do no such thing, and I'm not—I haven't—I can't—"

"Make up your mind what to say?" Shiloh asked politely. Nia hid her smile behind one hand.

"Oh! The conversations I've had today!" Cheney fumed. "I'm not going to talk to you for the rest of the day! I'm so tired of talking to crazy people!"

"Uh, Doc, I hate to tell you this, but you're the only one who's ranting and raving like a crazy woman," Shiloh said with an air of concern. "You having the vapors or something?"

"You—!" Cheney's eyes were a jade-green fire, her fists were clenched, and for the second time this day she abruptly wondered why she was acting crazy! She relaxed and began to giggle, then collapsed onto the ornate gold-and-white Venetian sofa. "Nia, maybe I should have taken that nap after all," she said, shaking her head.

"Yes, I know," Nia said primly. "Why don't you? Me and Dr. Irons will go see about these people."

"You two could drive someone crazy," Cheney scoffed, getting up and straightening her hat. "Let's quit talking nonsense and go to work."

★　★　★　★

Gowan Ford rode a fine black gelding, Shiloh rode his horse, Sock, and Cheney's horse, Stocking, was hitched to a small cart. Ford had brought up the cart and horses to the wide drive in the front of Les Chattes Bleues and was waiting patiently for them.

"How did you know to bring a cart?" Cheney asked Shiloh suspiciously. "How did you know I wouldn't be riding?"

"I figured Nia would talk to you, Doc," he answered, "and I also figured she'd want to come with us today. And I also knew—"

"Never mind," Cheney said with irritation. "You always know everything."

"'Bout you, I do," he said lightly. "Make it my business to."

Cheney looked up at him, startled at the turn the conversation had taken, but he was already talking to Gowan Ford.

"Have any trouble with Sock and Stocking, Mr. Ford?"

"No, sir. Good, sturdy horses they are, and amenable to being saddled or hitched either one, aren't they?" Ford replied. He adjusted his wide-brimmed hat, then swung easily up into the saddle of his horse. A rifle stuck out of a saddle holster, and Cheney wondered if he could shoot from the saddle with only one hand . . . she wondered how he managed to do most everything he did, so gracefully and seemingly without effort, with only one hand.

Shiloh helped Cheney and Nia into the little cart, then mounted, and Gowan Ford led them around the small, clamshell-paved road that circled Les Chattes Bleues and led to the miles of indigo fields.

"Thirty-five hundred acres, she is," Ford said proudly. "That's almost five and a half square miles. A great plantation. Rich soil, a growing season that's three hundred and thirty days long, and one of the most beautiful places on God's earth."

"I've never been on an indigo plantation before, never even seen one before," Shiloh told him. "I'd like to see everything. How the plants are processed and the dye extracted."

"Tough crop, and tough product to make," Ford said succinctly. "But a good cash crop, if you're good at indigo. And Elyse Buckingham

56

could make rocks sprout little pebble flowers and then make little stone seeds if she decided to."

"It's funny," Shiloh remarked. "She seems a little flighty, and Mrs. Edwards seems like the strong one. But that's not exactly the way it is, is it?"

"Not exactly," Ford said dryly.

Cheney smiled to herself; Gowan Ford was a man of few words, but he had no trouble making himself understood. "Mr. Ford, how many people are at Les Chattes Bleues now? Including all the sharecroppers, all the servants, and their families?"

"Twenty-nine, Miss Cheney."

"Is that all? Somehow I thought there'd be about twice that."

"There did used to be, Miss Cheney, and that's why you've gotten that impression. But some of the Negro sharecroppers just up and left after the war," Ford answered quietly. "Even though they were already free."

He turned to Shiloh. "The old vicomte learned some lessons the hard way about repression and slavery. First in France, and then in Saint-Domingue. So when he started this plantation, he started all the Negroes—and whites, too, my father included—on a sort of indentured servant basis. When you worked out your contract, you not only weren't indebted to him, but you'd earned some shares in Les Chattes Bleues. Then he worked out a sharecropping system, and you could either cash in your shares, or stay and go on the system. Thirteen of the Negroes were either indentured or were already sharecropping, but they just up and left. Most of 'em slunk away in the middle of the night like they were runaways or something. And we had eight white men sharecropping that joined the army." He shrugged. "I'm the only one that came back."

"But what about the families?" Cheney asked.

"The Negroes that went, all went," Ford answered with typical brevity. "Of the eight white men, John Court was the only one that was married, and Diana Court and her two children are still here, sharecropping sixty-four acres."

Cheney privately thought that she knew who did most of the actual crop work for this widow and her children, and she recalled again how much she liked and respected Gowan Ford. *The Lord is so good to have given* mes tantes *this man to look after them. . . . I wonder why Mr. Ford never married? Surely there have been ladies. . . . He was—is still—quite*

57

handsome, and such a good man. . . .

Cheney pulled herself out of her reverie and said, "I think today I'd just like to see—what did you say the lady's name is? The last one who came down with this sickness?"

"Dolly de Cheyne, and her husband Les de Cheyne." He turned in the saddle to smile at Cheney. "Dolly and Les always said that no matter what anyone was kind enough to call them, they were just poor scared slaves when the vicomte indentured them, and they begged his permission to take his name. There have been eighteen men and women who took that name because they wanted to, because it was a great privilege that the vicomte personally granted them, and because to them it was a name of honor. I hope you see it that way, Miss Cheney."

"Certainly I do, Mr. Ford," Cheney replied with dignity. "I'm honored by the de Cheyne name, too."

"From what I hear, Dr. Duvall, you've earned your own name of honor," Gowan Ford said gallantly. He turned back around, but Cheney could still hear him say clearly, "Just as all the de Cheyne women have."

They rode past indigo fields that stretched as far as the horizon. Though it was only the middle of February, the only month at Les Chattes Bleues that wasn't spent in production of the precious indigo was November. In December the fields were plowed and turned twice, January was planting, and by February the indigo plants—actually they were shrubs—were about a foot high. They flowered in March and produced all of April, May, June, and July—at Les Chattes Bleues, anyway. Ordinarily the entire plant was harvested to produce the dye. But at Les Chattes Bleues, the vicomte had produced such an energetic strain that twelve-inch prunings could be harvested in the months of April, May, and June, and in July the plant was harvested. August, September, and October were spent in processing, drying, and preparing for shipment. It was, indeed, a good cash crop; in fact, Les Chattes Bleues' indigo production was something of a miracle.

Looking out over the fields, Cheney frowned and muttered, "Why, I'm as ignorant as a bird about indigo plants, but even I can see that some of them are sickly!"

Ford and Shiloh turned to view the field on the left. The indigo, as small as it was now, could be seen as separate little shrubs growing in long sharp lines. The very symmetry of the fields was what drew attention to the withering plants with the brown leaves, although they were perceived only as blotchy flaws in the ruler-straight rows.

Shiloh sat up a little straighter in the saddle and narrowed his eyes. "It's not just a row here and there, or like . . . a bad ribbon of ground, is it?"

"No, Mr. Irons. It's single plants all over the place, with no rhyme nor reason," Ford said with irritation. "I've seen lots of crop problems before, you know, like a bad lot of seeds or like you said, when something goes wrong with the soil in a field or part of a field." He shook his head. "But this is just isolated plants, healthy, strong plants that suddenly get sick and die." He sounded desolate, for Gowan Ford loved Les Chattes Bleues. He felt that God had given them these special green plants, in this special place, to provide a good life for them all. It was a personal grief to him when something went wrong with Les Chattes Bleues' indigo.

Shiloh said nothing but continued to painstakingly scan the fields as they passed.

In the middle of the fields was a small home, a square of unplowed ground with great oaks shading a small cypress cottage. The four made their way carefully down a small road—really just a lane—between two indigo fields that dead-ended right in front of the cottage, which was surrounded by a perfect little white picket fence.

As Shiloh and Ford helped Cheney and Nia out of the carriage, a woman came out onto the front porch, drying her hands on her apron. Mr. Ford led them through the gate, doffing his hat as he walked up the little clamshell path to the house. "*Bonsoir*, Dolly. I'm glad to see you're up and around. Allow me to present to you Dr. Cheney Duvall, Mrs. Buckingham's and Mrs. Edwards' great-niece; her medical assistant, Mr. Shiloh Irons; and Miss Nia Clarkson. This is Mrs. Dolly de Cheyne."

The little Negro woman was very short and plump, with sparkling black eyes and gray-sprinkled hair pulled back into a tight bun. She nodded to the company and said a little nervously, "It's an honor to meet you, Miss—Doctah—Duvall, and you, Mistah . . . Mistah . . ."

"Just call me Shiloh," he said warmly, "and this is Nia. We aren't very formal folks. May I call you Dolly, ma'am? You look like a little dolly, I think."

The black eyes twinkled. "You're a one, ain't you? And sure, do call me Dolly—everybody does. Would . . . would you all like to come inside?"

Cheney stepped forward and spoke softly and very gently. "Thank you so much, Mrs. de Cheyne, but we certainly don't want to impose upon you, especially since you've been so ill. That's why we're here, you see. I'm a doctor, and I'm going to take care of everyone here at Les Chattes Bleues for a while. If you don't mind, can we just sit down here on the porch, and you can tell me about your illness?"

Dolly looked up at Cheney with wonder. Cheney was dressed in a robin's-egg-blue walking dress made of the finest silk, designed by Madame Martine of Lord & Taylor's in New York. Her white gloves were of the softest kid, her shoes were dyed to match her dress, her hat was a wide-brimmed white chip with blue satin ribbons and white satin rosettes. Expensive perfume floated in a discreet cloud about her, and her lacy white parasol had matching blue satin bows with white satin rosettes centered on the spines. Dolly de Cheyne thought that in her entire long life of eighty-four years she had never seen a lady that looked less like a doctor.

But this lady was kindly spoken and had goodly eyes, so Dolly said with great dignity, "Why, yes, ma'am, Dr. Duvall, please come up here and sit by me in this rocking chair. It's Les's chair, but I know if he was here he'd be glad to see such a fine lady, and a de Cheyne lady at that, resting in it for a spell."

Cheney smiled, thanked Dolly de Cheyne, sat down, and went to work.

5

UNWHOLESOME ATMOSPHERES, UNHEALTHY HUMORS

"This first course is gombo, and Marye insists upon making it herself. And it's no use asking her for the recipe, because it's a closely guarded secret that will go with her to her tomb," Elyse told the dinner guests.

"That would be a grave sin," Shiloh said, deadpan.

Victoria and Cheney groaned, Gowan Ford grinned, Richard chuckled, Irene smiled, and even Tante Marye's sharp blue eyes gleamed. But Elyse's expressive brown eyes opened wide as she said, "Oh yes, it certainly would be, Shiloh, because we can't inter people below ground here. The water table is so low, you see, that they float back up. It must be in tombs or crypts."

Shiloh's mouth stayed open as he stared at Tante Elyse. Tante Marye made a slight choking sound and dabbed at her mouth delicately with a black satin handkerchief. Gowan Ford rolled his single blue eye heavenward, Victoria and Irene were both blinking rather rapidly, while Richard was trying desperately not to laugh. Cheney, however, laughed out loud. "You know, Tante Elyse, you are the only lady I have ever seen who could render Shiloh speechless!"

"Thank you, *ma petite*," Elyse said with equanimity. Her dark skin seemed even more tinted by the gold of the candlelight, and she wore a white camellia in her hair. All of the ladies were dressed in fine gowns for dinner: Marye in black silk, Elyse in gray satin. Irene wore creamy white satin and had white rosebuds in her hair. Victoria wore pink and had a pink camellia in her hair. Cheney's dress was a golden-yellow color, and she had finally been persuaded by Nia to wear tiny yellow jasmine blooms secured in the curls arranged along the crown of her head.

Finally Tante Marye, after narrowly averting the danger of choking, drew herself up as straight and rigid as a Doric column. "Elyse, we are not now, and will never again, approach that topic at my dinner table. Cheney, you will not now, and never again, indulge her or countenance such indelicacies."

Cheney looked down and toyed with a steaming crab claw in her gombo. "But, Tante Marye," she said weakly, "Shiloh started it."

"No, he did not," Marye said sternly. "Elyse started it. Shiloh is a perfect gentleman, and you would do well to take note of the gallantry of his comportment, Cheney."

Cheney's eyes widened with outrage, and she almost made a quick retort—but she knew she would regret it, because Tante Marye allowed no pertness from anyone, not even Irene Duvall. So Cheney made a quick face at Shiloh, who was looking, Cheney thought, extremely supercilious. Then she lowered her eyes meekly and whispered, "*Tu as raison, ma tante. Je le regrette beaucoup, je serais très bonne.*"

"*Très bien, ma pauvre petite,*" Tante Marye said with approval. "Since you have apologized, and, more importantly, have promised to be good, may we have a conversation that does not include Louisiana burial rites?"

"Or French?" Richard asked hopefully.

The great dining room was only dimly lit by the dozens of candles on the table and sideboard. Stealthy shadows inhabited the corners of the room, and the diners' voices echoed strangely. Instead of mosquito netting Tante Marye had made ephemeral lace draperies for the open windows, and they rippled with an eerie slowness when the night air brushed them.

Monroe, dressed in a somber black suit, stiff white shirt, black tie, and spotless white gloves, served the diners. Molly stood silently at the sideboard, attending to the silver platters of food, polishing the covers, occasionally stirring a dish, cleaning the tureens and utensils after each use, sometimes whispering something to Monroe.

Cheney noted with interest that Monroe discreetly offered Gowan Ford each dish, and Ford would nod or shake his head. Then Monroe would return to the sideboard and whisper to Molly. Molly would then arrange Ford's plate and cut up all the food into bite-sized portions. Cheney was fascinated by the agility and ingenuity that Gowan Ford had been forced to learn with the loss of his right arm. She tried to imagine how the loss of an eye must affect one's vision and made a mental note to ask Mr. Ford if he would mind letting her study his vision and acuity.

Monroe and Molly's three children stood in a row on the other side of the sideboard, their hands folded in front of them, motionless, simply observing. The oldest was Corbett, who was eighteen and dressed in a suit exactly like his father's. He was a handsome young man, more dark-skinned than either of his parents, with strong features and secretive eyes. Adah, who was seventeen, looked like Molly, with her straight nose and warm milk-chocolate skin. She seemed almost painfully shy and shifted her gaze quickly downward whenever one of the diners happened to look in her direction. Chloe, however, shifted slightly from one foot to the other, her eyes darting to whoever was speaking, and she watched them obsessively: what the ladies did with their gloves, which fork and spoon they were using, how the ladies gestured and dabbed with their lace napkins. And Chloe's bright eyes rested often on Shiloh Irons.

Cheney, observing the formality of Monroe's and Molly's services and their silent dignity, rather missed Dally's warm bossiness and her earthy contributions to the dinner patter. Tante Marye, however, in whose veins seemed to flow only the cool blue blood of the *ancien régime*, would have disapproved of the Duvalls' familiarity with servants.

The gombo—a wonderfully piquant cross between a soup and a stew—was only the first course. Next came the entrée, filet of trout amandine, with a side dish of souffléd corn crepes with roasted corn. Monroe then began to move around the table with a silver platter piled high with curious golden flute shapes. As he bent to offer it first to Richard Duvall at the head of the table, Cheney cried, "Oh! Tante Marye! You made them for me—you didn't forget! Here, Monroe, bring them to me!"

Instead of scolding Cheney for her greediness, Tante Marye smiled indulgently. Shiloh had noticed that though Tante Marye was stern and often corrected Cheney—and anyone else in the vicinity who erred— her bright blue eyes stayed hungrily focused on Cheney's face most of the time. Tante Elyse, too, watched Cheney and smiled often to herself. "Well, I would like some too, please, Monroe," Shiloh asserted. "Whatever it is, it must be good, 'cause the Doc doesn't normally shriek for her food."

Cheney ignored his teasing as she urged Monroe to place two, then three, then four of the light golden flutes onto her plate. "Fried squash blossoms! Oh, how I love them, and Tante Marye's the only person who makes them, I think."

"Fried flowers?" Shiloh asked in surprise. "How decadent!"

"I prefer to call them *les fleurs frites*," Tante Marye informed them.

"She cooks my pansies, too," Tante Elyse said mournfully, "and my lemon geraniums, and my roses."

"All of the flowers I use in my cooking are grown in the kitchen garden, Elyse," Tante Marye scoffed. "It's not as if I go about pillaging your gardens."

"Oh yes, that's true," Elyse agreed suddenly, as usual throwing everyone a little off-balance.

"Speaking of pillaging the gardens," Gowan Ford, at the opposite end of the table, said grimly, "Diana Court told me today that she's got some sickly plants in her west field. I didn't get a chance to see them yet, but it sounds like our same old problem."

Shiloh watched Ford covertly, interested in the fact that he seemed to be much more a friend of the family than just an overseer. Cheney had told him that the vicomtesse had been a staunch believer in education—for children, adults, old people, poor, wealthy, regardless of social status or aspirations. All of the children at Les Chattes Bleues had been educated together until they were sixteen, and then the vicomtesse offered a classical education to those who wished to participate. Marye, Elyse, their three half brothers, Gowan Ford, and three other Les Chattes Bleues sharecroppers' children had all been educated together, with absolutely no different treatment for any of them in the schoolroom.

"We'll go see her tomorrow," Richard told Ford. "I haven't met Mrs. Court yet."

"Richard, now that you've seen what's happening to us, what do you intend to do?" Tante Marye demanded.

With deliberation Richard Duvall took a small bite of trout amandine, chewed slowly, then swallowed. "I can't help you with your crop, Marye, as much as I'd like to. I know nothing of the maladies of indigo plants. And, of course, I hope Cheney and Shiloh will be able to help with the illness—if anyone else gets it, though we pray not."

"I'm hoping that it was some sort of seasonal infection, short-lived and now gone," Cheney explained. "Mrs. de Cheyne—Dolly—was telling me some of the history of this area, and it sounds as if there is no place on earth more likely to foster sickness."

"I beg to differ, Cheney," Tante Marye said frigidly. "Les Chattes Bleues is clean and well-maintained and constantly attended. All of it. I do not hold with uncleanness and lack of fresh air and sunlight, for I believe that those unwholesome atmospheres provoke the most unhealthy humors."

"Yes, we all know, Tante Marye, that you are a most meticulous housekeeper and landlord," Cheney said patiently. "I'm not talking about Les Chattes Bleues in particular. I'm talking about the area, you see, and particularly New Orleans. That city has had more cholera, more yellow fever, more malaria, and more typhoid than any other city in the United States. More epidemics, more deaths, and more variances of each of these plagues—"

"That have rarely ever touched Les Chattes Bleues," Tante Marye asserted stiffly.

"But something has now, has it not?" Cheney countered.

"Why . . . yes . . . Cheney, I suppose that's true," Tante Marye said with one of her unnerving lapses into uncertainty. "But you can help us, can't you?"

"Oh yes, Tante Marye, of course I can!" Cheney said repentantly. "And Shiloh, too. He's probably a better diagnostician than I am! But if anyone else gets ill—oh—I do wish Dev were here," she finished disconsolately. Dr. Devlin Buchanan was practically an adopted son of the Duvalls and was an internationally known physician of prominence.

"Oh, so do I!" Tante Elyse cried. "I do love Dev so much. He's been almost like a son to me and Marye. He comes to Les Chattes Bleues at least twice a year and writes with great regularity. But, of course, you know that, don't you, everyone . . . except Shiloh, of course . . . but Cheney does, certainly, because you and Dev are still planning to get married, aren't you? And when is that, Cheney? I'm most unclear about it."

Shiloh's jaw tightened, but his expression of displeasure was quickly erased and replaced by heavy-lidded boredom. He glanced at Victoria de Lancie, whose blue eyes were wide and dark with some emotion she struggled to conceal by busily putting down her fork and arranging her napkin. Within moments she looked just as bored as Shiloh. By accident she caught his eyes, and a sudden understanding, a sudden sure knowledge of the other's feelings about Devlin Buchanan and Cheney Duvall getting married, passed between them. Both of them quickly looked away.

Cheney looked down and mumbled, "We . . . we haven't set a date yet, Tante Elyse. We simply have an . . . understanding."

"Well, I don't have any understanding," Tante Elyse declared.

"That is the greatest of truths, Elyse," Gowan Ford growled.

Tante Marye, as always, watched Cheney avidly. Her mouth tightened into a straight pink line, then she looked down and ostentatiously began to arrange ladylike bits of *fleurs frites* and trout on her fork.

Richard Duvall, who had been absorbed in his own thoughts and was unable to pick up the thread of the conversation, looked thoroughly bewildered. Irene watched Cheney sympathetically, but Cheney didn't look up. "Cheney and Dev both are so busy with their careers," Irene commented lightly. "Neither of them seems to be in any hurry."

An awkward silence fell. Everyone looked away from Cheney. Monroe collected the diners' Willow china plates—Cheney noticed he did it without making a single clink—and began replacing them with clean ones. Cheney stared down at the intricate Oriental design on the china and was reminded of Shiloh's Oriental scarf. She looked up at him, staring at him without realizing it. When he met her eyes he solemnly winked, and a smile tugged the corners of his mobile mouth. In spite of herself Cheney smiled and then ate her last *fleur frite*. Unnoticed by either of them, Irene Duvall's sea-green eyes noted the exchange, though she made no acknowledgment.

Finally Victoria asked coolly, "And what about the *vaudou*? Does anyone intend to do anything about them?"

"Of course, Mrs. de Lancie, I'm going to attend to that problem," Richard replied soothingly. He looked down the table at Gowan Ford. "Do you happen to know, Mr. Ford, the exact boundaries of Les Chattes Bleues? What I'm getting at is that we must establish that they are indeed trespassing, you see."

"No, I don't know the property lines, Colonel Duvall," he answered, then nodded to Tante Elyse. "Elyse does."

"The deed is difficult to interpret," Elyse sighed. "I read the entire thing when Papa died, but of course I wasn't reading it because of boundary disputes."

"Perhaps I might be allowed to read it after dinner?" Richard ventured. "It's important to establish that these people are in violation of the law, Marye, Elyse, or otherwise I wouldn't dream of intruding in your private affairs."

Tante Elyse laughed. "Oh, Richard, really! Everything we have is yours and Irene's and Cheney's for the asking—and even that is not enough, considering the care you take for us! But all of Father's most important papers are not here at Les Chattes Bleues. They're at John's office."

"John?" Richard prodded.

"John Law," Elyse announced importantly. "Our lawyer."

Richard blinked, fought back a smile, and said, "Elyse, John Law? Are you certain that's your lawyer's name?"

"He's been our attorney for thirty years," Elyse said huffily. "I should think I'd know his name by now."

"And what is so amusing?" Tante Marye said irritably to Cheney, who was giggling.

"Nothing, Tante Marye."

"He is a descendant of the great John Law of the Mississippi Company who practically founded *Nouvelle Orléans*," Tante Marye went on.

"Is he now?" Richard asked, his gray eyes glinting. "Then I have another reason for meeting him. I think I'll go into the city tomorrow and visit him."

"I shall send with you a letter of introduction," Tante Marye said coolly. "And, Richard, the man's name *is* John Law. Try not to burst out laughing right in his face when you meet him."

"Yes, Tante Marye," Richard said meekly, sounding much like Cheney.

"I cannot contain my curiosity any longer," Victoria said airily. "Mr. Ford, I demand that you tell me about these *vaudou* persons. Particularly their features and outward appearance and the kind of clothing they wear. Especially this Dédé woman."

"Yes, all the most important things such as that," Cheney agreed. "What is the latest *vaudou* fashion, Mr. Ford?"

Gowan Ford grimaced, and his fierce visage was dark indeed. "You ladies have never been exposed to these people, have you?"

"Certainly not," Irene said with distress. "At least I hope not," she added with a stern look at Cheney.

"No, Mother, I'd never heard of the *vaudou* before we arrived here," Cheney answered with a roll of her eyes.

"Nor had I," Victoria added.

"Then your jokes about them are forgivable, Miss Cheney, Mrs. de Lancie," Mr. Ford said heavily, "since they are made from a blessed ignorance. And I, and your father, and Mr. Irons, here, will pledge to do our best to keep you ignorant, ladies. Because those people are not a topic for light dinner conversation."

"But surely you're not afraid of them, Mr. Ford?" Victoria demanded.

Gowan Ford trained his singular gaze on Victoria. In the gentle candlelit gloom of the immense room, he seemed dark, a Vulcan presence, with his dark suit and thick black hair and black covering over his eye. "No, *madame*, I'm not afraid of them, and I don't think anyone needs to be afraid for their person. But the *vaudou* worship strange spirits, and they court evil, and I think that all Christians should be wary of them."

But *Madame* Victoria Elizabeth Steen de Lancie refused to be chastened. "Then if you won't explain their countenance to me, Mr. Ford, perhaps you'll explain their religion. Indeed, I think we should at least try and understand why they are doing what they're doing, as it is quite relevant to us here at Les Chattes Bleues."

Ford shrugged one shoulder carelessly. "The *vaudou* believe whatever the high priest or priestess decides they believe. They have no coherent code, no written set of laws or rules; it's all based upon African tribal beliefs, which are spread by oral tradition."

"And this woman, this Dédé, she is the high priestess?" Victoria went on irrepressibly.

Gowan Ford scowled but spoke gently. "Mrs. de Lancie—"

"Please, sir?" she asked in her most persuasive purr. "I appreciate your concern for our delicacy, but we wish to know what we face. Don't we, ladies?"

"Yes, we do," Cheney agreed. Irene frowned at her but remained silent.

"I already know," Elyse said smugly. "I made Gowan tell me all about them."

"I don't want to know," Marye asserted, "but it does seem that Mrs. de Lancie does, and as she is my guest, I will accede to her wishes. Tell us about them, Gowan. Since my sister didn't faint dead away, neither shall I."

"Oh, Marye, it's not like that," Ford muttered. "You ladies—all of you, Mrs. de Lancie included—are obviously made of stronger stuff than that! Very well. No, Dédé is not the high priestess. An old woman named Marie Laveau, who lives in New Orleans, is. But Dédé is a priestess, a *mambo*, and Doctor Sol is a *hoogon*. It was that delightful pair that I met up on the island. And as to why they're up there prancing about, I don't know, except what they told me."

"Well, it's going to be difficult—or impossible—to do anything about them unless they show up again," Shiloh said grimly. "I've been meaning to ask you, Mr. Ford, have they only been up on the rise that one time?"

Ford suddenly grew uneasy. Shifting restlessly in his seat, he looked down at his food. "No . . . no."

The silence was heavy as everyone waited for him to continue. Ford kept his head bowed, and in a low rumble like far-off thunder he said, "They were there last month, too. They came in the middle of the night, and Elyse and Marye never even knew it."

"*Mais, hélas!*" Marye whispered hoarsely.

"It's all right, Gowan," Elyse said softly. "I know why you didn't tell me, and I appreciate it."

Gowan Ford sighed deeply, then looked back up. His blue eye glittered in the flickering lights of the dozens of candles, and he searched each face carefully before speaking again. "Both times it's been the night of the full moon."

No sound was in the still air of the dining room. No one moved. An errant, lost wisp of a breeze floated in and made the candle fires bend slightly to the right in a flame-dance, then hiss slightly as they stood back upright.

Finally Shiloh murmured, "Tonight's the full moon."

★ ★ ★ ★

Gowan Ford stubbornly maintained that all that was needed for protective measures was that the dogs be allowed to roam the grounds of Les Chattes Bleues. "That's how I saw the *vaudou* last month, because the drums weren't very loud," Ford explained. "Riff came and got me."

"They don't bark?" Shiloh asked curiously. "*Can* they bark?"

"Certainly they can," Elyse huffed. "But it's just so impolite."

"*À la gare!*" Ford muttered softly. "Elyse, you know those dogs are trained not to bark!"

"Yes, I know," she answered sweetly. "I trained them."

"Just . . . don't listen to her," Ford said with exasperation to Shiloh and Richard. "It'd make a perfectly whole man into a blathering imbecile. Elyse, isn't it time for you to retire, since the other ladies have?"

"Hmm . . . yes, I suppose. Good night, everyone." She rose from the Venetian sofa, swept across the parlor, but suddenly, girlishly, bent over to whisper something in Gowan Ford's ear. He listened, nodded, and smiled up at her. Then she left the room.

He looked back at Shiloh and Richard, who were vainly trying not to look too curious, and chuckled. "That woman! She's been keeping the dogs in her room at night, you see, and Marye would skin her—all of us—alive if she knew it. Anyway, Elyse asked me to bring Mamie up to stay with her tonight. Mamie's Riff's and Raff's mother, and she's pregnant again." Ford grinned devilishly, crossed one booted leg over the other, leaned back in his armchair, and pulled a cigar out of his pocket. "Marye likely will keel over dead as a rock if Mamie litters tonight in Elyse's room."

Richard looked uneasy. "We'll just not tell Tante Marye if that happens, hmm?"

Shiloh and Ford both chuckled, and Ford cordially offered Shiloh and Richard a cigar. Richard declined, but Shiloh took one, and the men sat wreathed in lazy blue haloes of smoke.

"That Elyse is some woman," Ford said almost to himself, staring at the red hot end of his cigar. He looked up at Shiloh and Richard, and his single eye glowed with amusement. "At least she didn't ask me to bring her her pet raccoon or fox. They tear up the curtains, and Marye goes on for days."

"She has a pet raccoon? And a pet fox?" Shiloh asked in astonishment.

"Mr. Irons, that woman has a pet everything. Raccoons, foxes, squirrels, birds, cats, snakes—"

"Snakes!" Shiloh groaned.

Ford grinned. "Did you know that Elyse actually thinks she has a pet alligator?"

"I hope she is terribly mistaken in that belief," Richard said sarcastically.

"Calls her Sheba," Ford went on with a bemused air. "Found her on the bank of the bayou twelve years ago, orphaned, I guess. Elyse wagged her around until she got about a foot long and then put her back in the bayou. But Elyse still goes down there to visit her, she says, and feeds her scraps. Elyse says Sheba's shy and won't come out when I go down there with her. That's why I've never seen her."

"Dearest Lord," Richard groaned. "I don't know whether to pray that Elyse is telling the truth, or to pray that she's hopelessly insane."

"Just pray," Ford laughed. Richard and Shiloh joined in. Then the party grew sober again, and Ford went back to the beginning. "Anyway, I don't really like the idea of being obliged to post a guard on Les Chattes Bleues. I don't like to give those people that much acknowledgment. I think the dogs are enough."

Richard and Shiloh considered this. Then Shiloh frowned and asked, "But, Mr. Ford, don't you think that they've actually come over the lagoon to this property? Don't you think that they've got something to do with the problems with the indigo plants and the sicknesses?"

"I just can't think that, Mr. Irons."

"Why not?"

"Because," Ford argued, "I don't think those people would have come onto—and left—Les Chattes Bleues property without my knowing it. I think the dogs would have gone crazy. Now Riff and Raff are trained not to bark, but as I said, Riff came and got me up last month when those people were just cutting up over on the island. If a stranger had actually come on Les Chattes Bleues' property, I would have known about it."

Shiloh frowned. "But if they're trained not to bark . . . and if someone did come over the lagoon in a boat . . . it's so far from your house. . . ."

Ford nodded. "I know what you're thinking, Mr. Irons. But you've got to realize, those dogs are smart. Last month, when Riff came and got me, Raff stayed right up on the dock, watching the fires and listening to the drums over the bayou. If something like that would happen, one of the dogs would come get me. The other would stay wherever the trouble was."

"Smart dogs," Shiloh said with appreciation.

"Sure are. It's uncanny how smart they are," Ford agreed. "And I swear they understand every single word Elyse Buckingham says! Better than people do."

Ford's smile was so warm, his harsh, scarred features so soft, that Shiloh searched his face and listened to the deep baritone in his words even more carefully than usual. Suddenly the thought announced itself clearly in his head: *Ford's in love with Tante Elyse. Always has been, that's why he never married. He really does love her. . . .*

Richard and Ford were looking at him, and Shiloh realized he had missed a sentence or two. "Uh, sorry, sirs, I was just . . . uh . . . thinking. What did you say?"

Richard gave him a searching look and said, "You still look kind of tired, Shiloh, and it is late. Maybe you'd better go on to bed. Anyway, all I was saying was that I agree with Mr. Ford, that I'm not ready to admit that we need to stand guard. If the *vaudou* do show up tonight— and Mr. Ford has assured me that he will come wake me if they do— I feel that this is adequate. What do you think, Shiloh?"

Shiloh stirred restlessly in his chair. He didn't feel reassured, he felt uneasy, though he didn't know why. He didn't really think that the *vaudou* were going to come murder them in their beds . . . still . . .

"I don't . . . know, sir," he said at last. "I . . . I'm a little edgy. Maybe I could just kind of, you know, take a look around every so often."

Richard considered him gravely. As a soldier, Richard Duvall respected the power of men's intuitions. As a man, Richard Duvall respected Shiloh Irons' insight. "Shiloh, in the first place, the dogs would likely attack you. You've only been here for two days, and I don't think you're familiar enough to them yet. So if you feel that a watch should be set, we'll need to keep the dogs in and take turns."

Shiloh considered this, while Richard waited for his decision. Though it didn't occur to Shiloh, Richard Duvall's deference was quite a commentary on Shiloh's character. Gowan Ford did take note of the exchange.

Finally Shiloh shook his head slightly, then rubbed his eyes. "No, no, I don't think we need to get all the able-bodied men on the place up to stand a watch. And I do see that I can't dodder around outside with the dogs out. Maybe I'm just tireder than I think, and I'm seeing haints that aren't there."

Richard Duvall stood, stretched, then laid a hand on Shiloh's shoulder. "I'd rather see that than haints that are there, Shiloh," he grinned. "But instead, I'm going to bed. Maybe nothing at all will happen with the *vaudou* tonight—or ever again. At least, that's going to be my prayer."

★　★　★　★

The night was quiet. Riff and Raff, sleeping down in the gazebo by the lagoon, stirred in their sleep, their skin twitching, their paws moving, their jaws scissoring on hapless dream rabbits. They would wake up periodically throughout the night and make rounds of Les Chattes Bleues, sometimes running like rowdy boys, sometimes padding slowly, noses to the ground, always silent.

No candles lit Les Chattes Bleues after midnight, because the fear of fire was the only true fear that the inhabitants had. Surrounded by water, they would yet be as helpless as if they were standing in the Sahara if a fire should break out in the old cypress home. So the halls of Les Chattes Bleues were filled only with the warm, fragrant night.

Everyone slept soundly, except Mamie. In Elyse's room she stirred once and bared her teeth. But she was lying on a fine oushak rug by Tante Elyse's bed, the night was quiet and soothing, and the babies were heavy and sleepy in her belly. After long moments, as her black nose twitched and her ghostly blue eyes lit with mysterious fire, her eyelids began getting heavy again. She slept.

In the morning Monroe and Molly were always first to wake and come up the path through the gardens from their cottage to Les Chattes Bleues. When they saw what was on the gallery, both at the front door and the back door, Molly refused to enter the house. Monroe decided to wake Mr. Duvall first.

Then Monroe saw what was on the second-floor gallery, in front of every door, and he agonized over whether to just pick everything up and sweep everything away and scrub everything spotless and not tell anyone, as if it had never happened.

But that, of course, could not be done.

He knocked on the door to the Red Room, waited for Richard Duvall's sleepy answer, and slipped inside. Soundlessly, quickly, he glided over to the bed, pulled aside the mosquito netting, and whispered, "Colonel Duvall, come with me, please. Yes, now, please, *monsieur*."

Richard Duvall slid quietly out of bed, so as not to disturb Irene. He threw on a satin dressing gown and hurried barefoot behind Monroe toward the open door to the gallery.

Monroe stood on the gallery, looking down at the floor in front of Richard's feet. "Don't step on it, sir," he said gutturally.

Richard blankly looked down.

An odd, ugly little bundle was at his doorstep. It was a lump that had feathers, beads, something that looked horribly similar to human hair, and gummy red splotches that had to be blood. It stank.

Richard's jaw clenched so tightly it almost broke his back teeth. His nostrils widened until they were a bloodless white, and he looked as if he were going to be sick.

"*Gris-gris*," Monroe growled, still looking down.

Richard, with an exaggerated high step, got over the nasty lump and hurried around the corner so he could see down the gallery, where the doors to the other four bedrooms were.

"Oh, my sweet Jesus," he unconsciously prayed. "Dearest Lord, protect us."

Gris-gris lay in front of each door.

Richard jumped visibly when Monroe spoke behind his shoulder. "Colonel Duvall, there is more. Downstairs."

"More?" he asked bleakly. "More of those obscene things?"

"No, sir. It's . . . it's . . ."

"Never mind, I'll come." The two men hurried down the stairs without making a sound. Richard fervently hoped they could get the *gris-gris*, and the filth they left behind, cleaned up before all the ladies woke up.

In front of the great, gracious front door of Les Chattes Bleues was fashioned a three-foot cross made of wet salt poured about an inch thick. Approaching the door, the view of it was right side up; but viewing it from inside Les Chattes Bleues, it was upside down. In the middle of the crosspieces was a single bright red splotch of blood.

A House

of Defense

Bow down thine ear to me;
Deliver me speedily:
Be thou my strong rock,
For a house of defense to save me.

Psalm 31:2

6

LE SERPENT AND LE COCODRIL

"The bayou certainly has a wild beauty of its own, although it is undoubtedly hostile to man," Richard Duvall mused. "But then, many things that are quite beautiful are hostile to man."

"Like women?" Shiloh suggested.

Richard Duvall laughed heartily and was joined by the boatman, Octave. Shiloh narrowed his eyes as he considered the swarthy Acadian. *Absolutely refuses to speak English,* he thought irritably, *but I did hear him that first night. . . .*

But the thought occurred to Shiloh that while he, himself, spoke absolutely no French, he could understand some. Tante Marye and Tante Elyse often spoke French to each other, to Gowan Ford, and to Irene and Cheney. And Monroe and Molly spoke French to each other and to their children. Often Shiloh overheard certain words that translated easily—many French words sounded like their English counterparts—or else he caught a phrase that, to his surprise, he had absorbed, and he could clumsily repeat. Perhaps Octave was the same way.

"No, no, Shiloh, that's not what I meant," Richard grunted when he recovered. "I was thinking more along the lines of hurricanes, for example. They are quite a breathtaking spectacle . . . tigers are undoubtedly exquisite creatures, but they mean certain death to a man when their paths cross . . . some flowers, even, belladonna for instance . . ."

"Oh," Shiloh said lightly. "I see what you mean. But I still include women in this category."

"You don't fool me, Mr. Irons. Women like you," Richard said ingenuously.

"Maybe. But still, some of them are dangerous," Shiloh mused half to himself. He was thinking of Chloe Monroe, who was still bringing his coffee in the morning, still flirting outrageously with him, and was certainly dangerous. She was too young, too beautiful, and too inexperienced to understand the possible consequences of her invitations. *Not with me, of course,* Shiloh reflected, *but Les Chattes Bleues has three* garçonnieres. *And if the other two are occupied by men who are less sympathetic than I am to silly young girls . . .*

Shiloh was frowning darkly, and Richard Duvall watched him closely. Richard wondered if his daughter had something to do with Shiloh's ill-concealed bad temper with women this morning; usually Cheney did manage to be at the center of whatever controversy was going on at the moment. *I hope not,* Richard thought. *I hope she and Shiloh are getting on all right.* Then he wondered exactly why he hoped this so much. After some consideration, however, he dismissed all worries about Cheney and Shiloh. Like most men, he had a fairly simple and straightforward way of defining relationships. Richard Duvall knew Cheney and Shiloh were friends, and their little arguments generally meant nothing. That was good enough for him.

Shiloh stayed in his dark reverie, and Richard again searched the landscape sliding smoothly by the pirogue. The bayou was, indeed, sleeping water, as it seemed to have no current at all; yet Richard knew that it actually was flowing south, and Octave was guiding them north. The bayou was muddy, the color of milk chocolate, as if the earth had melted and begun to ooze. In places the water looked like green scum, but when the pirogue cut through it Richard could see that it was actually a tightly woven mosaic of tiny-leafed green plants that made a lush carpet upon the surface of the water. He scooped his hand down and came up with some of the plants—actually hundreds of them, for they were so tiny that a handful of them might hold as many as two or three hundred.

"*M'sieu,*" Octave said quietly, and when Richard turned around to look at the boatman, Octave shook his head once, twice, with great deliberation. Richard frowned, and Octave nodded toward the side of the boat. "*Le serpent,*" he pronounced clearly, as if to a child. He nodded over to the side of the bank. "*Le cocodril.*"

Though the words were oddly pronounced, Richard Duvall got the meaning very clearly. He searched over the side of the boat and saw no snake. He searched both sides of the bank and saw no alligators; but he crossed his arms, settled back, and decided to mind his own affairs.

It was not yet seven o'clock in the morning, and the bayou was eerily still. Enough light filtered through the always-overhanging trees that the night creatures had grown silent. A low carpet of smoky mist hovered over the still water, and occasional thin snaky tendrils rose out of it to waver up and curl around like beckoning wraith-fingers. Always the three men had to duck low-hanging Spanish moss and push aside vines and tendrils that seemed to drip from the low branches of the trees. In the gloom Richard could see, occasionally, plants he recognized growing in lush confusion on the banks: vines of Virginia creeper, palmettos with sword-sharp leaves, mounds of resurrection ferns that, though brown and dead-looking now, would soon be green again. Once they passed a great mass of Carolina jasmine, and Richard breathed deeply of the heady perfume. It reminded him of Duvall Court and home, and he sighed.

Shiloh roused and looked around, as if only now realizing where he was. "This is the sorriest-looking boat I've ever seen," he said lightly, "and the smoothest ride I've ever had in one."

"Scary-looking, aren't they?" Richard agreed. "And I wouldn't even try to step into one without an Acadian. It's like these pirogues are almost a part of them. I've yet to see anyone else handle one."

Pirogues were extremely light, delicate boats made from a single tree, usually cypress. They were hollowed out in the pattern of Indian canoes, but with a much lighter frame. Pirogues had a wide, low draft for the shallow waters of the bayous and swamps. At times the water seemed only to be an inch or two below the deepest part of the draft, but it never slopped over. It was said in southern Louisiana that a pirogue can ride on a heavy dew, and watching the strength and grace with which Octave maneuvered it, Richard could almost believe it.

"How is it that Octave got word to pick us up this morning?" Shiloh asked. "I thought we might have to ride over to the landing on the river by the Lefebvre plantation."

"Ford says that Octave comes to Les Chattes Bleues three times a week to bring the mail and the newspapers," Richard replied. "He's sort of . . . adopted Marye and Elyse, it seems."

"Really?" Shiloh stared over Richard's shoulder at Octave, who was grandly pretending ignorance of the conversation. "How'd that come about?"

"After the wreck of the *Creole Princess*, the mail steamers quit coming to Les Chattes Bleues. They had been coming down Bayou du Chêne twice a week, because there are three other plantations that have landings, too, and because it circles around back to the river anyway. Then last year Marye and Elyse were in New Orleans for some reason, and they couldn't beg or hire a steamer or a fisherman or a flatboat or a single pirogue to bring them back to Les Chattes Bleues—except for Octave. He brought them home that time, and he transports everyone back and forth to the city whenever they go, and he started bringing the mail and fetching supplies for Marye and Elyse whenever they needed something from the city and couldn't go in. And that's why he was on the lookout for you and Cheney when you arrived. Marye and Elyse had told him about you, and that you'd need to get to Les Chattes Bleues even if it was late."

"But why is Octave the only person who'll come up the bayou?" Shiloh asked in bewilderment. "I can see why the big steamboats don't anymore, but any small boat could make it easily."

Richard shook his head. "Ford really doesn't know. Marye and Elyse always pay well for services, so it's not that they wouldn't pay for the trip. He says that all Octave will say about it is something about ghosts and spirits—and the *vaudou*."

"Them again," Shiloh growled.

"Yes, them," Richard said mildly. "Maybe what you and Cheney saw on the hulk has scared everyone off."

"I gotta tell you, Mr. Duvall, that hulk's scary enough at midnight on the bayous, even without ghosts and spooky green lights."

At that moment they rounded the bend in the bayou, and the hulk loomed up in front of them. Octave rowed smoothly and evenly, with barely a rippling sound when he lifted the oar. Silently they slid by the wreck in the small pirogue, looking and feeling like three children sneaking by some evil giant's great blighted ship.

Shiloh strained to search the hulk as they glided by, and then he realized that it was almost as shadowed as it had been the other night in the dark of the midnight. He looked up at the narrow ribbon of sky visible above the eternal tree canopy and saw that it was lightening somewhat but only to a sullen gunmetal color. Unconsciously he shivered slightly and pulled his canvas coat more securely around him. He was going to need it today, and not just to hide the .44 Colt stuck securely in his belt.

Richard Duvall stared at the hulk as they passed, turning, exactly as Shiloh and Cheney had that first night, so that it would not be at his back. When he could no longer see it he turned back to stare straight ahead. "That thing looks accursed," he muttered. "No wonder Marye and Elyse are frightened."

"Yes, sir. It was hard to leave them today." Shiloh's mouth tightened into a thin straight line. "Even the Doc and Mrs. de Lancie have the jimjams. Only Miss Irene seems to be okay. . . ."

Richard and Shiloh had put off their trip into New Orleans for two days after the *gris-gris* and the salt cross had been found. The atmosphere at Les Chattes Bleues had been tense and irritable for the last three days, and Tante Marye had been a tyrant. Tante Elyse had disappeared each day until dinner, and Cheney, Victoria, Nia, and Zhou-Zhou had stayed together all day on Wednesday and Thursday. By this morning, however, Cheney was growing restless and the horror of the *gris-gris* was fading. She had planned to visit all the sharecroppers and servants today and get their medical histories started. Shiloh had offered to stay and help her, but Cheney had insisted that he go to New Orleans to see Miss Behring, saying it would be very good practice for Nia to help her, anyway.

"Yes, Irene is really quite tranquil and peaceful about this whole thing," Richard went on thoughtfully. "She doesn't look it, but she's a wellspring of strength."

"No, she doesn't look it," Shiloh said warmly, "but you can see it anyway."

"You can," Richard said shrewdly.

Shiloh shrugged. "Anyway, I'm really not too worried about leaving them just for the day. Seems like Mr. Ford's a good man to leave in charge."

"Gowan Ford is a good man," Richard agreed. "His father was a fine man, a strong Christian, who worked, and worked hard, for the vicomte all his life. Gowan was his only son, and he's just like him."

"Mr. Duvall, how long have Tante Marye and Tante Elyse been widowed?" Shiloh asked idly, his eyes wandering languidly over the gray and green landscape.

"George Buckingham died in the yellow fever epidemic of 1853. That," Richard said sorrowfully, "was a hard time, a terrible time."

"You were here?"

"No, but Dev and I came down when George died. The vicomte was not very strong, you see—not with yellow fever, but simply with age. He was eighty-two then, and he died that December. Anyway, Dev and I came down to help Elyse move back to Les Chattes Bleues—she and George lived in New Orleans—and to see if we were needed to help with the plantation. Which we weren't, because the vicomte had forbidden anyone to go into the city, and no one—not a single person—at Les Chattes Bleues got the fever." He turned and stared into the far distance. "That was the most awful sight I've ever seen. New Orleans during that plague. The very air seemed to crawl into your nostrils, it was so heavy with the stench of death and horrible sickness. They burned tar and pitch, and a great pall hung over the city, and they fired cannons, which sounded as dull as doom in the heaviness. People died in the streets and were left there, because they couldn't dig pits, you see, and lime them, and there were not nearly enough sepulchers. Not even close, because over ten thousand people died that summer."

"What did they do?" Shiloh asked quietly.

"Burned them," Richard answered. "And the reek hung over this land for months, Elyse said. We could smell it all the way to Les Chattes Bleues." With an effort he sat up straighter, pulled his caped greatcoat about him, and smiled. "Dark talk for a dark day. Anyway, as I was saying—or trying to say—Elyse was married to George Buckingham for twenty years before he died. She returned to live at Les Chattes Bleues, which I think she wanted more than her fine house in New Orleans, anyway."

"1853 . . . she must have been still very beautiful," Shiloh murmured.

"She always has been," Richard said simply. "She still is."

"And Tante Marye?"

Richard grimaced. "I'm glad you asked me about it, so I can warn you. All I know is that when Marye was twenty-eight she ran off with a man named Frank Edwards and was back at Les Chattes Bleues in two months. That's it, that's all of it, and don't bring it up in front of her."

Shiloh grinned. "Thank you, sir."

"You're welcome."

In two more hours they reached New Orleans, and Octave magically maneuvered the tiny pirogue through a maze of ships, steamers, flatboats, and fishing boats to dock at the southern end of the Garden District. He made an elaborate pantomime to let them know he'd stay on the docks and wait for them to return. Richard and Shiloh walked through the crowded, noisy bedlam of the docks and shouted to each other over the din.

"I'm going to Bank's Arcade, which is over there"—Richard waved to the northeast—"one block over from Lafayette Square. Do you know where that is?"

"No, but I guess any hansom cab driver will," Shiloh shouted. "After I see Miss Behring I'll go back to the square and wait for you." Shiloh was going to see Miss Behring, one of the three Behring sisters who had raised him in an orphanage in Charleston, South Carolina. One of them, the middle sister, had moved to New Orleans and was running an orphanage in a sizable house in the Garden District.

"All right. If I get through with John Law first, I'll wait for you there."

They reached the foot of Canal Street, Shiloh whistled sharply and waved, and a hansom cab came smartly to a halt in front of them. Richard Duvall climbed into it and went to the east, and Shiloh hailed another one and went west.

★ ★ ★ ★

The heavy oak door with the frosted glass read simply, "John Law, Esquire." It opened soundlessly.

A young man no more than twenty was hunched over the desk centered in the small receiving area. His name was Oliver Boyd, and he wore the uniform of all young law clerks: a cheap suit, a tight collar, round rimless glasses magnifying tired red eyes, and a worried expression. Looking up from a pile of dusty ledgers and books with impossibly small print, he saw a tall, distinguished man with leonine features and an unsmiling countenance. Boyd hopped to his feet, knocking over a thick green ledger in his haste. "Yes, sir," he said in a sonorous, hushed voice. "How may we be of service to you, sir?"

The man smiled briefly, removing his silk top hat to reveal thick silver hair. Throwing his greatcoat back over his broad shoulders, he removed his leather gauntlets, all the while handling his ebony cane with great grace. "Is Mr. Law in?" he asked in a quiet, strong voice.

"Yes, sir, he is. May I give him your card?"

"Certainly." Taking a slender silver case from his waistcoat pocket, he removed a white card and moved over to the desk. Boyd noticed that he had a very slight limp, though it made him look rather dashing, the young man thought.

83

The plain white card read: Richard Duvall.

Decidedly uninformative. Boyd looked uncertainly up at the man, who looked back with steady blue-gray eyes that held slight amusement.

Oliver Boyd decided that though this man had no appointment, Richard Duvall was definitely the type of man that John Law would want to see. "I shall inform Mr. Law that you're here, Mr. Duvall."

"Thank you." Ignoring the two chairs, both hands resting lightly on his cane, he stood with a negligent ease that bespoke a man who did not expect to be kept waiting long.

He wasn't. Boyd came back out the door as if he had been catapulted, and his smooth cheeks were slightly pink. He opened his mouth to speak, but a man shoved past him and scurried to Richard, his hand held out like a flag of surrender.

"Colonel Duvall, sir, it is a great honor for you to call upon me! I am John Law, and I am pleased to be at your service, sir! Most pleased!"

John Law, Esquire, was as pleasing-looking as his words. Short, rotund, expansive, he was nearing his fiftieth year but looked younger, perhaps because of his boyish, jolly face. His eyes were small, of a muddy hazel color, but they twinkled merrily. His cheeks were flushed and his hand was very warm, but his handshake was firm and businesslike. He was dressed somberly in black—suit, waistcoat, tie, shoes. The only relief was his starched white shirt, with a collar so stiff it was almost buried in the folds of his neck, and a heavy gold watch-chain that appended with just the right arcs from his waistcoat pocket.

"Colonel Richard Duvall!" he said again. "Please, please, come with me. Mr. Boyd, would you be so kind as to bring tea and coffee? No, no, no trouble, Colonel Duvall. No trouble. Please, sit down, make yourself comfortable."

Richard settled into one of the two elegant burgundy leather armchairs to one side of the desk, reflecting that John Law's office had all the somberness that his person seemed to lack. The lawyer's desk was massive, made of a beautiful teak, and piled high with papers, books, ledgers, and briefs. As it was an interior office at Bank's Arcade, it had no windows. Two murky paintings of severe-looking men in gray wool wigs adorned the wall behind the desk. The rest of the room was lined with bookcases that were crammed with thick, dull-looking books.

But across from the armchairs was a sofa made of teak with rich red velvet upholstery, and between the armchairs and the sofa was a teak tea table, a fine piece with gracefully curved legs. Richard did admit to himself that the lawyer had good taste in furniture.

"Now then, Colonel Duvall, I am at your service. Is this a business call—or perhaps an introductory social call?" Law asked with a hopeful gleam in his eye.

"It's business, Mr. Law," Richard answered. He drew a delicate piece of parchment, sealed with black wax and an ornate seal, from the breast pocket of his waistcoat. "I have a letter of introduction."

Law's pudgy hands shot up in the air as if the parchment were a burning firebrand. "No, no, Colonel Duvall, I am well aware of your status and your good character! No need to supply *me* with references as to who *you* are!"

Richard's expression did not change, and the parchment did not waver. "Please read it, Mr. Law."

"Certainly, if you wish, Colonel Duvall. Certainly." Law fumbled in his waistcoat, searched under papers, scrabbled in a desk drawer, his cheeks reddening even more. He frowned, and the effect was that of an eight-year-old boy sulking.

"Are you by any chance looking for these, Mr. Law?" Richard asked politely, pointing to a pair of eyeglasses half-hidden under a sheaf of papers.

"Yes, yes, thank you, Colonel Duvall. A vanity of mine. Can't bear to wear them unless I must read." Law looked quite embarrassed, and Richard thawed just a bit. Unobtrusively Richard studied his face as the lawyer read the short letter. Law read quickly, and when not deliberately posed, his expression was shrewder, more intense.

Law pursed his lips and nodded, then removed the offending eyeglasses. "Yes, yes, Colonel Duvall, as I said, I do know of your reputation, and I knew that Mrs. Buckingham and Mrs. Edwards are your wife's aunts. But I am happy to be of service to you in any capacity, Colonel Duvall."

"I wished you to read the letter of introduction because I am here on behalf of Mrs. Buckingham and Mrs. Edwards," Richard said mildly.

"Yes, yes. Happy to be of service."

"Since I must make some inquiries that might be considered a violation of Mrs. Edwards' and Mrs. Buckingham's privacy, I was certain that you would require some sort of recommendation from them." Richard's gray eyes were trained very steadily on John Law.

John Law was nothing if not quick on the uptake. His expression did not change, other than a quick flash in his hazel eyes. "Quite true, Colonel, I would never divulge any of Mrs. Edwards' or Mrs. Buckingham's personal affairs if I had not received permission first."

Richard was silent for a moment, but John Law's gaze did not waver. Richard nodded curtly, then asked, "I would like to ask you some questions about La Maison des Chattes Bleues."

John Law waited attentively but said nothing. Richard frowned, then asked with some difficulty, "Has anyone made inquiries to you about buying Les Chattes Bleues?"

His eyebrows flew upward, and then, to Richard's consternation, Law chuckled. "Oh! But that is amusing." When he saw the rigid expression on Richard's face, Law sobered quickly. "Your pardon, Colonel Duvall. It's just that Les Chattes Bleues cannot be sold, can never be sold—not for a long time, anyway. And certainly not by either Mrs. Buckingham or Mrs. Edwards."

"But why not? What do you mean, sir?" Richard demanded harshly. He knew that no liens existed on Les Chattes Bleues, and never had.

"Why, it cannot be sold. Not until the eleventh Vicomte de Cheyne reaches his majority." A shadow of satisfaction, a tinge of superiority, echoed in John Law's voice. Richard narrowed his eyes and determined not to let his dislike for this man show.

"Please explain, sir," he said with bland courtesy.

Law steepled his fingers together, leaned back in his chair, and assumed a lecturing voice. "It's because of two conventions in estate law, Colonel Duvall: primogeniture and entailment. The seventh Vicomte de Cheyne—I was his lawyer, too, as I am sure you are aware, for ten years—invoked primogeniture in his last will and testament, which meant that his eldest son would inherit Les Chattes Bleues."

"You mean Maxime de Cheyne actually owns Les Chattes Bleues?" Richard asked in astonishment. The vicomte's eldest son—Irene's uncle—was seventy-six years old and lived on the old estate in Varennes. He had finally decided to return to France in 1852 when Louis-Philippe Napoleon had decided that *aristos* were not such horrible creatures after all, which was most convenient, considering he was declaring himself Napoleon III, Emperor of France at the time. Louis-Philippe Napoleon had restored many of the old fiefdoms to the nobles of the Second Estate, including the de Cheyne properties in Varennes.

"Maxime-Louis-Augustin de Cheyne, the eighth Vicomte de

Cheyne, is the owner of La Maison des Chattes Bleues and all real property pertaining to it," Law recited prissily.

Richard sat back in his chair and stared unseeing at the painting of the grim man behind John Law's rounded shoulders. Richard was unaware of this, of course, and he was momentarily angry with Tante Elyse and Tante Marye for not telling him. Upon reflection, he decided with a sigh, they had no reason to march up and regale him with this information since he had not discussed with them his suspicions.

John Law watched him closely, his round little eyes alight with curiosity. When Richard did not speak, Law went on in a more normal tone, all the while watching Richard for his reactions. "Marye Edwards and Elyse Buckingham have a life tenancy proviso in the seventh vicomte's will. Also, they own all the personal property appurtenanced to Les Chattes Bleues."

Appurtenanced? Richard thought crazily. *Sounds like a petticoat or something* . . . With an effort he gathered his thoughts. "So they can't sell Les Chattes Bleues—and no one could force them to, under any circumstances?"

John Law licked his red button lips. "No, sir, not even the present Vicomte de Cheyne, because of the second convention I referred to earlier—entailment. The previous vicomte, Augustin de Cheyne, entailed the estate unto his fourth descendant. That means that no essence of the estate can be changed until the eleventh vicomte attains majority."

"I see." Richard went into a deep study, then looked alertly up at the lawyer. "What about the sharecroppers? Is there any possible way that they could make claim to the property?"

"None," Law said firmly. "Even without the vicomte's last will and testament—which I formulated for him, and I assure you, Colonel Duvall, it will stand up in any court in this land—the vicomte's sharecropping program assured that no sharecropper was apportioned shares in the physical property. They can only lay claim to proportionate monies earned from the indigo crops."

"Of course," Richard muttered.

"Am I to understand that you are trying to sell Les Chattes Bleues, Colonel Duvall?" Law asked innocently.

"Certainly not!" Richard roared, then managed to bring his voice under control when the little man actually flinched as if from fear of a blow. "No, Mr. Law, you misunderstand the nature of my inquiries,"

87

he said in a calmer tone, though something of the offense he felt still showed on his face. "We have had some problems at Les Chattes Bleues, and I am merely attempting to help Mrs. Edwards and Mrs. Buckingham."

"I am their lawyer, and have been for many years, Colonel Duvall," Law said in a weakly cajoling tone. "I would wish to come to the assistance of those gallant ladies in any way I can."

Richard considered telling John Law about all of the problems at Les Chattes Bleues, but he was quite reluctant to do so. He simply didn't like John Law. He was a social climber and was entirely too impressed—erroneously—with *what* Richard Duvall was rather than *who* he really was. At least, Richard thought that Law was mistaken in his flattery, because Richard Duvall was a modest and humble man. At any rate, flattery and fawning were two traits that Richard could not abide in a man.

Still, he is their lawyer and evidently has some standing here in New Orleans. And he probably hears gossip. . . .

Richard looked back up and unemotionally related everything that had happened at Les Chattes Bleues: the sicknesses, the indigo crop blight, the *vaudou*, the *gris-gris*. John Law never moved or changed expression as Richard spoke. When he finished, Law still sat unmoving, and Richard finished with, "So, you see, Mr. Law, I had thought—I had almost hoped—that for some reason someone might be trying to force Mrs. Buckingham and Mrs. Edwards into selling Les Chattes Bleues."

"Yes, of course. I apologize if I offended, Colonel Duvall, but I knew nothing of this," Law murmured. He focused intently on Richard's face. "Do you believe that the *vaudou* are responsible for the indigo and the sickness?"

Richard shrugged. "I did at first, but as there have been no more illnesses, I am inclined to go along with my daughter's opinion. She is a skilled and experienced physician, and she believes that it was simply some sort of short-lived contagion. As for the indigo plants, we simply don't know why they are dying, but to me that means that we need to rule out all natural causes before we accuse people of sabotage. I only mention them to you because I thought perhaps you might have heard of similar circumstances involving these *vaudou*."

John Law's eyes flickered slightly, but he smiled. "No, no, no, Colonel Duvall, I know very little about the *vaudou*. Indeed, why should I?

They certainly don't move in the best circles."

"No, I'm sure they don't," Richard said sardonically. "One thing I do know, however; they are responsible for those filthy things we found Wednesday morning, and since they must have placed them there, they are trespassing on private property. I want to know how I can put a stop to it."

"You can kill them, of course," Law said with shocking ease.

Richard narrowed his eyes with distaste, and Law grew visibly uncomfortable. "Pardon me for what you might presume to be coarseness, but put quite simply, that is the law, and that is the truth. Trespassers on private property—especially those with intent to do harm—may be shot. It is always ruled self-defense."

"I don't want to kill them, Mr. Law," Richard said tightly. "For one thing, I don't believe anyone is in mortal danger."

"That doesn't matter, you know," Law said with an air of confidentiality. "No one would ever question you, your motives, or your reasoning in such a situation, Colonel Duvall."

Richard ground his teeth and commanded himself to be calm and impartial. "Do I have any other recourse?"

John Law's smile was wide and cordial. "Well, Colonel Duvall, considering who you are, and your connections with the Secretary of War, I should think that you could convince General Sheridan to loan you a company to patrol Les Chattes Bleues. After all, it is only because of the high esteem with which General Grant holds you, and through your influence and intervention, that Mrs. Buckingham and Mrs. Edwards have been left in peace—and the estate has been allowed to remain intact and unmolested since the occupation."

Richard Duvall very nearly lost his temper at this little bit of smarminess. John Law made it sound as if he were one of those contemptible men with power who wielded it for personal gain—and Law obviously admired him for it!

The truth of the matter was that Richard—being personally acquainted with Phil Sheridan, commander of the Federal troops in Louisiana—had made formal application to him requesting that Les Chattes Bleues be spared from either seizure by the Federal Government, or from occupation by military forces for use as a headquarters or hospital. He had explained to General Sheridan that Tante Elyse and Tante Marye had absolutely no connection to any Confederates, as they had no blood relatives aside from two half brothers who lived in

France. He had told Sheridan that they were elderly and had no support from any family, but maintained themselves solely by their tenancy in, and income from, Les Chattes Bleues.

Phil Sheridan listened calmly for once and agreed to comply with Richard's wishes. The gruff little general did express doubt that any person—male, female, old, young, deaf, blind, crippled, and he had serious doubts about the horses—that lived below the Mason-Dixon line deserved any consideration, for he viewed them all as traitors and treasonous renegades; but he had no need of Les Chattes Bleues, anyway. New Orleans was a prime city for occupation, with many fine homes and hotels to accommodate his fifteen thousand soldiers, and besides, what would he do with a whole bayou full of indigo plants?

But John Law had managed to portray this bluffly cordial conversation with Phil Sheridan into shabby political maneuverings.

Richard rose and savagely yanked on his gloves. "I'll consider your suggestion, Mr. Law. I must take my leave now. Good day."

John Law hopped out of his chair and scampered around the desk, talking at a quick, nervous pace. "Such a pleasure to meet you, Colonel Duvall. Give my best to Mrs. Buckingham and Mrs. Edwards . . . so kind of you to call . . . thank you for your solicitations. . . ."

Colonel Richard Duvall crammed his silk top hat on his head, opened the door with the frosted glass and the backward lettering, and left the offices of "John Law, Esquire."

7

THE FOUNDLING

She sat in a rocker on the raised portico of the modest little home on Prytania Street, a book on her lap, a cup of tea on the table beside her. For an instant Shiloh felt as if time had rolled backward: he was eight years old and running to show Miss Behring the fool's gold he had found in the stream bed. He had known it was fool's gold, of course, but Miss Behring liked the dull rocks with the occasional flashes of brightness imbedded in them. She told Shiloh that they were worth no more, and no less, than real gold because they were God's decoration, and they were nice to look at, and after all, what else did real gold afford a person but something nice to look at? Shiloh had always brought her samples of the rocks when he found a nice one.

But now he was a man, strong, tall, and had seen the world and real gold, and Miss Behring was much older than in those long-ago days. Eyeglasses rested on her nose, her hair was completely gray, and the strong shoulders were slightly stooped. He walked up the steps, and she rose and nodded to him as if she were expecting him. But as he neared her she held out both thin, work-hobbled hands and smiled. Her eyes were still a bright, alert blue. "Shiloh! Oh, it is so good to see you again! I thought you might come today!" Her voice sounded the same: quiet, soothing, with only a slight staccato rhythm and more formal expression to mark her German heritage.

To Shiloh's surprise, she stood on tiptoe and kissed his cheek. It made him feel like a young boy again. "I'm so glad to see you, Miss Behring," he replied. "May I join you?"

"Certainly." She settled back into the rocker, took off her glasses, and put them and her book aside. Shiloh settled into a rocker identical to hers on the other side of the table. "Please, Shiloh, help yourself to some tea," she urged. "I would pour for you, but I have only just gotten mine cooled to how I like it. I'm getting old and crotchety, and I want to drink my tea." Her eyes cut slyly to him.

"You're not old, and you were always crotchety." He grinned. She chuckled as he poured himself a cup of delicately scented China tea. Staring down in the depths of the light green liquid, he was suddenly struck by the coincidence; the Behring sisters always drank China tea, not India, and all they had found with him in the SHILOH IRON-WORKS crate were some items of Oriental origin . . . perhaps Chinese. . . .

He looked up, startled, and saw Miss Behring watching him closely. "Is there some creature in your teacup, Shiloh?" she said tartly. "Or are you merely dazzled by my charm?"

"No, ma'am, and yes, ma'am, always," he replied gravely.

"This is odd," she countered, her blue eyes glinting. "You don't look dazzled. You look puzzled. What is it you see in the tea leaves?"

"No piece of a leaf would dare make its way into your tea when it was poured, Miss Behring. But a thought did occur to me . . . have you ever been to China?"

A half-smile made her look much less forbidding. "No, Shiloh, I have not, and neither have my sisters. Our parents preferred China tea, you see, and we inherited their taste for it."

"Oh." He settled back, took a sip of the tea, and reflected how China tea had a much more herbal taste, with a memory of flowers, in contrast to the strong, bitter India tea. He decided to begin drinking China tea. "Since you were obviously expecting me—perhaps to-day"—he smiled and lifted the extra teacup that had been waiting for him—"I assume you got my letter."

"Yes, and it was a lovely letter. The things you wrote, and the things you told me, were quite an honorable memorial to Linde. Thank you for that, Shiloh," she said formally. "And I am glad that you saw Etta in Charleston. She also wrote and told me that you visited."

"She's doing very well," he replied and considered her carefully. "Are you?"

"Oh yes, I'm doing much better than Etta!" she said mischievously. "I have thirteen children, but I have received scholarships from the Capuchin convent for the girls and from the Jesuit school for the boys! So I am not obliged to conduct school, you see, as all of my children are from eight years up."

Shiloh's eyebrows raised with surprise. "And how did you manage to wrangle scholarships for thirteen children from the Capuchins and the Jesuits? Their schools are real expensive, huh?"

"Really expensive," Miss Behring said sternly, both in agreement with Shiloh and to correct his grammar. "Really. And the Lord simply provided it."

"But you helped communicate the Lord's wishes in this matter to the Jesuits and the Capuchins, I'm sure," Shiloh teased.

"Surely," she said placidly. "Anyway, you see I am a lady of leisure. I know I don't have to work nearly as hard as Etta, because she has twenty-two now and still has school."

Shiloh reflected somberly that this was probably a good thing, because this Miss Behring was the middle sister and seemed to be aging more quickly than either Miss Linde had or Miss Etta. . . . Shiloh shook his head slightly, then asked abruptly, "Miss Behring, will you tell me your name? Since I'm over twenty now, your two sisters thought that I might be trusted to know their first names without abusing the privilege."

She laughed, a small, calm expression of joy that was most pleasing to hear. "Yes, I suppose we no longer have to worry about you being a scruffy, impudent boy who might call us by our first names. It's Tanzen. It means 'to dance.'"

"Tanzen . . . I like it."

"I'm glad you approve, young man," she said dryly.

He smiled, took another sip of tea, and leaned back in the rocking chair, which creaked with a familiar homey sound. The day was gusty, temperamental, with dark clouds writhing and racing in the heavens. The capricious breezes blew chilly, then warm, then cool again, and occasionally spit single lost drops of rain. But the storm had not yet broken.

"That reminds me . . . names . . ." he said with mock sternness. "Miss Behring, Miss Etta . . . told me that you tried to name me Count Storm von Frankenstein or something like that."

"Nonsense," she scoffed. "It was *Sturm von Drang*, for 'Storm and Stress.' And Frankenstein was the name of a character in a book written by Mary Wollstonecraft Shelley and published in 1818. And he was a baron, not a count."

"Can't argue with you there," Shiloh commented lazily.

"You've read it," Miss Behring said indignantly. "You know it."

He winked at her, and she muttered, "There! You are still impudent, though at least you are not scruffy!" Shiloh, as always, wore a working man's clothes, but they were always clean and pressed, and his hat and boots were always meticulously cared for. Today he wore his gray Confederate breeches with a gray muslin shirt, and his long canvas overcoat. His knee boots were carefully shined, and his gray wide-brimmed felt hat was brushed.

She was looking at him in a peculiar manner, and he met her eyes but waited patiently until she spoke. In the silence he thought languidly, *It's just the same, it hasn't changed . . . not with time, and not with the death of Miss Linde. I still feel more relaxed, more at ease, in the company of the Behring sisters than with anyone else in the world . . . except maybe the Doc . . . sometimes. . . .*

"Shiloh, are you trying to find out about your parents?" Miss Behring finally asked quietly.

"Yes," he answered without hesitation.

"And this—quest, is it very hard for you?"

Shiloh knew exactly what she meant, and he considered his answer carefully before he spoke. "No, it's not hard for me, and it's not hard on me. I'm curious, and sometimes I'm frustrated. But I can't say that I'm bitter or lonely. My life is good. I have friends that I care about, and a job that I care about."

"Thank you, Lord," Miss Behring breathed. She was still watching him closely, however, and she chose her words carefully. "So finding out about your parents is something you truly wish to do? Because it is possible that . . . that . . ."

"That knowing the truth about them might be much worse than having my dreams about them?" Shiloh finished the sentence for her, and she nodded vigorously. He shook his head slightly. "It doesn't matter. I don't care *what* they were. I'd just like to know *who* they were."

Miss Behring's shrewd eyes never left his face as he spoke, and when he said this she breathed easy and sat back, relaxed, in her chair. "*Das ist gut, mein Jungling*," she murmured. Often she expressed terms of endearment in German. "So I have something to tell you."

"You do?"

She met his eyes and smiled with warmth and, Shiloh thought, even with love. "There is a place here in New Orleans, a little to the west of here, down close to the docks. It's an iron foundry and blacksmith's shop. The name of it is Shiloh Ironworks."

★　★　★　★

94

Sitting alone in a hansom carriage that moved by fits and starts along the crazy-quilt streets of New Orleans, Shiloh was brooding and talking to himself.

"This is nothing to get excited about," he muttered. "Probably a coincidence. Probably can't help me at all. After all, what am I going to say? 'Hi, remember me? I was born in one of your boxes.'"

This dark nonsense went on until the carriage came to a stop at the entrance of one of the many off-street alleys close to the docks. It was not, however, a dank and fearful place, as many of New Orleans' lost and unnamed pathways were. The alley was narrow but clean, the old flagstones washed down, the buildings lining it well maintained. Across the entrance to the alley was posted a sign on a wrought-iron cross-piece: Spenser Alley.

Shiloh thought that the word *alley* was misleading, as many of these small pathways in New Orleans were actually sidewalks, or banquettes. Thousands of them dotted the city, many of them with gated entrances, many of them providing entrance to only one home or throughway from a single business to another.

This one dead-ended at Shiloh Ironworks.

It was a simple square wooden building, large but not imposing. Two stories, raised on pilings, it was whitewashed and had long French windows on either side of the door. Behind the building Shiloh could see the furnaces of the iron foundry belching black smoke, and he could faintly hear the far-off roar of the great ovens. In his nostrils was the coppery smell of smelted iron.

On the portico was a square black sign, trimmed with curlicues and embellishments of black wrought iron, with "SHILOH IRONWORKS" on it in white block script. Shiloh, feeling the first big threatening drops of rain thump on his hat, hurried up the steps and inside.

A bell jangled noisily when he entered, and a Federal soldier who was lounging lazily behind a desk looked up. His blue tunic was un-buttoned at the collar, and he looked sleepy. He didn't get up, but merely looked at Shiloh with boredom. "Yeah?" was all he said.

Shiloh took his time. He looked around the room, which was a long, narrow room spanning the length of the building. Three desks were lined along a low banister with swinging-door accesses, but the other two desks were unoccupied, forlornly bare. Behind the soldier was a line of businesslike filing cabinets. Shiloh noted that no entries were inserted into the title slots of the file drawers, and his heart sank.

Most all of the businesses in the South that had dealings with Confederates had destroyed their records before occupation. New Orleans had been occupied since 1862.

Shiloh folded his arms and looked back down at the soldier. The desk where he was carelessly sprawled was littered with coffee and remnants of *beignets* and was sprinkled messily with the white powdered sugar from the pastries. Not a single piece of paper littered his desk—or dining table, as it was.

"Who's in charge here?" Shiloh asked bluntly.

"General Phil Sheridan, commanding the Federal forces in Louisiana, is in charge here and ever'place else," he smirked. "You got any other questions, Johnny Reb?"

"As a matter of fact I do, bluebelly," Shiloh growled. "Is there anybody here that actually works? Here at the ironworks, I mean?"

The man, a private named Dennis Tilley, looked Shiloh up and down. He saw a tall man with broad shoulders, big hands, fighting scars, and mean eyes. Private Dennis Tilley decided that it wasn't worth the effort to have his afternoon intruded upon—perhaps by getting seriously injured—so he answered sullenly, "Yeah. Who you want? You looking for a job?"

"No, I'm just looking for someone who knows something," Shiloh said belligerently. He felt like a fool on a fool's errand, and he was taking it out on this dumb nick, but to tell the truth he didn't much care.

Dennis Tilley slowly unwound from the chair and without a word turned and went to a door in the back of the room. When he opened it, the thunder of iron-making got much louder. "Where's McDonough?" he hollered. "Send him in here!"

Tilley turned, shut the door, and swaggered slowly across the room and past Shiloh. He didn't say another word, but his dull brown eyes cut to his tall figure as he passed him, and when he was behind Shiloh he glanced nervously back over his shoulder. To his relief Shiloh was standing motionless and seemed not to have even seen him pass. With relief Tilley decided that Shiloh Ironworks could guard its own self for a while, as he felt a sudden need to go down to the Brazier Saloon and wash down those *beignets* with a beer.

Shiloh sat and decided to wait patiently, so he cleared all the grumblings out of his mind and willed himself to relax. *Like you told Miss Behring, it really doesn't matter. . . .* Deep down, Shiloh had a strong sense that one day he would find out about his parents. He didn't know when, and he didn't know how, but he just *knew* he would. So if today was the day, so be it. If not, one of his tomorrows would be the day.

The door opened, the din rushed in and then shut up as the man closed the door behind him. He was thickly built, burly, with coarse black hair and a full beard and mustache shot through with single strands of white. Dressed in a white shirt, black breeches, and red plaid waistcoat, he nevertheless looked like a working man caught in his Sunday clothes. He had a much-chewed pencil stub behind one ear and was holding a raggedy bunch of papers. His black eyes darted around the room once—searching for the vanquished Dennis Tilley, no doubt—then he walked with a slow firm step toward Shiloh.

He stuck out a meaty hand. "I'm Ian McDonough."

Shiloh stood and shook his hand. "I'm Shiloh Irons." He waited.

McDonough never missed a beat. "Are you, now? Quite a coincidence, eh?"

"Not really," Shiloh answered.

One of McDonough's thick black eyebrows went upward. "It's not?"

"No. That's why I'm here. Because I'm named after Shiloh Ironworks," Shiloh said, and was truly relieved, because it was so easy to say to this plainspoken man.

McDonough crossed his arms, encasing the papers in one thick arm, and looked at Shiloh speculatively. "You're named after Shiloh Ironworks," he repeated slowly. "Sounds like a story I'd like to hear. Care to sit down?" He looked down at Dennis Tilley's litter with disgust and waved toward one of the other empty desks. "Over there?"

"Thanks, I would." When they got seated, Shiloh said briskly, "I do have a story to tell, Mr. McDonough, but I don't want to waste your time. Have you been here long?"

"Twenty-five years. That long enough?" he asked with amusement.

Shiloh chuckled. "Sounds long enough for any man to be working iron. And it's long enough for me. If you wouldn't mind giving me a few minutes, I'd appreciate it."

"Sure, Mr. Irons. A pleasure to give a few minutes to a Confederate gentleman rather than one of Sheridan's ruffians for a change. You go ahead and tell me a story. Take your time."

In an unemotional tone Shiloh recited: "I'm an orphan. I was found on the beach after a shipwreck in Charleston, South Carolina.

I was just a baby, and I was in a crate marked 'Shiloh Ironworks.' "
Shiloh hesitated, considering what to say next, but McDonough nodded confidently and spoke.

"Mmm. November of 1843, was it? When we lost the *Ahava*, right off Morris Island."

Shiloh's jaw dropped, and McDonough watched him, his dark eyes crinkled with amusement. "You're what—twenty-three, twenty-four?"

"D-dunno," Shiloh stammered stupidly.

"O' course, you don't. Couldn't, could you? Been looking for us long, Mr. Irons?" McDonough asked, his laughter very near to bubbling out now.

"Y-yes. That is, no. I mean, yes. Sort of." Shiloh's mind stubbornly refused to stop its wild tilting and whirling.

McDonough finally laughed out loud, a rich, rolling sound that surely had been born hundreds of years before in the sweet air of the Scottish highlands. "I'm sorry, Mr. Irons," he said merrily, "it's just that I do know I can help you, and it's a pleasure to me to see it. I canna imagine how I'd feel if I'd been a foundling and had never known my parents. I may not be able to tell you who your parents were, but I can promise here and now that when you leave Shiloh Ironworks, you'll know more than you did when you walked in."

Shiloh managed a smile and simply said, "Please tell me."

"I was here then, blacksmith's apprentice just starting out," he began. "Man named Isadore Spenser—God rest his good soul—started Shiloh Ironworks in 1835. Named it after Shiloh in the Bible, you know? Mr. Spenser was a good Christian man, an honorable man, a hard-working man. His business thrived, and soon we were shipping iron all over the South and East. But shipping costs were so high, he decided to get into shipping, and he commissioned the *Ahava*. She was plain, just a sturdy and hardworking freighter, but Mr. Spenser loved the old girl. She never let him down, never missed a delivery, never slowed down. . . . She just died, I guess you'd say."

Shiloh sat up straighter in his chair, and his eyes blazed a fiery blue. McDonough's voice dropped to a hoarse rumble. "We got word quick. *Ahava* was loaded to the decks with some good pig iron Mr. Spenser had sold to a railroad firm outside Charleston." He shook his head sadly. "Next day we got a telegram from the Charleston harbormaster that *Ahava* had gone down. Seems like Mr. Spenser never had much heart after that . . . but he was ill, too, and he died three years later."

Glancing back up at Shiloh, who was listening hungrily to every word McDonough spoke, he chewed on his lower lip for a few moments, then said, " 'Course we all knew the *Ahava* went down in a storm, but I never really knew the details."

"First, Mr. McDonough, I need to know right now: Is there any chance I—a baby—would have been aboard the *Ahava*?"

McDonough's almost-black eyes grew as soft and tender as a woman's. "I'm awful sorry, Mr. Irons, but I think it's not very likely. Twelve men went down with the *Ahava*, all good men, men with families. They sailed when we had shipments, and when no shipping was going out, they all worked here in the foundry. Even Captain Rocklin. And the *Ahava* was a working ship, you know. No cabins, savin' a little closet for the captain. Just hammocks in a tiny little room for the seamen. And that ship was so loaded for that trip that e'en a wee babe couldn'a hid in it."

Shiloh said gratefully, "That's all right, Mr. McDonough. I didn't actually think that I was on the freighter, you know, but I wanted your best guess. I was pretty sure I was on the clipper."

Now it was McDonough's turn to look mystified. "Clipper? What clipper?"

Sighing, Shiloh murmured, "There was a terrible storm, yes. But the *Ahava* collided with a clipper, and that's what caused them both to go down. I see you don't know anything about that...."

"No, I didn't," McDonough said heavily. "I sure didn't know that. But Mr. Spenser didn't talk much about it, except when he called us all together and told us the *Ahava* had gone down. It was just a small company, you see, and we knew each other and everyone's families. Anyway, after that he never mentioned it again. So all we knew was what we gossiped and made up about it, I reckon."

This brought a little smile to Shiloh's face, and right then Ian McDonough made up his mind to help this young man if he could. "I'll tell you, Mr. Irons," he said very slowly, "we destroyed all the papers when the Billy Yanks came a-traipsin' into town. But Mr. Spenser kept good records, and I'd think the wreck of the *Ahava* would have been important to him, but not to the Federal Government. It may be ... it may be ..." His voice faded out, and Shiloh waited, trying to be patient and trying not to hope too much.

"Yeah, yeah," McDonough finally said decisively. "I might can find the file or report or whatever you call 'em. We burned all the papers for '60, '61, and '62, 'cause we'd been making lots of interesting things for the Confederate States of America. But we didn't burn all the old files, didn't figure we needed to, and didn't have the time nor heart to do it, anyway. You just wait right here, Mr. Irons. I don't think I'll be too long."

"Thank you kindly, Mr. McDonough," Shiloh said quietly.

McDonough got to his feet and gave Shiloh a shrewd glance. "I can't swear to finding it, Mr. Irons."

"That doesn't matter, Mr. McDonough. Thank you anyway. I'll wait."

Shiloh didn't have to wait long at all. McDonough went out the front door, and Shiloh realized that the stairs to the second floor were, as usual in New Orleans, on the outside. With surprise he saw that outside it was as dark as a new moon night, and fat droplets slapped against the French windows and trickled jerkily down the panes.

Sitting alone in the quiet, sadly empty room, he imagined how busy and how lively it must have been when Mr. Isadore Spenser was alive, before those twelve men from Shiloh Ironworks walked out that front door and never returned. He reflected how odd it was that he had never thought of all the other players in the drama in Charleston Harbor the night of that fatal tempest. Shiloh Irons, who was no fool, also reflected how very odd it was that he had been able to weave together the few slender threads of his past into the beginnings of his story. Those delicate strands might have been so easily, and so tragically, lost in the intricate tapestry of time. . . .

He was completely engrossed in this philosophical speculation when Ian McDonough returned, holding a slender leather binder. He had an odd light in his eyes. Without speaking he sat down across the desk from Shiloh and handed the binder across to him. Lettered in fine gold leaf on the front was *Ahava*.

Shiloh, his mouth suddenly going dry, opened the folder. It had several documents in it, and Shiloh could see that the first one was the building specifications for the freighter. But on the very top, loose, was a letter on fine parchment, and the letterhead tastefully announced that it was from Lloyd's of London.

It was a final report on a maritime assurance claim. The claimant was Shiloh Ironworks; the assured, the ten-ton freighter known as the *Ahava*.

Shiloh skimmed the tersely worded document at great speed. It was a synopsis of the weather and sea conditions in Charleston that night, the harbormaster's statement as recorded by the Lloyd's of London investigators, the investigators' explanatory notes, and then the final paragraph:

Conclusion: Ahava *went down on the night of November 2, 1843, at approximately midnight, with the loss of all twelve hands. Wreck is estimated to be four miles off Morris Island and unsalvageable.*

Probable cause: collision with Day Dream, *clipper ship (size/displacement unknown); last known harbor registry, New Orleans, Louisiana; home registry, San Francisco, California.*

8

TO NOTHING AND NOBODY

Luna sluggishly awoke to blindness. She thought that it was close to morning, but her bedroom was still cloaked in night. Rubbing her eyes, she felt the moistness on her cheeks and wearily realized she had been crying in her sleep again. Even though she was forty-two now, and Alexandre Bayonne had died thirteen years ago, and she no longer burned with longing and passion, she still cried in her sleep.

"Still dark," she said in a dead voice, "but I might as well get up." Luna knew she wouldn't be able to go back to sleep, so she rose and opened the shutters on the east window. No silvery gray promise of dawn showed on the horizon over the indigo fields, but Luna decided to get dressed anyway and go down to meet Octave at dawn. Today was Saturday, and he would bring mail and the newspapers.

Luna never got any mail, but she liked to read *The Picayune*, which was about the only bit of frivolity she allowed herself. Patterned after the northern penny press, *The Picayune* was filled with brief light articles that were even flippant in tone, poems, fiction, "cards" from readers, and social gossip. She always insisted on paying Octave the "picayune"—6 and 1/4 cents—for it, even though he told her that Mrs. Buckingham and Mrs. Edwards paid monthly subscriptions for each of the six newspapers that he brought to Les Chattes Bleues three times a week. That didn't matter to Luna. She was the only one on the plantation who read *The Picayune*, and she would pay for it.

Lighting a new candle, she dressed quickly in a shapeless gray cotton dress and plain white apron. Long gone were the fine morning dresses of satin in the negligible winter, and silk and muslin for the spring and summer. Sometimes she remembered them—as she did briefly this gloomy morning—but not with regret, only as frozen, faded daguerreotypes in her mind. Yawning, her eyes still stinging, she put on her shoes and went to fetch fresh water.

"Good rain yesterday, all day," she mumbled as she went to the cistern that served the sharecroppers' and servants' cottages. "Good thing . . . cistern was getting low. . . ."

As she filled two large earthenware pitchers, Luna kept talking but suddenly cut off mid-word. She reflected with dry amusement that she must be the only person in the world who talked to herself all the time but didn't listen to herself. Her ears had been registering voice noises, but she had no idea what she had been saying to nothing and nobody. A humorless smile turned up the corners of her full, well-shaped mouth.

Luna was an octoroon, the daughter of a white man and a quadroon woman. She looked whiter than many Creole women, with an ageless, smooth ecru skin and soft, wavy black hair that had burnished copper highlights and not a thread of gray. Without vanity she noticed her hands, as if for the first time; they were still fine, thin-fingered, soft, and bore no trace of the excruciatingly hard work she'd done for the last twelve years, making indigo.

"*Café brûlot diabolique,*" she said to the air. "Wonderfully romantic name . . . 'diabolically burning coffee.' " A better translation would have been "burned coffee." Rather than roasting fresh beans in the sun or in an oven, Luna actually cooked them over a high flame, so the *café brûlot diabolique* she made herself was thick, blacker than black, with a smoky, fired taste. She couldn't drink more than one cup of it at a time, but that occasional cup was good when she wanted it. She wanted it this morning, for she felt as if she hadn't slept in days, although she actually slept—or was in bed, at least—eight hours every night.

With a graceful economy of movement in the tiny kitchen, she made the coffee and sat down at the tiny wooden table with the single chair. It faced out a window, and she stared at the indigo fields and dawn-dreamed of long-ago, bright New Orleans days and sultry Creole nights.

With a start she realized that her half drunk cup of *café brûlot diaholique* was cold. It was almost dawn, and she had only drunk a glass of the fresh, sweet rainwater and had not eaten a bite. Still she decided to hurry down to the landing and meet Octave, although she wouldn't have time to read the paper and eat breakfast before she had to go to the drying barns. It didn't matter anyway. She was still strong, her body still lithe, and she often skipped breakfast when she lost the time, as she had this morning. It meant she would need to eat an early lunch, or she would be weak, but that was all right. No one looked over her shoulder and demanded that her time belonged to them. Never again.

She put on a plain straw sun hat and hurried out of her cottage. Les Chattes Bleues was lit with a pleasing pink light, and the gardens smelled green and fresh. Even though she was in a hurry, she stopped to breathe deeply and look at the eastern sky. Long scarlet lines, their edges fading to maroon and then pink, colored the horizon. The sky was already taking on an azure hue. The dreary February rains of yesterday were gone.

As she again made her way through the gardens, around the side of Les Chattes Bleues, she noticed that her forehead was a little moist, and she took off her hat to dab above her eyes.

"Odd," she murmured, "I actually feel a little chilled. . . ." But she was definitely perspiring. Walking quickly now, she jammed her hat back on her head and felt a bit queasy. Luna frowned. She was almost never ill, and the few times she had been it was generally only a little catarrh, or some sneezing and dripping in the springtime and autumn. She began to walk more slowly as she rounded the corner of the house. Her stomach was definitely rolling and lurching, and she swallowed hard. Again she felt a clammy moistness on her forehead . . . on her upper lip . . . on her arms, behind her knees . . .

Suddenly Luna's strong, well-formed legs felt as weak as a child's, and she twisted her ankle and crashed to the walkway. The path was laid with oyster and clam shells, and she cut her cheek, for she was so weak she was unable to control her fall in any fashion. Tears welled up in her eyes, but Luna was strong and proud, and she quickly choked them back. Slowly, shakily, she sat up and touched her hand to her face. Her delicate fingers came away bloody—much too bloody, she thought, for what had not seemed to be a serious cut. She wiped her cheek again, and blood dripped from her fingers, and she could still feel it running down her face.

Luna began to feel very, very frightened.

But the habits and manners of a lifetime are not easily tossed aside, even in moments of great stress, for a woman like Luna. It never occurred to her to call out for help. She simply sat on the path, wiping her cheek over and over again, swallowing down bile, and trying desperately to gauge if she could get up and walk back to her cottage. With deadly slowness the dizziness overtook her. She didn't even realize that what she was staring at blankly had begun to whirl sickeningly, until all at once a part of her mind registered that though her eyes were open, she was actually seeing nothing but a wavering, indefinite blur. Luna tried to say something, but within seconds she had, in truth, joined her constant companions: nothing and nobody.

★　★　★　★

Octave found her only minutes later.

He called Monroe, whose bronzed features turned a sickly yellow when Octave ran to the cottage and began banging on the door, calling out in urgent Gascon French. Monroe had some trouble understanding Octave, but he understood this. Both men ran back to Luna, but Monroe forbade Octave to move her or even try to make her more comfortable. She was still unconscious, and bright but thin red blood seeped steadily from the cut on her high, finely sculpted cheekbone.

Monroe ran for Richard Duvall; Richard immediately awoke Cheney and Shiloh, and within a few minutes all of them were gathered around Luna's pitifully crumpled form in the bright, cheerful garden.

"Don't touch her," Cheney muttered. "You haven't . . . very good, Monroe . . . Shiloh?"

They knelt on the path, one on each side of her. Shiloh reached out a tentative finger to dab some of the blood, but each time he wiped it away, it ran on and on. Shiloh's grave blue eyes met Cheney's over the still form.

Cheney felt Luna's pulse; it was fast and weak and erratic. Her breathing was shallow, almost an animal pant. Cheney pulled her stethoscope out of her bag and listened to Luna's heart as Shiloh ran gentle hands down both her arms and legs, and then down the back of her neck and along her spine. Luna had fallen over on her side, and Shiloh was careful not to jar her.

"Arms and legs okay," he muttered. "Back and neck—as far as I can tell—okay. Ankle's swollen. Maybe she wrenched it, fell, got dizzy? No . . . something's wrong."

"Something," Cheney echoed grimly. She looked up. A circle of pale men stood close around them, as if they were trying to shield Luna. "I want Shiloh to carry her to her cabin. Walk in front of him, Monroe, to lead and to make sure nothing will make him trip. Father, Octave, you walk close behind him to steady him. She's dead weight, she's a good-sized woman, and I want Shiloh to hurry. He can't be looking around to see where he's going."

"But couldn't we all carry her?" Richard Duvall asked. "It would seem—"

"No," Cheney replied firmly. "Shiloh knows exactly what to do. Just watch him, please, Father, and be ready to steady him if he stumbles."

Shiloh was already carefully turning Luna over on her back. She was still far under, and her light golden face was turning gray. Her skin was damp and too cool, and her eyes were rolled up to show a half-moon of white beneath the slightly opened lids. Shiloh squatted down beside her and slid one muscular arm beneath her knees, taking a moment to make certain that he had them in a good position and he had a good grip. Then he slid his right arm beneath her shoulders and crooked his arm upward to make a cradle for her head, which lolled as if her neck were broken. He lifted her until he was in a deep knee bend, straightened his back, and stood, seemingly with little effort. But it must have been a terrific strain, even for a man with Shiloh's great strength, for he had to support her entire upper body while cradling her head to keep it upright and steady.

As the group moved out, all of them walking quickly toward the servants' cabins, Cheney explained to her father in a low voice, "She's so deeply unconscious she could actually injure her neck—perhaps even break it—if Shiloh didn't hold her that way. And also, since she's in some sort of respiratory distress, he has to hold her up slightly, or she could swallow her tongue and suffocate."

Richard Duvall thought grimly, *What an awful way to be reminded how proud I am of Cheney . . . and what a good, steady man Shiloh Irons is. . . . I'm so glad she has him.*

Monroe called out in a low, strained voice, "Three steps up, Mr. Irons."

"Got it."

The odd caravan reached Luna's cottage. Monroe held the door open, Shiloh gracefully swept inside holding the unconscious woman, Cheney followed him, and Richard and Octave stayed outside on the porch.

With Cheney's help Shiloh laid Luna gently on the bed. The only bedclothes were a light cotton sheet and a fine linen coverlet. "See if you can find a quilt or blanket," Cheney told Shiloh. He was already kneeling in front of a small chest at the foot of the bed, but he quickly closed it and looked around the room.

It was a good-sized bedroom, but spare, with only the bed, a modest, plain armoire, a single bedside table, and the chest. Throwing open the armoire, he found two neatly folded handmade quilts, and he covered Luna with smooth, sure movements.

Cheney had propped her up slightly by folding up her thin pillow. She took Luna's pulse again and monitored her heartbeat through the stethoscope for a long time. Frowning darkly, she muttered, "Need to give her some digitalis, but we'd better make sure first that she doesn't have angina. Find out from Monroe if he knows, Shiloh, and if he doesn't, see if anyone at Les Chattes Bleues does. I don't want to give her anything until I get a little of her history . . . and this cut . . ."

With a worried look on her face she took clean linen bandages out of her bag and dabbed at the wound on Luna's cheek. "Shiloh, look . . . this is hemorrhaging entirely too much for this little cut. It's not even going to take a stitch."

Shiloh frowned. "It is strange . . . so much blood from that? Maybe it's real deep . . . still, it's odd. Jeremy's Paste?" A young man, Jeremy Blue, had developed an extremely effective styptic ointment that he had used when he was seconding Shiloh in his boxing matches.

"Yes, good idea," Cheney agreed. "I don't have any in my bag, do you?"

"Yes, but it's in my *garçonniere*. I just pulled on my clothes and ran. I'll go get it. What else?"

"See if she has any tea and honey in the house. If not, get some from Monroe." Cheney took Luna's pulse again and gently pulled up her eyelids. Only white still showed. "Start some hot water, if the stove's going. If not, get me a fire going. And . . . I don't want whiskey, too rough . . . ask Monroe if there's any brandy in the house. Good, smooth brandy."

Shiloh, to his surprise, found himself having a hard time listening to what Cheney was saying. He had just noted for the first time that she was still dressed in her gown, a fine white linen with ruffles trimmed with delicate white lace at the neck and throat. The buttons were made of tiny satin rosettes, and the top one was undone. . . . Cheney had a long, slender neck, creamy white and graceful. . . . She wore a matching white robe belted carelessly around her slender waist. Her hair was down, held back only by a white satin ribbon, and it tumbled in glorious disarray over her shoulders and down her back. *It's so beautiful, so shiny, so clean-looking,* he thought in confusion, *I bet it smells like flowers.* For a few seconds he saw his own hands, buried in the warm auburn depths of Cheney's hair, and bending down to bury his face in it and breathe deeply of that scent. . . .

"Shiloh!" Cheney said sternly. "Are you sleepwalking or something? Did you hear me?"

"Hmm? Oh, yeah, sure I did, Doc. Tea, honey, a fire, brandy, send Monroe in for history, and"—he turned at the doorway and looked at her with an odd light in his eyes—"I'll get Nia to come down with some clothes for you, and some shoes. You're barefooted, and I don't want you to cut your feet."

He spoke with great gentleness, his voice deep and caressing. Cheney caught her breath, but by the time she looked up, he was already gone.

★   ★   ★   ★

"Luna is a *gens de couleur libres,*" Tante Marye said.

"Well, all of the persons of color are free now, Marye," Elyse offered.

"She is an octoroon," Tante Marye went on. At Cheney's mystified look, Marye explained, "Her mother is a quadroon, one-quarter colored, and her father is white. A Creole."

"So Luna is one-eighth Negro?" Cheney asked.

Tante Marye hesitated, and she and Elyse exchanged uncertain glances. "Ye-es, dear," Elyse said airily, "but in New Orleans only pure-blooded Africans are referred to as 'Negroes.' "

Cheney, casting a look at Monroe's bronze, expressionless features, decided to ask Tante Elyse more about this later. "It doesn't matter, anyway. Does anyone know if she's had a history of heart trouble? Angina, even mild palpitations?"

Tante Elyse shook her head firmly. "Not that I know of. At least, she never told me if she does."

"She keeps to herself so much that I'm not certain anyone would know," Tante Marye sniffed. "I, myself, have not even seen her for weeks. I quite forget that she is even on the place."

"She's usually outside," Tante Elyse said seriously. "Not in the house. That's why you never see her."

"I go outdoors, to the garden, and on the galleries," Marye argued.

"No, you don't," Elyse said timidly. "You just think you do."

"Elyse, are you saying that I am delusional? That I think I go out-

108

side, but in fact I do not?" Marye demanded, her blue eyes sparking indignantly.

"Mm-hmm," Elyse hummed, taking a large bite of her potato omelet. Before Marye could release the torrent of words she was obviously preparing, Elyse changed the subject. "Anyway, Cheney, it's going to be difficult to find out exactly what she ate and drank for the last twenty-four hours, because Luna hardly ever eats with the other sharecroppers in the kitchen. They are responsible for their own breakfasts and lunches, you see, but they have a common supper prepared for them every night except Sunday. Luna rarely joins them, and I don't think she ate with them last night."

It was eleven o'clock, and Monroe and Molly had only now managed to get a meal together and served. In the confusion no breakfast was prepared, but Tante Marye would not have a household where three full meals were not offered to her guests. She announced that they would begin with *le déjeuner*, and have a light meal at *le thé anglais*, and tonight *un souper*. To Richard, Irene translated: their first meal would be a more elaborate cross between breakfast and lunch, their second meal would be at four o'clock, at teatime, and they would have a late supper. Gowan Ford had arrived on the scene rather late, and when he saw that Luna had fallen ill, he insisted upon visiting every cottage at Les Chattes Bleues, so he was not present at *le déjeuner*. But he would join them for *le thé anglais* and *un souper*.

Cheney had attempted to join the company in her working clothes, a plain black cotton dress and a clean white apron. But Tante Marye said decidedly, "I don't care what Irene does, this is my house, Cheney, and I shall certainly not allow you to dine costumed as a servant. I know you wish to change into a morning dress, and we will be happy to wait."

At that point everyone trooped obediently into the downstairs parlor to wait. Monroe hastily prepared tea and coffee while Molly fumbled to set up the warming candles and platters and match the great covers to each of the platters. Corbett and Chloe and Ada retrieved the fruit and compotes into covered containers and repacked the crushed ice into silver buckets packed inside larger buckets filled with sawdust.

Since Nia was staying with Luna, Cheney was obliged to change herself and arrange her own hair. Her hair flying and her cheeks flushed, she raced about the bedroom, strewing clothing, searching for stockings, finding only one shoe that matched her lavender morning gown. Finally, after an unconscionable time, she was fairly presentable and rushed back downstairs to the parlor.

Now they ate hungrily, and Shiloh gallantly said, "The food is always great here, but this is about the best I've had. The longer a hungry man waits, the better the food tastes."

Cheney shot him a grateful look, and he winked. Again Irene took note of their special little communications and smiled to herself. Richard, who was concentrating on his eggplant stuffed with rice and ham, saw and heard nothing.

"So Luna has the terrible Les Chattes Bleues malady," Victoria announced.

"It's worse with Luna," Tante Elyse said with a worried look. "The others had the same symptoms, but not as serious."

"Well, Cheney, do you have any idea what's wrong with this woman?" Victoria asked.

"None," Cheney sighed. "I've never seen anything like this before. The combination of symptoms is most unusual—thready pulse, erratic heartbeat, pale, cool skin, effusive sweating, acute hemorrhaging—"

"Cheney!" Tante Marye protested, her lips drawn downward with displeasure. "Irene! Cheney!"

"*Pardonnez-nous, ma tante,*" Irene said softly. "I suppose we've all grown accustomed to it."

"Sorry, Tante Marye," Cheney said weakly. "I forget."

"Sorry, Mrs. Edwards," Shiloh put in.

Her blue eyes darted toward Shiloh. "And what are you apologizing for, young man? You weren't even taking part in this distasteful little speech!"

"No, ma'am," Shiloh said, popping a grape into his mouth. "But I was thinking about talking about it. The blood and all. Boy, she was bleeding a lot!"

Victoria de Lancie pressed her napkin to her mouth, Tante Elyse giggled, Richard Duvall grinned, Irene sighed, and Cheney quickly ducked her head.

Tante Marye continued to stare indignantly at Shiloh, who tried hard to keep his expression blank but couldn't succeed, and grinned impudently at her. After a moment the merest twitch of the corner of her mouth betrayed her. She tried hard not to, but she smiled; it was hard not to smile when Shiloh did. "So, I see you were apologizing beforehand, Mr. Irons," she said with a grand air. "How gracious of you. Do you see, Cheney? Mr. Irons is prepared for any eventuality, as a gentleman with excellent deportment should be."

"Tante Marye!" Cheney exploded, but then everyone laughed, including Tante Marye, and Cheney realized her great-aunt was teasing her. At least, that was part of it. The rest of the story was that both of her great-aunts were quite foolish over Shiloh Irons, Cheney thought begrudgingly. *I thought Tante Elyse might like him, but Tante Marye!*

Cheney was staring at Shiloh with such ill-temper he put up his hands in a mock defensive gesture and leaned back. "Don't be mad, Doc. You're the one who civilized me, remember?"

"Am I?" she retorted sharply. "Remind me that we need to work on that some more. Now, if anyone here would like to have an adult conversation, I would like to know about Luna. How long she has been here, if she's ever had an illness like this before, if her parents were ill with any recurring diseases that might be hereditary."

Tante Marye nodded at Elyse, in effect giving her younger sister permission to speak. "She's been here twelve years . . . let's see . . . that would make her about forty? Forty-one? She's always seemed so healthy and vigorous. As far as I know, she's never ill. At least, she's never missed a day of work. And her parents . . ."

The severe lines of Tante Marye's face softened a bit, just in her jawline and a slight relaxation of the corners of her mouth. "Her mother lives in New Orleans. If it's truly important, Cheney, I suppose Mr. Law could find her and question her about recurring health problems. Her father is still alive, but I doubt very seriously if he would take kindly to questions being asked about Luna or her mother. He has a wife—his second—and fourteen children." She frowned as she thought how to put it delicately. "Fourteen children with his last name. The youngest is only seven."

"Oh," Cheney said uncertainly. "I suppose it's not that important. Luna, I think—I pray—will be able to tell me these things herself tomorrow."

"No, she won't," Elyse said in a low voice. "I mean, I pray she'll be able to, Cheney, but she won't talk about her parents even if she is. She won't tell you anything about her past at all. And it would offend her greatly if you asked, no matter what the reason."

"Wonderful," Cheney grumbled.

"She's already talking," Shiloh said airily, "and she's already offended."

"What?" Cheney exclaimed. "She was sleeping soundly when I left her with Nia, and I specifically instructed you two not to let her rouse and try to talk!"

Shiloh shrugged. "Nia was sitting by her bed, and I was in the kitchen fixing tea. I heard voices, so I went in there. Miss Luna got real mad, and she pointed at me. 'Get out!' she said. So I got."

Again Marye and Elyse exchanged dark glances. "She wouldn't like you much, Shiloh," Elyse said timidly. "I think Nia and Cheney and I will have to take care of her."

"But why?" Cheney said irritably. "Shiloh's done nothing to her except help her! Possibly save her life!"

"Cheney dear, Luna was . . . she . . . before she came here . . ." Elyse tried, then blew out an impatient breath. Finally she blurted out, "Luna's companion of eleven years was a man named Alexandre Bayonne. He was killed in a duel."

"So . . . so . . . does Shiloh look like him or something?" Cheney scoffed.

"No," Elyse replied gently, "he looks like the man who killed him."

"Figured something like that," Shiloh mumbled.

"What!" Cheney demanded.

"I told you you should have let me explain to you about the quadroon balls," Victoria said smugly.

"Victoria, I'm not an idiot," Cheney snapped.

"I disapprove of this conversation," Tante Marye suddenly decided.

"I'm having trouble assembling a conversation out of this," Richard mumbled. He had only been half-listening, for when he finally understood that Luna was going to be all right, his mind had wandered to his meeting with John Law yesterday. He had a lot of questions he needed to ask Marye and Elyse.

Irene patted his arm. "I'll explain it all to you later, dear."

"I will tell it now," Elyse said with the air of one who has made a momentous decision.

"Elyse, I don't—"

But for once Tante Elyse ignored Tante Marye and began speaking unconcernedly. "Luna's mother—her name is Avril—attended the quadroon balls with her mother and formed a liaison with a man named Jean-Michel Fleury. And don't fuss at me for telling his name, Marye, I don't owe that man any more—or less—respect than I do

112

Avril, or Luna for that matter. Anyway, *Monsieur* Fleury and Avril were lovers—"

"Elyse!" Marye clamored.

"—for eighteen years, but the only child they had was Luna," Elyse went on. "When *Monsieur* Fleury married, he made the usual settlement with Avril—he gave her a little house by the ramparts and a competence. Sometimes—most of the time—the quadroons use this money to begin businesses such as hairdressing or *modistes*, but the only business Avril ever undertook was Luna."

Elyse shook her head sorrowfully, and her voice was filled with pity. "Avril dressed Luna, she groomed Luna, she sent her to the Sisters of the Holy Family to receive a classical education, and in addition Luna had pianoforte, painting, tapestry, and carriage and deportment lessons every single day. When Luna was eighteen—not a moment before—she and Avril began attending the quadroon balls." Marye's fine nostrils quivered with distaste. "Avril turned down three substantial young men before she finally sold Luna to Alexandre Bayonne. Avril maintains that it is no different than an arranged marriage, but in my opinion it certainly is different, for no Creole gentleman ever actually marries his quadroon mistress."

"Elyse!" Marye protested again.

"Oh, Marye, do be quiet and let me tell it," Elyse said with unheard-of impatience. "No one here is having the vapors except you, and you never really faint all the way. Anyway, Avril got a handsome settlement, and Luna seemed to truly love Alexandre Bayonne, and he treated her exceptionally well. Of course, most men do treat their quadroon ladies very well, I believe. At least, that is my understanding."

"But they didn't live happily ever after, did they?" Victoria asked with quiet sarcasm.

"No, they didn't," Elyse replied. "In 1843 the Duke of Hesse-Posen visited New Orleans, and he attended both the white subscription balls at the St. Louis Hotel, and the quadroon balls at the Orleans Ballroom. In his entourage was a young Prussian soldier who fell in love with Luna."

"She still attended the balls?" Victoria asked curiously.

"Oh, certainly, but only escorted by Alexandre," Elyse answered. "Late at night, after the theater or the opera, one often sees gentlemen with their quadroon mistresses at the balls, and even in private dining rooms in fashionable restaurants. But this young Prussian soldier didn't understand the . . . the . . . strict code by which these relationships are governed. He simply showed up at Luna's house in the middle of the night and tried to make her let him in and insulted her. When Luna told Alexandre about it the next day, he challenged the Prussian to a duel."

Elyse was silent for a moment, and everyone waited expectantly. "Alexandre had no chance, none at all. The soldier simply walked up to him and buried his rapier in his heart. Alexandre died within minutes . . . but not before he whispered, 'Tell Luna I love her, and always will.'"

"Tragic," Irene whispered, her eyes downcast.

Elyse, who was staring down at the now-empty table, nodded, then looked back up. "Yes it is, but not for the reason you think. Luna didn't even know about the duel until she read it in the newspapers the next day. It was matter-of-factly reported that Alexandre Bayonne had been killed in *le charge d'honneur*. The article told all about how Alexandre was engaged to be married within two months, and how distraught his fianceé was. She was a young girl, only eighteen, from a fine family."

"What a terrible way to live," Cheney sighed.

"Yes," Marye said softly. "Luna told me once that every quadroon woman believes that her partner will prove an exception to the rule of desertion, and every white lady believes that her husband has been an exception to the rule of seduction, and they are both always wrong. So truly white and colored women were not so different after all."

"It is tragic for her to be so bitter," Irene said quietly. "Because not all men are like that." She smiled up at Richard, who clasped her hand and held it.

Cheney was eyeing Shiloh in a most uncharitable manner, and Victoria noted it. "It wasn't actually Shiloh who killed Alexandre Bayonne, you know, Cheney," she teased. "He only looks like this Prussian soldier."

"A-and why sh-should I be concerned if it was you?" Cheney stammered angrily at Shiloh.

"But, Doc, it wasn't," Shiloh protested, grinning. "Promise. I mean, I was in existence at the time, but you'll have to forgive me for that."

"Yes, Cheney, you really must," Elyse said with great seriousness, and then she turned to Shiloh. "But I don't think Luna will."

9

INTERLUDE

Luna fell ill on Saturday and was so stricken that Nia and Cheney and Tante Elyse took turns staying with her that night, the next day, and all Sunday night. By Monday morning, however, she had improved so much that Cheney felt assured that she would be all right staying alone—as Luna herself repeatedly requested.

Since it seemed that Luna would recover, and as no one else had fallen prey to the strange sickness, Richard Duvall and Gowan Ford decided to go into the city. Richard wished to send a telegram to Big Jim Clarkson at Duvall's Iron Foundry and wait for a reply. Gowan Ford had a newly readied shipment of indigo to sell and ship.

"Can we ride into the city?" Richard asked doubtfully.

"It's a ride and several swims," Ford said dryly. "I usually ride over to the Mississippi River landing at the Lefebvre plantation and catch one of the steamers."

"Then let's do that," Richard said with relief. "I can swim, but as Octave painstakingly pointed out to me, so can *le serpent* and *le cocodril*." Ford rode his black gelding, and Shiloh graciously offered to let Richard take Sock.

It was a two-hour ride, but Richard enjoyed it immensely. The day was sunny and cool, the woods and streams sweetly quiet, and Gowan Ford was not a man who insisted upon continual polite conversation. Richard had time to reflect upon the things that had happened, and the things he had learned, since he had come to Les Chattes Bleues. Even though he was a practical man, a strong man who never flinched at problems, he was dealing with an uncharacteristic personal difficulty. He was not afraid—certainly not. But he felt an untoward dread, curious premonitions of impending disaster. At odd times during the day, and sometimes when he awoke at night, he felt faint flickers of alarm. Like a bird's shadow that suddenly darkened a bright landscape,

115

the feeling came over him that something at Les Chattes Bleues was wrong. With a mental shrug he decided to ignore these feelings. Even if they were real, even if they were based in some fact he had yet to recognize, Richard knew all he could do—and should do—was pray, for his Lord was his rock and his fortress.

The Lefebvre landing was much more than a dock. In fact, there were three docks, one of them more like a pier to serve the large paddle-wheelers that rode the Mississippi. At the landing were stables, two stablehands, a gazebo with a silent Negro woman preparing food and drink, and even two sizable *garçonnieres*, although one of them was for ladies. They were evidently there for travelers to freshen up, and there were even hammocks provided in a back loggia for naps.

"This is quite an accommodation for a single plantation," Richard noted as they made arrangements for Sock and Ford's horse, who was named LaFitte, to be stabled until they returned that night.

"This landing actually serves four plantations," Ford explained, "including Les Chattes Bleues. All four families contribute to the buildings, the pay of the help, and the upkeep."

"So is this where you bring the indigo to be shipped out?" Richard asked as they repaired to the gazebo for a cool glass of lemonade.

"Sometimes, depending upon the size of the shipment. Indigo's not a high-bulk product like sugar and cotton. Sometimes we've even sent small shipments into New Orleans on Octave's big flatboat, and he brings his brother to help pole it." Ford shrugged expressively. "The vicomte contacted buyers all over the country, you see, and no one was too small for him to sell to. And Elyse has kept it up, too. We probably don't sell as much as if we factored it on the open market, but—"

"But also you aren't paying that middleman."

"True. More work for Elyse, but it seems that the size of the crop we produce is just exactly right for the buyers we have. Our shipments are always sold as soon as they're ready. It might be going to fifteen different buyers, or it might be going to two. But it gets sold, thank the Lord," Ford finished with satisfaction.

Richard took a sip of the iced, tangy lemonade, and his blue-gray eyes gazed into the far distance. "Mr. Ford, can you think of any possible reason, no matter how farfetched or unlikely, that someone would want to scare Marye and Elyse off Les Chattes Bleues?"

Ford's scarred face grew even darker. "I've spent a lot of time trying to figure that out, Colonel Duvall, but with no success. I can't think of a reason any person would mean harm to those two ladies."

"I thought at first that someone must want to buy Les Chattes Bleues," Richard told him, "and that they might be trying to scare them into selling." Richard watched Gowan Ford carefully; he wanted to see if Ford knew about the ownership of Les Chattes Bleues, but if he did not, Richard had no intention of divulging it to him.

Ford's firm mouth widened enough for a small smile. "Then they ought to be sending their ghosts and their indigo poison and their sicknesses to the vicomte's castle in France."

"I know," Richard said with relief. "But, Mr. Ford, is there a possibility that one of the sharecroppers would want Marye and Elyse to leave? Could any one of them actually think that they would somehow gain control of Les Chattes Bleues if that happened?"

"I'm the only one who'd have cause to think that, aren't I?" Ford asked blandly.

Richard gave him a penetrating look, then relaxed as he saw the twinkle in Ford's sharp blue eye. "Mr. Ford, if you've called out the *vaudou* and all their bag of tricks, would you please stop it?" he asked with an innocent air.

Ford took a long, slow drink of lemonade and then poured himself and Richard a fresh helping from the generous glass pitcher sitting on the table between them. "Sure would," he muttered, "if I had."

Richard grinned and nodded, and Ford went on. "The sharecroppers would be fools to run off Marye and Elyse. Elyse does all the selling of the crop and arranges for shipping, payment, and distribution of the monies. Marye attends to every single household's supply needs, from food and clothing to candles and chamber pots. Everyone at Les Chattes Bleues knows how good they have it, being in business with Marye and Elyse."

"Yes, I understand that very well," Richard agreed. "And from what I've seen of all the sharecroppers and servants, they understand it very well, too. But what about someone who might want to take over the land? I mean, they wouldn't have to actually own the land, if they could force Elyse to lease it all to them."

"In the first place, indigo is a difficult crop, Colonel Duvall. It's not like other cash crops. Riff and Raff could manage a sugarcane plantation, or a cotton plantation," Ford said with biting sarcasm. "But indigo is hard to raise, and hard to process, and hard to sell. I can't think of anyone who'd want to take over that plantation, because, as I said, Marye and Elyse are the very reasons it's so profitable." He shrugged. "Only people I thought might want to barge in there and grab it was the Federal Government, and believe me, they've done it to plenty of plantations around here. Treasonous Confederate traitors, you know, forfeiting their rights to land ownership, is the justification they use. I still don't know why they haven't bothered us at Les Chattes Bleues. Maybe because I'm the only treasonous Confederate traitor connected to it."

Richard said nothing about his intervention on behalf of Les Chattes Bleues; he hadn't even told Marye and Elyse, and never would. He leaned back, crossed his arms, and considered Gowan Ford carefully. "I'm thinking about requesting some Federal troops to patrol Les Chattes Bleues, if the *vaudou* show up on the land again."

Ford, unconsciously mirroring Richard Duvall, leaned back comfortably in his chair, but to Richard the empty right sleeve, the patched eye, the disfigured face suddenly loomed large in his mind. "That's sure your decision to make, Colonel Duvall," he said steadily. "And I'll stand by you, no matter what you do."

"Thank you, Mr. Ford," Richard said quietly. "It's good to know that Marye and Elyse have you to depend upon, and it's good to know that I can depend upon you, too."

"Thank you, sir, and yes, sir, you can, always," Ford said with obvious sincerity.

Richard sighed and toyed with his empty glass. "But we still don't know why these things are happening. Why the *vaudou* have suddenly started bothering Marye and Elyse."

"Only one reason left I can think of," Ford said succinctly.

"What's that?"

"That they really believe what they told me," Ford said, looking Richard straight in the eye. "That they actually think Les Chattes Bleues is land claimed by spirits. And that they have cursed it."

★ ★ ★ ★

For the next few days, life at Les Chattes Bleues seemed to slow down, to get more relaxed, to fall into a more normal pattern. After the shock and even fear that pervaded the plantation when Luna fell ill, a kind of lull set in, an interlude of dreamy numbness, and all of the people at Les Chattes Bleues unconsciously welcomed the respite.

Living on a plantation outside of the city was wildly different from living in Manhattan, Irene found. But she loved Tante Marye and found that she actually enjoyed the hard work, and she did learn a lot about plantation management.

Each day necessitated the mobilization of a task force of servants. Rooms were shut tight against the day's heat, or humidity, or both. Linens and other materials in armoires had to be aired or sunned each week for damp and mildew protection. Bureau drawers were kept smelling fresh with bundles of *vetiver* root, which must constantly be replaced with freshly picked and dried bundles. Flies, mosquitoes, and other nuisances were chased out of darkened rooms or tracked down manually; the appearance of even one insect made Tante Marye minutely inspect every curtain or drape for every window in Les Chattes Bleues. Mosquito netting for the beds was checked constantly for wear and tear and repaired immediately. The candlesticks and chandeliers had to be scraped free of wax every day and the candles replaced. Since it was early spring, the carpeting was removed and stored in the attic, where it was rolled in newspapers with tobacco and peppercorns for mothproofing. Woven grass mattings were tacked down to the floors for summer.

And these tasks did not even begin to account for the never-ending laundry and cooking. But by the time Irene had learned of all these chores, she didn't want to think of laundry or cooking, anyway. Ever again. But she did prove to be a great help, and much company, for Tante Marye.

Tante Elyse, as always, attended her gardens and her indigo fields. Each day she visited every sharecropper's and servant's cottage to see if they needed anything. She also monitored the indigo processing barns and drying barns and storage barns each day. Her eternal tasks were the bookkeeping, the bill-paying, the money-managing, and the correspondence; and these, in their right, were quite as taxing as any and all work that Marye ever did. But Elyse Buckingham didn't care. She was happy, and to her the work was not work at all, but it was, quite simply, her life and love.

Victoria wandered the gardens all day long. She kept finding new and delightful corners and hidden little paths and benches and arched trellises and even streams and small fountains. But she loved best the Japanese garden, a still and tranquil corner far away from the main house. She painted there and, to her surprise, did some quite presentable paintings of the pool, the rocks, the bamboo, and the spare but showy flowers Elyse had planted in carefully planned groups of three or five. Victoria was almost happy when she was alone in the Japanese garden, and she stayed there for hours at a time, painting and drinking lemonade and dreaming.

Chloe continued to attend to Shiloh, to his consternation. On Thursday morning she actually came up the stairs into his bedroom, pulled back the mosquito netting, and sat on the side of his bed. She giggled softly, which woke him with a start, and he almost knocked her across the room before he knew what he was doing. She seemed not to be afraid, however, merely flinching a bit when he threw a blind punch. Giggling again, she said softly, "Wake up, *Monsieur* Irons. Coffee is here, and I am, too."

"Go downstairs and sit down, Chloe," he growled. "Right now. Wait for me."

"*Oui, monsieur, certainement.*" Unfazed, she tripped lightly down the treacherous circular staircase.

When Shiloh had hurriedly gotten dressed—including his boots; he would have felt at a disadvantage, somehow, if he had been barefoot—he stormed downstairs. She was perched on the edge of a chair, waiting expectantly, her liquid brown eyes shining with mischief and laughter.

"Miss Chloe, I'm not going to mince words," he barked. "Either you behave yourself and leave me alone, or I'm going to address this problem to your father. If that doesn't work, I'm going to complain to Mrs. Edwards. Do you understand?"

Chloe smiled indulgently, got up, and with a provocative sway, went to stand in front of Shiloh, close. With a small, delicate hand, she toyed with one of the buttons on his shirt. Looking up at him, she pouted, "But no, Shiloh, I don't understand. What problem? Don't I serve you well . . . not as well as I could, maybe, but still . . ."

Shiloh took her by the upper arms—gently, for he still felt that Chloe was nothing but an ignorant, precocious child—and she took it as an invitation. Before he could react, she moved until her small body pressed against his and raised her face to his, putting both her hands behind his neck to try to bring him down to kiss her.

The door creaked open; Chloe had left it ajar.

Cheney stepped in, called, "Shi—"

Shiloh, his hands still on Chloe, looked at her in shock.

Chloe, whose hands were behind Shiloh's neck, looked around and frowned as if she were angry at Cheney's interruption.

Cheney stood, openmouthed, her hand still on the doorknob.

When Shiloh recovered, he pushed Chloe so hard she literally flew into the air. Luckily, she was standing directly in front of the chair she had been sitting in and landed in it.

"Doc, wait," he began angrily, "Doc, listen—Doc!"

Her cheeks flaming, Cheney disappeared, and the door slammed behind her.

Shiloh turned on Chloe, and now she was afraid. She shrank back into the great leather armchair and put up a trembling hand.

"You little witch," Shiloh growled hoarsely. "Now look what you and your stupid little games have done! I could kill you!"

"No . . . no . . . no, *Monsieur* Irons, don't hurt me!" Piteously she threw both her hands over her head and began to cry.

Shiloh, who was towering over her in a perfect rage, made a deep animal sound in his throat, whirled, and went to the door. Jerking it open, he snarled, "Don't ever set foot in here again while I'm here! Do you understand?"

Chloe only sobbed. Shiloh left his *garçonniere,* savagely banging the door *open,* so that Chloe would see that the time for chivalry was over, and he hoped that she and her shame would be seen.

★　★　★　★

Cheney walked fast and actually bit her lip until it bled so that she wouldn't cry. As if she were using her mind to erase a blackboard, and then write simple things back on it in big letters, she blotted out the vision of Shiloh and Chloe. She refused to even begin to think of what she thought of Shiloh, or what she would say to him; she denied herself any emotion at all. Summoning all her strength she thought only of taking this step, and that step—step here, left foot here, right foot there—

"Doc! Wait!"

His voice was still far off. If she could get to Luna's cabin, he wouldn't dare come in there. Cheney was almost running.

"Doc, wait, please . . . just wait."

His voice was near, right behind her.

Cheney kept up her fast pace.

"Doc—wait! Don't make me tackle you!"

Cheney stopped so suddenly he ran into her. She whirled upon him, her face white with high spots of color on her cheekbones. Her sea-green eyes had turned to an emerald fire, and her lips were swollen with temper. She looked absolutely beautiful, he thought helplessly.

"I don't care, I don't want to hear it, and this is the last time we'll ever speak of it!"

"No, we have to talk about it, Doc, 'cause you don't understand—"

"Of course I understand, you fool! I'm not stupid. I'm a woman, you know, not just a doctor!"

"I know, I know, Doc—I mean, Cheney—but listen to me—"

"Don't call me Cheney!" she railed.

"Uh . . . okay . . . Doc. Will you promise to listen to me if I just call you Doc?"

"No!" She turned and again stepped smartly away.

Shiloh cursed under his breath, took two long strides, and grabbed her arm. "Listen to me, please. . . . Please." The plea was so unmistakable, and so sincere, that it got through to Cheney even in her rage. She jerked her arm free from his hand—his fingers, though gentle, seemed to burn through the light linen of her dress—and turned very slowly.

"I shall give you a few minutes," she snapped. "But I'm on my way to attend to Luna. I'm in a hurry."

Shiloh took a deep breath, then stepped a little closer to her. She stepped back. He decided not to try this dance yet, so he tried desperately to think of what to say; then he decided not to use the usual polite euphemisms. The truth—plain and simple—always worked better for the Doc.

"Chloe's just a young, foolish kid," he said desperately, "and she's been trying to seduce me since the first day we got here."

"And she succeeded?" Cheney said stonily. Now her face was deathly pale.

"No! Doc, do you really think I'd be interested in a child like that?"

Cheney dropped her eyes, her shoulders sagged, and she nervously picked at her white apron. "She's young, yes, but she's old for her age. She's beautiful, she's . . . alluring, and . . . she . . . she looks like Maeva Wilding."

Shiloh was thunderstruck. It had never, not once, occurred to him that the young mulatto resembled Maeva Wilding, the woman in Arkansas he had once loved, who had been brutally murdered.

He was silent for so long that Cheney finally stole a look back up at his face. What she saw there—astonishment, disbelief, and yes, even great hurt—made tears well up in her eyes.

Then an ugly little voice inside her said nastily, *Don't be a fool, you can't trust him! How many times have you seen something like this? Maybe not a scene of so much intimacy, but how many times have there been these scenes—and more, much worse—when you haven't caught him? Always, everywhere, women watching him, women smiling up at him, women following him with their eyes, women pointing to him behind his back, women whispering behind their soft white hands about him. . . .*

Her face closed down as surely as she had slammed the door to the *garçonniere* only minutes before, and the tears in her eyes seemed to dry up as if they had never been. "I suppose you are telling the truth, but to be honest I don't care, Shiloh. It makes no difference. All I can say is that I'm glad I'm not attracted to a man like you. It's much too difficult, and you only make it worse, because you are so careless and reckless, and you never consider the effect you have on people. I'm so glad—so thankful!—that I have Dev. He's thoughtful, and kind, and would never get himself into some absurdly difficult, compromising, shabby situation such as this."

Shiloh, just as suddenly, and just as completely, shut down. His face became expressionless, his eyes became shadowed, his very posture became defensive and aloof. "Fine. As long as you understand that I didn't seduce that girl."

"Fine."

"Fine." Shiloh turned and stalked off.

Cheney turned and stalked off in the opposite direction.

And the tears began to flow.

★   ★   ★   ★

As soon as Shiloh was out of sight, Cheney went to a nearby gazebo to compose herself. It took a while, longer than she angrily intended that it should take, and much longer than she ever thought it would.

"Fine," she echoed belligerently to herself. "I don't need him, anyway. There are medical assistants everywhere, and in a year—or two—Nia will be perfectly adequate!"

With that she hurried to Luna's cabin, determined to put Shiloh and her own confusion and anger out of her mind. She was a doctor, and she had work to do.

To her surprise, Luna was up and in the kitchen, fixing tea, though it was early morning. At Cheney's soft knock, Luna came to the door, still pale but fully dressed and with her usual composure.

"Dr. Duvall, please come in," she said formally.

Cheney stepped in, and Luna nodded toward the kitchen. "I have fixed some tea. Will you join me?"

"Yes, thank you, Luna," Cheney said uncertainly. "But I didn't yet give you permission to be up and about. Perhaps I'd better serve the tea to you in bed."

"No, thank you, Dr. Duvall," Luna said firmly. "I feel so much better, and I need to get up in order to regain my strength. Isn't that true?"

"Yes, that's true," Cheney agreed reluctantly. She followed Luna into the kitchen, where the pungent fragrance of strong tea filled the room. The kitchen, like the rest of Luna's house, was sparely and functionally furnished. The few dishes were in precise arrangement in the cabinets, the towels and dishcloths hung in orderly rows on racks, the single chair was pulled up precisely to the center of the table. Cheney looked around questioningly. Another chair was forlornly consigned to a corner, and she pulled it up to the table. Luna served tea in a plain white earthenware teapot, with sugar and honey and a creamer full of fresh milk.

"How do you take it, Dr. Duvall?" she asked politely.

"Two sugars, heavy cream."

Luna nodded, then prepared her cup of tea with the grace of a duchess serving with a silver tea service. The cut on her cheekbone was still raw and sore-looking, but it would not leave a scar. Cheney realized that Luna had never even asked about a scar—usually the first question a beautiful woman asked when her face was injured. It occurred to Cheney that she had not seen a single mirror, large or small, in Luna's house.

"So you are feeling better," Cheney said briskly. "I'm so glad, Luna. But I must warn you: don't overextend yourself today or tomorrow. Get plenty of rest. Since I have no earthly idea what your ailment was, I also have no idea if you'll be subject to relapse."

Luna's almond-shaped eyes rested on Cheney's face. Cheney knew she was pale, and the evidence of tears was plain to see. But she also knew that Luna would never make any sort of comment or attempt to intrude on such a personal matter. Still, Cheney felt ill at ease under Luna's direct gaze. Finally Luna said in a clear, well-modulated voice,

"Then you have no idea what was wrong with me?"

Cheney started. "No, I don't. Do you?"

Now Luna's gaze went out the window and far away. "Not really. Except I do know it was the *vaudou*."

Cheney sat up straighter in her chair. "Oh? How do you know, Luna? Have you . . . spoken with any of them, or . . . seen them here?"

Luna shook her head with deliberation, once, twice. "No, Dr. Duvall. Never. But I know. I've known them for a long time." A wry half-smile twisted her full lips. "I recognize their handiwork."

Cheney was silent for a moment, but Luna continued to stare unseeing out the window that looked out over Les Chattes Bleues' indigo fields.

"Do you?" Cheney asked finally. "And how is that?"

"Because I used to be one of them," Luna answered matter-of-factly. "At least, I consulted with Marie Laveau quite often. I never attended their meetings, but to me Marie was doctor, consultant, and confidante."

Cheney groped for something to say. She wanted to question Luna extensively, but she also had already learned that Luna did not take kindly to prying. She could deftly turn aside any question that she did not want to answer in a most polite and inoffensive manner. But without waiting for Cheney to comment, Luna kept talking in an oddly distant and unemotional voice. Her eyes never left the benevolent and orderly scene outside her kitchen window.

"Marie Laveau has been voodoo queen for many, many years now. My mother took me to her as soon as I became a woman, and Marie gave me secret potions and ablutions to make certain I never conceived a child. Even though," she added with a tinge of sarcasm, "I rarely set eyes on a man until I was eighteen years old."

Cheney managed to remain silent, though she was tempted to lecture Luna on the medical facts. No secret potions existed that were a foolproof—or even partially effective—method of birth control.

"But when I did meet a man, and he became my lover, they certainly did work," Luna said in an eerie argument against Cheney's private thoughts. "Now sometimes I wish that they had not. . . ."

Cheney wasn't about to stand by and hear this most terrible of regrets—that a woman had refused to have a child until it was too late—based upon a needless guilt. "Luna, such things simply do not exist. I know. If you never conceived a child, it's because you are infertile, or because your lover was sterile. It's not because you took some concoction, or performed some outlandish ablution."

Luna's eyes came slowly around to focus on Cheney's face. They were strange eyes, both in their emptiness and in their color. They were brown, yes, but a light brown, almost tan, almost golden. "I had no children because the *vaudou* made certain I did not. With my permission, of course."

Cheney's face softened and her voice dropped to a sympathetic murmur. "Oh, Luna, you don't truly believe in such fantasies and superstitions, do you? An educated, intelligent woman such as you?"

One of Luna's arched eyebrows winged upward. "And you, Dr. Duvall? You are educated, you are intelligent, yet you believe in the superstition about God, don't you?"

Cheney took a deep breath. "Yes, I do believe in God, Luna, with all my heart. And I believe in His Son, Jesus Christ, who became a man and died for me, and for you."

"And this man, Jesus, He was a white man, wasn't He?" Luna said with only a touch of sarcasm. From Luna, however, it was the same as if she had shouted it in anger.

"No," Cheney answered with a little smile. "He was a Jew, actually, which means that he was probably more dark-skinned than you are. And His people—the Jews—have been enslaved, murdered, and downtrodden for many more ages than either your people or my people have. But that makes no difference. God is God, the Alpha and the Omega, the Creator of all, and His Son Jesus loves you and came to this earth to pay for your sins."

"Ah, but I do understand that the third Person in the Trinity is a spirit? The Holy Ghost, I believe you call Him?"

"Yes, that's true," Cheney said, a little disconcerted.

"Then you see, you and I and the *vaudou* are not so different," Luna said in a bored tone. "It's not that I don't believe in God. I do. It's just that He is another spirit, one of thousands, that are of this earth. When you worship one, you must worship all."

"No," Cheney countered. "You are mistaken, Luna, and you are terribly deceived."

Luna shrugged carelessly. "So all white people say. I say that you are deceived. You are the ones who have concocted this wonderful white God and shaped Him into what you wish Him to be."

"No, Luna," Cheney said gently. "There is one other thing that you have failed to take into account."

"And that is—?"

"Truth. Do you believe in Truth? That is, do you believe that there is such a thing as Truth, and that some people tell the truth, and others do not?" Cheney asked with great compassion.

"Yes," Luna answered angrily. "Some people are great liars."

"Then you know that there is evil, Luna, and if there is evil, there also is good. And God is good, Luna. God is love, and His Son came here to prove it. Just think about it, Luna. Because Jesus loves you, you see, just as much as He loves me, or white people, or Jews, or any other peoples. And God, our Heavenly Father, actually loves you as much as He loves His own Son, and the Holy Spirit will show you this, if you'll let Him, and you'll know that this is Truth."

Luna, staring at Cheney with her tawny eyes narrowed, seemed to be at a loss for words.

"I will pray for you, Luna," Cheney said and smiled. "It won't hurt you, I promise. And perhaps, soon, we can talk again."

10

THE VAUDOU

"Richard?"

"Yes, my love?"

A long silence ensued. Richard Duvall, with a sigh, got up from the comfortable chaise lounge—it was actually a lady's lounge, but he loved to stretch out his stiff leg and read at night—and went into Madame's Boudoir. At least, that was what Tante Marye and Tante Elyse called it. And they were serious.

Adjoining the master bedroom, Madame's Boudoir was likely the smallest room in the house, and probably the most luxurious. It had no outside entrance to the gallery, only the door leading from the bedroom. The walls were hung with hundreds of yards of blue satin, pleated as tightly as the thick material would allow. Underneath a bower formed by a crownlike valance, with swagged blue draperies trimmed in blue Valenciennes lace, was a daybed made of Saint-Domingue mahogany, intricately carved, lushly covered with blue satin damask. Along another wall was an immense dressing table, almost as large as a dining table, with a triple mirror mounted on it. On the dressing table were the most outlandish baubles Richard Duvall had ever set eyes upon: silver combs and brushes; boxes, large and small, of every shape, of silver and gold and shagreen and teak and mother-of-pearl and tortoise shell; silver candelabra; several different sizes of hand-held mirrors; at least a dozen delicate and exquisite colored bottles of perfume; tiny little ladylike books, their covers formed of silk and damask and velvet; a gold inkstand with crystal bottles; statuettes of birds, animals, and people made of jade and ivory; and other thingamabobs, the purpose for which Richard was certain he would never be able to guess. He sighed. He felt much more comfortable in the rather masculine master bedroom. In Madame's Boudoir he always felt tall and clumsy and boorish.

Irene sat at the dressing table, brushing out her long auburn hair. The candles in the ornate silver candelabra were burning low, and her hair looked jet, with the silver streak shimmering in the uncertain light. She wore a nightgown of white, rather plainly made but of the finest linen, and Richard could see through it, and admired the still-youthful curves of her body as she brushed her hair with slow, graceful strokes.

"Richard, dear," she said.

"Yes, my love," he replied. "I am at your beck and call, as always." He bent forward and brushed a kiss on her forehead, then went to sit uneasily on the edge of the daybed.

Irene's unlined forehead wrinkled slightly as she stared at herself in the mirror. "Have you noticed that Cheney and Shiloh aren't speaking to each other?"

"What?" Richard exclaimed. "But . . . yes they are! We were all talking today, about Luna, and they spoke to each other! Didn't they?" he suddenly added in confusion.

"Did they?" Irene repeated knowingly.

Richard looked back up at her guiltily. "No. I guess you might say they talked *at* each other, with me in between."

"Yes, I know," Irene murmured. "Exactly as it's been at dinner, which is, I've noticed, the only meal they both attend. Have you noticed?"

"Huh-uh," Richard said helplessly and reached over and picked up a jade figurine from the dressing table. It was a tiger, with ruby eyes, and he started tossing it into the air and catching it. "But they aren't mad, it doesn't seem like. I mean, they aren't fighting."

"I think they are, Richard," Irene said patiently. "I think they've had a terrible fight. Just because they aren't shouting at each other doesn't mean they aren't fighting. You and I certainly don't shout at each other when we fight."

"We never fight."

"Of course we do." Irene smiled.

"I never want to fight again, Irene," Richard pleaded.

"We're fighting right now."

"No, we're not. We are having a disagreement and, as always, you are persuading me to come around to your point of view."

"As always," Irene said mischievously, "I'm right and you're wrong."

"I love you more than anything, and that's at least one thing I do right," Richard said, grinning.

"True," Irene said softly and smiled at him. It still made his heart swell with pride and love when she smiled at him in that special warm way, and it was only with difficulty he returned to the original topic.

"This place . . . something's wrong with everyone," he finally said with rather dull helplessness. "No wonder Cheney and Shiloh are fighting. It's . . . tense and . . . oppressive here."

Irene set down her brush and turned to face him, her eyes wide with surprise. "Do you really feel that way, Richard? I hadn't noticed."

"Good," he muttered. "Maybe it's just me." He ducked his head and absently picked at the ruby eye of the tiger.

She went to him then, and knelt, and put her head on his knee. "I'm sorry, my love. You are my life, and I want to help you, always . . . I've been rather preoccupied."

His eyes warmed to dove-gray, and with a gentle hand he smoothed his wife's thick, lustrous hair. "I know, Irene. Don't you see? This, too, is uncharacteristic of you . . . normally you know before I do when I'm troubled."

"And are you troubled, Richard?"

"Yes, I am," he said in a low voice. "I feel that something is going to happen here, Irene, something—wrong."

Irene sat back on her heels and smiled up at him. "Then, Richard, we'll pray. Because I know that whatever it is our Father protects us always, and He especially protects you, because you bear the burdens for so many of us. Whatever comes, Richard, we are safe, hidden in the palm of His loving hand."

★ ★ ★ ★

First the drums began, an audible forewarning of what was to assault the eyes and ears of everyone at Les Chattes Bleues.

Shiloh woke up first and sat up in his bed.

Richard woke only seconds after him and sluggishly pulled aside the mosquitonetting to look around the room in confusion. Irene then woke.

Even though he was much farther away, Gowan Ford awoke next. He knew what had disturbed his sleep even before the dogs came running up onto his porch. He called out the open window in a harsh voice, "Riff! Raff! Stay!" and dressed as quickly as he could. It was difficult, with only one arm, but he had stubbornly taught himself the best and fastest ways to accomplish it.

Shiloh ran toward Les Chattes Bleues and saw that candles were being lit in the downstairs parlor. Far to his left he saw a square of light in one of the open cottage doors. Monroe was coming to the main house too.

Shiloh reached the front door and burst in without knocking. In the front parlor Marye, Elyse, Irene, Cheney, Victoria, and Richard were gathered. Marye and Elyse sat on the sofa, close together, and Elyse clasped one of Marye's hands securely in both of hers. Tante Marye was pale, her face drawn and looking even older, and quite frail. Tante Elyse looked calm, but her lips were pressed together tightly. Irene was watching Richard with worried eyes as he stood at the French window, gazing to the north. Cheney looked almost ill; she was so pale and had dark shadows beneath her eyes that the low candlelight only accentuated rather than softened. Beside her, Victoria sat straight upright in a delicate Louis XIV chair, her feet tucked primly to the side, her silver hair dressed immaculately. She looked at Shiloh gravely as he entered, but she was still, composed, not fidgeting as Cheney was.

Without saying anything Shiloh joined Richard at the window. The drums were growing louder, a wild, savage sound that had no place in their world. There was nothing, however, to be seen except the moonless night and occasional silent flashes of far-off heat lightning.

No one spoke for long moments. Shiloh and Richard continued to stare toward the island till their eyes hurt from the strain. Once Richard pressed the heels of his hands momentarily to his eyes. When he looked up again, he saw it, and knew it was real; a sickly green flash, brief but unmistakable. Then another, and another. Then a steady orange light began to glow at the top of the rise on the island, and faintly Shiloh and Richard could see thin dark lines, which they knew were the massive trunks of the oak trees that crowned the little hill.

Gowan Ford hurried into the house, with Riff and Raff at his heels. Wordlessly he stood behind Shiloh and Richard, while the dogs went to greet Tante Elyse and then sit in front of her as if they were the great guard lions of Trafalgar Square.

Ford, Shiloh, and Richard stood at the window. The glow on the hill grew brighter, and the green flashes grew so large and intense that sometimes the men's faces reflected the putrid hue.

"I'm going over there," Richard said in a low voice. "Shiloh, Mr.

Ford, I'd appreciate it if you'd accompany me."

"Of course, Colonel Duvall," Ford said instantly.

"Yes, sir," Shiloh muttered. He was angry, and his voice was thick with it.

Richard turned to study his face. "Shiloh, I'm going to speak to them. I don't want anyone—you or anyone else—to lose his temper and do something foolish. Can you do this?"

Shiloh, his jaw rigid, his eyes flaming, still nodded with certainty. "Yes, Mr. Duvall, I'll do whatever you say. But I won't stand by and allow you or Mr. Ford to get hurt."

Richard shook his head. "They won't hurt anyone. They wouldn't dare." He asked Gowan Ford, "How do we get over there?"

"Boat, moored in a little cove close to the landing."

"Good." He turned back to the ladies and noted for the first time that Monroe had come in, fully dressed in his ever-present suit and tie, and was calmly lighting more candles as if in preparation for an after-dinner gathering in the parlor. "Monroe, I'm glad you're here. Will you stay with the ladies until we return?"

"Yes, Colonel Duvall."

"Thank you, Monroe." He turned back and looked at Gowan Ford and Shiloh. All three of the men were fully dressed, with sturdy boots. Shiloh wore his long canvas coat, and Richard knew that he was carrying his gun. He also knew he could trust Shiloh not to use it unless—God forbid—he had to. Gowan Ford, he figured, had left his rifle outside. Richard had no intention of carrying a gun, but he decided that it might not be a bad idea if Ford and Shiloh did. This was a fair warning as to how serious these men were.

He turned back and said simply, "Don't worry, ladies. We'll be back soon." He smiled at Irene, who smiled tremulously back. Then Shiloh, Richard, and Ford left for the island where the fires grew hot and the flames rose high.

★　★　★　★

Richard put up his hand, and as he expected, both men behind him stopped in their tracks without a verbal command. It would not have been heard, however, by anyone, for the beating of the drums and the wild cries of the *vaudou* were deafening. They stood in the shadows of the trees and surveyed the scene on the top of the hill.

Two fierce fires were built at opposite sides of the clearing, in great squares built of bricks. In between, an oblong table was set up, a rude and hasty construction of boxes for a base and cypress boards laid atop them. At one end of the table, in a cage, was a white cat, and at the other end of the table was a black cat. Both were yowling and spitting, and their fur stood on end. In the center of the table was a sizable box with cabalistic signs upon it. On the box was a keg with a small tree planted in it. Hung from the tree was a black doll with a dress decorated with cabalistic signs and emblems, and a necklace made of the vertebrae of snakes and alligator's teeth.

To Richard's dismay, he counted about sixty people dancing and screaming and chanting. At the far end of the clearing a woman—a young, curvaceous quadroon—danced, and a group of men stood clapping, swaying, and chanting. Richard saw about six white men in the group. At the end nearest to where Richard, Shiloh, and Ford stood were the drummers, six of them. Three of them sat cross-legged upon the ground, beating small drums, and three of them stood in front of drums about four feet tall. Directly in front of them was a huge Negro man, muscular, tall, strong, dressed only in a white loincloth. He danced and whirled and jumped incredibly high in front of two young girls, both white, draped in scarlet sarongs that left their arms and shoulders bare and only reached to their knees. More people gathered in a loose circle about the clearing, some dancing frantically, some swaying and moaning, some kneeling and touching their foreheads to the ground in a mindless rhythm.

The rhythm, the intensity, the continuous assault upon the ears, made Richard grit his teeth, and the evil sights made him ill. With determination he swallowed back bitter bile, and with a slightly shaking hand he wiped his mouth. He actually felt dirty.

Gowan stepped close and muttered in his ear, "That's Dédé." He pointed to the beautiful young quadroon in white.

With no further hesitation Richard stepped into the clearing, followed closely by Shiloh and Ford. He stopped, expecting the music and the dancing to stop and everyone to stare at them. But no one even gave them a second look, and the sickening drums went on and on. Finally Richard strode through the crowd and went to stand in the circle formed by the men watching Dédé dance. Shiloh and Ford stood behind him.

She kept dancing, wildly and suggestively, and once even smiled at Richard. He crossed his arms and frowned and stood his ground. She whirled and swayed and reached out her arms, her body moving shamelessly. Though the white drape she wore was elaborate, and reached from her throat to her ankles, it was made of thin silk, and her body was completely visible by the lurid light of the flames. Weaving over to the fire, she reached into a hidden pocket, took out her hand, and with a flourish threw something in; phosphorescent green flames shot high up to the sky, and a noxious smell pervaded the air. Dédé threw back her head and screamed, her arms raised high. Then she pulled her arms down tightly, dropped her head, and threw herself down on one knee.

The drums stopped. The cats still hissed, and the *vaudou* still chanted, a mindless, maddening thrum that made Richard's head ache.

Slowly Dédé got up and looked at Richard, Shiloh, and Ford, her dark eyes heavy-lidded, her mouth turned upward in a feline smile. With deliberate slowness she swayed toward them, and behind her, like a huge, threatening shadow, moved the Negro who had been dancing with the drums.

To Richard's surprise, Dédé completely ignored him, walking right past him to stand in front of Shiloh. She looked up at him and held his eyes for a long time, then, with maddening slowness, she reached up to caress his face. Shiloh visibly flinched but allowed Dédé to touch him. Richard was frozen with disbelief. Shiloh looked down at Dédé, his face twisted with disgust, his shoulders taut with anger. But he seemed unable to move. One hand was inside his coat, and Richard was certain it rested on the butt of his .44. Beside him Gowan Ford watched with uncertainty, fingering his rifle.

Suddenly, Shiloh made a hoarse noise in his throat and slapped Dédé's hand away. The Negro man stepped forward threateningly, but Dédé merely threw back her head and laughed, a full, rich, wild laughter that barely sounded human. "What's the matter, big man?" she taunted Shiloh in a low, musical voice. "You came to see Dédé, did you not? And my friends?" She was making movements, or signs, with her arms, raising her left one to square in front of her, and waving her other hand and fingers in a hypnotic motion over it.

Richard finally recovered from his shock and stepped back to see what Dédé was doing. She had her back to him, and the Negro man stood in his line of vision. When he came even with them, he was horrified.

On Dédé's warm bronzed arm crawled a small snake. It was completely white—a sickening, pale, color, the color of death itself—and its eyes glowed red in the firelight. It seemed to follow Dédé's waving hand, and slithered oh, so slowly along the length of her arm, toward her fingers . . . and her fingers were pointed toward Shiloh.

Shiloh's face drained, his eyes grew wide with unreasonable, uncontrollable fear, and he stumbled backward in horror. Dédé, her face now contorted into a rictus of a smile, suddenly leaned forward with the very quickness of a striking snake and hissed at him, "You, big man, had better stay away from Dédé. You are the worst of cowards because you're just like us, but you're too afraid to admit it, even to yourself!"

"Stop it!" Richard roared and stepped between Shiloh and Dédé. This brought him close—much too close—to Dédé, but he managed to control the shudder that rose up from deep inside him. The black man growled gutturally and took a step toward Richard, but Dédé put up her hand and backhanded him in the chest.

"No, Doctor Sol," she murmured, the infernal chanting an insane background to her careless tone. "These men are here to see me, and it is with me they must speak." Her eyes now fixed on Richard, they again grew heavy-lidded with seeming boredom. With sickly sensuous movements she picked up the white snake, put it to her lips, kissed its mouth, and held it to her chest. It slithered quickly into the sleeve of her tunic. Richard fought down his nausea again, and behind him he could hear Shiloh actually gagging.

Dédé looked Richard up and down, propping her hands on her full hips. She stepped even closer to him, and it was all Richard could do to keep from backing away from her. Her scent was wild and musky, and he could actually feel the heat from her body. The hair rose on his forearms and the back of his neck, and his gut rolled and lurched. He was trying to speak, but he felt so ill that he was afraid to try, so he kept swallowing convulsively.

Dédé saw his discomfort and chuckled, a glottally dark sound made low in her throat. "I know who you are," she breathed, "and I know what you are. You don't belong here. You have no right to be here. You will leave now and never come back."

Richard spoke in a voice roughened with loathing. "It is you who doesn't belong here, and I will tolerate your presence on this land no longer. Leave. Leave before I make you leave. I'm warning you, and I do not make such threats lightly."

She cocked her head as if he were discussing the latest gossip. "Oh,

135

but you, noble man of war, you would never hurt a woman. Besides," her voice dropped with disdain, "you see, I told you, I know you. You're not so different from me, proud warrior. You also get down on your knees just like a peasant to worship the spirits."

Richard drew himself upright, his gray eyes flashing like struck flint. "Get thee behind me, woman!" he growled harshly. "I, and my family, and my friends, and all those under my protection have no part of you! Leave, I tell you! And never come back!" He whirled and muttered to Ford and Shiloh, "Let's go. Don't turn your back on them, and, Shiloh, come here and stay close to me."

They walked warily through the still-chanting crowd, and with every step they took, the chants rose in tone and intensity until it was more like a thousand horrible screeches. Every single person watched them, looked through them, and each face was distorted, ugly, inhuman. Shiloh moved blindly, repeatedly wiping his mouth and touching his fingers to his face where Dédé had caressed him. Richard clung to his arm with a grip of iron. Gowan Ford half-raised his rifle as they stumbled and backed to the treeline.

Dédé stepped forward and called out in a loud, half-hysterical voice, "Ah, so, you'll come back to fight this battle all by yourself, warrior? Do so, I beg you!" She took a little step, then ran toward the three men, but stopped warily while she was still some distance away. Gowan Ford glared at her, but she only stared with huge, insane eyes at Richard Duvall. "You'll lose, warrior! You're weak, and you endanger your mortal soul . . . and if you lose that, you'll die!"

Richard said nothing, didn't even look at her. He was only concerned with helping Shiloh, who seemed to be almost blind, as he lurched along and occasionally threw up his hands to guard himself against things that weren't there. Gowan Ford stopped. At Dédé's last screamed words, he yanked his rifle in a swift up-and-down motion, which threw the bolt, which chambered a cartridge, then threw his rifle up to his eye and aimed directly at her. Now she looked at him, and horrible fear showed on her face.

Ford stood motionless, the clenching of his jaw over and over again the only movement he made. Richard stopped and looked at him, but said nothing.

Finally Ford lowered the rifle, slowly. "Nah," he murmured as if in deep thought. "Not worth wasting a bullet."

Then the three men disappeared out of the circle of orange firelight.

Soon the drums began again.

IN THE NEW

PART THREE

MOON

Blow up the trumpet in the new
moon, in the time appointed,
On our solemn feast day.
I removed his shoulder
from the burden:
His hands were delivered…

Psalm 81:3, 6

11

RETREAT AND REGROUP

The white faces of the women seemed to be ghostly apparitions floating in the gloom of the parlor. Monroe had hastily lit two four-branched candelabras before hurrying to prepare hot tea for the ladies. Somehow the candlelight seemed dull, unable to sever the darkness with sure light.

Victoria sat completely motionless, her composure complete, staring out the French windows, her hands folded gracefully in her lap, her back never touching her chair. Of all of them she looked the most ethereal, with her silvery blond hair and pale heart-shaped face that had never been exposed to sunlight without a veil or a parasol's protection. The only evidence of her tension was a slight distention of her thin nostrils and her shallow breathing.

Irene Duvall stood in front of the window, a delicate shape occasionally outlined in the faint reflections of green flashes from the island. Her face was still and calm, and with her usual grace she laid a tiny white hand on the frame, listening to the malignant sounds of the far-off drums. After a time she returned to her chair, sitting straight and still. Occasionally she bowed her head slightly and closed her eyes in prayer, and then looked back up with renewed strength.

Tante Marye and Tante Elyse sat huddled together on the sofa. Marye was so pale, and clung so obsessively to Elyse, that Elyse finally ordered Monroe to bring her some sherry. Tante Marye took two sips, then another, and finally drained the glass. She sat back a little, closed her eyes, and sighed. Elyse could see some color return to Marye's chalk-white face and signaled Monroe, who immediately served both of them a small glass of sherry. Elyse sipped hers and spoke in low tones to Tante Marye, urging her to sit back, tuck a coverlet around her, and sip her second glass of sherry slowly. After a while Tante Marye seemed to be slowly retreating from the edge of hysteria.

Cheney would have driven everyone insane had they not been so preoccupied with their own thoughts and prayers. She sat for a while, obsessively worrying the material of her dressing gown. Then she jumped up and began to pace, restlessly circling the chairs and furniture like a caged panther. She stood at the window, straining so hard to pierce the darkness that she began to see spectral shapes making phantom movements. Whirling about and pressing her fingers to her eyes she muttered, "I should have gone with them."

"No, Cheney, my love, you should not have," Irene said in soothing, cool tones. "Please, come sit here by me."

Obediently, as if in a dream, Cheney sank into the chair by her mother. Irene reached out and took her hand; Irene's was soft and cool, Cheney's hot and dry. Cheney was instantly reminded of when she was a child, and sick. *Mother's touch always cooled me when I was fevered,* she thought dreamily, *and Father's voice always warmed me when I was chilled.*

Men's boots sounded on the steps, and men's voices sounded on the porch. Everyone froze, then their faces swiveled toward the front door. Irene rose calmly and glided to the door quickly enough to beat Monroe. By the time Cheney had shot out of her chair, everyone was already coming into the parlor.

Irene came in first, her face twisted with concern. Behind her Richard and Gowan Ford supported Shiloh's massive frame. His head was lolling, his knees kept giving way, and his steps were shambling.

"Shiloh!" Cheney cried. "Oh, Shiloh . . . what . . ."

She rushed to him, rudely pushing past her mother. Cradling his head between her hands, she lifted up his face and stared into it. He was ashen, his eyes a dismal smoke color, his expression dazed. Her eyes wide with fear, Cheney held open his coat and ran her hands on his chest, his neck, his back. "Has he been shot? Is he—how is he hurt?"

"Let's get him over to the sofa," Richard murmured. With some difficulty—although Shiloh was obviously trying to help himself—the two men half-walked, half-dragged him across the room. Tante Marye and Tante Elyse scattered like frightened doves.

Shiloh collapsed onto the sofa in a half-sitting position. With effort he laid his head back and took a deep breath. Cheney still stood in the middle of the room, staring at him in shock. Richard came to stand in front of her, taking her upper arms in a firm grip and forcing her to look at him.

"Cheney, calm down," he ordered firmly, but kindly. "Shiloh has not been shot. He has not been seriously injured. Do you understand?"

Cheney's hands went to rest upon her father's arms, his strong, comforting arms. She took a deep breath, nodded, and immediately her eyes cleared of the look of stark fear. "Yes, Father. Has he been hurt in any way?"

Richard Duvall grimaced with a deep pain. "Yes, he has . . . but . . . it's like shock, I suppose, Cheney. You need to look him over and help him before I explain."

Cheney asked no more questions. Squeezing her father's arms lightly, she nodded again and went to Shiloh. "Mother, find some firm pillows. Take them off the furniture if you have to. Father, come help me get his feet up on the sofa. Yes, I know he's too tall, but that's why we need the pillows, to prop him up to a comfortable sitting position. Monroe, go get some whisky."

Cheney knelt by Shiloh, unbuttoned the top button of his shirt, then reached down and yanked the Colt .44 revolver out of his breeches. Tante Marye and Tante Elyse made horrified noises, but Cheney expertly popped the breech, emptied the six cartridges into her hand, snapped the breech shut, and held out the gun and cartridges to Gowan Ford, who took them without a word. Then she turned back to Shiloh, who was leaning back against two velvet and tasseled pillows with his eyes closed.

Cheney laid her hand across his forehead and he murmured, "That's nice . . . your hands are soothing . . . always make me feel better."

Cheney looked startled, then a half-smile flitted across her face. "Be quiet," she whispered. To her surprise, Nia knelt down next to her with her medical bag, reached in, and handed Cheney her stethoscope.

"Good, Nia, thank you," she said. The room was deathly quiet as she listened to Shiloh's heartbeat. It was strong and even, though strangely slowed down. Cheney frowned, then took his pulse, which was the same: stable but torpid. His respiration was the same: he was breathing slowly but not erratically. Shiloh watched her through clouded, half-closed eyes.

"How do you feel?" she asked quietly.

"Like a fool," he said faintly.

Again she smiled fleetingly. "Can you see? How many fingers?" She made a V-sign.

"Two," he said obediently, then dizzily reached out, grabbed her hand, and put it to his chest, with his hand on top of hers. He took a deep breath and closed his eyes again. To Shiloh it was just a gesture, reaching out for comfort, but Cheney could hardly bear it. His shirt was unbuttoned, his chest was bare, and his skin was warm and golden. Cheney managed to stay still for a few moments, though she could feel her cheeks flaming. Then gently she pulled her hand free, and Shiloh turned his head all the way toward her in surprise.

Suddenly Cheney jumped up and bent over him. "What's this? Monroe, bring those candles! Quickly!" Monroe hurried to hold the candelabra directly over Shiloh's head. With deft movements Cheney turned Shiloh's head until his left cheek was highlighted in the candle's weak glow.

Underneath the V scar, three long red lines marred Shiloh's smooth skin. Tiny blisters were already forming all along them. When Cheney barely touched it, Shiloh flinched slightly. "Burns," he muttered. "Her fingers . . . felt dead . . . but it burned. . . ."

"Do you know what this is?" Cheney turned and asked her father calmly. "Was he burned?"

Richard and Gowan Ford exchanged worried glances. "Not . . . with fire," Richard said finally.

Gowan Ford's nostrils were distended with disgust. "She probably had some kind of irritant on her fingers," he muttered blackly.

Cheney narrowed her eyes as she looked back at Shiloh's face. If it was some kind of acid, it could keep burning, keep working away down to the bone. If it was acid she needed to act fast.

Gently, softly, she turned Shiloh's face toward hers and bent over until her lips were almost touching his. "Listen to me, Shiloh. Can you hear me?"

"Sure, Doc," he answered weakly, opening his eyes all the way.

"This is very important. Is this burn an acid burn? You know, if it's some kind of acidic compound, it will keep burning. Does it feel like that?"

"No . . . no. Not like that. Feels like . . . it stings."

"That's it!" Ford said suddenly, and though he had not called out, his voice sounded loud in the room. "Stinging nettles!"

"Could be . . . yes, wax on her fingertips," Richard said in a thoughtful voice. "That way her skin wouldn't be affected . . . then dip her fingertips into some juice from stinging nettles, when she was playing with that witch's bag of hers."

Cheney didn't care how it happened. She only wanted to make sure that was really what the red marks on Shiloh's face were. "Did you hear?" she asked him anxiously. "Does it feel like stinging nettles?"

"Yes," he said with puzzling relief. "Must have been . . . sure, it feels just like it." He sounded stronger and looked slightly less pallid.

"That's good," Cheney said with relief. Nia was watching helplessly, and Cheney said kindly, "Nia, all we need to do right now is clean those red marks with some witch hazel. It's in a green bottle in my bag, and it's labeled. Then we need to put some sodium bicarbonate paste on them. You'll find some sodium bicarbonate—it's a powder—in small ampules in a black leather case in my bag. It's marked $NaHCO_3$ and—"

"No, it's not," Shiloh interrupted faintly. "It's marked 'Sodium Bicarb.' Makes some sense."

"Thank the Lord," Nia breathed, her eyes never leaving Cheney's face.

Cheney smiled indulgently at Shiloh. "You are feeling better."

"Better than dead," he said distantly.

Cheney turned back to Nia. "Anyway, you just mix the sodium bicarbonate with water until it makes a spreadable paste."

"I can do that," Nia declared, getting up and almost running toward the back of the house.

Cheney went to the sideboard and poured a small tumbler about half-full of whiskey, then, wrinkling her nose at the strong smell, returned to Shiloh. "Here. Just sip this very slowly, Shiloh. No jokes, no tossing it back. Very slowly."

"You don't have to make me, Doc," he sighed. "I don't like to drink on an empty stomach, and believe me, I think my stomach's about as empty as it's ever been." He pulled himself up to a sturdier sitting position, then caught sight of his muddy boots propped up on Tante Marye's white-and-gold Venetian sofa. With an effort he swung them off onto the floor, ignoring Cheney's sharp order to sit still, then turned himself around into a sitting position and gazed contritely at Tante Marye.

"Mrs. Edwards, please forgive me," he apologized. "I wish I'd fainted into that brown horsehair armchair instead."

Tante Marye smiled tremulously. "I forgive you."

Everyone looked around rather helplessly for a moment. Finally

145

Richard said, "Let's sit down, shall we? I know . . . I have some explanations to make."

Irene gave him a puzzled look; his voice was heavy with sorrow and laced with guilt. Still, she sat down on the sofa facing Shiloh, and Richard sat down close to her and took her hand. Ford settled into the horsehair armchair, Tante Marye and Elyse returned to the sofa, in spite of Shiloh's muddy boots, and Cheney and Victoria took the seats they had before.

Even as Richard opened his mouth to speak, the drums and the faint rhythm of chanting ceased. Everyone sat up alertly—except Shiloh, who still looked slightly dulled and dazed—as if it were the beginning instead of the end of the noisome sounds. After a few moments Richard began again to speak in a halting, hoarse rasp that barely resembled his normally strong, mellifluous voice.

"There were about sixty of them. We just walked into the clearing, where they were dancing and chanting. Ford pointed out Dédé to me, and I approached her. But she ignored me at first." He looked at Shiloh, and his face was distorted with grief. "She . . . went to Shiloh, and . . . touched him. We were all so shocked . . . we couldn't . . . didn't react . . ."

"A man can hardly slap down a woman that's decided to touch him," Gowan Ford growled.

Cheney's face suddenly drained, and she shot an agonized look at Shiloh. He didn't see her, however, as he was staring blankly out the French windows. Now they only reflected back the low candlelight in the parlor. The island fires had gone out.

"It's my fault," Richard said numbly. "It's all my fault."

Shiloh turned back to stare at him. "Your fault? Begging your pardon, Mr. Duvall, but that's crazy! That witch had that sickening little snake"—he shuddered convulsively—"and I got scared, and got sick, and that's it! It's no more your fault than it is mine!"

Richard Duvall shook his head sorrowfully. "You don't understand, Shiloh. How could you? It's more than that, and it's worse than that."

Irene's face suddenly registered comprehension, but everyone else looked completely confused. Irene took Richard's hand, smoothed it, and murmured, "It's all right, Richard. We can overcome this, and we will. And remember, you will never, as long as you live, ever have to bear this or any other burden alone. God is your strength, an ever-present help in time of trouble."

"Yes, Irene, you're right, thank the Lord." Richard sighed, dropping his head and lifting Irene's hand to press to his lips. Then he looked back up, and though he still was grieved, his voice grew more even as he explained. "You see, I made two terrible errors tonight. The first one was underestimating, or misunderstanding, what we faced when we went against the *vaudou*. Their true threat is not in making the sharecroppers ill or poisoning the crop. The real danger is, quite simply, their presence here." He turned to look at Gowan Ford's scarred face. "You said it, Mr. Ford. They court evil, and that makes them a far worse menace than just being sick or having a poor crop."

Irene said softly, her eyes focused on the far distance, "For we wrestle not against flesh and blood, but against principalities, against powers. . . ."

"Yes," Richard nodded, and Gowan Ford's single blue eye grew sharp with comprehension, and he glanced at Shiloh. "Yes," Richard said again so quietly that everyone heard only a deep whisper floating on the still air in the room. "That was my second, most terrible error—taking Shiloh."

All eyes turned to Shiloh, who looked thoroughly bewildered.

"Because, you see, Shiloh," Richard continued, his shoulders rounded with heavy guilt, "Mr. Ford and I were protected, because we put our faith and trust in the Lord Jesus Christ. But you were not, and I knew it—and Dédé knew it. I never should have taken you with me to face the *vaudou*."

★　★　★　★

"Elyse, come here," Tante Marye ordered in that particular tone of voice that meant no delays.

Tante Elyse, who was escaping out the front door with an empty basket and some scissors to cut flowers, obediently turned and followed her sister into the parlor. No one else had come downstairs for breakfast yet.

Tante Marye sat stiffly on the edge of the Venetian sofa, which had been duly cleaned of Shiloh's muddy bootprints by Molly. Elyse sat across from Marye on the red divan and listened warily as she spoke. "I simply cannot bear for Richard to be so burdened, Elyse. It's been very difficult for him the last two days, since those *vaudou* persons came," Marye said irritably, as if it were all Elyse's fault. "I want it to stop."

"We all want all of it to stop, Marye," Elyse ventured.

"And I intend to do something about it," Marye went on, continuing the conversation as if Elyse had not spoken, as usual.

Elyse waited, but Marye only eyed her with faint accusation.

"Um . . ." Elyse hummed.

"Well? Speak up, Elyse! I can hardly hear you!"

"We could go to the city," Elyse said tentatively. "After all, our guests haven't had a very good time here at Les Chattes Bleues, have they?"

"Yes . . . yes," Marye murmured, frowning as if she were considering a particularly complex military maneuver. "I suppose we could. I need to make market, anyway. And Mrs. de Lancie and Cheney and Irene wanted to visit some dressmaker . . . although I hardly think that would cheer Richard up. He does make awful faces when Irene and Cheney talk about visiting the dressmaker."

Elyse, her dark brown eyes alight, sat up straighter in her chair. "But, Marye! Oh, how could we forget?"

"I have forgotten nothing," Marye sniffed.

"Marye, don't you know what it is?"

"What . . . what is, Elyse? Make sense!"

"Well, I had forgotten anyway," Elyse giggled, then bounced out of her chair to grab Marye's hands. "It's next week! Tuesday is Mardi Gras!"

Tante Marye's reaction would have, and did later, surprise everyone. Her blue eyes seemed bluer, her cheeks flushed pink, and she smiled with genuine pleasure. Rising from her chair, still holding Elyse's hands, she nodded, "Yes, Elyse, that's it. We must attend Mardi Gras."

They hurried outside and upstairs to the bedrooms, Marye at a sedate and dignified pace and Elyse bouncing from step to step. Marye went to the Red Room, and Elyse went first to Cheney's room, and they both went to Victoria's room. Soon the four of them—Marye, Elyse, Cheney, and Victoria—with Zhou-Zhou and Nia also in tow, went back downstairs. The chorus of ladies' voices, chattering sometimes in French, sometimes in English, sounded incongruously light and cheerful in the misty morning stillness.

In the Red Room, Richard cocked his head as the genteel commotion out on the gallery filtered through the louvered shutters of the French windows. Irene had just returned from stepping out onto the gallery for a few words with Tante Marye. "Are your aunts up to something, Irene?" he demanded.

"You make them sound so disreputable, darling. Like smugglers, or pirates," Irene teased.

He sighed and struggled to pull on his boot. His long-wounded leg felt stiff and ached slightly. "Wonder how Shiloh is this morning," he said halfway to himself.

Irene, who was already dressed for breakfast, went to Richard and pushed on the bottom of his boot while Richard pulled on the uppers. "He's . . . fine. Just like he's . . . been . . . since yesterday morning," she gasped. Irene was not very strong, and she pushed on the boot with all her might. "There! Now, let me see you." With a critical eye she inspected her husband. He was wearing a gray suit with a blue waistcoat, blue tie, and his spotlessly shined boots. Richard was a handsome man, normally vigorous and healthy-looking, with a clear eye and a year-round tan, for he took long rides every day. But now he was pale, his face lined, and his eyes weary as he obediently stood for Irene to look him up and down.

"Richard, I think you look marvelous," she said, putting a slim finger to her chin thoughtfully, "because you are a marvelously handsome man."

A smile of genuine pleasure lit his tired face. "Thank you, wife. Glad you still think so, after twenty-seven years."

"And since you are so handsome, I want to show you off. I think we'll go to town and get you two new suits, a white one and a cream-colored one. Both in that new cotton-wool blend, I should think," Irene decided.

Richard's shoulders drooped slightly, and he looked weary again. "Irene, I don't want to go to town. What if—"

She moved quickly, glided across the floor to place her forefinger on his lips, then stood on tiptoe to kiss him gently. "Please?" was all she said.

It was all she had to say.

12

ONLY FOR LOVE

"I think I've been duped."

Richard Duvall pushed his silk top hat far back on his head, propped his hands on his hips, and stared up at the silk banner strung across the four massive Tuscan columns at the grand entrance to the St. Louis Hotel. In bright scarlet letters it read: "VIVE LE MARDI GRAS!"

Beside him, Gowan Ford looked amused. "You mean you didn't know tomorrow is Mardi Gras?"

"Sure didn't," Richard replied wryly. "And somehow Irene—and Cheney, and Mrs. de Lancie, and Marye and Elyse—all forgot to mention it when they were begging us to bring them to town."

"Oh, but you're mistaken, Colonel Duvall," Ford said, chuckling deep in his throat. "It's all they've been talking about for the last two days."

Richard sighed. "In French, right?"

"Right."

The women were still chattering in French in a tight little knot— or rather, a large noisy group—directly behind Richard and Gowan Ford. Though the party was staying for only two nights, they had brought a veritable mountain of trunks and cases. Tante Marye seemed to be having an altercation with one of the drivers of the hansom cabs. It had taken two cabs to transport all of them from the docks, and the other cab driver had run back and forth by Richard and Gowan Ford six times, carrying trunks into the hotel. Then, in a pleading whisper, he asked Richard for the two-dollar fare and hurriedly escaped Tante Marye's eagle eyes and sharp tongue.

Shiloh appeared beside Richard, and the three men resolutely kept their backs turned and their faces straight, although they listened with great enjoyment to the genteel tirade and accompanying pleas and chatter going on so volubly behind them.

"Can you understand any of what they're saying?" Richard asked Shiloh curiously.

"None," Shiloh admitted. "And neither can that coachman. I was getting ready to help him with the bags, and I asked him if he spoke French. He doesn't."

"Marye thinks it's a law that you aren't allowed in the French Quarter unless you speak French," Ford grumbled.

The poor defenseless coachman was backed helplessly against his hansom cab's door. Tante Marye loomed over him threateningly while the other ladies formed a solid bulwark behind her.

"If you really want to know," Ford went on idly, "Marye didn't like the way he tied the trunks to the top of the cab, Elyse didn't like him whipping the horses, and Miss Cheney has accused him of leaving her doctor's bag down at the docks." In fact, Shiloh was holding Cheney's doctor's bag, and had been ever since they left Les Chattes Bleues.

"Poor fella," Shiloh muttered. "Hard going to earn two dollars."

"Marye will give him two, and Elyse will sneak him two more," Ford grumbled. "She thinks money's just paper that's got printing on it."

"Uh . . . well, what else is it, exactly?" Shiloh asked.

"Good point," Ford replied.

After a few more tough moments for the coachman, Shiloh, Richard, and Gowan were joined by their ladies: Irene, Cheney, Victoria, Tante Marye, and Tante Elyse. Obediently following were the ladies' maids. Victoria had insisted that without Zhou-Zhou she would not be able to make herself presentable within two days' time, and she would miss Mardi Gras altogether. Cheney had insisted upon bringing Nia, for Nia had not yet seen New Orleans. Tante Marye had insisted upon bringing Molly to wait upon her, and Tante Elyse had insisted that Molly bring Adah and Chloe for her own odd reason.

"That will make us a party of thirteen," she had sniffed haughtily. "And I say à la diable with those vaudou persons and gris-gris and curses and such silly superstitions."

As they went into the hotel, Richard cast a worried look up and down St. Louis Street. It was much more congested than usual, with throngs of people, carriages, and horses. "I'm not so sure we should both have left Les Chattes Bleues, Mr. Ford," he said uneasily. "What if the vaudou come back tonight or tomorrow?"

"They won't," Ford reassured him. "Believe me, they won't miss a chance to sell their *gris-gris* and love potions and good-luck charms to all the suckers coming into town for Mardi Gras. And besides, Monroe and Corbett can handle Les Chattes Bleues very well for a couple of days."

Richard frowned but said no more, and Gowan Ford exchanged a worried look with Shiloh behind Richard's back. Duvall had been tense and depressed ever since the night of the *vaudou*. Both Ford and Shiloh hoped that Irene was right, and that getting away from Les Chattes Bleues for a couple of worry-free nights would help her husband come out of his melancholia.

The block-long St. Louis Hotel's exterior was simple and dignified in design, but its interior was lavish both in architecture and in furnishings. The principal entrance on St. Louis Street opened into a vestibule 127 feet wide and 40 feet deep. In the center of the building was the rotunda, a circular apartment that rose a breathtaking 88 feet above the main floor and was surmounted by a magnificent dome 65 feet across. In the rotunda auctions of all sorts of property, including slaves before the war, were held. As they entered the main lobby they saw a sign lettered with embellished calligraphy announcing a grand showing of art works and photography in the rotunda at eight o'clock that evening Winslow Homer's paintings and Matthew Brady's photographs of the late war would be featured. After that a ball was to be held in the grand ballroom on the second floor.

"Oh, I want to see that exhibit!" Cheney exclaimed. "I've seen some of Mr. Homer's work, and I like it very much. But I've never seen Mr. Brady's photographs, and I hear he is a wonderful photographer."

"I'd like to see if he is," Richard said dryly. "We certainly saw a lot of him during the war, but I never saw any of his photographs."

"That's settled, then," Irene said with satisfaction. "We're going to the tailor right down on Chartres Street and the dressmaker over on Toulouse. Then Tante Marye must make market—she'll only patronize the French Market, and we've arranged to meet Octave there to transport everything to Les Chattes Bleues. We should be finished in time for dinner—"

"At Antoine's on Royal," Tante Marye finished with satisfaction. She had joined them after speaking briefly with the innkeeper. "We shall dine there tonight, as the crush will be too horrible on Mardi

Gras. I have instructed *le concierge* that all of our meals will be served in the Vicomte's Suite tomorrow."

"The Vicomte's Suite? Is that yours and Mrs. Buckingham's suite?" Victoria inquired, her eyes bright.

"Oh yes, Mrs. de Lancie," Tante Marye nodded as she led the party up and around the magnificent circular staircase. "Our father was quite a good friend, and a patron, of the architect J. N. de Pouilly."

"And the vicomte and vicomtesse stayed here often?"

"Yes, they did, and so did we." Tante Marye smiled. "In fact, the Vicomte's Suite was never rented to anyone else while he was alive. But after he died, Elyse and I gave them permission to rent it, except for Mardi Gras."

"So you always attend Mardi Gras?" Victoria asked in amazement.

"*Oui, certainement,*" Tante Marye answered with amusement. "My father and mother had as much fun as we children. My father was a Huguenot, and my mother was a devout Catholic. They disagreed, volubly and often, about religious matters. But one thing they did agree on was that Mardi Gras was a time for celebration and joy, and a respite from the cares of this world. We had parties at Les Chattes Bleues before Mardi Gras parades began in 1857. Then, on Ash Wednesday, we always fasted the entire day and had our own private family service on Thursday morning. It was neither Protestant nor Catholic, but simply a thanksgiving and worship service."

"That sounds wonderful," Victoria said with finality. "We should celebrate exactly the same way this year at Les Chattes Bleues."

"A very good idea, Mrs. de Lancie," Tante Marye said. She cast a worried look over her shoulder at Richard Duvall's rounded shoulders and drawn face. "I think it would be good for all of us."

★　★　★　★

On April 22, 1722, the engineer La Blond de la Tour submitted a plan for the new capital of *Louisiane*, which was to be called *Nouvelle-Orléans*, to John Law and his Company of the West, which was the possessor of a monopoly of the new French colony. De la Tour's projection was of a simple gridiron of streets with a public square in the center, four square blocks extending in each direction above and below and six blocks back of the river. The blocks flanking the public square were marked with a fleur-de-lis, indicating that they were to be reserved for royal use, and on the block facing the square, a site for the parish church was designated. The streets were given such names as Royal, Bourbon, Chartres, Conti, St. Peter, St. Ann, St. Philip, and St. Louis, probably to flatter the owners of the new territory, the French court and the church.

But the new city underwent many changes in the years after the work had begun, and in view of the nature of these changes it was odd that the Vieux Carré maintained a distinctive French air. But French it began, and French it remained, so much so that "Vieux Carré" is commonly translated, and believed to mean, "French Quarter," although the literal meaning of the words is "old section."

In 1762 Louis XV ceded *Louisiane* to his Spanish cousin Charles III, but the Treaty of Fontainebleau was kept secret for a year and a half. More time passed before Spain reluctantly took possession, and the inhabitants of *Nouvelle-Orléans* found out that they had been Spanish possessions for nearly two years. With typical Gallic shrugs, they kept on speaking and believing and being French.

On March 21, 1788, a great fire desolated *Nouvelle-Orléans*, destroying 856 buildings—most of the French colonial city. During the years 1793–1794, the city was struck by three hurricanes, and many more of the oldest buildings simply disappeared. On December 8, 1794, a second great fire destroyed practically all the remaining buildings left by the French. But as fire purifies and water washes clean, what was destroyed in these disastrous years was an irregular, haphazard, rudely built French town; what was rebuilt was a stately Spanish city, exotic and ornate in detail but graceful and dignified in proportion.

In 1800 Spain retroceded Louisiana to France by the Treaty of San Ildefonso, but again the people who lived in this political chesspiece of a colony were not to find out who, exactly, owned them for another three years. Finally, in 1803, Napoleon deigned to send a Colonial Prefect to let Louisianians know, by the way, that he was their emperor. In May of that year the United States purchased the colony, but by this time Louisiana and particularly New Orleans were so haughtily self-contained that it didn't matter to them that they didn't find out until August that they were supposed to be Americans. It made no difference, anyway. Their home was in *Louisiane*, in *Nouvelle-Orléans*, and the people of the Vieux Carré barely noticed in 1812 when Louisiana became a state.

As the company of thirteen from Les Chattes Bleues set out on their walking tour of the French Quarter, Richard Duvall was, as always, amused and bemused by the other-worldly air and ambiance of this most unique of cities. He told Shiloh of its checkerboard history and rainbow heritage. The three-block walk down Chartres Street to the tailor was a visual synopsis of the exotic potpourri that was New Orleans. Well-dressed quadroons and octoroons paraded gracefully down the street, their expressions haughty, but their gazes never quite meeting anyone else's. Filthy children ran barefooted, weaving their way between the men in cream-colored morning suits and the finely coiffured women. Two men in cheap black suits and worn top hats passed, gesticulating energetically and speaking passionately in French. Negro women in all colors of *tignons* pushed carriages, carried bundles, hurried on errands, and sometimes dawdled along, staring longingly at the goods displayed in the windows of the tiny shops.

"It is odd," Shiloh mused. "You can see that this architecture and design is Spanish. But the people are certainly French and believe everything here is French."

The buildings were predominantly of stucco, mostly white, but some of them were painted a rich cream color, or even pastels, an unmistakably Spanish conceit. Lacy wrought iron was everywhere, forming balustrades on great second floor galleries and ornamenting the tiniest windows. The streets were honeycombed with passages leading into interior courtyards, sometimes private, sometimes shared by four or even six buildings. Most of the buildings were small, but almost all were two or three stories, with a number of businesses on each floor, as evidenced by the different signs in each window. Nearly all of the signs were in French, although some supplied an English equivalent in small letters underneath—an obvious afterthought.

"I must say," Gowan Ford said thoughtfully, "that the French Quarter is the most beautiful part of the city."

Shiloh and Richard exchanged grins behind his back.

They reached the tailor's, which was discreetly announced by a tiny white sign above the doorknob that read in fine script: "Monsieur Beluche." Irene took Richard firmly by the arm and announced, "I'm going in with him, or he'll come out with only a new handkerchief or top hat."

Tante Elyse grabbed Gowan Ford's arm and commanded, "Gowan, come with me. You're going to order a new morning suit, too, and— no, be quiet. You'll look quite handsome in . . . hmm, a tan broadcloth, I think . . . or perhaps a cream color. . . . I don't think white, it's much too impractical for riding, isn't it?" Her strident voice faded as she marched into *Monsieur* Beluche's hauling Gowan, who looked as helpless as a kidnapped child.

Cheney looked speculatively at Shiloh, who put up his hands and backed up two steps. "Huh-uh, Doc, not me. I don't want one of those fancy-pants white get-ups—"

"Come along, Shiloh," she said briskly, taking his arm. Victoria took his other arm, and Tante Marye gave him a haughty nod before leading the way. Zhou-Zhou and Nia exchanged shrugs, Adah hovered close to her mother, Molly. But Chloe took a step toward the door, her eyes sharp and bright as she watched Shiloh being led into the small shop.

"No, Chloe," Molly said sharply. "We wait out here."

"But—" Chloe began, making a pouty mouth.

"No," Molly repeated. "You don't belong in there."

The door to *Monsieur* Beluche's tailor shop closed with finality, and Chloe moved to the window beside the door to stare hungrily inside.

Monsieur Beluche's tailor shop was as discreet and understated as his sign. The room was small and rather dark, as the two windows on either side of the door were high and narrow, and fronted with black ironwork grilles. Along the back wall was a long table, and the only items on it were three top hats tastefully arranged at one end on stands of different heights. Along one wall were bolts of cloth, symmetrically displayed by color: black, charcoal gray, light gray, navy blue, dark brown, light brown, tan, cream, white. Along the other wall was a long glass-enclosed counter with an array of buttons, cufflinks, handkerchiefs, and ties.

White curtains stirred at the back wall behind the table, and *Monsieur* Beluche emerged. He was a small man, only a few inches over five feet, with his shoulders thrust back and his chest puffed out, and he walked with high, rather mincing steps. Cheney stifled a giggle; he looked exactly like a rooster as he made a precise turn around the table and headed toward the crowd of eight people assembled in the front room of his shop. His hair was black and heavily pomaded and parted exactly in the middle. Above his pressed-thin mouth was a precise little black mustache, and a monocle was stuck firmly in his left eye.

He stopped before Tante Marye, who had arranged herself, as it were, as the figurehead of this noisy group, and bowed, removing his monocle and gesturing dramatically with it as he did so. "*Bonjour, mes-*

dames et messieurs. Je suis Monsieur Beluche, à votre service."

"*Bonjour, Monsieur Beluche*," Tante Marye nodded. With a dismissive gesture at Richard she asked, "*Parlez-vous anglais?*"

"Yes, *madame*, I do," *Monsieur* Beluche answered with a small sniff. Cheney thought he looked as if his funny little mustache was tickling his nose. "How may I be of service to you ladies and gentlemen?"

Tante Marye opened her mouth, but Richard interrupted with a mischievous glance at Irene. "I'll have a handkerchief."

Shiloh announced, "I'll have a pair of socks."

Gowan Ford's mouth twitched. "I'll have one cufflink." *Monsieur* Beluche eyed Ford's empty shirt sleeve without humor, his little button eyes already busily sizing the three men.

Ignoring them grandly, Tante Marye continued, "These three gentlemen all require three-piece morning suits, *Monsieur* Beluche. As you take their measurements, we ladies shall decide upon suitable fabrics."

"*Certainement, madame*," *Monsieur* Beluche responded with another small bow. Planting the monocle back firmly in his eye, he looked each of the three men up and down severely and slowly walked in a circle around first Richard, then Shiloh, and finally Gowan. "Mmm, mmm," he hummed to himself, and the timbre of his humming changed as he studied Gowan's empty sleeve.

"I only have one arm," Ford asserted clearly. "Does that mean I get a discount?"

Shiloh and Richard chuckled, Tante Marye continued to ignore him, Cheney and Irene hid smiles behind their gloved hands.

Tante Elyse asked, wide-eyed, "Well, does he?"

"Certainly not, *madame*," *Monsieur* Beluche answered stiffly. "It will be much more difficult to make his suit fit properly. Quite a nuisance—"

"To me, too," Ford agreed dryly.

"—but I can make a suit that will flatter him," *Monsieur* Beluche continued, almost to himself. "Some additional padding on the right shoulder. . . . He is still well-proportioned, I think, and his shoulders are wide. . . . Yes, *monsieur*, I can make a fine suit for you, and it will be well worth the money."

"Good," Tante Elyse said with finality. Ford frowned darkly but stood still under Monsieur Beluche's assessing gaze.

"And, you, sir, you are a good size, tall, but very well-proportioned for a man your age," the little tailor said, giving Richard another up-

and-down look. "No need for disguising a fat belly on you." He shuddered theatrically, then turned a jaundiced eye on Shiloh. "But you! *Que faire?* You are so tall, such long legs! I think the cream broadcloth. That is the only one of which I believe I have enough fabric in stock!"

"The cream broadcloth will do very well," Cheney said decisively. Shiloh was fidgeting like a guilty schoolboy and rolled his eyes.

"This way, gentlemen," Monsieur Beluche asserted firmly, as if he were directing the prisoners to the dock. "It will take much time to get precise measurements. All of you are too tall."

"So sorry about that," Shiloh muttered as he followed the prancing little tailor behind the curtains in the back of the room.

Richard and Gowan Ford followed obediently, and when they had disappeared behind the curtains, the ladies all smiled. "Such a fuss," Tante Marye commented. "Men are so much trouble."

"They are worth it, though," Irene said with a secret smile.

"Not all of them," Victoria scoffed.

"But some of them are," Tante Elyse countered. "Like Richard, and Gowan, and Dev. And I think perhaps Shiloh is one of those who is well worth all the trouble, don't you, Cheney?"

Cheney turned to face her great-aunt, and behind the women she saw Chloe staring in through the window. Cheney's eyes narrowed and turned a dark jade green.

She was dismayed by the intensity with which she disliked the young girl, but she couldn't seem to overcome it no matter how severely she lectured herself. Cheney had been dismayed when she found out that Tante Elyse had told Molly to bring Chloe—she had avoided the girl assiduously since the morning she had witnessed the scene in Shiloh's *garçonniere*—but she could hardly protest. She would never think of telling her great-aunts—or anyone else, for that matter—about Chloe's sordid little games of seduction, and she had not mentioned it to Shiloh after that morning. She and Shiloh had slowly regained some of the old ease in each other's company, although they both were conscious of a new tentativeness and restraint in their conversation and manner. Cheney blamed Chloe for this, although at times she still viewed Shiloh as flirtatious and irresponsible.

"Sometimes he is," she finally murmured, staring at the heart-shaped face silhouetted in the window, "and sometimes I think he's entirely too much trouble—for everyone."

"What?" Tante Elyse asked plaintively. "I couldn't hear you, Cheney. What I asked was—"

"Yes, I know, Tante Elyse," Cheney interrupted hastily and turned her back to the window. "Never mind. Let's look at this great quantity of cream broadcloth, shall we?"

★　★　★　★

Irene Duvall ordered three suits for her husband: one of tan broadcloth, one of a slightly darker buff color, and—against Richard's protests that he'd never keep it clean for five minutes—one of a fine ecru linen. Tante Elyse insisted on a buckskin-colored broadcloth for Gowan Ford, and Cheney was satisfied with the cream-colored broadcloth for Shiloh.

The company promenaded up Iberville Street, walking slowly and breathing in the exotic air of New Orleans. As they walked they often changed walking partners, for it was necessary to walk no more than three abreast on the narrow banquettes, and the ladies in particular swirled back and forth along the long line of thirteen people in what seemed to be a leisurely choreographed dance. The three men generally tried to bring up the rear, but Molly kept stepping deferentially around behind them, keeping Adah and Chloe beside her. Adah stayed close to Molly and rarely spoke, but Chloe continually either hurried her pace or lagged deliberately in complicated maneuvers that resulted in her staying close behind Shiloh.

"I'll look like some kind of big ol' muffin, fol-de-rolin' around in that white suit," Shiloh complained to Cheney.

"It's not white," Cheney argued. "It's cream."

"That's what I said. A big ol' creamy muffin."

Behind them, Chloe murmured seductively, "I love muffins with cream. . . ."

Walking beside Chloe, Molly's head whipped around, her eyes huge with outrage. Chloe pretended not to see her and sashayed along directly behind Cheney and Shiloh. Shiloh pretended not to hear, as did Cheney, but Cheney could feel her cheeks reddening with a sudden, choking surge of anger—but she told herself it was with embarrassment at Chloe's crudeness. Resolutely she turned to stare down a small street lined up to the curb with two-story buildings. At the end of the alley they could see the graceful lines of the St. Louis Hotel.

"That's Exchange Alley," Shiloh told her, his voice reflecting none of the tension that Cheney felt in the air surrounding them. "That's the only place in New Orleans I saw when I was here before. Except for the docks."

"You've been here before?" Cheney asked in surprise.

"Once, when I was eighteen. For a fight with Jamie Jakes. They brought me here, to Exchange Alley, to work out the day before the fight." Shiloh nodded to the uniform line of buildings in the narrow passage. "That used to be known as the street of the fencing masters, because several of them had their ateliers there. That's where I worked out, in one of the ateliers. Even tried fencing." He grinned down at her. "Too girly for me. All that prancing and prissing."

"Yes, you would prefer just to knock people around with your fists, wouldn't you?" Cheney snapped.

"Nah. Actually I prefer your method."

"What? My method?"

"Yeah, Doc," he replied, his eyes glinting a mischievous cornflower blue. "Shootin' 'em."

"Shiloh! I have never actually shot anyone!" Cheney exclaimed, rather too loudly, for Irene turned around, her eyebrows winging upward.

"I should hope not," Irene murmured.

Richard turned and winked surreptitiously at Shiloh. "Have you almost shot anyone, Cheney?"

"Well, there was this one time—" Shiloh began, but Cheney pinched his arm fiercely, and with a small yelp he shut up.

"This conversation is absurd," Cheney said firmly, though she didn't meet her father's gaze. "Father, Shiloh was just telling me about Exchange Alley and the ateliers. Very interesting."

"Yes, very," Richard agreed with a grin, and he turned back around with no further comment.

As they got farther away from the Mississippi River and the commerce nearest the docks, the street traffic lessened somewhat, but the throngs of people crowding the banquettes did not. Occasionally an Indian family walked by in single file, always with the man in front, the woman behind him, and the children from the tallest to the smallest following. They kept their dark eyes trained straight ahead.

A chubby, cheerful Negro woman called out in a musical chant, "*Bels calas, bels calas, tout chauds! Tout chauds!*" She walked past them, her hands on her hips, a wide basket balanced on her head.

Cheney told Shiloh, "A cala woman! She's calling, 'fine fritters, fine fritters, very hot!' 'Cah-lahs' are a rather coarse rice fritter, made by dropping a rich yeast batter into deep hot fat. They're delicious."

"Want one? I'll treat you."

"No, thank you, I don't care for one right now," she said formally. Shiloh shrugged.

They also saw a blackberry woman, who called "Bla-a-ck berries, berries very fine!" A vegetable peddler, savior to the housewives who couldn't get to market, balanced an immense basket on her head, piled so high with all kinds of glossy vegetables that she was obliged to steady it with one hand, the tendons in her strong neck corded from the weight. A chimney sweep passed them, smiling and bowing and tipping his trademark battered silk high hat to all the ladies, all the while singing, "*R-r-r-ramoner la cheminée!*" The clothespole man passed them, walking down the middle of the narrow street, his bundle of saplings neatly trimmed, with the V-notch cut at one end to raise the clotheslines. "Clo-o-othes-poles, *mesdames!*" he cried out. "Clo-o-othes-poles!"

At the corner of Bourbon and Bienville was a woman who sat with a basket, covered with a white cotton tea towel, on her lap. She didn't call out, or even look around at passersby. Slowly she waved a palmetto fan over the top of the basket.

"Mmm, the praline mammy!" Cheney cried. "Can you smell them?"

"Sure can smell something good," Shiloh replied. "What's a praline?"

"Come with me," Cheney said, hurrying to the silent woman. As they stood over her she said nothing, but pulled the cotton napkin aside. Inside were flat wafers of delicious candy—brown pecan pralines and white and pink coconut ones. The sweet aroma made Cheney's mouth water.

"Bet you'll let me treat you to one of these," Shiloh teased.

"One of each!" Cheney said greedily. The woman, still silent, held up three gnarled fingers, and Shiloh gave her thirty cents. She was a very old woman, her face creased with a thousand wrinkles, and she had no teeth. She smiled up at Shiloh and gave Cheney the three largest pralines: one brown, one pink, and one white. Shiloh watched in amusement as Cheney broke each precisely into halves, then broke three of the halves into quarters. She ate a quarter portion of each one, gave the other quarters to Nia, then wrapped the three halves in her handkerchief and placed them carefully in her reticule. "Thank you, Shiloh," she said with the same formality as before.

"Welcome, Doc," he said easily, but a shadow crossed his expression for a brief moment. Although Cheney was obviously not still angry with him, neither was she as open and comfortable with him as she had been before she'd found him and Chloe clasped together.

Even though the truth is I was pushin' while Chloe was pullin', Shiloh thought darkly. *The Doc's a strong woman . . . independent . . . stubborn, a woman with her own mind and her own ways. It's gonna take some time to win back the ground I lost over that little minx!*

They came to Bourbon and turned east. As they passed the corner of Bienville Street, Gowan Ford looked longingly down the block. "Absinthe House is right there. They make a drink called absinthe frappe—"

"Never you mind," Tante Elyse said firmly. "It won't kill you men to take this promenade with us."

"Absinthe what?" Shiloh asked, licking his lips.

"No," Cheney said shortly.

Shiloh muttered something under his breath that sounded suspiciously like "bossy women," but he obediently trooped on, Cheney clasping his arm as if she were afraid he might break into a run.

Along Bourbon Street they passed Conti and St. Louis Streets as they headed for the dressmaker on Toulouse. Most of this area was residential, although there were still the tobacconist shop, the cafés and occasional saloon, the barber, and the pharmacy on each block. The homes were of varied size and elegance, though all were obviously of Spanish design. Some were palatial estates of pink or coral stucco, enclosed in wrought-iron fencing, built in squares that enclosed luxurious courtyards. Some were precariously narrow two-story dwellings that fronted the streets directly, but even the most humble of these usually had some ironwork, and almost all of them had window boxes with riotous blooms of every shape and color.

At the corner of Bourbon and Toulouse, directly across the street from the French Opera House, was a narrow two-story white stucco house, rather plain, although it did have pretty white grillwork over the windows and a small gallery on the second story with a white ironwork balustrade.

"This is Angelique's," Victoria announced. "She's a dressmaker, quite exclusive, which is why there is no vulgar sign or advertisement. You gentlemen will be obliged to wait."

"We could go over to the *Café des Exilés*," Gowan Ford suggested hopefully.

"Yes, we could do that," Richard said in the same pleading tone, staring down beseechingly at Irene.

"You don't even know what the *Café des Exilés* is," Irene teased.

"I could go find out."

"They'll speak French."

"So will I," Richard said, grinning. "I'll say, '*café*.'"

"Go on with you," Irene said, giving him a playful little shove. "We have lots of work to do. Mr. Ford, please take responsibility for my husband, and whatever you do, don't let him speak French. There is no accounting for what he might say, and these Creole gentlemen are so high-tempered!"

With undisguised relief the three men trooped off to the café, and Victoria led the way to the plain whitewashed door of the cottage. "Zhou-Zhou, come with me. In fact, all of you—Nia, and Molly, and you two girls—what are your names again? —yes, yes, Chloe, Adah, you come too. Angelique is exclusive, but her designs are for everyone. I think you'll find something you like here."

Victoria imperiously knocked on the door, and almost instantly it was answered. A beautiful quadroon woman —or a girl, really—stood in the doorway. She was small, with a tiny waist and small delicate hands. Her skin was a tawny gold color, and her round dark eyes were heavily fringed with long thick lashes. Her mouth was wide and sensuously full, but her expression was open, with no hint of the conscious sultriness that many of the quadroon women affected. She smiled warmly when she saw Victoria, and quickly she stepped forward to clasp Victoria's hands in hers. Then gracefully she kissed both of Victoria's cheeks and murmured in a soft voice with a heavy French accent, "Madame de Lancie, how very good it is to see you! Please, please come in."

All ten of the ladies followed Angelique into the house. The entire first floor was a showroom. Every wall was draped with red velvet, with graceful swags formed to frame the long narrow windows. The floor was of white marble, and along the back wall was a small raised platform. On each side of the room, angled toward the back, were two red velvet couches with tea tables at each end. Between these were single

163

chairs, white Queen Anne chairs with red velvet upholstery, four of them arranged around two low white marble pillars that served as tables.

Gracefully Angelique waved her hand toward one of the couches. "Madame de Lancie, if you will please make yourself comfortable here.... *Bonjour, madame,* I am Angelique...." With quiet grace she went to each lady and introduced herself, then delicately suggested where everyone might be seated. Cheney observed that Angelique treated each person in the same gracious manner, and that she spoke just as courteously to little Nia as she did to Tante Marye. Victoria, Cheney, and Irene were seated on one couch, Tante Marye and Tante Elyse on the other, and Zhou-Zhou, Nia, Molly, Adah, and Chloe were seated on the chairs.

"Please make yourselves very comfortable, *mesdames et mesdesmoiselles*," Angelique said, nodding with a queenly gesture. "If you will excuse me, I will make some arrangements, if you ladies would be so gracious as to have tea with me."

"Very well, Angelique," Victoria said.

The girl disappeared behind the heavy curtains through an unseen door, then returned quickly. "Tea will be only a few minutes," she said, addressing everyone.

"Good," Victoria said briskly. "Now, Angelique, I like very much what you've done here. This room is simple, elegant, and has the kind of intimacy that ladies like when they are taking their time deciding on their wardrobe."

"Oh, thank you, Madame de Lancie," Angelique breathed, "but it was because of what you told me last time—about ladies preferring to have an ... an ... air like this—that I thought of this room, and of presenting my dresses. Well ... I will show you, if I may." Her eyes were a soft deer-brown, startling in their depths, and her gaze never left Victoria's face. Cheney couldn't understand the strange currents of intimacy between her friend and this quadroon dressmaker; she hoped that Victoria would tell her about Angelique later.

"Of course, Angelique, that is why we are here," Victoria retorted with a tinge of haughtiness. "I am certainly in need of some summer dresses, and I think I shall give Zhou-Zhou a new dress. I also want to present my gracious hostesses, Mrs. Buckingham and Mrs. Edwards, dresses as a thank-you gift for their kindness and hospitality."

"Oh no, Mrs. de Lancie, that is quite unnecessary," Tante Marye said stoutly. "It has been our pleasure—"

"Oh, thank you, Mrs. de Lancie!" Tante Elyse interrupted with childlike delight. "I should love a new dress! You and Irene and Cheney are always dressed so smartly, and Marye and I are so dowdy!"

"Elyse!" Marye protested. "Really!"

"But to be in good form, one must accept gifts properly offered," Elyse said slyly.

"That is true, Mrs. Edwards," Victoria said with a small smile. "It would give me great pleasure if you would accept this small token of gratitude from me. So that's settled. Now, Angelique, how do you present your designs?" She looked curiously about the room. "And where are the fabrics?"

"If you will allow me, I have thought of a new way to present my dresses," Angelique said shyly. "I have not had an opportunity to try it yet, but I should like to now, since you are so kind, Madame de Lancie, and will give me a fair opinion of my idea."

"All right, Angelique," Victoria said indulgently. "Let me hear of this new idea."

"*Mais non*, you must see it, *madame*." She hurried to stand beside the small platform and called out softly, "Jacqueline."

A woman, tall and slender, came soundlessly through the draperies to stand on the small platform. She was an octoroon, her face slightly averted, her eyes downcast, but she moved gracefully and gestured slightly with her long-fingered hands as Angelique said in a quiet, even tone, "This is one of my designs for evening, a dress made of sea-green glacé silk, trimmed with dark green satin ruching, with an overskirt of white Alencon lace. The neckline is slightly off the shoulder, and I have also fashioned a matching mantelet of dark green satin with a sea-green lining. The gloves are dark green to match the satin, and I would suggest that Madame Duvall would look lovely in this color; and with emeralds in your hair, *madame*, you would glow."

Irene Duvall smiled brilliantly. "You are too kind, Angelique, but I must admit that sea-green is one of my favorite colors. And the dress is perfectly lovely."

"Thank you, *madame*," Angelique said gratefully. "Thank you, Jacqueline. Now please allow each of the ladies to see the dress closely. Leonie!"

Another quadroon, this time a short, curvy girl who could not have been more than sixteen, swept out from behind the curtains and pirouetted prettily on the platform. She wore a peach-colored linen walking dress, with a matching parasol, and peau-de-soir shoes dyed to match. Then came Madeline, who wore a dramatic black satin evening dress and a black velvet cloak trimmed in ermine. After her was Tammy, who modeled a morning dress of white percale trimmed with pink lace and with a delicate white embroidered overskirt.

After all the ladies had seen all the models and dresses, and had delicately fingered the fine satins and percales and linen, and had looked over the needlework with critical eyes, the models disappeared behind the draperies once again. Then the heavy red velvet curtains behind the platform were drawn open to reveal the very back wall of the room, which was lined with bolts of fabrics, and a long marble pedestal table displaying four especially fine satins and silks. To the side an easel was set up, and Angelique's patterns were displayed. Cheney noted that instead of sketches, Angelique did each design in expert watercolors. As one, all of the ladies hurried to see the fine fabrics— the sheer chiffons, the glazed chintz, the heavy brocades—and to admire the rainbow shades from deepest black velvet to finest, sheer white chiffon.

Victoria discreetly took Angelique aside as the ladies were poring over the fabrics. The four models, still dressed in their finery, showed the fabrics to them and expertly told them of the qualities of this batiste and that damask and the other satinet, the shortcomings, the drawbacks, the qualities, the best uses. All of the models were seamstresses who worked for Angelique. Madeline and Tammy disappeared for a few moments and returned with two plain but elegant silver services, one for tea and one for coffee, each with a selection of tea cakes and ladyfingers. The ladies and the mannequins drank tea and coffee and sampled the delicious sweets while they discussed the delights of Angelique's shop.

"I am impressed, Angelique," Victoria said warmly. "I like the idea of the live mannequins; one can truly see how the fabrics move, how they flow, the true effect of the colors, and the life of the different textures. It's so much more vivid on models rather than on stiff bolts of cloth."

"Oh, thank you, *madame!*" Angelique cried. "I have been so worried that it would seem . . . forward . . . or . . . vulgar."

"Nonsense," Victoria retorted. "It's an excellent idea, and women will like it, so continue to present your dresses in this way, no matter

166

who the patroness. Believe me, when other dressmakers hear of this they will do the same thing, so don't tell anyone. Keep it your secret for as long as you can."

"*Oui, madame,*" Angelique said humbly. "I appreciate so much your advice."

"Now, I must suggest some changes in your designs, Angelique," Victoria went on almost brusquely. Any kind of emotion, even gratitude, made her slightly uneasy, and at once she became distant and cool. "Do you see these new designs from Paris that I and Mademoiselle Cheney and Madame Duvall are wearing? I have observed that here in New Orleans women are still wearing full crinolines, but I assure you that as soon as civilization returns after that awful war and this absurd occupation, you will see no more of them. In Paris, London, and New York the silhouettes have slimmed down, and evening dresses are quite form-fitting through the hips."

Angelique studied Cheney's dress thoroughly but unobtrusively, then Irene Duvall's. "*Oui, madame,*" she finally replied. "I see, and I already have some ideas for designs."

"Yes, very good, Angelique," Victoria said encouragingly. "You must make your dresses adhere to current fashion, you see, but your designs are unique. Don't ever just copy what you see, and never make more than one dress of the same pattern. You are very creative, and your special flair is the reason you can charge more for your work. Now, we are all wearing day dresses, in rather plain patterns. You do see that Cheney and I have small bustles in the back"—Victoria turned slightly so Angelique could observe the back of her dress—"and this is sometimes formed by gathering the material and adding padding—as mine is—or sometimes by specially shaped crinolines." She frowned. "Personally I don't care much for them, and I shall probably not indulge in bustles that are too large. But it does seem that they are already getting larger. I think it looks ridiculous, to have such ... such ..."

"Exaggerated posteriors?" Angelique suggested doubtfully.

Victoria laughed, a silvery sound that made Cheney look over at her and Angelique and smile. Cheney decided to join them, and as she came up she heard Victoria ask imperiously, "—very expensive? How are you faring?"

"Oh, quite well, Madame de Lancie," Angelique answered, her eyes

167

shining. "And I must thank you again, and always, for your kindness and generosity—"

"Here's Cheney," Victoria said hastily. "You really must have that navy blue cambric for a traveling suit, Cheney dear. With the lawn, I think, for a blouse, trimmed with the Brussels lace. . . ." Taking Cheney's arm firmly, she steered her back to the table to rejoin the other ladies, and Angelique followed.

Irene Duvall asked, "Leonie, may I see those shoes again? Oh, they are charming! Angelique, did you design the shoes, too?"

"*Oui, madame*, and I personally mix the dye to match the fabrics."

"Very good, Angelique," Victoria said approvingly. "You have noted that now the tops of the shoes may be—indeed should be—seen."

"Scandalous," Tante Elyse remarked dryly. "Now men may begin to suspect that we actually have legs."

"Ladies do not say that word in public," Tante Marye said automatically.

"What? 'Scandalous'?" Tante Elyse asked with wide-eyed innocence.

"No, Elyse, and it won't work," Tante Marye retorted, though her blue eyes twinkled. "I'm not going to say it."

Everyone laughed, even the servants, for they had been put completely at ease by Angelique's graciousness and by the fact that the ladies easily included them in all the discussions of fabrics and design. Zhou-Zhou and Nia chattered incessantly and felt of every single one of the materials, while Molly was quite reserved, though she smiled faintly and occasionally asked the seamstresses a question. Adah hung back, smiling shyly whenever Molly showed her a fabric, but Chloe was everywhere, eavesdropping on Angelique and Cheney and Victoria, running her hands over the fabrics, and insisting that Leonie show her how to pirouette so prettily and gesture the way the mannequins did when Angelique was showing their dresses.

"I'll have the black taffeta," Tante Marye decided.

Victoria countered, "Mrs. Edwards, I refuse to present you a gift of another black dress." She turned to Angelique and said with determination, "Mrs. Edwards will have that dark purple damask. Zhou-Zhou will have one of the peach linen that Leonie is wearing, and I suppose—"

"Oh, *madame, madame*, may I have the shoes to match, too?

Please?" Zhou-Zhou cried, clasping her hands in dramatic supplication.

"—she will need the matching shoes, Angelique," Victoria finished without even glancing at Zhou-Zhou. "And as I am confident that Mrs. Buckingham will not try to be a wallflower in black taffeta, I shall allow her to choose her own fabric."

"Mmm, I love this flowered organdy," Tante Elyse said dreamily. "But do you think it's too young for me, Marye?"

"No, dear Elyse," Tante Marye answered with rare affection. "Nothing is too young for you, for you are young at heart, and always will be. I think the organdy is perfect."

After three hours, the meticulous measurements were taken and the momentous decisions made. Victoria, Irene, and Cheney each ordered two summer dresses in fine pastel linens, and Victoria persuaded Cheney to order the navy blue traveling dress. Cheney ordered a white sprigged muslin for Nia, and Marye and Elyse ordered a cream-colored taffeta for Molly, a pink-flowered percale for Adah, and a blue-striped percale for Chloe. All together, the women ordered fourteen dresses from Angelique, and her gratefulness was touching.

As they were leaving, Victoria asked Angelique, "I assume you received my message? Were you able to get those items ready?"

"*Oui*, Madame de Lancie," Angelique answered. "I hope you are satisfied with them."

"I'm quite certain I will be, Angelique. Have them sent to the St. Louis Hotel, Room 204. I will certainly come back before I leave Les Chattes Bleues, and I shall expect to see some new sketches."

"*Certainement, madame.* And thank you, thank you from the bottom of my heart, Madame de Lancie," Angelique said, again clasping both of Victoria's hands in hers. "I can't tell you how grateful I am to you." Her eyes shimmered with tears.

"*Pas du tout.*" Victoria shrugged and pulled away from her rather quickly.

Cheney observed this scene at the door of Angelique's shop, and as Victoria turned to leave, Cheney fell into step beside her at the end of the line of ladies.

"You and Angelique know each other well, do you not?" Cheney asked.

Victoria smiled without humor and gracefully opened her parasol. "Not well, no. I have known her for some time, however."

"Oh, I see," Cheney said quickly, though she did not.

In a careful monotone, without looking at Cheney, Victoria continued, "My husband, Lionel, knew Angelique quite well. When he died there was a provision for her in his will"—she gave Cheney a narrow-eyed, sidelong glance—"including a one-story white house on Rampart Street and a sum of money. So I came here not long after Lionel was killed to . . . meet her."

Cheney was so shocked she could frame no reply. After a few moments Victoria went on in the same tuneless voice, "There was another woman, too, in New York, that Lionel left some money to, but she had moved to Venice by the time I traced her down. I did find Angelique, though, and she was so . . . so . . . very young. And alone."

"But he . . . he was your husband!" Cheney finally stammered.

"Yes, he was, and I was glad to marry him, and I think he was glad to marry me," Victoria replied carefully. "But Angelique truly loved him, you see. And I did not."

"I just don't understand, Victoria," Cheney said in a small voice. "It's hard for me to imagine living like that."

Suddenly Victoria's sky-blue eyes grew sharp and slightly green-tinged. "Oh? Then listen to me and understand: that is what happens when you marry the wrong man, Cheney. Remember that." Victoria quickened her step so as to catch up with the other ladies, and Cheney hurried to stay alongside of her. "Remember that," Victoria repeated in a hard tone, her eyes searching straight ahead. "You must marry only for love, Cheney."

Softly, thoughtfully Cheney repeated, "Only for love . . ."

13

EXILES, PIRATES, AND LOVELY LADIES

"I suppose I ought to call on Mr. Law again," Richard grumbled. "At our last meeting I forgot to get the deed to Les Chattes Bleues."

"It's in French, you know, Colonel Duvall," Ford said mildly. "And now it really doesn't matter, does it?"

"What do you mean?"

Ford shrugged carelessly. "Well, we wanted the deed to establish the property boundaries to Les Chattes Bleues so that we could determine a course of action if the *vaudou* were, indeed, trespassing."

Richard Duvall stared blankly at Gowan Ford's dark visage.

"I would say that leaving *gris-gris* right on the galleries of the house constitutes trespassing," Ford continued acidly.

Richard shook his head with irritation. "Of course. Now we don't need to establish that they are trespassing on the rise across the lagoon."

"To say nothing of trespassing on my face," Shiloh added sarcastically, rubbing the left side of his face as if to erase the memory of Dédé's cool dead fingers tracing down it. Though the red streaks and the tiny blisters had disappeared within two days, the memory of that night, and the snakes, and the voodoo priestess's touch still gave Shiloh a frisson of dread.

Richard sighed with a trace of regret, which made Shiloh feel guilty, so he looked around and said lightly, "I sure like this place. Not much like the saloons I've been in."

Ford grinned his lopsided grin. Because the right side of his face was not as responsive as the left, that corner of his mouth never quite turned upward. "Gaston, over there, would have a few things to say to you, Monsieur Irons, if he heard you call his place a saloon."

"Yeah?" Shiloh said gamely, grinning over at the short, plump proprietor. "Like what?"

"Like you are a crude and boorish *Américain,* probably a *Kaintock* with no manners, and if you were any kind of a gentleman he would be obliged to challenge you to a duel to avenge the reputation of his establishment. But since you are obviously only semicivilized and have no honor, he cannot challenge you." By now Shiloh and Richard were chuckling at Ford's foolishness and the vision of the short, plump Gaston shouting up—far up—at Shiloh in his high voice that carried all over the small coffeehouse.

The *Café des Exilés* was typical of many of the oldest and most genteel coffeehouses of the Vieux Carré. The interior was dark and cool and smelled of cigar smoke and chicory coffee. The floor was sanded, and small tables were scattered about the room. Rather than a long bar where men "bellied up" to toss down rough whiskey, in front of the wall that housed the collection of fine wines, port, sherry, and brandy was a counter with a sink where Gaston made and served coffee and tea during the day and mixed aperitifs or after-dinner cordials during the evening. The *Café des Exilés* did not even serve beer.

In the early part of the century, the *Café des Exilés* was patronized mostly by Frenchmen who, like the Vicomte de Cheyne, had fled France during the Revolution, or Saint-Domingue during the slave uprisings. They gathered each evening to argue politics or discuss commercial affairs, and to commiserate for the losses each had known, whether in business or, in the Vicomte's case, in family, friends, and home.

Now the café's clientele had changed somewhat. Most of the patrons were Creole gentlemen who had been staunch Confederates, and they had lived in an occupied country since 1862. Bitter in defeat, dispossessed of their businesses, many of them stripped of their homes and personal possessions, they banded together at the *Café des Exilés.* Once again the coffeehouse was home to men who were exiles, albeit in their own country.

But to Shiloh Irons, Richard Duvall, and Gowan Ford on this warm afternoon, the *Café des Exilés* held none of these poignant associations; they were merely glad to be in an unmistakably male atmosphere, where they could sit down and rest and talk about man things instead of clothes and fabrics and laces and fittings. There were about a dozen other men scattered about the room, sitting in groups of two or three at the plain square tables, talking in low voices, almost all of them in French.

Suddenly Gowan Ford sat up a little straighter and leaned forward with an intent look on his face. Shiloh and Richard watched him curiously and could see that he was eavesdropping on the conversation going on at the table nearest them. The table was behind Shiloh and Richard, and they didn't turn around or attempt to hear the conversation, as it was in French.

After a few moments Ford relaxed, sat back, and took a cautious sip of his steaming chicory coffee. "I know one of those men slightly," he told Shiloh and Richard as they looked at him expectantly. "I've met him once or twice, anyway, here and in the City Exchange. His name is Emile Bertin, and he has a small sugar plantation over near Lafayette."

"Did I hear him say 'La Maison des Chattes Bleues'?" Shiloh asked.

"That you did," Ford answered.

"I couldn't catch a word," Richard grunted. "Hate French. Words all run together, and they talk so fast."

"That's because the words have no accents, as in English," Ford replied, his eyes sparkling devilishly. "Supposed to be a smooth, flowing language, they say."

"Girlie, you mean," Shiloh asserted. "Hard to talk like a man when all the words sounds like 'foo-foo' and 'bon-bon.'"

The men laughed, then Richard asked, "Well? Would you mind, Mr. Ford, telling us what they were saying in spite of the fact that Shiloh here just insulted your manhood?" Ford's French was impeccable.

"Always sounded girlie to me, too," Ford admitted. "My mama and Doña Isabella almost had to beat me to get me to say it out loud when I was a boy. Anyway, all they were saying was that old rot about the treasure at Les Chattes Bleues."

"What?" Shiloh and Richard exclaimed in unison.

"The treasure," Ford repeated with amusement. "For years there've been rumors of treasure hidden at Les Chattes Bleues. Last I heard the place was overrun with pirate gold and jewels. Funny. I'd almost forgotten those old stories ... heard them a lot when the vicomte was alive, but it seemed like they kind of petered out after he died."

"How in the world did a ridiculous story like that get started?" Richard demanded.

"Well, he was a vicomte, you know, and to commoners I suppose that automatically means great wealth. And he did know Jean LaFitte.

The vicomte received him and General Jackson at Les Chattes Bleues after the Battle of New Orleans."

"I didn't know that!" Richard exclaimed.

Ford went on, his single glittering blue eye gazing into a remote past. "When I was a boy, we used to think the vicomte trafficked with Blackbeard the Pirate. I don't know why we decided that, especially considering that Blackbeard died in 1718, and the vicomte wasn't even born until 1771. But we used to tell each other scary pirate stories about him, and play pirate games, and hunt for all the buried treasure. . . ."

"You sure these rumors don't have some basis in fact?" Shiloh asked. "Seems to me like it would take a lot of money to keep Les Chattes Bleues going."

"It does, Mr. Irons," Ford answered solidly. "It always has. And just as it's always been, indigo—and hard work—are what pay for it."

The door opened, and a sliver of bright afternoon sunlight knifed through the pleasant dimness of *Café des Exilés*. All the men blinked several times, then every man in the place stumbled to his feet.

Tante Elyse came sailing in, looking around with curiosity, her eyes crinkled with amusement. Behind her, in a slice of sound as the door opened and closed, Tante Marye's strident voice sounded, "Elyse, I absolutely forbid you to—"

"Hullo, Gowan," Elyse said pleasantly. "Hullo, Richard, Shiloh." Again she surveyed the dark masculine confines of the coffeehouse. "Are you gentlemen ready to go? I suppose you are . . . too bad . . . I should like to have a *café au lait.*"

Ford hurried to her side and with exaggerated care took her hand in his and made a singular motion, which Shiloh had noted was his way of signaling Elyse to tuck her hand in his arm. "Elyse," he said with a great show of patience, "if you stay in here more than thirty seconds, Marye will have an apoplexy."

"I know," Elyse giggled. "It wouldn't be nearly as much fun if that were not the case."

They turned and Elyse allowed Ford to lead her to the door, although she deliberately took slow little mincing steps. "Mother used to always send her maid in here to fetch Father, and I've always been curious about this place. It's very nice."

"Nice," Ford repeated gutturally. "Nice for gentlemen. Not nice for fine ladies."

"You know I'm not really a fine lady, not like Marye," Elyse said ingenuously.

"You're wrong on two counts," Ford argued stiffly. "You are a very fine lady, and I do know it."

Elyse paid no attention either to Ford's unnatural manner or to the words he said with such difficulty. But behind them Shiloh heard and felt the depth of emotion that Ford worked so hard to hide from Elyse Buckingham.

He pitied Gowan Ford. Shiloh, with his uncanny intuition about people, knew that Ford believed Querida Elyse de Cheyne Buckingham was much too fine a lady for an overseer, much too delicate for a commoner, much too beautiful for a scarred and crippled man. He knew all this as well as if Ford had told him outright. But Gowan Ford had not, and probably never would, say a word about it to Shiloh or anyone else. Shiloh, who had seen many men crippled and scarred in the war, and who had tried to heal their minds and self-worth as much as he did their bodies, wished that he could do something to help Gowan Ford realize that he was still a man, a good man, a man that a woman could love and honor.

I think Tante Elyse could, if her eyes were opened, he speculated. *But just as she doesn't see him as a scarred and broken man, neither does she see him as a man who could—does—love her.*

After rejoining the ladies and calming Tante Marye down, the troop walked straight down St. Ann Street back toward the river. Along the way they passed the firstborn block of *Nouvelle-Orléans.*

"La Place d'Armes," Tante Marye said, waving toward the great public square.

"Jackson Square, you mean," Tante Elyse corrected her with a mischievous light in her dark eyes.

"La Place d'Armes," Tante Marye repeated in an ominous tone.

The old square had been the seat of government since the eighteenth century, and had been called La Place d'Armes even though most of the reigning governments had been Spanish. But in 1803 the fleur-de-lis had disappeared forever from the square, and in 1856 the great equestrian statue of General Andrew Jackson had been erected and the square renamed in his honor. Tante Marye knew this, of course, but to her it would always be La Place d'Armes.

"The Illustrious Cabildo," Tante Marye announced grandly to the group. The central building of the square, an edifice that looked almost like a cathedral with its mansard roof and Gothic spires, had housed the governing body of the Spanish regime, which had been called the Illustrious Cabildo. Now the building itself was commonly called "The Cabildo."

"The Cabildo," Tante Elyse said, pointing to the building, mirth making her voice tremulous.

"The Il—" Tante Marye began stubbornly, then, with a warning glance at Elyse, began again. "Elyse, if you don't behave yourself, I shall charge Molly with returning you to the hotel and making you stay in your room."

"Yes, Marye," Elyse said humbly.

Soon they saw the first arcades of the French Market. Situated on the levee near Jackson Square, the market house held more than one hundred stalls and extended along the levee all the way from the foot of St. Ann Street to St. Philip. With its low-pitched tile roof and arcaded sides, it was—as was so much of New Orleans—unmistakably a Spanish structure from foundation to chimney pots. As early as three o'clock in the morning the market was crowded with people from every part of New Orleans and even from Algiers and other outlying areas, for nowhere else could one find the abundance and variety of the articles sold in the stalls.

Even now, late in the afternoon, shoppers thronged the market. Hundreds of people went about their business throughout and outside the arcade, for many of the vendors were too poor to lease a stall and simply sat down on the levee surrounding and leading up to the market, displaying their wares on crude blankets on the ground.

The ten ladies hurried forward together, but soon were milling about by twos or threes as they wandered to whatever sight caught their eyes. The three men hung back, trying to keep their women in sight, then realizing that they'd do better to split up and try to keep at least one escort with each group of women. Hurriedly they gathered everyone back together and planned, should they be separated, to meet at the foot of St. Ann Street in two hours. Shiloh was detailed to look after Cheney, Victoria, Zhou-Zhou, and Nia. Richard would stay with Irene and Tante Marye and Tante Elyse. Gowan Ford was to go find Octave and then join Richard.

Molly and Adah dutifully followed Tante Marye and Tante Elyse, but Chloe kept darting about from here to there, squealing loudly when she saw something exciting, and sometimes giving a furtive look around and scooting over to wherever Shiloh was. Gowan Ford frowned; he might be half-blind but he wasn't dumb. He could see Chloe's infatuation with Shiloh and how foolishly she acted around him. Ford had observed long ago that Molly and Monroe had trouble controlling their youngest daughter. He gave a mental shrug and went to look for Octave down by the levee. Chloe, at any rate, was not going to get far from Shiloh's protection.

Shiloh followed Cheney and Victoria and their maids from a distance, watching everyone and everything around them carefully, but not intruding upon them. Chloe tagged along beside him but was careful not to prattle, for he had been brusque to her all day. Still she managed to stay close to him, making wide circles around him and looking at all the stalls in his vicinity. Shiloh resignedly kept an eye on her, too, to make sure no one bothered her.

Cheney, Nia, Zhou-Zhou, and Victoria stopped outside the market to look at some jewelry displayed on a rag of a blanket by an old man who seemed to be asleep. The jewelry was silver and had turquoise stones, and Cheney was fascinated. She'd heard of these colorful rocks from the western territories, but she'd never seen any. She didn't much care for the jewelry the old man had, as it was rather crudely finished and she thought the stones much too large, but she did like the rainbow of blues in the stones.

She noticed that Victoria was not at her side and looked around curiously. Nia said, "She's over there, Miss Cheney, by those Indian squaws."

Through the crowd Cheney saw Victoria standing in front of two Indian women, who were displaying their wares on the ground. Zhou-Zhou stood close behind her, and Cheney hurried over to them.

Victoria stood stock-still, watching the women, who looked at her without curiosity—seemingly without any emotion at all. Their faces were impassive, their eyes guarded, and neither of them spoke. Cheney could smell the spices they sold; many Choctaws came from their homes near Bayou Lacombe in St. Tammany Parish, across Lake Pontchartrain, to the French Market to sell herbs, roots, and especially "filé," which was pounded dried sassafras leaves used in making gombo. Several cleverly woven baskets were arranged on a brightly colored blanket in front of the women, and the strong spice of sassafras rose like a puff of fragrant smoke to Cheney's nostrils.

"Victoria?" she asked breathlessly. "Don't tell me you're going to buy some filé and learn to cook gombo!"

"No . . ." Victoria murmured in an absent tone, as if she hadn't really heard what Cheney said.

The Indian women were kneeling at the back of the blanket. One of them was older, with skeins of gray showing in her hair, and wrinkles at the corners of her eyes and mouth. The other girl—probably her daughter—was about twenty, and in the fullness of the beauty of youth. Her shiny black hair was parted in the middle and pulled back into several braids that were anchored by strips of woven leather and a small bunch of white feathers. Her eyes were dark, impenetrable, and her skin was a cinnamon color, warmed and darkened by the sun. She was holding a baby. Now Cheney could see that Victoria was not staring at the women, but at the child. Although it was tiny, it was obviously a little boy. He had a thick fringe of hair, and his infant eyes were already focused and had that stillness that many Indians seemed to have. Clasped in his hand was a bauble made of beads and string, but he merely held it tightly and watched Victoria without expression.

"He's . . . he's beautiful," she said in a strangely hoarse voice.

The two Indian women exchanged cautious looks; Victoria was a fine lady, dressed in exquisite clothing, with aristocratic hands that had obviously never known a day's work. Such people were so far removed, so alien, from these Indian women's lives and experience that they hardly knew how to speak to them, much less carry on a conversation.

"Thank you," the young girl finally said uncertainly.

Victoria watched the little boy hungrily, her blue eyes locked with his. Suddenly he cocked his head and grinned, a baby's toothless smile, open and sweet and spontaneous. Victoria's eyes lit up, and he gurgled a little with delight. "Oh . . ." Victoria made a little choking sound, and her hand fluttered to her breast.

"Victoria, dear, are you all right?" Cheney asked. "It's . . . it's rather warm out here; perhaps we should sit down for a few minutes."

Victoria said nothing, and Cheney saw, to her astonishment, that her friend's normally icy blue eyes were shimmering with tears. Helplessly she wondered what to do or say. Meanwhile the older Indian woman asked patiently, "Will you have some filé, *madame*? Some mint? Some bay leaf?"

"What? Oh . . . oh . . ." With a visible effort Victoria drew herself up, and immediately her expression settled into the familiar lines of boredom and haughtiness. She blinked several times, then answered in a careless tone, "Yes, some filé. Yes, that much is fine . . . here . . ."

With jerky movements Victoria pushed a five-dollar bill into the older woman's hand, and she looked down at it in amazement. Victoria snatched a small cheesecloth-wrapped bundle from the blanket and hurried off, with Zhou-Zhou almost running to stay close behind her. The Indian woman called out, "But, *madame—madame!*"

"Never mind, keep it," Cheney told her. "I guess she wanted you to have it."

Cheney followed after Victoria, and as she caught up to her, she said, "Victoria, I think we need to talk."

"Do you?" she asked coolly, slowing down to a sedate walk. "I think there is nothing to say. Come over here, Cheney, I want to look at these fruits. Don't those strawberries look unreal? Strawberries in February!"

With a sigh Cheney obediently admired the strawberries.

In just about two hours the group, except for Shiloh, who had faithfully stayed close to Cheney and Victoria until the last few minutes, met back at the foot of St. Ann Street. Nia, Zhou-Zhou, Molly, Adah, and Chloe all carried bundles. Cheney had surrendered to her impulse and bought a turquoise hat pin from the old man, who had indeed been asleep until Cheney shook him. Victoria bought a quart of strawberries and insisted upon bringing them back to the hotel instead of sending them to Les Chattes Bleues with the other perishables and foodstuffs. Irene had bought a cake of handmade peach-and-glycerin soap. Tante Marye had bought fruits, vegetables, dried beans and peas, flour, rice, and herbs for Les Chattes Bleues, but she adamantly refused to buy meat from the butcher because she couldn't abide the stench and flies in the open stalls. Les Chattes Bleues had no livestock, but Tante Marye bought chicken, pork, and beef from a neighboring farm. At the last minute she had decided to buy a lovely black lace mantilla for herself.

Tante Elyse bought, of all things, some rubber knee-high boots that were actually made for a little boy. Tante Marye was, of course, horrified, which was probably why Tante Elyse decided to take them back to the hotel instead of sending them back to Les Chattes Bleues with Octave. Secretly Tante Marye was so relieved that Elyse didn't insist on *wearing* them back to the hotel that she relented easily when Elyse handed them to Molly to carry.

Finally Shiloh came running up, carrying the largest and most untidy bouquet Cheney had ever seen.

"Here you are!" he said as he peered out from behind some particularly long stalks of carnations. "I had to have these flowers—for all ten of the lovely ladies of La Maison des Chattes Bleues!"

Feminine voices trilled laughter, and choruses of "Oh, thank you, Shiloh! Thank you! May I have the camellias? May I have the white carnations? And the pink ones, too? These roses . . . for me? Oh, thank you . . ." All ten women crowded close around him, their faces flushed with pleasure.

Standing by themselves, Richard and Gowan Ford looked helplessly at each other. "How does he do it?" Richard mumbled.

"Dunno," Ford sighed, "but I'm watchin' and learnin'."

14

THE FOREVER SHILOH

Their errands done, the market made, the perishables transported to Les Chattes Bleues, the tailor's fittings and dressmaker's orders given, and Antoine's duly patronized, the party from Les Chattes Bleues met at the entrance to the rotunda at eight o'clock precisely. All of the ladies—even Tante Marye—wore Shiloh's flowers in their hair, for he had insisted on it.

"Good," he said with satisfaction and raised a delicate fluted glass of champagne as the ladies joined him and Gowan Ford in the vestibule. "I believe that we escort the most beautiful, charming, and graceful ladies in New Orleans tonight, gentlemen."

Tante Marye, who looked girlishly pleased at Shiloh's words, had consented to wear lavender with only a black stripe instead of her usual black widow's weeds. In her gleaming white hair were a few discreet violets. "Thank you, Mr. Irons," she said with dignity.

He went to her and raised her soft, blue-veined hand to his lips. "Mrs. Edwards, I'm glad to see that you've put aside your mourning for tonight and, I hope, for tomorrow night," he said formally.

Her blue eyes shone with mischief. "Oh, but, Mr. Irons, I'm not in mourning."

"You're not?" he asked with astonishment. Tante Marye always wore black or dark gray, even at the rather formal dinners in the privacy of Les Chattes Bleues.

"No, Mr. Irons," she said gravely. "It's not mourning, you see. It's a warning."

The party was silent for a few seconds, and then everyone burst into laughter. Shiloh grinned, bowed his head in acknowledgment, and commented, "I stand warned, Mrs. Edwards, but it has done no good. I still think you are a lovely and gracious lady."

"You, Mr. Irons," she said with a glint in her old eyes, "are much too charming, and I am very wary of you."

"Excellent idea," Cheney muttered, but only her mother heard her and gave her a sharp look. Cheney was glowing in a rather simple blue silk with matching gloves. Nia had managed to wave her hair and smooth it into a delicate frame around her face, and then pull the back into long, shiny ringlets that fell well below her shoulders, with six white rosebuds at the base.

Irene's dress was pearl-gray silk, trimmed with silver cord and black lace. Anchoring and twining through the fall of ringlets at the nape of her neck were delicate tufts of narcissus blossoms and their long graceful leaves. Richard Duvall, who had escorted all the ladies downstairs, could still hardly tear his gaze away from his wife.

Shiloh was teasing Tante Elyse about breaking every man's heart in the place, and Gowan Ford watched them with a jaundiced eye. Tante Elyse did glow in a fawn-colored satin that set off her rich olive skin and her expressive brown eyes. Her still-dark hair was parted in the middle and pulled up to a mass of curls at the crown, which was wreathed with purple and yellow pansies.

As usual, Victoria stood slightly aloof, an exquisite living ice sculpture, with her silvery blond hair and cool blue eyes. She wore a pastel pink satin, so light it was almost white, and a single pink camellia in her hair. Shiloh went to her, kissed her slender white-gloved hand, and smiled. "You look ravishing, Mrs. de Lancie. That color becomes you, and that camellia is the only possible thing that could add to your beauty."

One of Victoria's perfectly arched eyebrows rose slightly. "But, Mr. Irons, you don't have to pay me such extravagant compliments, you know. I'm already in love with you, as every other woman is after knowing you for more than a few minutes."

Everyone except Cheney laughed, and Shiloh chuckled good-naturedly.

"Not every woman," Cheney muttered under her breath.

"Really, Cheney," Irene whispered. "Are you going to be in such an ill temper all night?"

Cheney sighed. "No, Mother, I'm not really in an ill temper, and I'll do better."

"Thank goodness," Irene said severely. Shiloh came to them and kissed Irene's hand lightly. "You are always breathtaking, Miss Irene, and tonight even more so than usual."

"Thank you, Shiloh," Irene said warmly.

He turned to Cheney, his hand held out to her. But she merely nodded perfunctorily and said loudly, "I believe everyone is going into the rotunda. Are we ready?"

Perhaps two hundred people had been milling around the great vestibule, and the crowd was moving in the general direction of the rotunda. All of the Les Chattes Bleues party joined in the genteel crush, and Cheney hurriedly pushed ahead by herself. Shiloh, frowning, followed her with his eyes for a moment, then shrugged almost imperceptibly and offered his arm to Victoria, who smiled warmly at him and accepted his escort.

The immense round room, lined all the way around with twelve-foot arched doorways with twenty-foot Corinthian columns between them, was decorated and arranged handsomely for the art and photography showing. Instead of lining up the art works and photographs in rows, the mounting easels were arrayed in a large circle around the room. In the center, directly under the soaring height of the great dome, was the most spectacular centerpiece Cheney had ever seen: a great flower arrangement, loosely conical in shape and at least ten feet tall at the pinnacle. The circular base was about twenty feet in diameter and was surrounded by three-foot white marble benches with lavish arrangements of crimson roses in brass urns in between. Every flower that Cheney had ever seen, including drawings in books, and some she had never seen before, was included in the breathtaking centerpiece. She stood wide-eyed and drank in the sight for a few moments, and breathed deeply of the heavily fragrant air. Her sensitive nose could pick out roses, hyacinths, jasmine, lavender, and gardenias. The sight and scent were simply stunning.

An orchestra of pianoforte, six violins, two cellos, and a harp played under one of the great vaulted doorways. In the immense room, however, the music was almost lost, and an occasional measure or two of Chopin was all that reached the ears. Solemn Negro men in black suits with tails, stiffly ruffled white shirts, white ties, and white gloves offered trays of champagne to the guests, bowing slightly whenever a drink was accepted. Since the room echoed continuously with even the slightest sound, the guests unconsciously kept their voices down, resulting in an unbroken low hum of men's voices accompanied by the lyric tenor of ladies' speech.

Cheney looked around, trying to decide where to start in the circle of works to be viewed, and she noted with approval that Homer's vivid, large paintings were interspersed with groupings of three or four of Brady's stark black-and-white photographs. She finally walked to the nearest painting and studied it. About two feet by two feet, the foreground of the painting was stark and finely detailed, the background smoky and clouded ominously. Two mounted cavalrymen, the Confederate in gray, the Union soldier clutching a red-white-and-blue standard, were fighting with sabers. Cheney looked at the small card at the corner, which read: "The Fight for the Standard, 1865. Artist Unknown." For some reason, the fact that the artist had been lost in that terrible time, which he had so painstakingly recorded, made Cheney feel sad.

"Hello, darling," her father said at her elbow. "Enjoying the show?" She smiled brilliantly up at him, admiring how very dignified and regal he looked in his black suit and white tie.

"This is only the first one I've viewed," she admitted. "I've been gaping at that magnificent floral centerpiece."

"Breathtaking, isn't it?" Richard agreed, looking back over his shoulder at the riot of flora towering above their heads. "May I accompany you on your journey of discovery, Dr. Duvall?" he joked, smiling down at her. "Irene's speaking French again."

Cheney caught sight of her mother and Tante Marye standing in front of a painting, nodding and gesturing toward it with graceful hands. "Of course, Father," she replied. "I'll take pity on you. Besides, perhaps you could tell me more about some of these paintings or photographs. When I met General Forrest, I was appalled at how ignorant I was about the Great War." Cheney had been absorbed in medical school at the Women's Medical College of Pennsylvania all during the war.

As they drifted toward the next group of photographs, Richard murmured, "I doubt that I could explain anything better than these works do, Cheney. From what I've seen, these paintings and photographs are quite an eloquent depiction of the truths of that terrible time."

Slowly they studied the art works, many of them single works by artists Cheney and Richard had never heard of, all of them quite good. Other photographers besides Matthew Brady were represented, too, although Cheney finally said, "I must admit that Mr. Brady's photographs are by far the best. They are so clear, so vivid, so . . . so . . . self-explanatory. One hardly need read the captions."

Richard smiled wryly. "Mr. Brady was quite an active participant in the war, in his own right. He was everywhere, it seemed, and proximity to battles didn't faze him, even though we warned him over and over again that Rebel snipers wouldn't care that he was carrying a camera instead of a rifle. He just laughed."

"I notice that he's in quite a few of his own photographs," Cheney remarked mischievously. "He must have had brave assistants, too."

"Many of them," Richard replied irritably. "They were everywhere, too, and quite insistent. Trying to make their own names, I suppose."

Cheney stared at the grouping of Brady photographs directly in front of them. The central photograph was of General Grant and several of his aides and generals, with two smaller pictures of Grant's headquarters on either side. "Father, you haven't appeared in any of these photographs!" She looked up at him accusingly. "Did you hide every time someone set up a camera?"

"I had work to do," he growled. "I didn't have time to lounge about posing for photographs."

Cheney laughed with delight. "Amazing! You must have been running the headquarters for the entire Army of the Potomac—since General Grant obviously had time for photographs!"

Richard's cheekbones colored slightly, and he looked sheepish. "Oh, Cheney, I just didn't have much heart for all that foolishness. And neither did General Grant, but they hounded him unmercifully, and sometimes he'd consent to a photograph just so they'd leave him alone. You'll note"—he made a wide encircling motion with his hand—"that there are many badly blurred photographs of him, because he wouldn't stay still, and only a few that he posed for."

"True," Cheney agreed, still giggling at Richard's shyness when it came to cameras. He hated posing even for family portraits.

They viewed another painting, then another grouping of photographs, and Cheney suddenly pointed and cried, "Why, there you are, Father! Someone did catch you, too, only—" She bent closer to look at the four photographs. "Oh, for goodness' sake! Did you know that photographer was there? Your back is turned in every single one!"

Richard looked amazed, then he frowned. "That's at Massaponax Church, when we set up headquarters. All there was for miles around was that little brick church. General Grant didn't want to have a council of war in a church, so he ordered the pews brought outside.

Hmm . . . some blamed photographer was in the church, up in the choir loft, hanging out one of the windows with a camera! And we never knew it! Blue-deviled people, couldn't leave a man his privacy for even one day!"

The photographs were indeed from a bird's-eye view, Cheney saw, and about twenty men were seated on church pews gathered in a rough circle under the shade of two great oak trees. General Grant had obligingly, though unknowingly, seated himself across from the sneaking photographer, and was the central figure of each photograph. In a pew at right angles to where he was seated were General Meade, Colonel Richard Duvall, and two other men. In the series of photographs, Richard had his back turned to the camera, but his arm was propped along the back of the pews, and the full colonel's silver eagle insignia on his shoulder was unmistakable. Cheney, however, would have known him by the set of his head, the proudly squared shoulders, and the way his thick hair came down over his collar.

"Well, Father, I must say that is quite a striking war portrait of you," she joked. "Very flattering. Your eagles are shining, your hat is on straight, and the back of your collar is very clean."

"Most flattering photo I ever was in." Richard grinned.

Cheney stared at him oddly for a moment, then asked quietly, "Would you like to sit down with me for a few minutes? There's something I'd like to ask you."

"Certainly, Cheney dear," Richard said agreeably. He guided her to one of the marble benches; since it was early in the show, no one was seated yet. The crowd moved in a surreal carousel around them, the music floated in and out of their hearing, and the scent of flowers was overwhelming. For the rest of her life, Cheney recalled this conversation, and always the music of Chopin and the smell of flowers were as vivid to her as the story her father told.

"Father, when we were in Charleston," Cheney began in a low voice, "I mentioned once, when I was having dinner with General Forrest and Shiloh, that you had never had a field command. They looked . . . confused, and Shiloh changed the subject." She stared up at him intently.

Richard looked down at her and smiled slightly. "And you would like to know if, in fact, I ever had a field command?"

"Yes," Cheney said hesitantly.

Richard's steady gaze never left her face. "What you're really asking,

Cheney, is if I actually fought and killed men in the war. Isn't that so?"

Almost inaudibly Cheney whispered, "Yes, Father. I . . . I've thought about it, and I would like to know."

Richard's mouth grew firm, and his gaze grew stern. "All right, Cheney, I'll tell you, since you've given it some thought. I never mentioned it to you before, for the simple reason that I didn't think you needed to know. And also because I didn't—and still don't—believe that it was my greatest and most honorable contribution to the war."

"Neither do I," Cheney said softly.

He smiled at her again. "Good. Then I have no hesitation in telling you, since you seem to understand already." He looked, unseeing, at the slow-moving circle of people around them. "It was in the Wilderness. Do you know what that was?"

"It was a terrible two-day battle in Virginia, wasn't it?"

"Yes . . . and I think it was the worst I ever saw," Richard said in a voice hoarse with remembered pain. "The worst . . . It was summer, and hot, so hot. And it was, quite simply, a wilderness. Thick woods for miles and miles, with impenetrable undergrowth. We were outnumbered, two to one, and the Confederates were attacking savagely and pushing us back and around and in circles." He shook his head and shut his eyes tightly. "Fires everywhere, and smoke so thick that you couldn't see for more than a few feet. Gray phantoms just loomed up right in front of the boys' faces. . . . They had to get flat down on their bellies to fire and roll over on their backs to reload." Opening his eyes again, he stared into a smoky, bloody distance.

"The boys, when it was time to retreat and regroup, simply couldn't find their way. They just wandered and scattered, and then were too disoriented—and frightened—to call out and try to locate their companies and commanders."

"Horrible . . ." Cheney muttered, but her eyes never left her father's face.

"Yes, it was, all of it, both days, and long after. . . . But anyway, we completely lost touch with V Corps, because they were scattered over a two-mile thicket that was on fire, and no one could find General Warren, who was V Corps' commander in the field. So General Grant asked me to find an aide and send him into the Wilderness, and to tell him not to come back until he found General Warren, alive or dead."

"But you went instead, didn't you?" Cheney said with sudden comprehension.

"I did," Colonel Duvall admitted, "but only because all of the runners were either already out or wounded or about half-dead from smoke inhalation and heat prostration. So, without bothering General Grant, I decided to go find V Corps and General Warren myself. Instead of taking a couple of aides, I took a bugler and a drummer. We rode to the highest point I could find—it was just a little rise in the middle of the woods—that overlooked that burning thicket. I started calling for the men to rally, and the bugler played, and that poor little drummer beat his heart out on that snare drum. Pretty soon the men from V Corps started stumbling in, and we rallied for a countercharge. It was enough to get the Rebels off that break in the line for a little while, and we also found General Warren. He'd been thrown from his horse and was stunned, and he was suffering from acute smoke inhalation." Richard sighed. "It was a miracle he didn't burn to death . . . so many of them did. . . ."

"So . . . you only . . . commanded that particular . . . charge?" Cheney asked with difficulty.

"No, I had to take field command of V Corps the next day, too," Richard answered in a monotone. "General Warren was so ill he was unable to take command, and General Grant asked me to take the field. He said that out of two full corps, only the men under my command— about brigade-strength—had managed to get themselves found and turned around in time to bite the Rebels back. He said he'd like to go with that little bit of luck, if I'd agree. And of course I did."

Richard fell silent. Cheney bit her bottom lip and stayed deep in thought for a long while, and Richard waited, merely watching her. Finally she turned her face up to his and leaned close enough to rest her cheek on his shoulder. "Thank you, Father. I'm glad you told me. Somehow it makes me feel that I . . . just see you more . . . clearly."

Richard smiled warmly at her. "It's a sign of your growing wisdom, Cheney. I'm very proud of you. But I think that you generally see people, including me, pretty clearly."

"It's just that I never thought of you as a warrior," Cheney said, half-teasing.

Suddenly Richard's face grew sober, and his eyes grew thoughtful. "But I'm not a warrior," he muttered, almost to himself. "Dédé kept calling me that . . . but it wasn't about being a colonel, and the war, was it?"

"What?" Cheney sat up straight and stared at her father in confusion. "What do you mean, Father? I wasn't asking you about being a colonel."

"No, no, nothing, Cheney," he said hastily, though his brow was still wrinkled, and his eyes still searched inward. "It's . . . not you. I was thinking about something else . . . someone else . . ."

Cheney was going to question him further, but suddenly Tante Elyse popped up in front of them. "There you are, Cheney!" she said, almost breathless with excitement. "Where is Shiloh?"

"I don't know. It's not my turn to watch him," Cheney said rudely. Richard frowned at her, but Tante Elyse took no notice.

"Oh, my dear, you must go look!" she cried. "Over there!" Wildly she waved in the direction of a painting, about two feet high and three feet long, with a small knot of people, including Tante Marye, Victoria, and Irene, standing in front of it. "Oh, there he is, with all those girls!" Tante Elyse laughed and then whisked away.

Cheney and Richard stood up, and Richard went to join Irene, but Cheney turned around and watched Tante Elyse. On the other side of the room she saw Shiloh's tall figure—he could never hide in a crowd, he was always taller than everyone—in the middle of a group of two men and three ladies. The men were dressed in dark suits and white ties and held champagne glasses with careless grace, but they were obviously left out of the circle of ladies fluttering about Shiloh. All three of them were wearing light pastel dresses with impossibly wide hoop skirts and tiers and tiers of lace. They had jet black hair adorned with white camellias. One looked slightly older and was very curvaceous. She stood closest to Shiloh, looking up at him, smiling, her neck a long lovely line, her shoulders and face and bare arms that lovely golden hue peculiar to Creole women.

Unknowingly Cheney grumbled, "Hmph!" and was startled when her father again spoke in her ear.

"Cheney! You must come see this painting!" he said. When she turned around he was grinning like a young boy.

With one last look at Shiloh—Tante Elyse had swept into the little circle and was literally pulling him away by one hand—Cheney turned around to go view this painting that seemed to make everyone so excited. When she saw it, she realized why.

It was of Shiloh.

Cheney's lips parted in amazement, and her sea-green eyes opened wide. For a moment she stood, frozen with surprise.

"Shut your mouth, dear," Tante Marye murmured, and Cheney did manage to close her mouth and swallow.

Shiloh came up then; the crowd of people parted on either side of him and looked expectantly at him, instead of the painting. The people who didn't know him stared with amazement and couldn't look away, for Shiloh had—quite unknowingly—struck the exact pose that Winslow Homer had captured on canvas forever. Shiloh frowned, his head slightly tilted to one side, one hand propped carelessly on his hip, one leg slightly forward, the knee bent. Exactly the pose of the central figure in the huge painting. A lady murmured, "It's him! It's really him!"

The painting was entitled "Prisoners from the Front." The dominating figure was a Confederate cavalryman, dressed in dark gray, cavalry knee boots, and a gray kepi. It was Shiloh. He was tall and had long legs and wide shoulders, and the same squared jaw, thin nose, and firm chin. The kepi hid his eyes, but no one who looked at Shiloh doubted that the man in the painting must have had the same icy blue eyes.

Cheney looked up at him. "It's you!" she said accusingly.

"Huh," Shiloh said in a voice that sounded only mildly interested. "Imagine that."

Cheney looked back at the painting. Everyone else looked at Shiloh.

"Were you ever taken prisoner?" Cheney demanded.

"Not hardly!" Shiloh scoffed. "See, this was painted in 1866, after the war. Mr. Homer must've just done this from a combination of scenes he saw and sketched . . . but I can't figure where he ever saw me."

"Well, it is you!" Cheney insisted, again sounding as if she was accusing him of some outrage. "Except for the mustache and goatee!"

Shiloh shrugged, and his disdainful look—unknown to him—was exactly how the Shiloh in the painting was looking at the young Union major who had captured the prisoners. "Actually, Doc, I did have a mustache and goatee then."

"Oh, I think you looked marvelous with a mustache and goatee, Mr. Irons!" a high-pitched voice sounded breathlessly.

Cheney whirled around. Behind Shiloh were the three ladies—or girls, really, the oldest could not have been more than twenty—that he had been surrounded by when Tante Elyse found him. The youngest one was looking up at him, her eyes shining, her cheeks pink, and Cheney decided it was she who had simpered at him. Cheney looked the three ladies up and down, and they looked at her. No one spoke. They had not been introduced, after all.

"Huh, fancy that," Shiloh drawled again. Then he turned around, having lost interest in the fact of his likeness—evidently considered by the most famous artist in America as being the epitome of the dashing, gallant, rebellious South—being put on canvas for all time.

"Pardon me, ladies," Shiloh said and bowed to the three girls. The youngest one giggled. "Dr. Duvall, may I present to you Miss Leila Calvé, Miss Sarah Calvé, and Miss Anna Calvé. Ladies, may I introduce you to Dr. Cheney Duvall, my friend and employer."

Miss Leila Calvé's almond-shaped brown eyes blinked several times at Shiloh's words. "Oh?" she asked in a soft drawl. "You are a doctor, Miss—it is Miss, is it not?—Duvall? And Mr. Irons is your—" Delicately she left the sentence unfinished and waited expectantly for Cheney to explain herself.

"Yes," was all the explanation Cheney cared to give.

"Oh," Miss Leila Calvé said in quite a different tone.

All of the ladies nodded slightly to one another, and Shiloh offered his arm to Cheney. "If you ladies would excuse us, please, I promised Dr. Duvall that I'd view some of the photographs of her father, Colonel Richard Duvall, with her. It's been a very great honor to meet you, and a pleasure to talk with you, ladies." Cheney reached for his arm—almost grabbed it—but it was too late; Miss Leila Calvé was much faster on the draw than Cheney Duvall ever was, or ever would be.

"Oh, but no, Mr. Irons," Miss Leila said with delicate urgency and managed to insert herself squarely between him and Cheney at the same time. Taking possession of Shiloh's arm, which he had not snatched away from her quickly enough, she turned her back on Cheney and looked up at him with great, soulful Creole eyes. "Please, I and my sisters have a favor to ask of you. Don't we, sisters?" she asked sweetly.

Miss Sarah, the middle sister, swiftly said, "Oh yes, Mr. Irons. Please, it is a matter of grave import."

The youngest sister, Anna, who was only sixteen, looked as if she were having great difficulty working out the turn the conversation had taken, but Miss Leila went on quite unperturbed. "Yes, Mr. Irons, we simply must request a few more moments of your time." With only half a glance over her shoulder she said, "I'm certain you don't mind, Miss Duvall?"

"It's Dr. Duvall, and I see that you are certain," Cheney replied in a syrupy sweet tone to the back of Miss Leila's lovely neck.

Little Miss Anna looked positively lost, but Miss Leila swept them all away, trilling up at Shiloh the entire time. Cheney watched them until they disappeared through one of the great arched doors, and then she turned around and looked at Shiloh, the soldier—he of the grim face, the rebellious, disdainful stare, the arrogant stance. The Shiloh in the painting—the forever Shiloh.

15

KING'S KISSES

"Victoria! *C'est moi!*" Cheney announced gaily as she knocked on the door to Victoria's suite.

The door was cautiously cracked, then flung open. Zhou-Zhou paused in the doorway, her brown eyes sparkling, and she pressed her hands to her flushed cheeks. "Oh! *Mademoiselle* Cheney! You look like an angel!"

"She does, doesn't she?" Nia, almost hidden behind Cheney, complacently agreed. It had taken Nia almost three hours to dress Cheney and do her hair. Even now she reached up to arrange a curl that fell down Cheney's back, and Cheney smiled at her warmly.

"Zhou-Zhou! Don't keep them out in the hallway, let them in, you silly girl!" Victoria ordered.

With a petulant bounce of chestnut curls, Zhou-Zhou moved aside and curtsied as Cheney and Nia entered Victoria's suite. Immediately Zhou-Zhou and Nia began to compare notes and comments on their ladies' *toilettes*, which had been a nerve-wracking undertaking for both. Victoria was fussy and demanding when she was dressing for a formal event, and Cheney was always fidgety and impatient. Zhou-Zhou and Nia had worked hard for long hours to produce the grand ladies standing before them.

"Victoria! You . . . you . . . look . . . stunning!" Cheney stammered.

"Do you think so?" Victoria asked with affected boredom. "I've never worn a dress like this before. It is rather daring, is it not?"

"You look wonderful," Cheney said warmly. "Yes, the effect is quite startling, which I am sure is exactly what you wished to achieve. And you are so beautiful, you can get away with it."

Complacently Victoria studied her image in the full-length cheval mirror. She did, indeed, look startling, for her gown was entirely of crimson velvet. It made her skin look as pure as the finest cream, and her hair the color of spun silver.

The hue of the dress was not bright, but deep, and the material so thick and lustrous that all shades of red from magenta to the deepest scarlet seemed to flow in and out of the folds as Victoria moved. Her gloves reached four inches over her elbows and were made of the same red velvet, and her shoes had been covered with the thick fabric. The top of the dress was formed by sewing on a separate shawl-like length of the material, attached at the top of the bodice, so that the wide gathered loop of material formed the neckline and fell to a graceful arc on Victoria's shoulders. Fitted tightly through the bodice and tailored to a V point in the front, the pattern accentuated Victoria's already-small waist. The dress had an overskirt and underskirt, but instead of being in two different fabrics, both layers were made of the red velvet. The overskirt was gathered at the sides up to Victoria's waist with a black satin braided cord, which was tied in a graceful knot with three descending loops, and the cord was finished with intricate tassels reaching to the exact length of the underskirt. In the back the overskirt was padded slightly to form a bustle and fell to an elegant midlength train.

Cheney moved close beside Victoria and smiled at their reflections in the mirror. "We certainly contrast, Victoria dear. But no one will be looking at me, I'm afraid. I pale in comparison."

"Nonsense," Victoria murmured. "You, Cheney, are a striking beauty, no matter what you wear. And you do look just like an angel."

Cheney's dress was pure white. The underdress was made of heavy satin, so white it seemed to radiate light, with an overdress of spidery-thin Brussels lace with a delicate appliqué design. The satin underdress had a low décolleté, but the net of the overdress rose to a high neckline with a fitted collar of the white satin edged by tiny seed pearls. Cheney's bustle was formed by a separate length of the white satin, gathered and padded, and attached only at the back of the waist and trailing down to form a heavy train, a gleaming white river of satin of such fullness of body that it seemed of its own accord to shape itself elegantly when she stood still.

"We do contrast, but we complement each other admirably, I think," Victoria finally said with a touch of smugness. "I am the mysterious lady in red, and you—"

"And I am just your mysterious pale companion," Cheney laughed, giving her a quick hug around the waist. "As usual!" Cheney and Victoria had a history of making rather startling entrances. The first had been at one of Shiloh Irons' pugilistic competitions, and they both had been dressed from head to toe in black and heavily veiled. Needless to say, they had made quite a stir at the warehouse where the fights were held. Cheney had always excused her unconventional behavior on the grounds that she was only Victoria's mysterious companion.

"And speaking of being pale," Cheney went on in mock sternness, "why in the world did you tell me not to wear any jewelry? And why aren't you?" Cheney put her hands on her hips and turned to face Victoria. Cheney wore only small diamond stud earrings, and Victoria wore small twinkling rubies.

"Listen, Cheney," Victoria said excitedly, "I have a surprise for you! Guess what we're doing tonight!"

"Oh no," Cheney moaned.

"No, no, listen, Cheney! Look!" Victoria hurried over to the four-poster bed. It was piled high with petticoats, shawls, shoes, and toilet articles. Boxes of assorted sizes spilled over onto the floor, some of them with the tops awry and delicate tissue spilling out of them. "Where are they, Zhou-Zhou? Look at this! If you've lost them I'll—"

"Here they are, madame," Zhou-Zhou said calmly, rolling her eyes in a see-what-we-have-to-put-up-with? signal to Nia, and then taking three boxes out of the hidden depths of the top shelf of the great cedar armoire. "I put them up here, madame, for safekeeping."

"Come here, Cheney," Victoria commanded. "Sit down." Imperiously she pointed to the low backless bench in front of the triple-mirrored dressing table.

"What?" Cheney said suspiciously. "I'll tell you right now, Victoria, I'm not going to do anything while I'm here to scandalize *mes tantes*! Or my mother! Or my father!"

Victoria sniffed haughtily. "Hmph! As if I would try to involve you in anything shameful or disreputable!"

"Well, Victoria, there have been times . . ." Cheney teased, her sparkling green eyes belying any offense. With a certain wariness, however, she moved to sit down at the dressing table.

Victoria motioned to Zhou-Zhou, who brought the boxes. But as Victoria reached for one of them, Nia hurried up and said breathlessly, "No, let me, please, Mrs. de Lancie?"

"Of course, Nia. You've arranged her hair so beautifully, you should put it on her." Victoria smiled and moved aside.

"What are you people doing?" Cheney demanded. "I dislike it when people speak of me in third person when I am in the room!"

"Do be quiet and sit still, Cheney!" Victoria fussed.

Then Nia placed a crown on Cheney's head.

For long moments the room was silent. Cheney's eyes grew round and darkened to a deep jade green with surprise. Her hand went to her breast, and she took a deep breath. It was a tiara, but it was a full circlet instead of a half-circle to be inset on the top of the head, so that it was like a crown. Made of gold wrought so delicately into a basket-weave pattern that it seemed as if it was spun, it was set with hundreds of tiny starry diamonds.

"Now me," Victoria cried. She pushed Cheney over on the bench and sat precariously on the edge next to her. Zhou-Zhou, her smile dreamy, put another tiara on Victoria's shining silver hair. It was a true tiara, and Zhou-Zhou carefully placed it exactly at the crown of Victoria's head. Zhou-Zhou had pulled her mistress's hair back rather severely and had arranged the length of it in tight ringlets in the back. But the tiara was a perfect frame that made Victoria's already ephemeral features seem even more fairylike. The tiara was of heavy gold, a plain design, with a huge square-cut ruby centered in the front and three smaller square-cut rubies on each side.

"Good gracious!" Cheney finally breathed. "Where did you get these?"

"They're your great-aunts', Cheney," Victoria replied and took Cheney's hand. "They were your ... um ... well, they were Doña Isabella's, and now this one belongs to Mrs. Edwards and the one you're wearing belongs to your Tante Elyse. Your great-aunt Marye insisted that we wear them, because tonight we're leading the carriage masker's parade, and our carriage has the Vicomte de Cheyne's coat of arms on it! So we have to look like princesses, you see, Cheney!"

"And you do," Nia said, and Zhou-Zhou nodded vigorously in agreement.

"But ... but ..." Cheney stammered. "The carriage masker's parade? But ... but ..."

"Really, Cheney, your conversation has grown most tiresome in the last few moments," Victoria chided her with mock severity. "You are repeating yourself."

"But ..."

"See? Zhou-Zhou, please get *Mademoiselle* Cheney some mineral water, she seems to be quite breathless." Victoria rose and smoothed her gown, then hurried over to the bed. "Now, Cheney, listen. We have

196

a busy night planned, and you really must get yourself pulled together. First we shall be in the carriage parade, you see, and here are our masks! Aren't they beautiful? Angelique made them for us. I ordered them last week when I decided that we should attend Mardi Gras. I thought, you see, that I should be wearing the black, for I knew you were wearing white—your mother told me—and I wanted to wear black, but Shiloh absolutely refused to wear red! Anyway, it's all worked out beautifully, because I do love this dress—"

Cheney took a long drink of the iced mineral water that Zhou-Zhou brought her on a small silver salver. But when Victoria said the part about Shiloh wearing red, she choked slightly, and Victoria turned to her with concern. "Cheney, are you all right?"

"No!" Cheney managed to say in a hoarse voice. "Whatever are you prattling on . . . and on . . . and on . . . about, Victoria?"

"Why, our plans for the evening, of course," Victoria answered impatiently. "Here. Look at this mask. It's perfect."

She held out a mask to Cheney, and automatically Cheney took it, but held it and looked at it blankly as if it were an alien, unknowable object. It was beautiful. It was an eyepiece mask, made of stiffened white satin and shaped with the ends curling upward flirtatiously. Covered with clear and black glass beads, it was patterned in small one-inch squares for a checkerboard effect. The wand was made of a sturdy wooden dowel and was covered with small black and white satin cords woven into an intricate checked pattern, with the dangling ends of the cords finished with three beads each. As if in a dream, Cheney held the mask up to her eyes, looked in the mirror, and smiled. Everyone loves a masquerade.

"See? See mine, Cheney?" Victoria demanded, childlike. Her mask was identical to Cheney's except that it was patterned with red and black beads and cords. "Do you see? Do you see the theme?"

Cheney laid the mask in her lap and turned to Victoria with barely concealed impatience. "I do not see, Victoria," she said with ominous slowness. "You have made absolutely no sense for the past few minutes."

"Of course, you'll have to see Shiloh," Victoria agreed—nonsensically, Cheney thought with irritation.

"No, I won't," she said shortly.

Victoria looked at her curiously and started to say something, but a firm knock at the door interrupted her.

"Hello? Would somebody please let me in before I get arrested in this get-up?" Shiloh sounded exasperated. Zhou-Zhou hurried to the door and opened it before Victoria could say a word.

"Ooh, *Monsieur* Irons! You do look *très dangereux!*" Zhou-Zhou's red mouth was pursed into a little cupid's bow, and her eyelashes fluttered as she looked adoringly up at Shiloh.

"I am," he grumbled. "I'm in danger of falling over this sword and looking like a blinkin' fool." He stepped into the room and shut the door solidly behind him. " 'Course, I don't guess I look as much a fool as some I've seen out there. This thing—" With irritation he fumbled with the saber hanging at his side. "No wonder General Forrest wouldn't let us carry these bloomin' things! We coulda killed ourselves ten times over, just stumble-bummin' around with 'em! Saved the Yanks a lot of trouble!"

The room was quiet, and Shiloh looked up suspiciously. "What?"

Cheney cleared her throat. "You look . . . you look . . ."

"Don't pay any attention to her," Victoria asserted. "She seems to be having some sort of speech impediment tonight. I hope it's only temporary. You, Mr. Shiloh Irons, do look dangerous. Dangerously handsome and striking."

Shiloh was dressed in solid black. His shirt was open at the neck and had wide gathered sleeves and French cuffs with onyx cufflinks. His tight-fitting breeches were black broadcloth with a black velvet stripe down the side and were tucked into his black kneeboots. He wore a black mask, a simple strip of linen with embroidered eye-holes that was fashioned with small white cords that tied under his long blond hair. The saber at his side was hung from a black leather belt with a silver buckle, and the sheath was of patterned silver with stones of onyx inset along the curved length.

"I feel like a dangerous idiot," Shiloh grumbled. "And I dunno about wearing the vicomte's saber . . . looks real valuable . . . and besides, I feel like I'm impersonating a . . . a . . ."

"A king?" Victoria suggested. "But you are. And here's your crown." Out of the third box Zhou-Zhou held, Victoria drew out a coronet, those golden circlets worn only on state occasions by the aristocracy. It was the traditional vicomte's coronet made of a thin band of gold, patterned with a simplified rendering of the de Cheyne coat of arms, with small seed pearls mounted atop.

Shiloh put up his hands and started backing toward the door. "Oh no . . . huh-uh! Not me! Huh-uh! Tell her, Doc!"

Cheney sat, her mouth slightly open, still staring at Shiloh.

"Don't be ridiculous," Victoria declared, advancing on the still-retreating Shiloh. His back came up against the door with a thump. "It's a masquerade, silly, and of course you're impersonating a king! That's the idea! You're the Black King, I'm the Red Queen, and Cheney's the White Queen!"

Finally Cheney recovered, and she jumped up and clapped her hands together. "Oh! Now I see! Chess and Checkers! One of the themes of the parade is 'Blessings of the Future,' and 'Games and Fun' is the title of one of the Comus floats!"

"Of course," Victoria sniffed.

"No," Shiloh moaned.

"Oh yes," Cheney said, her eyes positively sparking green flames. "The Black King. And here, Sire, is your crown."

"But, Doc—"

"Go sit down over there, Shiloh!" Cheney commanded, pointing to the bench in front of the dressing table and snatching the coronet out of Victoria's hands.

Shiloh looked mutinous for a few moments, then he grinned lazily, crossed his arms, and leaned negligently back against the door. "That's 'Your Majesty' to you. Or 'Your Highness' will do."

"I really hate to tell you this," Cheney taunted, taking his hand and pulling him over to the dressing table, "but I was crowned before you were, and besides, the queen is more powerful than the king, you know. Now sit down, and you'd better be nice, because I'm not certain how men do this. Ladies do it with hairpins," she finished sweetly.

"Doc, please, no hairpins," Shiloh begged. "Please?"

"And how do you propose to keep this crown on?" Cheney said, the corners of her mouth twitching. "With tacks?"

"That'll be fine," Shiloh urged. "Tacks are fine. Anything but hairpins."

"*Mademoiselle* Cheney, if you will allow me," Zhou-Zhou said silkily, moving up to stand behind Shiloh and caress a lock of his long shiny blond hair. "I know how to do this."

Cheney's face flashed rebellion for a moment, then she quickly smoothed it out into carelessness and shrugged. "Certainly, Zhou-Zhou. But you'd better hurry, while we have him cornered."

"*Oui, mademoiselle*," she purred, taking the coronet and placing it carefully on Shiloh's head. Then, resting her hands on his shoulders, she leaned far over to gauge the placement in his reflection in the mirror. "But perhaps he will be good for Zhou-Zhou, *non*?"

"Oh yes, I'm sure he will," Cheney said with acid sweetness, frowning darkly.

Catching sight of her forbidding reflection, Shiloh moaned, "Good grief," then closed his eyes to blot out the sight.

★　★　★　★

"Fine carriage for a pug like me to be drivin'," Shiloh drawled. " 'Specially with those hoity-toity shields on it."

The black carriage had the de Cheyne coat of arms posted on each side. The device was simple, as it was one of the oldest recorded in French heraldry, and had never been quartered to incorporate other armorial bearings joined to the de Cheyne family through marriage, as was a common practice. The de Cheyne coat of arms, since the thirteenth century, had been a simple device of a shield divided *per bend sinister*—from top right to bottom left, looking straight on—with a plain azure field in the bottom quarter and an oak tree drawn in black on a white field in the top quarter. Instead of a helmet and crest, the coat of arms was displayed with only the vicomte's coronet at the top. The carriage coats of arms were made of a frame of very light iron with painted canvas stretched over it, but the coronet on top was made of real gold, with real pearls, and the shield itself was outlined in gold. In deference to their "Chess and Checkers" theme, the lantern posts alongside the driver's seat flew large silk banners, one with a red-and-black checkerboard weave, and one with a black-and-white chessboard theme.

"The king can't drive his own carriage," Cheney objected strenuously.

"Of course not!" Victoria said indignantly.

"Well, I'll just get one of my coachmen, then," Shiloh said sarcastically. "Um . . . by the way . . . where are all of my coachmen?"

"Here," Victoria replied smugly. A small Negro man, dressed in the unmistakable attire of a coachman—the many-tiered topcoat, the gray top hat, the pegged pants—peeped shyly around the prancing black horses. He was holding them, and as Shiloh, Cheney, and Victoria had hurried up to their coach, he could not be seen.

"Heah, suh," he volunteered. "I drive these heah hosses."

Shiloh folded his arms, frowned, and looked the small man up and down. Shiloh looked dangerous, indeed, but the little man merely smiled up at him. "I been drivin' this heah coach in ever' Mardi Gras parade since the fust one in 1857, suh," he insisted. "I'll take good care of these ladies, and the hosses, too."

"What's your name?" Shiloh asked.

"Dean. Dean Bly. I'm Mayor Pitot's driver, and this here's his carriage, and his hosses. But," he added slyly, "they thinks they's my hosses, and they mind me good."

"Mayor Pitot insisted that we use his coach and driver," Victoria explained to Shiloh. "I had hired a five-glassed landau, but when Tante Marye told Mayor Pitot what we were doing, he insisted that we use his open barouche. More fun in a parade, I should think." Tante Marye and Tante Elyse were old friends of the mayor, and they had a standing invitation to observe the parades from the private gallery at his home on Royal Street. As the St. Louis Hotel had no galleries, and the streets were entirely too crowded, Tante Marye and Tante Elyse always watched the parades from the mayor's home.

"Oh, this is going to be such fun!" Cheney cried. "You aren't really mad, are you, Shiloh? Because we made you wear the coronet?"

"Nah," he said, grinning infectiously. "I'm getting to like it. Think I'll ask Mrs. Edwards if I can borrow it for a while . . . you know, wear it at Les Chattes Bleues. At dinner."

"She'd probably let you," Cheney scoffed. "Here, Victoria, I know, you and I'll sit together—" Cheney pointed to the two facing seats of the open barouche.

"No, no! It's a parade, not a ride in the country, Cheney!" Victoria argued. "Haven't you ever seen a parade?"

"Well . . . well . . . not this kind of parade." Cheney looked uncertainly up at Shiloh. They had seen a parade, all right, in Charleston, of the Knights of the White Rose, but it was nothing at all like a Mardi Gras parade, Cheney was certain.

"We all sit up there," Victoria directed, pointing to the top of the seats facing forward. "You and I on either side, Shiloh in the middle, of course. And you must wave, Cheney, and smile at everyone. And here, see what I've gotten for us!"

Victoria opened one of several lumpy-looking pouches sitting on the floor of the barouche. "Look!" She held up her hand, revealing a pile of little curly streamers. Shiloh and Cheney looked at her blankly.

Victoria made a face. "Don't you know what this is? It's confetti!"

Still Shiloh and Cheney looked mystified and exchanged uncertain glances.

"Oh, for heaven's sake, where have you two been? What have you been doing all your lives?" Victoria exclaimed.

"I've been a doctor, working my heart out, and Shiloh's been in the war, and he's worked as hard as I have—" Cheney bristled.

"Yes, yes, I know how very noble you both are," Victoria interrupted, then thrust the curly streamers toward them, as if explaining a new toy to children. "It's called confetti. You throw it at the crowds, and it creates an atmosphere of gaiety. You know, gaiety? Fun? Laughing?"

"Oh, that," Shiloh shrugged, then grinned hugely. "You mean we actually get to throw things at people? This is sounding like more fun all the time!"

Victoria laughed, and Cheney joined in. "I hardly think even you could bean someone satisfactorily with those bits of paper, Shiloh," Cheney teased.

"I can try."

"Then let's go, shall we?" Victoria clamored. "It's Mardi Gras, and it's time to parade!"

Down the block in front of their carriage, the last float of the Comus Parade was just disappearing around the corner of Conti Street. Behind them were about thirty carriages in a line down the block and snaking around the corner. The coachman Dean jumped up onto his seat, saw that his passengers were securely settled, then, with a flourish, raised a bugle to his lips and rang out a single loud, raucous note. Behind them Cheney and Shiloh and Victoria heard cheers and catcalls, and the Mardi Gras Carriage Masker's Parade of 1867 began, following along closely behind the Comus Parade.

The Mystick Krewe of Comus, the first New Orleans carnival organization, had begun in the dark recesses of the Gem Café on Royal Street near Canal in 1857. They had sponsored a parade, with floats, each year except the war years from 1861 through 1865. The Krewe had produced a splendid parade in 1866, but had vowed to top it this year, as the war remembrances waned and the people of New Orleans slowly began to recover—even though Federal soldiers were still occupying the city in great numbers, and General Phil Sheridan ruled the wayward state of Louisiana with an iron hand.

On this night, however, it appeared that the people of New Orleans and the soldiers in blue had reached an amicable truce, for they mingled together in huge numbers in the streets along the parade routes. In fact, both General Sheridan and the distinguished Creole Confederate General P. G. T. Beauregard were riding in the carriage parade, though General Sheridan was attending the ball at the St. Charles Hotel, and General Beauregard the ball at the St. Louis Hotel.

The Mystick Krewe of Comus this year was sponsoring a parade with thirty-one floats and a grand pageant at the St. Louis Hotel. The theme was "The Past, the Present, and the Future." The largest floats presented such grand tableaux as "The Blessings and Beauties of Peace," "Horrors and Sorrows of War Past," and the "Hope of a Smiling Future." Some of the smaller floats were representative of more trivial themes, such as "Picnics on the Levees" and "Pirogues upon the Still Bayous," and the one Cheney had mentioned, "Games and Fun in the Vieux Carré." Cheney and Victoria felt that their "Chess and Checkers" theme was perfectly appropriate, even though Victoria was still fussing that the red should have been a king, as the red pieces were "kinged" in checkers. No one else seemed to notice, or to mind.

"By the way, what is the parade route?" Cheney asked Shiloh.

"We're going up Conti to Royal, then along Royal to Gravier," Shiloh explained. "Around the block where the St. Charles Hotel is, then back down Royal all the way to Esplanade."

"Oh no!" Cheney said in mock horror. "The dread American section! I'm surprised that Tante Marye would let her coat of arms and her coronets cross Canal Street!"

Soon they were nearing the corner of Conti and Royal Streets, and the crowds were beginning to turn into a throng. The noisy laughter, singing, and shouting were deafening. The streets were well-lit, as every single gaslight was turned up full-glow for the parade. The night was cool, but as usual the air was wet, and in their nostrils was the rich dank smell that was New Orleans.

As the lead carriage moved into the streets where the people were crushed along the banquettes by the thousands, Cheney's eyes grew big and she felt uncertain; there were a lot of people, and they were quite noisy and rowdy. Unconsciously she moved a bit closer to Shiloh and looked over the edge of the carriage with unease. She and Victoria were, after all, quite close to the raucous crowds. On these narrow streets they were easily within touching distance.

Shiloh looked down at her quizzically, then took her hand and squeezed it. She could feel the warmth of his fingers and the strength in his touch, even through her gloves. "Don't worry, Doc," he said quietly. "I won't let anyone even brush up against you, or Mrs. de Lancie either. Besides, I found out before the parade that soldiers keep the crowds back off the streets during the Comus Parade and the carriage parade. Then they let them join in on foot after the last carriage has cleared."

"All right, I'm fine," Cheney said with a touch of impatience. She was a little embarrassed that Shiloh had seen her discomfort and awkwardly pulled her hand away from his. He didn't seem to notice, merely smiling and turning to tell Victoria the same thing, though Victoria's eyes glittered with excitement and her cool white cheeks were flushed delicately. She didn't look at all uneasy.

They rounded the corner of Conti, and sure enough, soldiers lined the parade route, though the crowds were not at all pushy. They seemed content to stay crushed along the banquettes, waving and shouting and smiling at the paraders. Cheney and Victoria held their masks in place and smiled and waved, and Shiloh grinned and tossed confetti everywhere. The crowds were delighted, for the previous year some of the maskers had tossed small open bags of flour, which was funny as long as you didn't happen to be the one hit. Being covered with the bright curly streams of paper was much more fun.

Many people were wearing costumes, some as simple as a handkerchief with rude eye-holes cut, some quite intricate head-to-toe costumes. One man's costume was a wine bottle actually made of glass. Cheney wondered how in the world he wore it, and how long it would last before it got broken, and how many people would be hurt. But soon he disappeared in the swirling, noisy crowd, and Cheney forgot him. One man sauntered along the banquette dressed all in black, including a black hood, and carried an executioner's ax; one man was on stilts about five feet high and teetered precariously through the crowds; a man carried a huge platter with an enormous cooked fish on it, and people paid a penny for a bite; a woman dressed as a shepherdess, crook included, led a very angry sheep on a leash; two men led a fat pig with a huge red ribbon round its neck and a golden earring in its ear. A young couple stood on either side of an enormous bull with huge white horns, though it looked docile enough. Its massive neck was wreathed with red and white carnations, and a small child rode on its back, a lollipop stuck in his mouth and his eyes wide as he watched the parade. Four men dressed in clever harlequin's costumes hopped and skipped, and the bells on the ends of their silly three-pointed hats jingled.

The parade went on and on, and Cheney smiled and laughed and waved until her face and shoulders ached. Shiloh waved and occasionally threw kisses at impudent women who called out to him, though the first time he did Cheney poked him sharply in the ribs with her elbow.

"Hey, Doc, it's only Mardi Gras fun," he grumbled. "You know, smiling? Laughing?"

"Flirting," Cheney snapped.

"I'll only flirt with you," he murmured, suddenly grave, "if you want me to."

Cheney's mask dropped suddenly, and she turned to look up at Shiloh. He looked down at her and moved closer to her, and for a dizzy moment she thought he was going to kiss her. The cries of the paraders faded away, and she felt her cheeks flush, and her mind spun off erratically into dozens of inconsequential little thoughts. For a moment she couldn't move, then with a jerk she thrust her mask back in front of her eyes, turned, and waved to the crowds. "Nonsense," she said stiffly, as if her mouth was numb. "Don't say such ridiculous things, Shiloh. You'll always be an incurable flirt, and besides, I . . . I . . . d-don't c-care whom you flirt with."

Shiloh sighed, then narrowed his eyes and shrugged slightly. Reaching down, he grabbed a huge handful of streamers and leaned far over Cheney to toss them in the air toward two young girls who were calling out, "Hey, Your Majesty! Give us a kiss, love!" Then, with great deliberation, he pressed two fingers to his lips and flung his hand toward the girls.

"There you go, ladies!" he called. "King's kisses cheap tonight!" Glancing down at Cheney, his blue eyes sparking recklessly in the slanted eye-holes of the mask, he growled, "Right, Doc? King's kisses cheap, but I'll tell you the White Queen's kisses are much too dear for any man!"

With that he turned to speak to Victoria, and she laughed prettily at something he said. But Cheney found herself biting her lip, and blinking back tears, and wishing that the parade was over, so that the White Queen could go home.

16

Combat and Noncombatants

By the time the lead carriage in the carriage masker's parade had reached the American section, Cheney had managed to recover from her upsetting exchange with Shiloh and regain some of her enthusiasm for Mardi Gras. Shiloh, too, seemed to have forgotten the tension between them and had resumed his easy manner.

The parade wound around the splendor of the St. Charles Hotel and then crossed Canal back into the tiny streets of the French Quarter. The crowds were more tightly packed here, but still no one tried to push past the soldiers' blockade into the streets, although they did call out rowdily.

"Look, Shiloh . . . look, Victoria! There are Mother and Father and Mr. Ford! And Tante Marye and Tante Elyse!" Cheney cried. All three turned to look up and wave at the second-floor gallery of the fine home at 630 Royal Street.

Tante Marye and Tante Elyse were seated grandly in the center of the gallery, and Gowan Ford's figure loomed behind them like the grim avenger. Irene was seated to one side, with Richard standing behind her, waving and smiling broadly. Irene smiled and nodded elegantly at them. Tante Marye nodded, but Tante Elyse waved frantically and called out, "Hulloooo, Cheney! Hulloooo, Shiloh! Hulloooo, Mrs. de Lancie!" Tante Marye's shoulders stiffened with horror, and she turned to say something to Tante Elyse, who merely laughed and kept waving until the carriage was out of sight.

Finally they crossed Esplanade, and the parade dissipated. Cheney, Shiloh, and Victoria settled into the seats of the barouche with relief and ordered Dean to take them back to the St. Louis Hotel.

"Oh! That was exhausting!" Victoria declared, then smiled brilliantly. "But such fun!"

"Yes, it was," Cheney agreed.

"You two ladies are the most beautiful queens I've ever seen," Shiloh said slyly. He was seated by Cheney and slid his arm along the back of the seat while he grinned down at her engagingly.

"And how many queens have you seen, Shiloh dear?" Victoria hummed.

"None. But you two would still be the most beautiful."

"Thank you," Cheney said uncertainly.

"Welcome."

The streets were now crowded with people on foot, as the soldiers had allowed the revelers to take to the streets as soon as the parades had passed. Coming to a dead standstill at the corner of Royal and St. Ann, Dean looked back mournfully. "So sorry, ladies and sir. It looks like it might take a while to get back to the hotel."

"We're in a hurry, coachman," Victoria called imperiously. "Just get us there as fast as you can."

"Yes, ma'am," Dean said resignedly, then turned and began a rhythmic chant that provided buzzing background music to their conversation during the entire trip back to the hotel. "Move along there, get along, comin' through, comin' through, please, move on along there, please . . ."

Finally they reached the hotel, though the crowds were thick and merry all throughout the Vieux Carré. Cheney and Victoria patted each other's hair and assured each other that their faces didn't need any attention. Shiloh offered an arm to each of them, and the three grandly swept up the staircase to the ballroom on the second floor. At the entrance—great double doors ten feet wide and twelve feet high— a footman, resplendent in powdered wig, satin knee breeches, and slippers with bows, stepped forward and gave them a deep bow.

"Good evening, ladies, sir," he whispered reverently. "Would you be so kind as to present your cards of invitation, please?"

The cards had been delivered to their rooms while they were at luncheon in the Vicomte's Suite late that afternoon. Each card was hand-lettered in gold ink with their name and a command for them to appear at the Mystick Krewe of Comus Pageant that night in the Grand Ballroom. Obediently they handed the cards to the footman, and he slipped through the doors, with a plea that they wait for the majordomo's appearance to escort them in. Through the cracked door the tantalizing music of a waltz drifted through, along with the silvery sound of women's laughter and the faint baritone of men's voices.

Cheney could smell flowers and perfume and the hot waxy scent of hundreds of candles burning.

"Great," Shiloh muttered. "A majordomo. That's one of those men with the stick that bangs it and hollers out your name, huh?"

Cheney and Victoria laughed, and were still laughing at Shiloh's grumpy expression when the doors opened slowly. The music sounded louder, the scents grew heavier, the voices more defined, and the majordomo bowed deeply. He wore a black coat with tails, a high starched collar, and striped gray pants, and of course he was carrying his "stick"—an ebony cane with a silver lion's head. He turned to face the crowd in the ballroom and gave the traditional three raps on the floor.

"*Mademoiselle* Cheney Duvall," he called out in an impressive bass. "*Madame* Victoria Elizabeth Steen de Lancie. *Monsieur* Shiloh Irons."

The music went on, the waltzers still circled, the voices still ebbed and flowed over the enormous ballroom, but quite a few people did take note of the announcement and look up. Tante Marye and Tante Elyse came forward in full steam, with a crowd of people in their wake to be introduced. Soon Victoria and Cheney were mingling with the crowd, thirstily sipping fruited ices. Shiloh, with a glass of champagne, searched over people's heads for Richard and Irene. He saw them and made a signal to Cheney, who was standing a few feet away from him, and she nodded that, yes, she'd be there as soon as she could make her way. He nodded understanding, turned, and walked toward the Duvalls.

In her ear Victoria said in a *faux* whisper, "Oh, look! There are the three fatted Calves!"

Cheney whirled around—rudely turning away from the lady who was inquiring about her stay at Les Chattes Bleues—and saw that Miss Leila Calvé had planted herself in Shiloh's path, and he was flanked by Miss Sarah Calvé and Miss Anna Calvé. Cheney clenched her teeth and took a step forward, then recovering herself, hissed to Victoria, "You know it's pronounced 'Cal-vay,' Victoria. And I don't care if they are talking to Shiloh, anyway."

Cheney turned back to the matron, and as Victoria walked away she heard her whisper, "Don't you, Cheney? Well . . . perhaps I care. . . ."

With determination Cheney apologized and continued her conversation with the lady, who was tittering rather nervously at Cheney's inattention. Sternly Cheney ordered herself not to pay any heed to what Shiloh Irons was doing, whom he was dancing with, or whom he talked to during the ball.

The matron's son—Cheney had already forgotten her name, and promptly forgot the son's name as soon as she heard it—appeared and claimed Cheney for a dance.

Gentlemen she had just been introduced to claimed every one of Cheney's dances for a solid hour. After that time she was so thirsty and hot that she promised a young man of about eighteen who was begging her for the next dance that she would dance with him in an hour; then she slipped away. Grabbing a tall, frosty glass of mineral water from a table set up by a small set of French doors, she hurried outside the ballroom onto the gallery of the rotunda. Still, Cheney found the air stuffy, and quite a few people wandered about out on the galleries, so she hurried downstairs and went to a side entrance of the hotel to step outside and get some fresh night air.

She stood on the steps at the small entrance that faced down Exchange Alley. Small crowds of people still passed back and forth, but the night was cool, and a freshening breeze stirred the damp tendrils of hair on Cheney's neck. Closing her eyes, she lifted her face to the night and breathed deeply.

"*Mademoiselle* Duvall," a curiously hoarse voice croaked out of the darkness. "Yes, so it is. And pardon me. It is Dr. Duvall, isn't it?"

Cheney started and peered into the gloom at the side of the stairs. The voice had seemed to come from there. Yes, when her eyes adjusted to the shadows she could see a movement. Then she heard a tap—tap—tap of wood upon the brick banquette, and a very old woman came out of the darkness to stand at the side of the stairs, still hanging back in the shadows.

The woman's shoulders were terribly stooped with age, and she wore an old-fashioned bonnet that shadowed her face. She walked painfully slowly, leaning precariously on a gnarled wooden cane. Cheney drew back in spite of herself. She knew this frail, ancient woman couldn't possibly hurt her, but she was so bent, so disfigured, her voice so coarse . . . and the hand that grasped the knob of wood that formed the handle of the cane was horribly like a claw, stretched and dried brown skin over spiky bones.

With a guttural groan the woman straightened up somewhat and lifted her face. To her shame, Cheney flinched slightly. The woman was ancient, and her nose had dropped into a downward-pointed beak, while her chin—as she'd long ago lost all her teeth—curved upward almost to meet it. Her skin was brown, but as blackened with age as old rotted leather. Her eyes, buried deep in the recesses of the ravaged face and the shadows of the grimy bonnet, glittered with a fierce light. "Dr. Duvall?" she croaked again, shuffling another step forward. "I'd like to speak to you."

"How . . . how do you know who I am?" Cheney stammered. She swallowed hard and made herself take a step down toward the speaker. She felt guilty for being so openly repelled by the woman's ugliness.

The dark eyes focused first on the glittering tiara on Cheney's head, then on Cheney's face. "I know you. I sent for you."

"What?" Cheney asked, bewildered. "For me? What . . . what . . ." To combat her confusion, Cheney took a deep breath, then the thought occurred to her. "Oh, did you mean you need a doctor? Is that it?"

To her consternation, the woman grinned. It wasn't a pleasant sight. Her mouth stretched open, but to Cheney it just looked like a black slash across the desolate face. Still, Cheney, trying desperately to retain her good manners, refused to step away from the woman, even though as she neared Cheney, the smell repelled her: revolting, old, unwashed body and another deeply disturbing herbal smell . . . not of pleasant, seemly herbs, but of something else, something noxious, something that smelled of disease and death. . . .

Cheney gritted her teeth and made herself take another step toward the woman. She still thought that the woman needed a doctor, or had come for someone who did, and this was what Cheney was concerned with first and foremost. She would never turn away from human beings who needed medical help, no matter how personally unpleasant she found them.

But suddenly, with a terrible strength, the woman reached out her hooklike hand and clasped Cheney's arm. Cheney had taken off her gloves as she came outside, and the woman's filthy, unkempt nails bit into Cheney's flesh. Cheney shuddered and pulled back, but the woman kept a death-grip on her and leaned forward. She could smell her foul breath and almost gagged.

"My name, dear Dr. Duvall, is Marie Laveau. Ah, you have heard of me, haven't you, my dear doctor?" Again she smiled, and Cheney, in alarm that was quickly turning into fright, thought that she looked upon a demon's face, a shadow demon, with glistening stone eyes and a dark pit of a mouth.

"Now you listen to me," the old woman muttered, then coughed, spraying Cheney's arm with her wretched sputum. Cheney actually had to clench her jaw to force the bile in her throat back down. She couldn't move, and Marie Laveau went on in a tone that dropped to an unearthly growl dripping with menace. "You better leave La Maison des Chattes Bleues. You leave, and you take your whole accursed family with you. I, Marie Laveau, am warning you, Dr. Duvall, that if you don't leave Les Chattes Bleues soon, and forever, you will pay—not with your life, or your wealth, but with your immortal soul!"

Cheney was paralyzed with horror and revulsion, and the shadows and faint glow of gaslight began to spin sickeningly around her. Still the woman kept her grip on Cheney's arm as she stared at her. In Cheney's faintness it seemed that the woman's misshapen face was first close to her own, then far away....

"Hey! You! Take your filthy—"

A dark shadow seemed to take flight and land in front of Cheney, and the woman's grip on her arm was loosed. Cheney shook her head, desperately trying to regain her equilibrium, her mind, and her clear vision. Shiloh stood in front of her, blocking her sight of the old woman. Cheney felt weak and helplessly clasped his waist with both hands and stumbled to his side. He put his arm around her, and she thought she'd never felt such welcome warmth, such strength, or such security.

"Get away from her," he growled, the threat in his lowered voice unmistakable. "And get away from here."

Cheney watched as Marie Laveau, who merely gave Shiloh a look of black hatred, turned, and shuffled away. When she was a few feet from them, she turned back and spat on the banquette. "I'll leave, but not because I fear you, you fool! Don't forget my warning, Dr. Duvall! Because I won't! I certainly won't!" She hobbled into the darkness of Exchange Alley.

Shiloh turned, took Cheney's upper arms, and searched her face anxiously. "Did she hurt you?"

"I ... I ... just want to sit down," Cheney said tremulously, "and I need some water, please."

Shiloh studied her face, and Cheney only now noticed that he still wore his mask and the crown, and he looked like an ancient medieval lord. "Can you walk?" he asked anxiously.

"Oh yes, yes ... Just ..." She rested her hands lightly on the sides

211

of his hips, and Shiloh could feel her fingers trembling. Faintly he heard her whisper, "Just don't leave me for a few minutes, please."

"Cheney, I'll never leave you," he said hoarsely. Still her head was down, her face averted, like a woman in a violent storm. His jaw clenched tightly, over and over again, but he willed himself to relax and continue in a soothing voice. "Here, walk with me, Doc. Let's go inside, and I'll find you a nice quiet place to sit down and get you something to drink."

"Th-thank you, Shiloh."

"Welcome."

Firmly he clasped her about the waist, and they went back into the hotel. Cheney straightened her shoulders and raised her head proudly, though she was pale, and she kept rubbing her arm. Shiloh's eyes took on a hard mica glint when he saw the unmistakable red marks from four fingers on Cheney's forearm. But he said nothing.

They crossed the vestibule, where a few of the guests of the hotel were milling about, sipping drinks. Shiloh grabbed a glass of water off a tray from a passing waiter and led Cheney to the entrance to the rotunda. There were three people there, observing the paintings and photographs, but they were quiet and the room was cool.

Shiloh led Cheney to one of the stone benches in the center of the room, and she sank down on it gratefully. He knelt in front of her so he could see her face and held up the tall glass of water. "Here, Doc, just relax and be quiet and drink this. You okay?"

"Yes, I'm fine, thank you. Would you . . . like . . . to sit down?" she asked awkwardly.

"Sure." He sat down close beside her and watched her anxiously. She sipped the water slowly and looked around the room. He gave her several minutes to calm down before he spoke. "Who was that old crone?"

"Her name is Marie Laveau."

"Oh yeah? The old witch herself, huh . . ." he said in an ugly voice.

Cheney sighed gently. The soft sound echoed in the still room. Now there were only two people, a couple, walking around, looking at the photographs and paintings, and they didn't speak. Dropping her head, Cheney fidgeted with her gloves and felt tears sting her eyes. Tears of shame and tears of self-disgust. "I . . . I . . . was afraid of her," she said, her voice hoarse. "She . . . she . . . frightened me."

Shiloh put his arm around Cheney's waist again, and helplessly she leaned against him and rested her head on his shoulder. "Doc," he said with great tenderness, "I'm a big, strong man, and she scared me, too. Even her little girlfriend Dédé scared me. There's something about those people, something wrong, and something frightening."

"Evil," Cheney whispered. Shiloh said nothing, merely tightened his hold on her waist.

I will fear no evil. . . .

"What?" Cheney said, startled. Looking around, she saw that the couple had left the rotunda, and she and Shiloh were alone. She knew he hadn't said anything, but . . . something . . . Someone . . .

I will fear no evil, for Thou art with me. . . .

Cheney drew a deep breath, then smiled and closed her eyes. *Yes, Lord, I hear. I will fear no evil, for Thou art with me. Your rod and your staff, they comfort me. You make me to lie down in green pastures. . . . You anoint my head with oil . . . my cup runneth over. Surely goodness and mercy shall follow me all the days of my life, and I will dwell in the house of the Lord forever. . . .*

Shiloh and Cheney were still, and quiet, for a long time. The lights in the rotunda had been dimmed, so the room was shadowed. But the lights nearest the paintings were turned up, so that they were highlighted. Cheney saw now that they were sitting directly across from the "Forever Shiloh" painting, as she called it privately.

Rousing a bit, she narrowed her eyes, and Shiloh followed her gaze. He hadn't noticed that they were seated across from his likeness, and now he looked at the painting curiously again. Even though he hadn't thought too much about it, it was odd to see himself in that painting.

Cheney cocked her head. "Shiloh?"

"Hmm?"

"Is that uniform you're wearing in the painting accurate?"

"Uh . . . you mean, was that my uniform?"

"Yes."

"Well, yeah, it is. That's what's so strange. That thing's gotta be a painting of me, 'cause that is my uniform. But I still haven't figured out where that rascal saw me. . . ."

Cheney turned to him and regarded him intently. "The insignia on your sleeve. It's a cross."

A faint flush colored his high cheekbones. "Well . . . yeah."

Cheney waited, watching him.

Shiloh fidgeted with the saber at his side, his eyes on the painting.

When he spoke, his voice was distant and so soft Cheney could barely hear him. "I was a medic, you see. In fact, I was the only medic we had when we went on raids—long ones, or tough ones, at night. We hardly ever took the whole headquarters and staff with us. . . ."

"Yes," Cheney said in a low tone of encouragement.

He shifted uneasily, a curiously awkward movement unlike Shiloh's usual easy grace. "I wouldn't wear an armband."

"You mean a white one? With the red cross? Why not?"

"Aw . . . you know, Doc. Medics are supposed to be noncombatants."

Cheney's expression changed to sudden comprehension. "You mean, they wouldn't shoot at you if you were wearing an armband."

"Somethin' like that."

"And you refused to take the part of a noncombatant, even though you had a perfect right to."

Shiloh shrugged carelessly. "General Forrest made me wear that insignia, anyway." A sudden smile lit his face. "He said that he figured it wouldn't hurt for a wounded man to see that cross, even if he didn't know if I was a chaplain or a medic."

"He was right," Cheney said firmly. "You know what I think?"

"Most of the time," Shiloh replied, deadpan.

Cheney ignored his lightness and stared deeply into his eyes. "I think that the hand of the Lord God Almighty is on you and on your life, Shiloh. I think that He has a great plan for you, and He has given you some very special gifts . . . some wonderful gifts, and that one day you'll use them for Him."

For long moments he stared at her soberly, and Cheney held his gaze. Then she smiled, and he smiled back at her and nodded. She knew what that little gesture of acknowledgment meant—Shiloh listened to her and respected her and her thoughts, but he was his own man, and he would go his own way. *I was wrong . . . that painting— the soldier, the grim man of war, the prisoner of rebellion—that isn't the Forever Shiloh . . . One day*, Cheney thought, *he'll see that he has nothing without the Lord. . . . I have to believe that one day he will. . . .*

"You're feeling better, huh, Doc," he commented.

"Yes, much better, thank you. And . . . thank you for . . . being there."

"I'll always be here, Doc," he said lightly. "You know, I knew something was wrong with you."

"Hmm? What . . . what do you mean?"

He shrugged carelessly. "I just knew. I know stuff like that, sometimes. I was kinda looking for you in the ballroom, and I couldn't see you. Then I got kinda anxious . . . and then I knew. Something was wrong. So I went to find you, and I walked right out the door to where you were."

Cheney stared at him and had no earthly idea what to say.

He glanced at her, and his expression grew intense. His jaw clenched once, twice, and his eyes, behind the mask, grew hooded and secretive. Long moments passed. Then he clenched his fists once convulsively and drew away from her.

He looked at the painting and laughed, a careless, rowdy sound that made Cheney sit up and smooth her gown self-consciously. "You know, I just walked off and left Miss Leila Calvé waltzing all by herself! Maybe I better not go back to the ball. Might get into trouble, and I'm sure outnumbered by those Calvé sisters. . . ."

Cheney laughed with him, then rose and drew on her gloves with impatient, jerky movements. They would hide those red marks quite well. "Nonsense! I want to go back."

"You do?" he asked, rising to his feet.

"Yes, of course. I haven't danced with my father yet, and I'm going to bully Gowan Ford into dancing with me, and I—" Cheney hesitated, watching Shiloh intently.

"Yes? And?"

"And I hoped, Shiloh," she said quietly, "to have the last dance with you."

MUCH FINE
❉ P·A·R·T F·O·U·R ❉
GOLD

The fear of the Lord is clean,
Enduring forever:
The judgments of the Lord
Are true and righteous altogether.
More to be desired
are they than gold, yea,
Than much fine gold...

Psalm 19:9–10

17

To Stand

As if to reinforce that the rites of spring were finished and the toils of summer must begin, Nature, on Ash Wednesday—which fell on March 1—decreed that it would be hot. The sun was blazing in the Vieux Carré by seven o'clock in the morning, mercilessly spotlighting the dingy remembrances of Mardi Gras. Every street in the French Quarter and those parts of the Garden Section that the parades had crashed through were littered with food, torn and dirty masks, manure from countless horses and livestock that had been paraded, forlorn leavings of confetti, and even some desolate human beings who had passed out in the alleys.

In the St. Louis Hotel, however, business was as usual, though most of the clients rose rather late and their servants rose rather early. Molly, Adah, and Chloe were up before dawn packing for Tante Marye and Tante Elyse; Nia had packed most of Cheney's belongings the night before, but she was up at dawn anyway. Zhou-Zhou had tried to ready Victoria's things as well as she could the night before, but by the time Madame de Lancie had whirled in at three o'clock in the morning and had undressed and then dressed for bed, Zhou-Zhou's careful preparations and neatening of Victoria's things were in vain. Zhou-Zhou merely shrugged, went to bed, and slept late the next morning. She knew that by the time Madame de Lancie dressed for breakfast and then changed for the journey back to Les Chattes Bleues, everything would be in a jumble again anyway.

A sleepy company of seven met in the Vicomte's Suite at eleven o'clock. The suite was grand; it was, indeed, more like a small house than a hotel accommodation. The main room was a combination sitting room and dining room, with a main bedroom on each side and a small connecting room for servants on either side of those. Cheney was the last to arrive, for she had slept later than anyone else.

"Good morning," she said to the assembly, then yawned with a jaw-cracking sigh.

"Cheney, you must learn not to yawn so hugely in public," Tante Marye said sternly. "Ladies must pout a yawn, you see, and pat their lips daintily. Twice, and twice only."

"Yes, Tante Marye," Cheney replied with drowsy vagueness. Only a moment later she yawned again, hugely. Tante Marye's sparse white eyebrows shot up, but everyone else laughed out loud, and her severe expression smoothed out.

Cheney looked around, mystified. Irritably she dismissed this inappropriate early-morning humor and demanded, "Aren't we having breakfast?" She dropped into a chair and waited. Her mother and father were seated close together on a divan; her father was reading *The Daily Crescent*, and her mother was looking over his shoulder. Shiloh sprawled in a great leather armchair next to her, drinking coffee and rubbing his unshaven beard contemplatively. Gowan Ford was in a matching armchair on the other side of him, reading *The True American*. Tante Marye and Tante Elyse were seated on the other divan, as Tante Marye always "poured" and Tante Elyse always fussed with the service as she did, which afforded Tante Marye the opportunity of telling Tante Elyse that she didn't know how to serve properly. Victoria, subdued and tired-looking, stood at the window, looking down on the relatively quiet street. Puzzled, Cheney double-checked the dining table; it was set for seven and the sideboard was laden with several dishes, with tantalizing aromas rising in the bits of steam that escaped from around the covers.

Tante Marye smiled her brief smile at Cheney. "Elyse and I and Mrs. de Lancie planned to fast today, and Richard, Irene, and Gowan have decided to join us. Elyse and I are following a long tradition modeled by our mother and father. Tomorrow we will have a private service at Les Chattes Bleues and break our fast. But, of course, Cheney, we don't require—or expect—anyone else to observe Ash Wednesday as we do, unless you wish to."

"No, I think it's a good idea," Cheney said slowly. "I shall fast, too. After all the wild frivolity and excitement, it will be good to fast and pray and call to mind the other things in our lives that are as important as fun and laughter."

"Very true," Richard said with approval. He was tired—as was everyone, for the Comus pageant had gone on until the small hours of the morning—but somewhat to his surprise, his mind had been eased by the careless merriment of the last two days.

"Well, I'm not promising that I won't eat anything today," Shiloh drawled. "Eating is a fairly important thing in my life, you see."

"Quite all right, Mr. Irons." Tante Marye nodded. "As I said, we don't expect anyone to fast who doesn't wish to, and we would be rude indeed if by our abstinence we made anyone uncomfortable. We shall all go to the dining room table now. Mr. Irons certainly needs to eat, and we can drink juices and coffee."

"That's okay," Shiloh said. "I've already had breakfast, Mrs. Edwards. I would not, by the same token, want to offend all of you, so I ate early at Maspero's."

"It was very gracious of you to do that," Tante Marye said approvingly.

Cheney stared at Shiloh, her mind beginning to clear from its sleep fugue. "Yes, so gracious of you to eat breakfast, Shiloh. Wonderful."

"Cheney, I do believe you are not yourself this morning," Tante Marye pointedly observed. "I do not know exactly who you are, but it appears to be a person with very little sense and no manners."

"I know," Cheney admitted disarmingly. "I'm sleepy."

"Goodness, I wonder how your patients fare when you're sleepy, Cheney," Tante Elyse mused thoughtfully.

"Elyse, you have no idea how absurd you are at times," Marye rasped.

"Oh, yes I do!" Elyse argued.

Everyone burst out laughing, and finally even Tante Marye chuckled. For an hour the company drank coffee and juice, while the servants toiled mightily to get the ladies' belongings packed. By noon they were ready to go to the dock and find the lone boatman who dared to enter Bayou du Chêne and take them home.

By the time they reached La Maison des Chattes Bleues, the ladies were wilted and exhausted, and Richard, Shiloh, and Ford were almost as spent. All of the thirteen people who had gone to Mardi Gras, including the servants, took long naps. Then everyone wanted baths, and by nightfall they were growing tired again. Tante Marye suggested that they have warm milk out on the gallery and gaze at the milky Louisiana night sky and the lazy, fuzzy stars.

Shiloh politely declined to join them. *Just can't do it*, he grumped to himself. *Seems like I'd be kinda—hypocritical, I guess. So now I gotta eat, even though I'd rather just sit outside with them and have some warm milk. . . .*

He decided to go to the kitchen and scrounge himself a light snack. The kitchen was a long, low brick building directly behind the kitchen gardens. In many large Southern houses, the kitchen might be a walk-out basement, insulated and cooled by being half-buried in earth. But since the water table in southern Louisiana was sometimes as shallow as three feet, this was impossible. Also, as the main house was predominantly wood, it was much wiser to keep it separate. This way, should a fire start in the kitchen, the entire house would not burn.

Adah was the only person in the kitchen; when Shiloh entered, she ducked her head and nervously stirred an enormous pot of gombo that was simmering on top of the great iron cookstove. It was warm in the kitchen, but generous windows were open on every wall of the building, and pleasant cross-breezes heralded a cool night.

"Hello, Adah," Shiloh said pleasantly. "Mind if I have some of that gombo? It smells delicious. No, no, I can help myself. I see bowls and stuff."

The kitchen, like all kitchens that served great houses, was pleasantly cluttered but efficiently arranged. Open shelves lined the walls, and everything was easy to find. Shiloh got a brown earthenware bowl, a plate, and a spoon, and Adah ladled out a generous portion of the rich gombo. "W-would you like some bread?" she stammered nervously, not looking up at him.

"Sure, but I see it. I'll help myself." On the long oak worktable in the center of the kitchen was a loaf of fresh-baked bread, a sizable wheel of yellow cheese, and a platter of grapes, apples, and cherries. At the far end of the kitchen was another serviceable oak dining table with six chairs. Shiloh settled himself down and began to eat. Wordlessly Adah brought him a glass of frothy milk.

"Thank you."

"Yes, sir," she whispered and almost ran across the long expanse of the room to continue stirring the gombo.

The door opened, and Chloe's petulant tones echoed in the kitchen. "Mmm, I'm starving! Now that we're finally through slaving over the Big Bugs' baths—"

"Chloe," Adah murmured and jerked her head toward the other end of the room.

Chloe saw Shiloh and her eyes lit up; deliberately she assumed a sensuous look, complete with heavy lids and pouting mouth. "Mmm, Shiloh! I'll join you for supper."

Molly came in, carrying two heavy buckets of water, and murmured, "Chloe, you'll do no such thing. Help me with these, child. Good evening, Mr. Irons. I'm so sorry you aren't being served properly—"

"No, no, Molly, it's really okay," he said, hurrying across the room to grab the buckets from her. She looked up in surprise, but with relief allowed him to take them. "Where do you want these?"

"Over there by the stove will be fine."

"I'm hungry, Mama, and I'm going to eat," Chloe announced.

"All right, child," Molly sighed. "But don't bother Mr. Irons."

Grabbing a plate, Chloe helped herself to some of the bread and cheese and a sizable pile of cherries. Then she hurried to sit down across from Shiloh's place. Ruefully he realized he'd been outmaneuvered and sank back down at the table.

Chloe picked up a cherry by the stem. Deliberately she dipped it in Shiloh's glass of milk, ran the cherry across her lips, and finally nibbled it, staring hungrily at him all the time. Stolidly Shiloh ate, barely looking at her, but she kept on performing this little pantomime. With irritation Shiloh wondered where in the world this young girl had learned such lasciviousness.

"Something wrong with the cherries, Chloe?" he asked. "You're making faces like they taste funny."

But Chloe was unquenchable and unstoppable. "Oh no, they're wonderful, Shiloh," she murmured throatily. "Would you like for me to feed you some? One . . . at . . . a . . . time?"

Adah had disappeared; Molly was now at the stove tasting the gombo and adding spices and stirring. Though she couldn't possibly have heard Chloe's soft words, she evidently sensed something and looked across the long expanse of the room and frowned.

Chloe ignored her mother, but Shiloh was uncomfortable. "No," he said brusquely, then lowered his eyes and began to eat as methodically and quickly as he could.

"You're going to fall in love with me, you know," Chloe whispered. "You won't be able to help yourself, Shiloh. You might as well admit it. Don't you feel it? I know you do, but you're just fighting it because I'm young. . . ."

Without looking up, Shiloh said tonelessly, "I will not fall in love with you, Chloe. In fact, I don't even like you. Would you please go away?"

"No," she giggled, "I won't."

"Won't what?" Molly demanded, suddenly looming over the table. Shiloh didn't look up. Steadily he spooned the gombo into his mouth.

Chloe cut her eyes slyly to him. "Fast, of course," she told her mother in a tone that just barely touched on disrespect. "I think it's dumb, and so do Adah and Corbett."

"Chloe!" Molly moaned. "You keep your sassy opinions to yourself. And you're bothering Mr. Irons—"

"Shiloh thinks fasting is dumb, too," Chloe said in a bored tone.

With that Shiloh threw down his spoon and jumped up. Chloe smiled a satisfied little kitten's grin, and it only made him more angry to realize that he had let her upset him—which seemed to suit Chloe just fine, in lieu of his falling for her seduction, or asking her to marry him, or whatever it was that she wanted from him. "Thank you, Molly, for a good supper. The gombo was delicious," he said in a curt tone. Without a backward look he banged out of the kitchen.

Molly watched helplessly as Chloe jumped up and ran to the window to watch Shiloh walk back to the house.

Even as Chloe was watching his back adoringly, Shiloh was muttering, "That does it! Next time I fast!"

★　★　★　★

"Put on the whole armour of God,
That ye may be able to stand
Against the wiles of the devil.
For we wrestle not against flesh and blood,
But against principalities,
Against powers,
Against the rulers of the darkness of this world,
Against spiritual wickedness in high places.
Wherefore take unto you the whole armour of God,
That ye may be able to withstand in the evil day,
And having done all,
To stand."

Richard closed the Bible and looked gravely around at each person who sat in the library at La Maison des Chattes Bleues on Thursday morning. Tante Marye met his gaze with level, unflinching eyes, pressed her mouth into a thin determined line, and nodded. Tante Elyse smiled sweetly at him. Gowan Ford raised his chin proudly, his single blue eye glowing with an inner flame. Victoria de Lancie looked pale, but stubbornly determined, and nodded acknowledgment to him. Beside her Cheney smiled warmly, easily, and Richard knew that she—like her mother, who sat close beside him—had no fear and no doubts.

Richard rose to his feet and said quietly, "I will stand. By the grace and power of God, I will stand."

Gowan Ford immediately stood up, and the ladies rose slowly. Ford said hoarsely, "In this house, we will all stand with God—and with you, Colonel Duvall."

Moving as if by unheard direction, they all drew together in a close circle, joined hands, bowed their heads, and prayed.

As he had done for the past hour, Shiloh Irons stood alone on the lagoon landing and stared up at a thin, dirty trail of smoke rising from the accursed island, so near to him, yet so bitterly out of his reach. His eyes were a fierce, savage blue, his nostrils pinched white, and his mouth was a straight hard slash against his firm chin. To an unseen observer, this man looked anything but afraid; he looked wrathful, he looked formidable.

But though these observations were truth, Shiloh Irons was decidedly afraid. He was afraid of what that noisome gray smoke portended; he was afraid for the safety of Cheney and her parents and everyone else at Les Chattes Bleues; he was afraid for himself. He tried to make himself climb into the small boat and go over to the island, but he remained motionless, closing his eyes and clenching his jaw over and over again.

I can't, he thought, seething. *I just can't. Those snakes . . . and that disgusting woman . . . all of them were just . . . just . . . sickening! And I got so ill . . . so ill, for no reason. . . .*

But deep within himself, Shiloh knew there was a reason why he had been ill. He knew—although he rarely let himself dwell upon it or analyze it too closely—that Richard Duvall was right. He, Shiloh Irons, had no business trying to fight this fight. He simply didn't possess the right weapons for an offensive stance; he didn't even have a defense.

Opening his eyes, he stared back up at the smudges against the hot blue sky. *One thing about it, though*, he suddenly realized, *if I admit that I gotta stay out of this fight, then it wouldn't be the right thing to do to go stompin' over there. And I do know that there's no shame in turning and running from a fight you're sure to lose. There is honor in living to fight another day. . . .*

Shiloh decided to wait until Richard Duvall and Gowan Ford were through with their prayer service, then tell them of the fire on the island. He relaxed and felt his anger fade in the glow of the sunlight as surely as the tatters of dark smoke above him were burned away.

Shiloh watched the burning for a while. Suddenly he felt something cold and wet on his hand, and he jumped. Beside him stood Riff and Raff, wagging their tails and looking up at him expectantly. He and the dogs had made fast friends after their one unfortunate misunderstanding when they'd first met.

"Hey, boys! Breakfast time, huh?" He knelt and petted them for a while—he had to be careful to pay the same exact amount of attention to each dog, or the neglected one would knock him down to bring it to his notice.

"Be nice to eat with everyone again, won't it, boys?" Shiloh told the dogs. Riff and Raff seemed to be in agreement with him, although they certainly never ate in Tante Marye's house. What Tante Marye didn't know, however, was that Tante Elyse usually brought them at least one meal a day, and she would sit down on the floor of the back gallery and companionably snack on something while they ate, all the while talking to them in an unbroken flow of conversation. Shiloh had caught her at this once, and after that he asked Tante Elyse if he could join her and Riff and Raff for their lunch. Tante Elyse was delighted, and the dogs seemed amenable, too. Shiloh grinned. "Yeah, you know, boys, it's kinda nice for us old scruffy men to get to eat with the nice ladies. Not much fun to eat all by yourself, huh?"

As Riff and Raff escorted Shiloh back up the long avenue of majestic oaks, Shiloh reflected that it was odd. He was quite as hungry as if he'd been fasting for a day. A quiet voice buried deep within him whispered, *Even more odd . . . you, the orphan, the proud loner, Shiloh Irons, who doesn't need anyone or anything . . . you were lonely when you weren't included. . . .*

Shiloh's head snapped up in a deliberately dismissive gesture, and he stared at the graceful lines of La Maison des Chattes Bleues. "Hey, you thugs! Riff! Raff! Wait up!"

Then he broke into a run.

18

DEV

Very early on Friday morning the brass knocker on the front door sounded. Cautiously Monroe opened the door, hesitated for a fraction of a second, then bowed. "Dr. Buchanan, sir," he intoned. "How good it is to see you again."

"I'm glad to be back here at Les Chattes Bleues, Monroe," Dev Buchanan replied. Removing his hat and gloves, he nodded toward the dining room. "I see no one is down for breakfast yet."

"No, *monsieur*, but *Madame* Edwards, *Madame* Buckingham, and Colonel and Mrs. Duvall are in the library, waiting."

Dev nodded understanding; Cheney must be late again. "There is no need to escort me, Monroe. If you don't mind I'll just go along to the library and announce myself."

Monroe nodded and said solemnly, "They will be surprised, *monsieur*. And pleased, if I may be so bold as to say so."

"Thank you, Monroe, you are kind," Dev replied with his customary formality. He hurried through the parlor into the library and paused at the great arched entrance that was the only division between it and the front parlor. Irene and Richard sat on a couch in front of a long window, and the sun haloed them in brightness. Tante Marye was fussing with the coffee service, and Tante Elyse was bending over the table that held it, helping herself to one, two, then three lumps of sugar.

"Hello, everyone," Dev said quietly.

Four faces turned toward him, and immediately Irene broke into a dazzling smile. Richard and Tante Marye looked stunned. Tante Elyse looked surprised, then bounded toward him, her arms held open. "Dev! Dev! You surprised us!" she cried.

Everyone hurried to him, and after all the greetings he settled on the couch by Irene, who watched him avidly, her eyes shining. "I thought I would surprise you in New York," he told Richard and Irene, "but instead I was surprised. I arrived a week after you'd left." He looked over at Tante Marye and Tante Elyse. "I was planning on visiting you next month anyway, so I decided to come a little early."

"Oh! I'm so glad you did!" Tante Elyse exclaimed.

"I'm glad too, Elyse," Marye said irritably.

"Marye's glad, too," Elyse told Dev.

He smiled, and deep dimples showed. Dev was very handsome but rather stern-looking, with his dark eyes and saturnine, but well-shaped, eyebrows. His hair was blue-black, thick and wavy, but he kept it cut short and refused to indulge in the long thick sideburns that were so fashionable, though he had recently grown a well-manicured mustache. When he smiled and the dimples flashed, however, he still looked incongruously boyish.

"You've grown a mustache," Irene said softly.

"Do you like it?"

"Yes, very much."

He took her hand and pressed it to his lips. "Thank you, Miss Irene. I had already determined that if you didn't like it, I would immediately shave it off."

Irene positively glowed, and Richard watched her fondly. Devlin Buchanan had a very special place in his wife's heart, and Richard had come to love him as though he were his own son. When Dev was six years old, Richard and Irene Duvall had assumed responsibility for him and his young widowed mother. They had supported them financially, but more than that, they had made them both feel as if they were family.

Dev and Cheney studied together under the same tutor until Dev was eighteen and she was twelve. Dev's mother died that year, and the Duvalls then sent Dev to England, where he graduated from the prestigious Hospital of University College in London. In the years since, Dev gained prominence both in England and in America as a highly respected physician and scholar. For the last year and a half he had been on full fellowship at Guy's Hospital in London, studying the relatively new disciplines of preventive and corrective surgeries with some of the most renowned physicians in the world. In fact, Devlin Buchanan, M.D., had joined their ranks and could now be considered one of them.

Cheney came sweeping in and broke into a run when she saw Dev. "Dev! It really is you! I thought I heard your voice, but—"

Dev rose slowly to his feet and began an elegant bow, but Cheney bowled into him, throwing her arms around him with abandon. Two streaks of color appeared on his cheekbones, but he smiled, hugged her, and gave her a chaste peck on the cheek. "Hello, Cheney. It's good to see you again."

"Oh, Dev, I've missed you terribly," she chattered, standing back, clinging to his hands, looking him up and down. "You've grown a mustache! I like it! You look so forbidding!"

"I'm so glad you think so," Dev said dryly. With spare elegance he handed her into a chair near his.

"Oh, I think you look terribly handsome, and you know that you are," Cheney scoffed. "Now, what have you been talking about? I insist that you repeat every word you said before I came in—and why didn't someone come and get me and tell me you were here? Why didn't you let us know—"

"Cheney, dear, Dev only just arrived," Irene chided gently.

"All we've been talking about is his mustache," Richard grumbled.

"I do think it's so luscious, don't you, Marye?" Elyse purred.

"I hardly think 'luscious' is how Dev would like his facial features described, Elyse," Marye retorted scathingly. "Of course Dev is a well-favored man, and—"

"Oooh, luscious," Cheney teased. "Dev's luscious! Perfectly luscious!"

"I'd almost forgotten the singular joys of feminine company," Dev asserted with a touch of exasperation.

"That's what you get for hobnobbing only with those dusty old male doctors at Guy's," Cheney declared. "For the last *seven* months! Dev, how could you? Running away from Manhattan last year in such a peculiar manner—even though you did horsewhip that horrible Philip Teller. But no one knew about it, anyway! Except the Marquess of Queensbury, and Mr. Chambers, and Victoria and I knew, and I believe that His Lordship told Shiloh—"

"Cheney, cease that chattering this instant!" Tante Marye commanded. "What is this? Dev, you actually horsewhipped someone?"

"Oh no," Dev moaned with a horrible grimace at Cheney. "Tante Marye, it was a . . . difficult situation, and a . . . long story. . . ."

"Oh, how wonderful!" Tante Elyse cried, scooting to the very edge of her chair. "Tell, Dev, tell! Or perhaps Cheney should tell—"

"No, Cheney will not tell," Irene asserted with an unusually severe glance at Cheney. "No one will tell this story right now; there are more important things for us to talk about. Such as—" She turned to Dev and took his hand again, smoothing it lightly with her own. "How long can you stay, Dev?"

With immense relief Dev smiled a thank-you to Irene and answered, "I hadn't decided yet, as my plans have been rather turned around. But my leave is for a month."

"Oh, wonderful!" Irene murmured. "Then you'll stay here at Les Chattes Bleues until we go back to New York, and you can return with us then."

"Perhaps," Dev replied noncommittally. "As I said, I had intended to come here anyway. And I do have some . . . things I must attend to." He glanced at Cheney, who looked surprised for a moment but smiled at him warmly. "Tante Marye and Tante Elyse wrote me a rather odd letter," he went on, staring at them with some concern. "So I thought I'd better plan to come here and make certain you were all right. Is that why you are all here?" he asked Richard.

"I'm here because the Doc made me come," Shiloh announced, wandering into the library. "But I'm glad she did." Dev got to his feet, and he and Shiloh shook hands. "You've grown a mustache," Shiloh observed.

"I wish I hadn't," Dev responded. "Hello, Irons."

"Good to see you, Dr. Buchanan," Shiloh replied easily.

After they seated themselves, Richard finally answered Dev's question. "Yes, Dev, we came because Marye and Elyse are having some problems here at Les Chattes Bleues. We'll tell you all about them at breakfast—by the way, is Mr. Ford joining us this morning?"

"Yes, and I can't think why he's not back yet," Tante Elyse answered irritably. "We've already met to talk over the day's work. He said he was going to run out to the stables to check on Sock and Stocking— he's quite fond of them, you know—and then come right back."

"I just came from the stables," Shiloh informed them. "He wasn't there. In fact, I didn't see anyone stirring out on the grounds."

"Hmm? What?" Tante Elyse said alertly. "No one? Not even Luna or Corbett?"

"Not a soul."

"Elyse, sit down," Marye snapped as her sister almost jumped out of the chair. Elyse immediately sat. "I doubt that everyone has disappeared from Les Chattes Bleues, and Dev is here."

"Yes, and if they have disappeared, Gowan will know," Elyse agreed. "If he hasn't disappeared too. . . ."

"What is she talking about?" Richard muttered to Irene.

"Nothing, dear," Irene answered soothingly.

Dev was grinning at the two elderly sisters. "A good thing you have two doctors here, if Les Chattes Bleues is affected with some sort of disappearing disease."

"No, it's not a disappearing disease," Elyse told him earnestly. "It's a *vaudou* disease."

"I don't think so, Tante Elyse," Cheney said stubbornly.

"What's a boodoo disease?" Dev asked in bewilderment. "I've never heard of it!"

"No, no, it's French," Tante Elyse said.

"It's a French disease?" Dev asked plaintively.

"Down here it'd be Creole," Shiloh put in smugly.

"What are they talking about, Irene?" Richard demanded.

"Nothing, dear."

"But—" Dev began.

"*Vaudou*, Dev," Tante Elyse repeated informatively, if a trifle belatedly.

"*Vaudou? Dev?*" Victoria's normally cultured tones sounded harsh. She hurried into the room and stopped abruptly midstride when she saw Devlin Buchanan. Her blue eyes grew wide, almost stricken, and her face turned ashen.

Dev turned, saw her, and shot to his feet. He stared at her in disbelief, stiffening his shoulders and clenching his hands. "You! Here!" he said between tightly clenched teeth.

"You . . . you . . ." Victoria said faintly, pressing a tiny, white-fingered hand to her breast.

Shiloh sat up alertly and glanced at Cheney, who looked completely bewildered. Irene looked puzzled also, then sudden, shocking comprehension jarred her smooth features for a moment. Then she, too, anxiously watched Cheney.

Abruptly Shiloh jumped up and drawled, "There you are, Mrs. de Lancie. Am I glad to see you! I'm starving!" In two long strides he was by her side and with lazy grace took her arm. She was trembling, and Shiloh thought with dread that this woman might have the actual, the real, the serious vapors right here in the library. He cast a quick glance

231

at Devlin Buchanan, silently pleading with him to get control of himself and this situation.

Dev's Grecian face smoothed out as if he had suddenly turned to highly polished marble. Stiffly he went to Victoria, took her limp hand, and brushed it against his lips for the merest second. "Mrs. de Lancie, I am at your service, as always. Please accept my grave apologies for my rudeness; I was surprised by your unexpected presence here at Les Chattes Bleues." His voice was deep, but completely without inflection.

Victoria drew a ragged breath. Then, with visible effort, she pulled herself erect and nodded, a queenly, controlled gesture. "It's my pleasure, Dr. Buchanan," she said with colorless cordiality. "I can understand your surprise, for I am equally surprised to see you. I assume you gave no notice of your visit?"

"No, and I heartily regret it," Dev growled. He and Victoria stared at each other: Dev with some inexplicable anger, and Victoria with barely concealed rebellion.

"Will you accept my escort into the dining room, Mrs. de Lancie?" Shiloh said with heavy politeness, pressing her arm slightly.

"Oh . . . oh yes, thank you, Shiloh," she said quietly, turning to lead the bewildered company in to breakfast. "Thank you so much," she added under her breath.

" 'S'okay," Shiloh answered carelessly but very quietly. "You looked kinda weak there for a minute."

"Weak is the word," she replied sarcastically, as if she were speaking to herself.

Shiloh said nothing more.

In silence they went to the dining room and seated themselves. Cheney still looked mystified, and Irene watched her closely. Tante Elyse looked upset, and Tante Marye only a little less so. Richard, though he might not pay attention to every word in a conversation, had certainly seen the tension between Victoria and Dev. What it meant he had no idea, but he was anxious that no one should be distressed.

After everyone sat down—each person except Irene with eyes downcast—Richard said firmly, "I will say grace." Without waiting for a response, he bowed his head and prayed, "Dearest Lord and Savior, this morning we want to say thank you that Dev is here, and thank you for keeping him safe on his journey. And all of us, Lord, thank you for him, because all of us here love him, and his arrival reminds us that you have given us all—each of us—a family that loves us, and cares for us, and that will always draw close in time of need. We are, Lord, your sons and daughters, and we all thank you for giving us sisters and brothers in You. Amen."

"What a perfectly marvelous prayer, Richard," Tante Elyse said happily. "Especially for breakfast!"

Everyone laughed, though not a soul there had the foggiest notion what Tante Elyse meant. It did, however, serve as a sign of release, as everyone had taken time to recover from their discomfort as Richard had prayed. Now they all rose and, chattering companionably, went to the sideboard. Breakfast at Les Chattes Bleues was usually buffet-style, and this morning the platters held fruits, biscuits, bacon, pork chops, boiled eggs, and an assortment of croissants and pastries. Monroe and Molly were still in careful attendance, Monroe pouring coffee and juice, and Molly servicing the dishes on the sideboard.

Dev found himself at Victoria's side, waiting as Tante Elyse, Tante Marye, and Irene served their plates. "I had no idea you were coming here, Mrs. de Lancie," Dev said with difficulty.

"And I didn't know you were coming," Victoria retorted frostily. "I am sorry to have caused you so much distress. I assure you that Mr. and Mrs. Duvall asked me to accompany them, and your great-aunts have made me very welcome."

"I didn't intend to imply that you are unwelcome. I merely was not—didn't—did not—" Dev cleared his throat uncomfortably and began again. "I hope you have been well."

"Very well, thank you."

"Good. That's good."

"And you?"

"Fine."

"I'm happy to hear it."

Behind them Shiloh rolled his eyes and cast a quick glance at Cheney, who stood a little apart from them, watching them with obvious dismay. Finally Cheney stepped up to Dev's side and took his arm. Leaning across him, she spoke to Victoria, on his other side. "Dear Victoria, isn't it wonderful that Dev's here?"

"Yes, Cheney, I know you and your parents and your great-aunts are so happy to see him again," Victoria said politely.

"You are, too, aren't you?" Cheney asked, almost pleaded.

"Of course."

"Here, Cheney, allow me to help you." Firmly Dev stepped up to the sideboard and began to comment upon the food in a low tone. Behind him Victoria sighed and dropped her eyes for a moment. Shiloh could see a small, sad smile play on her lips. But in a moment she roused herself and, assuming her normal slightly distant expression, began a polite conversation with him.

When everyone was seated, Tante Elyse said, "Oh, Dev! I'm so glad you're here. You can help Cheney, although no one has fallen ill since Luna."

"Thank the Lord," Cheney asserted.

"One moment," Dev protested. "I admit I am a little wearied by the journey, so I don't wish to have too many nonsensical conversations. No offense, Tante Elyse, but 'no one has fallen ill since luna'? Since luna *what*? A luna moth? The lunar cycle? The lunar eclipse?"

"Actually, I think it was the full moon, was it not?" Tante Elyse asked Cheney, who began to laugh.

"The word 'lunatic' comes to mind here," Dev said sarcastically to Cheney, who kept on giggling and refused to pay any attention to him. With exasperation he turned to Richard. "Sir, would you mind just giving me a synopsis? In English, please?"

"Richard doesn't speak French," Tante Elyse twittered, which made Cheney go into a fresh spasm of laughing. Even Victoria's eyes shone, and she hid her smile behind her napkin.

"I don't know what they're talking about, anyway," Richard said complacently, winking at Irene. "I never do. I don't know anything about the lunar cycle."

Dev rested his head on one sensitive, long-fingered hand for a moment and closed his eyes as if he were in pain. Irene was smiling but looked compassionately at Dev. He did, truly, look tired, even though he was exaggerating his ire, playing along with Tante Elyse. That was one reason Tante Elyse loved him so deeply, because he put aside his normal severity to play silly games with her.

"Poor Dev," Irene teased. "Just remember, 'tribulation worketh patience.' "

"I didn't know I needed this much work," Dev groaned.

Wide-eyed, Tante Elyse exclaimed, "Oh! But I thought a famous doctor like you, Dev, would have lots and lots of patients!"

A shout of laughter greeted this bit of idiocy, and Tante Elyse looked markedly pleased with herself. Even Tante Marye was looking amused.

When the chuckles died down, Cheney observed superciliously, "Dev's not *im*patient. But he's not *patient*."

"Cheney, I swear you sound just like Tante Elyse," Dev remarked.

"Thank you," Tante Elyse said sweetly.

"*Malédiction!*" Dev said under his breath, and then mock-glowered up at Shiloh, who sat across from him. "Irons, do you suppose you could talk some sense to me?"

"Sure," Shiloh shrugged. "Only way I've kept my sanity around here is to talk sense. 'Course, I've been talkin' it to myself, and answerin' myself, so there is some doubt. . . ."

Again laughter swept the diners, and even Monroe smiled faintly.

Shiloh was meticulously observing Victoria de Lancie and Dr. Devlin Buchanan. At no time did their eyes meet; they studiously avoided each other's gaze. Once Victoria observed Shiloh's watchful look and quickly dropped her eyes when he saw her.

As the laughter died down, Tante Marye evidently decided that this was enough nonsense, for she announced, "Elyse, I forbid you to say a word for the next few minutes. At least until Richard finishes telling Dev what's been happening around here. Richard?"

Dutifully Richard began to explain to Dev who the *vaudou* were, and of the strange happenings at Les Chattes Bleues since they had first appeared on the island.

But he was interrupted by a commotion at the back door of the dining room. Gowan Ford came crashing in, his boots muddy, his hat still on, and his expression severe. Hurrying up to the dining table, he nodded perfunctorily at Tante Marye, who had her mouth open to— no doubt—chide him for his appearance. But for once Gowan Ford had no patience for Tante Marye's rules.

He suddenly saw Dev, and a measure of relief lessened the tension in his face. "Hello, Dr. Buchanan. I'm glad you're here."

"Hello, Mr. Ford. Is something wrong?"

"Yes." He turned to Tante Elyse, who stood expectantly and smoothed her skirt. "Grand-mère Journée is sick. And so is Becky Colton."

Tante Elyse nodded and went to fetch her hat. "Cheney and Dev are here," she said to Gowan as she passed him. "It will be all right."

Dev rose and immediately took charge. "Monroe, send someone

to fetch Cheney's and my bags." Monroe hurried off, and Dev turned to Gowan Ford. "Who are the two people?"

"Grand-mère Journée—"

"And how old is she?"

"I don't know. Quite elderly. She's very ill."

"And the other?"

"Becky Colton. She's only four, and also very ill, but Grand-mère Journée—" Uneasily Ford shook his head.

"Where are they?"

"Grand-mère Journée lives in one of the sharecroppers' cottages out back. The Coltons' place is about half a mile from here."

Dev turned to Cheney and Shiloh, who had come to stand close beside him. "Cheney, I will go see the old woman, and I think Shiloh should come with me, since he knows about the sickness, and I don't."

"That's fine, Dev," Cheney agreed. "Nia can come with me."

"Nia?" Dev's finely shaped eyebrows shot up.

"Yes, she's a good assistant," Cheney said a little defensively.

"All right," Dev nodded. "Then either I or Shiloh will join you, depending upon the old woman's condition."

"What can we do?" Richard asked, his arm around Irene's shoulders.

"Stay here, sir," Dev decided. "We'll all be back as soon as we can, and I expect Tante Marye and Irene would feel better if you'd stay here at the house with them."

Victoria's eyes flickered when Dev did not express the same concern for her. It seemed he had so effectively determined to ignore her that he had completely blotted out her existence. But she said nothing.

"All right," Richard readily agreed.

Irene looked at him curiously for a moment, for she had thought that Richard would insist on at least riding out with Cheney. But suddenly she realized what Richard had already recognized. She knew it as one knows things in dreams; there is no visible evidence, and yet she was certain.

This was not Richard Duvall's work to do.

But his time, and his task, would come.

19

HEALING HEARTS, HEALING MINDS, HEALING HANDS

"I haven't moved her. I haven't even touched her," Luna told Dev. "All I did was cover her with the quilt."

Dev nodded absently. Staring down at the tiny shrunken form of Grand-mère Journée, he touched the side of her neck lightly with two fingers. At least she was still alive; she looked dead.

"Find me another pillow. Or two," he muttered. Shiloh's and Luna's eyes met over the bed, and Luna nodded. Grand-mère Journée's home was comfortably but sparely furnished, and no other pillow was in sight in the single bedroom.

"I'll go get mine," Luna said and hurried out of the cottage.

"Who is she?" Dev asked. He bent over the still form and pulled up one of Grand-mère Journée's eyelids. Only white showed.

"Her name is Luna," Shiloh answered. "She's one of the share-croppers. Her cottage is next door. Luna's the last one that got sick."

Dev frowned. Grand-mère Journée lay on her side across the width of her narrow bed. Her thin legs hung awkwardly over one side. She was fully dressed, including stockings and a clean apron and white ker-chief, and her shoes were on. Certainly she was in an awkward position, but Dev didn't dare turn her over on her back until they could prop her up enough to keep her from swallowing her tongue. She was in a deep coma.

Frowning, Shiloh touched one of her hands, then the other. "Cold and dry..." Suddenly he straightened and said hoarsely, "Listen, Buchanan, if there's something—if you suspect something besides nat-ural causes here, don't say anything in front of Luna."

"What?" Dev asked in puzzlement.

"I can't explain right now, but unless this is just a normal everyday plague or something, don't say anything about it to—"

Luna came back in with two pillows. With a last warning glance at

Dev, who still looked bewildered, Shiloh took them from her and began to attend to Grand-mère Journée. Since she was lying on her side, he loosened the ties of her apron in the back, then rolled her over and propped her up. With gentle fingers he removed the kerchief from her head, revealing sparse white hair done up in a tight bun. Shiloh withdrew several hairpins and loosened her hair. Then he pulled the apron loose and removed it, took off her shoes, and placed them neatly underneath the bed. Finally he covered her with the coverlet. All of this took him a scant minute.

Dev stepped back, took his stethoscope out of his bag, and waited impatiently until Shiloh had finished and then brought him a kitchen chair to set by the bed. Only a part of his mind noted how quiet Shiloh was, how deft and sure were his movements, how unobtrusive his attentions.

Settling into the chair, Dev listened for long moments to Grand-mère Journée's heartbeat, frowning. Then he took her pulse, staring down at his watch, and timed her respiration. Shiloh noticed that her breathing was almost imperceptible. Gently Dev felt of both of her hands, then her forehead, then ran both hands down her neck and under her chin.

"You found her?" he asked Luna.

"Yes. I came over to check on her this morning after I had breakfast. She didn't answer the door, so I just came in. As I said, I found her just as you saw her."

"When was the last time you saw her?"

"Last night. We had supper together, late . . . about nine o'clock. She was fine." Luna suddenly sounded defensive, but neither Shiloh nor Dev seemed to take special note of this, so imperceptibly she relaxed.

Dev grimaced. "Then we know nothing about any symptoms leading up to this condition. She's definitely in a coma, and has heart arrhythmia, and may be in vascular distress."

Luna bit her bottom lip. "I . . . I think she vomited." Dev and Shiloh looked up alertly. "But I . . . I . . ."

"You cleaned it up?" Dev growled.

Luna nodded. This doctor was quite formidable and stern, and she thought now that she had done something unforgivable.

"'S'okay, Luna," Shiloh said gently. "Just tell us what happened."

Luna dropped her head and spoke almost inaudibly. "It was in her water bucket, in the kitchen. I emptied it and just rinsed it out when I went to find Mr. Ford, and I left it outside. I was going to clean it good later. I'm sorry if I did something wrong."

Dev said nothing; he was staring down at Grand-mère Journée with narrowed eyes. With an impatient glance at him, Shiloh said again, "It's really okay, Luna."

"You were sick last, is that correct?" Dev asked abruptly, staring up at her with penetrating dark eyes.

"Yes, sir."

"What were your symptoms?"

Luna swallowed hard. "I got dizzy and fell."

Shiloh said quietly, "Dizziness, and she sprained her ankle, fell on the walkway, and cut her cheek. Abnormal bleeding from the cut. Nausea, slow heartbeat, depressed respiration, slight fever, unconsciousness. Two days of nausea, dizziness, weakness."

"Did she vomit?"

"Yes, for three days, irregularly."

Luna still stood with her head down, and Dev said in a slightly kinder tone, "Luna, is that about it? Any other symptoms you had that Shiloh didn't mention?"

"No, sir."

"Any recurrence of any of the symptoms?"

"No, sir. After three days I felt better, but weak. I got stronger every day, and now I'm back to normal. I feel just fine." She shrugged.

"What about the bleeding? Had you ever had this particular problem before this last incident? Excessive bleeding from cuts or injuries?"

"No, sir."

Dev stared out the window, his brows knit together, his mouth pressed into a firm line. Shiloh stood quietly, his arms crossed, and waited. He'd worked with Dr. Buchanan before, and he knew that though Dev could move fast enough in an emergency, he normally took his time and concentrated on diagnosis and treatment.

Finally Dev stood up, took his stethoscope from about his neck, and meticulously placed it back in his bag. He turned back around to frown at Luna forbiddingly. "I must ask you to leave now, Luna," he said firmly.

Luna's eyes widened. "What? But I think that, surely, I should stay! I'm her friend! A woman should stay with her!"

"No," Dev said coolly. "I'm a physician, and Mr. Irons is a trained medical assistant. You will do as I say, Luna. I don't want you here while I examine this lady; you are distracting me, because you have no sickroom experience."

Drawing herself up to her full height, her smooth features distorted with hate, Luna blustered, "Oh, yas, suh, Massa, suh!" Whirling on her heel she stamped out of the cabin.

Dev looked defiantly at Shiloh, but Shiloh merely stared back at him with heavy chagrin. "I should have known it," he growled. "Me, of all people! I should have known it!"

"You mean you know . . . you understand . . ." Dev stammered with surprise that Shiloh evidently knew what Dev suspected.

"Now I do," Shiloh grunted with self-disgust.

"Good, then I don't have to instruct you," Dev said with relief, bending to remove the coverlet from the tiny old woman. "Help me, and hurry. We need to check her—every inch—and then go to Cheney."

★ ★ ★ ★

It was half past midnight before Cheney, Dev, Shiloh, and Gowan Ford returned to Les Chattes Bleues. Victoria, Richard and Irene, and Tante Marye and Tante Elyse were in the library, but Tante Marye had instructed that Monroe leave out a cold supper in the dining room, so they decided to go and get a report from Cheney and Dev while they ate.

Wearily Cheney, Dev, and Shiloh sank into chairs alongside one another at the great dining room table, while Gowan Ford took his customary seat at the far end. Cheney rested her head on her hands; she had a grinding headache. Dev slumped back, his arms crossed, and stared into space. Gowan Ford threw himself tiredly into his chair, laid his head on the high back, and closed his good eye. Slowly, as if his arm were heavy, he reached up to adjust the black eye patch and leather strap that held it around his head.

Tante Marye and Irene hurried to the sideboard and prepared plates for them, a cold but appetizing supper of thin ham and roast beef slices, dried apricots and figs, almonds, fresh bread, cheese, and poppyseed cake. Tante Elyse chipped ice from a block, and Victoria poured and served them all tall glasses of sweet tea.

Shiloh took one look at Cheney, then got up and stood behind her chair. Bending over, he whispered something to her, and she leaned

240

back slightly and closed her eyes. In the gloom of the dining room, the few candles that were lit played strangely on Cheney's white face, upturned slightly as if in prayer. Shiloh began to rub her shoulders and the back of her neck, and lightly massaged her temples. The corners of her mouth turned up the tiniest bit. Her headache was already subsiding.

Across from them, Richard smiled. When Shiloh was staying at Duvall Court with them, Richard had awakened one morning in considerable pain. His wounded leg hurt, and the pain seemed to burn a river of fire around to the small of his back and up between his shoulders. He could barely walk, even with his cane. Shiloh had noticed at breakfast that Richard was in pain and had given him a long back massage that morning. Richard had immediately felt the pain subside, and by lunchtime he felt completely whole again, pain-free and energetic. *I know Cheney and Dev have healing hearts, and healing minds,* he thought, *and I suppose Shiloh does, too, even though he has no formal training . . . but some people, like Irene, just have healing in their hands. Shiloh certainly does . . . what a wonderful gift from God.*

Everyone got seated. Cheney, Dev, Shiloh, and Ford all began eating slowly, then hungrily, for none of them had eaten all day long. The others sipped tea and spoke of trivial things until the four were sated enough to converse comfortably.

Dev looked around at everyone. "Thank you for being so kind, to give us an opportunity to eat . . . it's been a terribly long day for all of us, but I know that you must be frantic to know what we . . . know."

"Which isn't much," Cheney sighed.

"Certainly not enough," Dev murmured. "At any rate, Becky Colton is gravely ill, but I think she will be all right. She's a healthy, strong little girl, and though it may take her a while to recover completely, I think she'll be fine in a couple of weeks."

"Oh, thank you, Lord," Tante Elyse said under her breath. "And Grand-mère Journée?"

Dev shook his head slightly, his face grave. "I don't know. She's very old and very weak. At this point I can't surmise what other systemic problems she may have, but I do know that her heart is not in satisfactory condition. She may not make it."

"But you must do something, Dev," Tante Marye demanded. Concern, and even fear, made her more exacting. Tears sprang to Tante Elyse's soft eyes.

241

With compassion deepening his voice, Dev replied, "I'm sorry, Tante Marye, Tante Elyse. I know that Grand-mère Journée has been here at Les Chattes Bleues since long before you were born. I know that she was one of the women here who took a hand in raising you. I know you care for her very deeply. But under the circumstances I can do nothing at all for her."

Doña Isabella had brought Grand-mère Journée—who was simply called Journée, or "Day," then, at sixteen—to Les Chattes Bleues when she married the vicomte. She had been the cook at Les Chattes Bleues for years and had retired comfortably to her cottage in 1850. Grand-mère Journée still made lovely, delicate lace and read constantly. Tante Elyse visited her every single day, and Tante Marye often invited her to tea in the afternoon, where they would compare laces and gossip.

A long silence reigned in the dining room. The shutters were opened, and the lacy drapes billowed occasionally. The candles on the sideboard blew out, but no one noticed. The candles in the six-branched candelabra at the center of the table flickered, and weird shadows played upon the faces of the nine people seated there. The black-and-white chessboard tiles could be seen close around the table, but the rest of the room was shrouded in darkness, and the dining table seemed to be a dim island on a surreal black sea. Far-off thunder rumbled, ominous bass notes that permeated the atmosphere in the great echoing room with mysterious threats.

"We can pray for her," Richard said quietly. "In fact, I feel that we should pray right now." He bowed his head, closed his eyes, and everyone did the same. Briefly but passionately, he prayed for Grand-mère Journée and Becky Colton: for healing, for peace, and for protection. When he said "Amen" everyone looked up and took a deep breath of release. Even the room seemed lighter.

"Now, Dev, tell us the rest of it, please," Irene said.

He looked at her gravely, then his eyes met Richard Duvall's. "It's all right, Dev," Richard said kindly. "All of us here stand together, and we have asked the Lord's protection on this house. No one here is ruled by fear."

Still Dev hesitated; he cast a quick glance at Shiloh, who looked grim but nodded. Dev muttered, "Poison. They've all been poisoned."

To his surprise, Richard nodded slightly; Irene looked sad but not at all shocked. Tante Marye paled and exchanged a worried glance with

Tante Elyse; Victoria sighed and looked down at her hands, clasped together tightly in her lap.

"Have you told anyone about this?" Ford growled. "Any of the servants or sharecroppers?"

"No—thanks to Irons," Dev replied heavily. "And considering the circumstances, it's a good thing we didn't say anything to anyone."

Cheney moodily fashioned crosshatching in the soft poppyseed cake with her fork. "We thought—Dev and Shiloh thought—that it might have been snakebite." A shocked gasp sounded round the table, but Cheney never looked up. She just kept methodically pressing the flat of her fork down in her cake. "But neither Grand-mère Journée nor Becky has any kind of bite."

"I still say it's just like snakebite," Shiloh said crossly, evidently returning to a previous argument with Cheney and Dev. "I oughta know! I've been snakebit twice, after all!"

Cheney rolled her eyes and said irritably, "Then you also know, Shiloh, that snakebite causes progressive local edema and rapid development of ecchymosis!"

"And what does that mean, Cheney!" Tante Marye demanded. "Speak English!"

"Excess fluid accumulation, extravasation of blood under the skin—" Dev muttered automatically.

"Be quiet, Dev," Tante Marye ordered. "You're just as bad as Cheney!"

"Swelling and bruising," Shiloh interposed.

Tante Marye's flashing blue eyes turned on him, then she smiled wickedly. "Thank you, Shiloh. I see that you are quite as proficient a doctor as you are excellent in gentlemanly bearing and conduct."

"That's me, all right," Shiloh agreed complacently.

"Great blue skies," Dev muttered ill-humoredly.

"Isn't it disgusting?" Cheney commented to him.

"Cheney, you are rude," Tante Marye announced. "Now, Dev, if you think you can be polite enough to speak in terms that can be readily understood by the persons you are addressing, you may continue."

"Yes, Tante Marye," Dev replied with at least a semblance of humility. "To return to Shiloh's hypothesis . . . er, theory, of snakebite. The symptoms are very similar—"

"The symptoms are identical," Shiloh interrupted. Cheney looked expectantly at Tante Marye for his comeuppance, but she merely nodded encouragement at Shiloh, so he continued, "And I thought maybe, with Luna especially, it might have been just a prick on her ankle, because it was swollen. Kind of unlikely that she would get that ill from just a pinprick amount of venom, but . . ." He shrugged expressively. "Snakebites can affect different people different ways. Just like insect bites. Some people have a more violent reaction than others."

"Interesting," Tante Marye muttered. "But of course Luna would have told us if she'd been bitten by a snake."

"Of course," Shiloh sighed. "And so would Becky, and so would all of the others. But no one has been."

"My point exactly," Cheney reminded everyone sourly.

"I still think it might be spiders," Dev remarked thoughtfully.

"Oh, horrors!" Victoria moaned, and Dev suddenly looked repentant. Victoria de Lancie, after all, was not as inured to discussions of medical horrors as the Duvalls, and Tante Marye and Tante Elyse had a certain earthy strength in spite of their blue blood; a legacy from their sturdy, no-nonsense Spanish mother. When Dev looked around the table, however, he did notice that even Irene looked distressed. Tante Marye swallowed convulsively, and Tante Elyse looked troubled.

"You did want to hear," he reminded everyone awkwardly.

"I've changed my mind," Tante Marye announced.

"No, you haven't," Tante Elyse mumbled.

"I beg your pardon?" Tante Marye asked, rounding on her with outrage.

"Just a moment, ladies," Richard said hastily. "I, for one, feel that we need to discuss this problem, because I heartily agree with Shiloh that no one should be told of Dev's and Cheney's—and Shiloh's—suspicions. I can see how it would cause a near panic if either snakebites or spider bites are the cause of these mysterious illnesses, but . . . in a way, it would be worse if the servants and the sharecroppers found out that those are the symptoms, but that Dev and Cheney can't find a cause."

Sternly he searched the shadowy faces around him and waited until comprehension dawned on Tante Marye, Tante Elyse, and Victoria.

"They'll think it's the *vaudou*," Victoria said in a low tone. "A curse . . . because of the *gris-gris*, perhaps."

"And I saw smoke on that accursed island yesterday," Shiloh grunted. "I told Mr. Duvall and Mr. Ford, but by the time we had finished breakfast, it was gone. So we decided not to go over there, or say anything to anyone. But if I saw it . . ." He shrugged.

"Then someone else may have seen it," Cheney murmured, "and the very next day two people fall ill. . . ."

"Yes." Richard nodded. "And I think that the only people who can deal with this without being afraid of *vaudou* curses are the people here in this room. But if anyone here is too uncomfortable, I want you to know that I believe that Cheney and Dev, and Shiloh, and Mr. Ford and I can, and will, take care of it ourselves."

Tante Marye sniffed. "It's my home, Richard," she argued, though she was in effect reversing her stance. "I certainly am going to stay and take part in the discussion and do whatever I can to help."

"That's . . . very . . . strong of you, Marye," Richard said, hiding his grin. "Now, Dev, Cheney, what about this? Spiders? Is that a possibility?"

Dev, Cheney, and Shiloh exchanged rather helpless looks. "Maybe," Dev answered cautiously, "but it is rather unlikely. The only poisonous spiders that I know of in this region are black widows and the brown recluse. Bites from a black widow cause symptoms very different from those of the people here at Les Chattes Bleues who have fallen ill. Bites from a brown recluse result in a delayed local reaction that consists of a painful, reddened area with overlying blister formation and a surrounding area of ischemia—"

Tante Marye's intense gaze automatically swiveled to Shiloh, and obediently he interpreted, "It makes a big sore."

"—and no one's evidenced any type of necrosis," Dev finished.

"No one's had any kind of a sore," Shiloh told Tante Marye.

"Then why, may I ask, do you think it might be a spider bite, Dev?" Tante Marye asked.

Dev didn't meet her eyes or look directly at anyone else at the table. He gazed out the far windows as eerily silent lightning flashed suddenly. "Because it does appear to be poison, and it does bear similarities to snakebite poisoning. Because it is possible that there is a spider, or another type of insect . . . or . . . or . . . perhaps a lizard with a poisonous bite that Cheney and I know nothing about. Because . . . because . . ."

"Because the alternative is unthinkable," Richard finished for him in a deep baritone.

No one said anything. Dev gave him a sharp look.

"But we must think it, Dev," Richard said wearily. "You have said that the people here are being poisoned. You have said that the poison is very like a snakebite, only there is no evidence of any kind of bites at all. Isn't this true?"

"Yes," Dev said reluctantly. "But there must be another answer. That just doesn't make any sense."

"Oh, but it does," Richard countered, dread deepening his voice. "If they haven't been bitten by snakes, then—" His mouth moved, but he seemed unable to finish.

"Aw, man!" Shiloh growled. "Then that means they've ingested it!"

"What?" Tante Marye and Tante Elyse almost shrieked. Irene and Victoria both moaned something inaudible, and Cheney drew in a sharp gulp of air as if she'd been holding her breath for a long time.

"They've swallowed it," Shiloh said brutally. "They've swallowed snake venom."

A sudden gust of wind tore at the light window drapes and blew out the candles, and the room was darkened to pitch. Victoria screamed. Cheney started but managed to keep from crying out. Shiloh got to his feet so quickly he knocked over his chair and cursed under his breath. Irene drew in a startled breath, but Richard slipped his hand around her shoulders and she immediately relaxed. Gowan Ford got to his feet and began making his way in the general direction of the sideboard.

Dev calmly got up and went to Victoria, knelt by her chair, and took one of her hands. It was icy cold. He spoke in quiet, soothing tones, and she clung to him in the darkness as if he were life and breath.

Tante Marye started and let out an odd yelp. Tante Elyse rose calmly and patted her shoulder as she went by on her way to the sideboard. "Funny we didn't notice that the candles on the sideboard had gone out," she remarked to Shiloh as they literally felt their way along.

Shiloh took her arm. "I'll hold on to you if you don't mind," he said.

"Are you scared, Shiloh?" she asked. He could hear the teasing note in her voice.

"Yes, ma'am," he answered. "Scared I'll stomp you with my big ol' feet in this ink."

"Please don't," she begged. With a thump she ran into something. "I found the sideboard," she told Shiloh unnecessarily.

"Yes, ma'am. I assume there's some matches here somewhere?"

"Left-hand cabinet, bottom shelf." Shiloh bent down on one knee, opened the cabinet door, and cautiously started feeling around. Tante Elyse started patting the top of the sideboard and finally found the six-branched candelabra.

"Here—" a deep voice thundered behind her.

"Yaaah!" she screamed, whirled, and blindly struck out with the candelabra.

Every woman in the room started screaming.

Shiloh jumped to his feet and groped in front of him, trying to feel—since he couldn't see—what was going on. Something barely slapped against his hand, and then something heavy thudded down right across his forearm—twice. "Ow! Ouch!" Blinking and flailing against empty air, he backpedaled quickly to the left; a cacophony of shrieks and whumps and thumps and deep groans and sounds of "Hey—ow! Yow! Oh—ow!" sounded close to Shiloh's right.

A match flared in the darkness. Abruptly the women stopped screaming.

Gowan Ford, a foot away from Shiloh, glowering, held the lit match. Close by Ford, Tante Elyse stared up at him, holding the candelabra, her eyes huge dark pools.

"Elyse, d'ya think I might light one of those candles?" Gowan asked calmly. "That is, if you're through beating me with it."

"Yes, I'm through," Tante Elyse said hastily, shoving the heavy silver candelabra toward him.

"Sure am glad of that," Ford said dryly. He lit the candles and immediately the room turned from a fearfully dark cave into a dining room again.

Suddenly Shiloh burst into laughter. "You sure got me, Tante Elyse! Did you get Mr. Ford, too?"

"Well, yes, I did," Tante Elyse admitted, "but only on the right side, I think. Right, Gowan?"

"Yep. If I'd had an arm you woulda broke it," he replied with disgust.

"But you don't," she retorted with satisfaction, as if that closed the argument.

Tante Marye jumped to her feet and sailed over to the sideboard. "Elyse! This time you have gone too far! Poor, poor Shiloh!"

"Poor Shiloh?" Gowan repeated sarcastically. "I'm the one she almost beat to death!"

"You scared me," Elyse said complacently.

"I noticed."

"But Shiloh didn't!" Tante Marye said stoutly, reaching Shiloh and taking his arm to pat it comfortingly.

"So she had a reason to beat me, but not Shiloh?" Gowan asked. But as it was a rhetorical question, no one bothered to answer.

Tante Marye "helped" Shiloh back to the table, cooing and patting him, while Elyse sailed triumphantly to her seat and Gowan Ford stumped back to his. The others were still laughing, but Dev, standing close to Victoria's chair, seemed frozen. When the room had gone dark, Victoria had jumped to her feet and screamed. Dev, without thinking, had jumped up, thrown his arms around her, and pulled her close. Her scream had been immediately silenced, and she clung to him. Dev closed his eyes and—for only a moment—imagined that he didn't have to let her go. Then the light had shone again, and he dropped his arms and stepped away from her as if she burned him. Now he couldn't tear his gaze away from her, though she was seated and half-turned away from him, and seemed to have forgotten the moment of intense closeness between them.

With a start he turned on his heel and stalked back to his chair. No one had taken note of him, for which he felt immense relief. Studiously he avoided glancing in Victoria's direction, though her cool blue eyes rested on him often.

"You're all right? Quite certain?" Tante Marye asked Shiloh anxiously as he handed her back into her chair.

"I'm fine, really, Tante Marye," Shiloh said as he took his seat. "She just winged me, is all."

"I'm fine, too, in case anyone wants to know," Gowan Ford put in sarcastically.

"You mean after that savage attack, no one needs immediate medical attention?" Cheney giggled, winking at Tante Elyse, who looked as innocent as a lamb.

"I think you were wonderful, Mrs. Buckingham," Victoria commented. "If I'm ever in any danger I shall call you to my aid."

"If you think she's good with a candelabra, you ought to see her with a broomstick," Gowan Ford remarked.

"Gowan! You know that was all your fault too!" Tante Elyse cried.

"Elyse, it was not my fault that a weasel got into the hen house," Gowan asserted.

"But it was your fault that your head got in the weasel's pathway," Elyse countered.

"It was the broomstick's pathway that bothered me," Ford grunted.

"Oh, you big baby, it was only two small lumps," Elyse said wrathfully, "and it was certainly your own fault."

"Oh yes," Ford sighed. "I've got to learn to quit ramming my head into your broomstick. And smashing my ribs into your candelabra."

"Yes, you really must," Elyse sniffed.

After the laughter died down, Dev said quietly, "Well, I hate to be a damper, but I must remind you all of something. I still haven't heard about all the incidents here at Les Chattes Bleues. All I know about is the sickness. Remember?"

"Oh yes. Richard was telling you when Gowan came in at breakfast," Tante Marye said thoughtfully. "Was that breakfast just this morning? It seems so long ago. . . ."

Murmurs of assent sounded throughout the room. But even though it was late, and everyone was so tired, no one seemed ready to leave. There was a pleasant intimacy between these people on this night, and with each passing moment they could feel it growing stronger and more secure. All of them were reluctant to break their special feeling of closeness.

As if someone had spoken the thoughts out loud, Tante Marye nodded firmly. "Proceed, Richard. Tell Dev about everything."

Richard told Dev of the sickened indigo plants, and of the night that the *vaudou* had beat the drums and danced on the island. Dev listened closely, only asking a few brief questions as Richard related the events. He didn't describe what had happened to Shiloh, but he did say that Shiloh had gone with him and Gowan Ford to the island.

Once Dev glanced at Shiloh with understanding and sympathy, but quickly he returned his full attention to Richard Duvall.

Buchanan knows, Shiloh thought with sudden certainty. *He may not know the details, but he knows I got into trouble that night. That's strange . . . Mr. Duvall hardly even mentioned me. Never thought of Buchanan as being that sharp. . . .*

Devlin Buchanan was certainly extremely intelligent, but because of his natural reticence and a rather stiff dignity, he didn't appear to have much empathy. But Shiloh admitted to himself that he truly didn't know Buchanan very well. He realized Richard was finishing his story and returned his attention to the conversation.

" . . . but we still have no idea why anyone would deliberately be trying to scare Marye and Elyse," Richard was saying. "Perhaps it is like Mr. Ford says, that truly the *vaudou* believe all that . . . that . . ."

"Offal," Tante Elyse offered sweetly.

Richard grinned. "—offal they are saying."

"In that case we have a genuine problem," Dev said thoughtfully. "If it truly is their aim to make everyone leave Les Chattes Bleues so that the . . . uh . . . things, spirits, can take over . . . then we have no bargaining chip. Nothing to give them, to satisfy them—"

"I would not give them a drop of water if they were on fire," Tante Marye bristled. "Horrid people."

"I don't mean you should accede to their wishes, Tante Marye," Dev explained a trifle impatiently. "You didn't let me finish. I merely meant that if they were after money, for example, that could be dealt with, and we could make an end of it. But this insistence that everyone leave Les Chattes Bleues . . . it makes no sense, really."

Everyone looked at everyone else, baffled. Finally Shiloh rasped, "Maybe they want to look for the pirate treasure. That would be simple."

Tante Marye turned on him indignantly. "I beg your pardon? *Pirate treasure?*"

"Uh-oh," Shiloh mumbled, realizing that perhaps Tante Marye and Tante Elyse didn't know of the silly rumors of pirate treasure on Les Chattes Bleues' land; also that perhaps they might not care to know that people gossiped about their father, the illustrious Vicomte de Cheyne, being in cahoots with bloodthirsty pirates. Indeed, both of them were staring at him; Tante Marye sternly and Tante Elyse blankly. "Uh-oh," Shiloh again mumbled helplessly.

"Oh, Shiloh, don't worry, it's quite all right," Irene said calmly. "It's just those silly rumors about the treasure here at Les Chattes Bleues. They've been circulating forever, it seems."

Tante Marye's icy blue gaze and Tante Elyse's deer-brown eyes swiveled to Irene, who smiled. "Perhaps you haven't heard, dear aunts. But it is quite common, you know, for such rumors to get started about any house. Particularly one built so long ago, and particularly one so fine."

"That's right," Shiloh said with relief.

"Ridiculous gossip," Richard muttered.

"Yep," Ford sturdily agreed.

"Absurdities," Cheney pronounced.

"Childish games," Victoria sniffed.

To their utter astonishment, Dev was staring, hard-eyed with accusation, at Tante Marye and Tante Elyse. "Tante Marye?" he growled in a tone of warning. "Tante Elyse?"

"What?" Richard asked anxiously.

Tante Marye suddenly looked confused, but Tante Elyse began to look very peculiar—guilty, she looked—and dropped her head as if she were a small girl in trouble in the schoolroom, casting timid glances up at Dev.

"Uh-oh," she said in a tiny little voice.

"Tante Elyse! Tante Marye! You didn't!" Dev thundered.

Bewildered, everyone looked at one another, then back at Dev. He ignored everyone else, his burning gaze fixed on Tante Marye and Tante Elyse.

"What?" Richard demanded. "What are they talking about, Irene?"

"I don't know," Irene whispered.

"You don't?" Richard was dumbfounded.

"*À la gare!*" Ford blustered, his single blue eye opened wide with sudden comprehension.

Shiloh watched Ford, then Dev, then Tante Marye and Tante Elyse; his expression changed from speculation to one of complete, almost comical amazement. "There is?" he gulped almost inaudibly.

"Huh?" Cheney mumbled as she stared at him, and then she glanced at Victoria, who looked almost as stupidly lost as she.

"Well? Did you?" Dev roared. Tante Elyse flinched a little, and even Tante Marye blinked several times.

"What!" Richard shouted. "Did they do what!"

Dev never looked around. "Tell someone," he finally answered through clenched teeth. "Tell someone about the gold."

20

GOLDEN NIGHT, DARKENED DAWN

Tante Marye stared at Dev defiantly. Tante Elyse peeked at him timidly. Dev—and everyone else in the room—just stared.

Straightening her shoulders, Tante Marye made a haughty gesture with one thin, blue-veined hand. "I told no one, Dev," she said primly. "Elyse must have told."

"I didn't! Never!" Elyse declared.

"Wait," Richard said helplessly. "Wait. Do you two mean to tell me that there actually is gold here? At Les Chattes Bleues?" He looked around in bewilderment, as if piles of gold might have been just behind him all the time.

Tante Marye continued to look prim, and Tante Elyse said in a small voice, "Dev told us never to tell anyone."

"Tante Elyse!" Dev boomed. "You can tell now! We're talking about it!"

"Well, you're the one who started talking about it," she said airily. "So you tell, Dev."

As if they were gunsights, every eye in the room trained on Dev. With a long exasperated breath he rasped, "Oh, there's gold here, all right. Lots of it. Big, heavy gold bars."

Long, pregnant moments passed. Richard blinked continually. Irene's mouth was slightly open, and her eyebrows winged far upward. Gowan Ford's head thumped back on his chair as he muttered blackly, "Oh boy, oh boy, oh boy . . ." Cheney's jaw positively dropped. Shiloh bit his lip. Victoria looked coolly amused.

Tante Elyse looked around, first with chagrin, and then she began to titter nervously, though she tried hard to keep it from escaping. Then Irene began to giggle, ever so lightly, and pressed her hand against her lips. Soon Richard chuckled, and Shiloh laughed out loud. Then Cheney and Victoria—rather helplessly—joined them. Even

Gowan Ford grinned his gargoyle's grin and shook his head in amazement, over and over again.

"And just what," Tante Marye demanded haughtily, "is so very amusing, may I ask?" But everyone only laughed harder; now even Dev was chuckling.

Finally, when everyone had recovered—Richard was wiping his eyes—Ford gasped, "So there is pirate treasure at Les Chattes Bleues! Marye, I never would have thought it of you!" The vision of Tante Marye dressed up like a pirate—complete with scarlet kerchief knotted above one ear, a giant golden earring, an eye patch, and a parrot on her shoulder—occurred to everyone, and gales of laughter rang out eerily in the great room.

"But what about me?" Tante Elyse prompted Ford.

"Oh yes, Elyse," he stammered, "I can see you perfectly!"

"I hesitate to point it out, Gowan," she said with mock politeness, "but you are the only one in this room who looks like a pirate! Except you, of course, are missing an arm instead of a leg—I believe that is customary, is it not? The stick leg?"

"P-p-peg—" Cheney tried to say between giggles.

"Peg leg," Shiloh managed.

"Oh?" Tante Elyse said with such an intent look that Cheney simply couldn't bear to look at her anymore. "Peg leg," she repeated thoughtfully. "Peg leg . . ."

"Stop it," Cheney said helplessly.

"Yes, do," Tante Marye ordered ominously. "All of you stop it this instant."

Although this proved to be impossible, the giggles and chuckles finally died down and Tante Marye turned back to Dev, whose eyes still flashed with dark amusement. "I would hardly have believed you to indulge in such foolishness, Dev."

"Yeah, Dev," Shiloh chimed in.

"Yeah, Dev," Cheney echoed mischievously. "Behave yourself. After all, you are the one who gave it away."

"Spilt the beans," Shiloh suggested.

"Gave up the goods," Ford growled.

"Ratted on—" Shiloh began.

"Stop it," Dev ordered. "Stop it, and I'll tell the rest."

Immediately everyone fell silent.

"I visited here in 1862," Dev began. "Remember that summer? I was asked to come down to the Touro Infirmary and advise them on how to arrange the hospital so as to separate civilian care from the enforced Federal care."

"I remember," Cheney said softly.

Dev shrugged. "Tante Marye and Tante Elyse were having severe financial problems."

Richard and Irene stared accusingly at the two ladies, who stared back at them defiantly. "You didn't tell us," Richard muttered.

"We didn't have to. Because we didn't have a problem," Elyse scoffed.

"We had the gold," Marye asserted with satisfaction.

"That's right," Dev grunted. "There they were. They had no cash, and though they had plenty of indigo to sell—and plenty of markets available—Tante Elyse just couldn't get it shipped. The occupation, you know, and shipping was in a terrible mess."

"Our regular shippers either weren't here, or wouldn't come to New Orleans after the occupation," Tante Elyse complained. "And the others—" She made a terrible face. "The docks, and every ship in the port, of course, were completely controlled by Union soldiers. They wouldn't listen to me. They just swatted me aside like a little bluefly or something."

"I'm sorry, Marye," Gowan Ford said bitterly. "I'm so sorry, Elyse. I should have been here."

"You probably would have been jailed as a Confederate traitor," Elyse retorted.

"I won't hear of this, Gowan," Marye said sternly. "You should *not* have been here. You did exactly what you had to do, which was go to war for your home and your country. And besides, we had the gold."

"Yes, let's talk some more about this gold," Shiloh said, his eyes twinkling like frosty blue diamonds. "This is really interesting."

Dev shrugged. "They asked me if I could get them some money for a gold bar. So I did."

"Gold bars are very cumbersome," Tante Elyse sighed.

"Good heavens!" Cheney exclaimed. "Tante Elyse, you . . . you . . . make it sound like an unwanted pet or something!"

"But I have no pets that are not wanted," Elyse argued. "Except by Marye."

"Elyse, stop it," Marye insisted. "These people don't want to hear about your absurd menagerie. We were telling them about the gold."

She addressed the table again. "But what Elyse said is true. I mean, it's not as if you can take it to market and ask, 'Here, do you have change for a gold bar?'"

Everyone laughed heartily again, while Tante Marye looked pleasantly surprised at their amusement.

"That's true," Dev agreed. "They're both right. It's a lot of trouble to actually spend a gold bar."

"Then what did you do with it?" Cheney demanded.

"I took it to the United States Mint right up there on Esplanade," Dev replied. "I asked them if they would buy it from me for the current price of gold per ounce. It caused a stir, I must say—it's funny that they seemed to view their little pieces of paper as more . . . uh . . . valid than that gold bar I was frantically waving around."

Irene smiled at this ridiculous exaggeration; Dev never waved his arms or made any extravagant gestures. "But I assume they did finally buy it."

"Yes, they did." Dev looked around, baiting everyone.

"Well?" Richard finally blustered. "You might as well tell us! You have to tell us! How much?"

"Six thousand dollars," he murmured in a low tone.

A gasp went around the table; even Shiloh drew his breath in sharply. "And you . . . you . . . have several of these lying around?" he asked Tante Marye wide-eyed.

"We don't know how many," she said, frowning. "As Elyse said, they are quite cumbersome. We don't exactly take them out and play with them."

This so confounded everyone that no one said anything for a while. Finally Gowan Ford rasped, "But where? Where in the world are these gold bars? I've been over every inch of this house—and this plantation—and I can't think of a single place where 'several cumbersome gold bars' might be hidden."

"They're right here, Gowan," Tante Elyse smiled. "Here, in the dining room. Underneath one of the tiles."

Everyone looked at the floor.

Tante Marye continued, "It's quite a lot of trouble to get to them, and I dislike having my dining room torn to bits."

"*Malédiction!* Marye, it's only one tile," Elyse fumed.

"But I dislike—"

"We know," Elyse interrupted, then addressed the table in a woeful voice, "which explains perfectly why we don't take them out and play with them very often."

"But wait—the house is raised six feet," Richard muttered. "You mean they're sitting on the ground underneath the flooring?"

"No, Father was actually very sly when he thought of this," Elyse said, beaming. "One of the floor joists is hollowed. It has a nine-inch-by-nine-inch opening on the top, and one of these tiles is directly over it. The tile is sealed with black wax, you see, and the seams are not at all noticeable."

"Yes, they are," Tante Marye said stubbornly.

"No, they're not," Elyse said under her breath.

"Anyway, you get the picture, Colonel Duvall," Dev said hastily. "You lift one of these tiles, and there is a nine-inch opening underneath, directly into the hollow floor joist, which is a ten-by-ten. But the gold bars are laid horizontally in the joist—not stacked at the opening—and though I felt more inside the joist, I have no idea how many are pushed back in there."

"Neither do we," Tante Elyse said happily. "Isn't that just the cleverest thing you ever heard?"

"Not exactly," Gowan Ford growled. "The vicomte didn't tell you?"

Tante Elyse shook her head. "No, he just told us where it was and warned us only to use it if we got into trouble."

"That's right," Marye agreed for once. "He told us his father just shipped it to him in Cap Français—with a very short note for him to keep it until such time as it could be retrieved—in April of 1792." She frowned heavily. "That was the year the Reign of Terror began, you see. And Grandfather was guillotined that summer."

Dev said thoughtfully, "The French Republic was seizing all the nobles' lands—"

"And their heads," Tante Elyse added with gusto.

"Elyse!" Marye exclaimed.

"—that summer, and I suppose the vicomte thought he might send some of his most valuable personal property out of the country and retrieve it after the Reign of Terror died down," Dev finished thinking out loud, ignoring the great-aunts' interruptions. His dark eyes focused again, and a small smile played on his wide, sensitive mouth. "It was . . . a striking sight," he admitted. "I'd never seen a gold bar before. And the de Cheyne crest was stamped on it, in exquisite detail."

Cheney's eyes sparkled. "Let's get one," she clamored. "I want to see!"

"All right," Elyse smiled, childlike. "Let's!"

"No!" A chorus of both male and female voices resounded in the room.

"You're not digging up my dining room!" Tante Marye blustered.

"But Cheney wants to see it," Elyse argued.

"No, she doesn't," Richard countered. "We can't, can we, Irene?"

Irene merely raised her eyebrows, and to Cheney's everlasting astonishment, said, "I want to see it, too, Richard."

"Huh? But . . . but . . ." Richard gave up.

Irene smiled. "Tante Elyse, are you certain that the gold is still there? Have you checked it?"

"No, not since that time—when did you say it was, Dev? 1862?" Tante Elyse frowned with concentration.

"Do you mean to tell me that you have gold bars, here, right in this room, and you don't even look at them?" Shiloh asked in amazement. "For years? And years?"

"Well, they do have a certain beauty, I suppose," Tante Elyse said thoughtfully. "But, after all, if you've seen one gold bar—"

"—you've seen them all," Shiloh finished for her, his shoulders shaking with laughter. "My view exactly."

"Exactly," Tante Elyse echoed with satisfaction.

"This has to be the most . . . absurd, most . . . unreal conversation I've ever had the misfortune to be a party to," Gowan Ford mumbled.

"No, Gowan, remember the conversation we had about the New Zealand storks?" Tante Elyse corrected him, accompanied by a fresh wave of laughter around the table.

Ford laid his arm down on the table and rested his head on it. "I'm tired . . . so tired . . ." came his muffled tone.

"But you said that that was the most absurd conversation you've ever—" Tante Elyse insisted.

"Tante Elyse, please," Irene gently prompted her. "I think we're all tired. In fact, I think we're all so tired that we're getting a little delirious."

"And look," Richard said softly. "Isn't it getting just a bit lighter outside?"

Everyone stared, astounded, out the windows. Though it was certainly not light outside, neither was it the unrelenting blackness of the night. It was, perhaps, a shade of charcoal-gray.

"Good heavens," Tante Marye said, standing slowly, grimacing. "I'm going to bed. Right now. I haven't stayed up all night since—"

"The Dark Ages," Tante Elyse said promptly, bouncing to her feet. "I'm tired too. Could we get the gold later?"

"Yes . . . yes . . . later," Richard said hastily. "Everyone must get some rest. I can't believe we've kept Cheney and Dev and Shiloh and Mr. Ford up all night!"

Cheney yawned prodigiously. "But we really should go check on Grand-mère Journée and Becky. . . ."

"No, Cheney," Dev said stubbornly. "They are fine, I'm certain. Nia is sitting with the Coltons, and Luna is with Grand-mère Journée," he told everyone. "They would have come for us if there was any substantial change in anyone's condition."

"We could leave a note for Monroe to send someone to relieve Nia and Luna until noon," Cheney agreed wearily. "I think all of us ought to rest at least that long."

"Agreed," Dev voted.

"Sounds good to me," Shiloh said, stretching so high he almost touched the ceiling with his fingertips. "Boy-o, I didn't realize how tired I was!"

"I'll stop by Monroe's on my way," Ford asserted. "He won't mind if I just wake him up an hour or so early."

With that, the party—suddenly stunned and stupefied with weariness—broke up. Cheney and Victoria ascended the staircase, yawning and blinking, while Irene practically hung from Richard's arms. Tante Elyse still moved energetically, but she did help Tante Marye. Shiloh and Dev made their way to the *garçonnieres*; Dev's was the one right next to Shiloh's.

"I still haven't worked it all out yet," Shiloh mused as they walked through the dim gray-shaded garden. "How these people are getting poisoned . . . the gold . . . what it all has to do with the *vaudou* . . . if it does at all."

Dev shrugged. "I don't know either, Irons. In my opinion, none of us is thinking too clearly right now. Human powers of reasoning and analysis are at their lowest ebb after loss of an entire night's sleep."

Shiloh wearily grinned. "You said it, Dr. Buchanan."

"Yes, well, good night, or good morning, rather." Dev hurried into his *garçonniere* and shut the door firmly.

"G'night," Shiloh said sarcastically to empty air and then went into his own retreat.

★ ★ ★ ★

Half an hour later, as the horizon was beginning to lighten from charcoal-gray to dove-gray, a door on the second-floor gallery of Les Chattes Bleues opened quietly, throwing an amber rectangle of light out into the grayness. A small, slender figure slipped out onto the gallery and hurried down the stairs and then down the great oak bower toward the lagoon. She glided silently as a wraith, her white clothing glimmering softly in the shadowy hour between darkness and the dawn.

As fleet as a doe, as light as the wind, she hurried down the long walkway to the gazebo at the lagoon landing. It was still black inside, though it was an open gazebo. Dawn had not yet touched the shadows inside with its first tentative touch. Across the lagoon the rise loomed up, a black hump crowned with mysterious flat black stencils of trees. But the woman didn't hesitate; indeed, she hurried her light footsteps even more, as a bird flies straight and true to shelter in a storm, passed through the gazebo, and almost ran to the pier. She stopped at the edge, stared down into the murk of the sleeping waters, and sighed deeply.

"Victoria!" a deep voice whispered hoarsely.

Victoria started, then strained to look across at the shadowy figure that emerged from the trees on the bank. "Dev? *Dev?*" she cried, first with relief, and then with something akin to anger.

Devlin Buchanan strode forward and stopped five feet away from her as if he'd hit an invisible wall. His expression, too, was stormy. "What are you doing?" he growled. "Why did you come down here all by yourself?"

"I might ask the same of you," Victoria replied spiritedly.

"No, you may not," Dev retorted angrily, taking a half-step toward her and then hastily back-stepping away. "You shouldn't be down here by yourself. You shouldn't be wandering around anywhere on the grounds at night! Riff and Raff would tear you up!"

"Perhaps," Victoria countered angrily, "if they weren't in Mrs. Buckingham's room!"

Dev opened his mouth for an angry retort, then said lamely, "Oh, I didn't know that."

"Obviously not."

Dev gave her a keen look. "But still, you shouldn't be out here by yourself, Victoria. It's not . . . wise, considering everything that's been happening."

"But I'm not by myself," Victoria said in an odd tone. "You're here with me."

"No, I'm not," he replied in confusion, taking another backward step. "That is, I'm . . . I'm not . . . I was just leaving."

Victoria turned to him. "Would you please stay with me for a few moments?" she asked, her tone cool, her face expressionless.

"What?" Dev exclaimed, then turned away, shut his eyes tightly for a few moments, and took a deep breath. When he turned back to her he had regained his composure. "I suppose," he answered with remote cordiality. "I will stay for a few moments."

"Thank you, Dev," she said softly and turned to stare at the island across the lagoon.

He studied her profile and found her to be lovely. With her smooth, pale complexion, her straight small nose, her classical features, her long slender neck, Victoria Elizabeth Steen de Lancie was the loveliest woman he had ever seen. The thought made his voice harsh again.

"Why aren't you resting?" he demanded. "You must be exhausted."

"Again, I might ask the same question of you, Dev," she said dreamily, then turned to him. "But I will answer you, as you have been so kind to consent to stay with me." She hesitated, searching his face intently, and then said, her voice dropping to a tone of warm intimacy, "I came out here because I couldn't sleep. Not only was I unable to sleep—I couldn't sit still at all."

"Oh?" Dev responded in a deliberately bored tone. "I'm sorry to hear it."

"Yes," she said, her voice so soft that it was almost like a sigh of the wind. "And I couldn't sleep, or rest . . . because of you."

Dev's head jerked around to face her, and he looked astounded.

"You, Dev," she repeated. "I couldn't—and can't—and won't stop thinking about you." She took a small step closer, her passionate gaze hypnotizing him. "And I think that you are here for the same reason . . . that you can't stop thinking of me."

"I have to!" he groaned, clenching his fists. "I left New York last year because of you! To get away from you and Cheney! To think, to straighten out my mind!"

"But, Dev, you kept thinking of me, did you not?" Victoria pleaded, stepping even closer to him. "Dev, please—"

"No," he muttered. "We—I—can't. We can't." In his confusion, he tried to walk by her, away from her. But Victoria had already broken the unspoken covenant of silence between them, and she was not going to let it be in vain. Deliberately she stepped directly in front of him.

He brushed hard against her, then quickly took her by the arms to steady her . . . but somehow it turned into a caress, and Dev felt as if slow, tightening bands of strength bound him and this woman together. She moved to stand encircled in his arms, close, as closely as she could, and lifted her face.

With a hoarse sound of surrender, Dev lowered his head and hungrily kissed her. Victoria's small white hands slid up to his neck, and then the back of his neck, as she urged him closer.

"Well, how about this?"

Footsteps sounded on the wooden dock; long strides, hard steps, heavy boots. Shiloh Irons stopped very close to the entwined couple. His face was hard as steel, and his hands were jammed savagely into his pockets. Both Dev and Victoria could clearly see the tense, straining muscles and tendons in his powerful forearms. "Ain't this a pretty picture!"

Dev and Victoria stumbled apart. Victoria pressed both hands to her mouth, as if she could hide the kiss that Shiloh had already seen. Dev grimaced, then drew himself up to his full height. But he felt small anyway—he was a full four inches shorter than Shiloh—and he realized that it wasn't simply a difference in size that made him feel bitterly outmanned.

"Irons, wait," he rasped. "I'll . . . I'll make explanations to you if I can . . . but . . . ." Helplessly he looked at Victoria. "Go," he said roughly. "Don't say anything. Just go."

Hot tears scalded Victoria's eyes, and one trickled down her cheek. She looked from Dev's harsh features to Shiloh's furious expression and silently pleaded with him. . . . But Shiloh merely looked at her with curious distaste, as if she were a struggling insect he had pinned underneath the edge of his boot. With a strangled cry, Victoria turned and stumbled away.

Shiloh watched her go, then turned back to Dev and crossed his arms. Devlin Buchanan had a feeling that Shiloh did that in order to keep from breaking his jaw right then and there. Dev tried to think of something to say, but his mind whirled, his throat burned, and his eyes stung. He could say nothing.

"You know," Shiloh said in a deceptively calm voice, "I don't even think I'm going to ask you any questions."

"But, Irons, I have to—"

"No!" Shiloh thundered, and in one stride stepped so close to Buchanan that Dev unintentionally leaned backward from the threat looming so close to him. "I—don't—want—to—hear—it." Shiloh's words were so fraught with anger that Dev felt as if he were seared. Making a tremendous effort, Dev straightened and looked up into Shiloh's eyes. Tentative beginnings of the dawn glimmered, and Shiloh's blue eyes looked a violent purple in the uncertain light. Dev knew that he'd never faced such heated anger.

Shiloh drew in a deep breath and deliberately relaxed his body, though he still stood close, a towering threat. "I just have one thing to say to you, Buchanan," he breathed quietly, the words still edged with menace. "And I'm just going to say this once, so you listen real good."

Dev narrowed his eyes, crossed his arms, and nodded curtly. "I'm listening."

"She—Doc—Cheney—" Shiloh said throatily, almost choked, and began again. "Cheney Duvall loves you, and she believes you care for her. You asked her to marry you, Buchanan . . . and . . . and she's counting on that."

"I know, Irons—"

"Shut up!" Shiloh said in a harsh croak. "I'm not through!"

"All right, Irons," Dev said placatingly.

Again Shiloh stepped up to him and very slowly and deliberately placed his hand on Dev's shoulder. Shiloh's hand was hot and seemed to weigh a ton, and it took every ounce of Dev's strength not to flinch. Shiloh bent down so his face was only inches from Dev's. "You—aren't—going—to hurt—Cheney Duvall. Or I will hurt you."

Dev looked straight in his eyes and managed to keep his voice still and calm. "Yes, Irons, I understand."

"I don't think you do, Buchanan," Shiloh said quietly, then ever so slowly his grip on Dev's shoulder started tightening. After only a few seconds the grip agonized Dev as Shiloh's powerful fingers dug a burning hole in the back of his shoulder, and his thumb pressed so hard against Dev's collarbone that he truly thought Shiloh might break it.

Still, his gaze did not waver from Shiloh's, though his lips tightened with pain.

Shiloh grinned, and it was not a pretty sight. "You see, Dr. Buchanan, I'm the one who's going to make sure that you don't hurt Cheney. So if I were you, I'd keep away from Mrs. de Lancie."

Dev said nothing; truth to tell, he was trying with all his might to keep from crying out from the torturous pain in his shoulder. He felt as if Shiloh's hand were a fiery clamp on his bare skin.

Suddenly Shiloh released him, turned on his heel, and walked with slow deliberation back across the dock. He stopped, turned, and spoke again as if he'd simply forgotten to say good-bye: "Don't forget, Buchanan. I'm going to be watching you. And I don't miss much."

He turned and quickly disappeared up into the still-shadowed peace of the oak bower.

Dev stared after him blankly for a long time.

21

The Ways of Women and Men

Victoria Elizabeth Steen de Lancie was still sobbing—deeply, wrenchingly, uncontrollably—when the knock came on the door. The discreet sound barely touched her tortured mind.

"*Madame!* Oh, *madame*, please, please let me in!" came Zhou-Zhou's urgent plea.

Victoria eventually registered that Zhou-Zhou was at the door, and could hear her crying, and was distraught, and would never go away and leave her alone. Slowly she rose from the bed and staggered to the door. Before she opened it, she straightened her shoulders, rubbed her face roughly with a towel, and ran a shaking hand down her skirt in a futile attempt to straighten it. Then, assuming an impassive expression, she opened the door.

Zhou-Zhou immediately threw her arms around Victoria and cried, "Oh, *madame, madame*, whatever is wrong? What has happened?"

"Nothing, you silly girl," Victoria said brusquely, disentangling Zhou-Zhou's arms from around her neck. "Stop it, Zhou-Zhou, I can hardly breathe."

Obediently Zhou-Zhou stepped back and gave Victoria a knowing look. Victoria's eyes were almost swollen shut, and her exquisite ice-sculpture face was marred by ugly red splotches. Her nose was swollen and running prodigiously, and Zhou-Zhou was certain that Victoria was trembling. "I know something is wrong, *Madame* de Lancie," she pleaded. "Please let me help you."

Victoria hurried to the bed and sat down, rubbing her forehead with one shaking hand. "Yes, I will let you help me, Zhou-Zhou. You may help me by doing your job. We are leaving today, so you must get me packed. And hurry. I'm tired of dawdling around this place, and I want to catch the noon steamer at Lefebvre Landing. Go and find Monroe and tell him to have a carriage ready to convey us to the landing at ten o'clock."

"But . . . but . . . *madame*," Zhou-Zhou pleaded, "you aren't well! Please, what is wrong? You look . . . you seem . . ."

"I . . . I . . . have a terrible headache," Victoria admitted in a faint voice, with none of the bluster of the speech before. "But . . . it . . . doesn't matter, Zhou-Zhou. We have to leave. Now. This morning."

"All right, *madame*," Zhou-Zhou said soothingly, as if to a small, frightened child. "I will take care of everything, don't worry. Here, just let me loosen this. . . . Why don't you change into your bedclothes and rest for a while?"

"Yes . . . yes . . ." Victoria said almost inaudibly. "Oh, Zhou-Zhou . . . it's bad . . . this pain, it's getting bad."

Zhou-Zhou was removing Victoria's shoes and noticed that they were covered with mud, as was the hem of her dress—the same fine green silk dress she had worn to dinner the previous night. Zhou-Zhou looked up at her curiously and saw that Victoria's face had gone paper-white, and her lips were pressed together into a pale line. "Oh, *madame*, do you have—are you—?" Zhou-Zhou whispered with dread.

"No!" Victoria exclaimed, and then clutched the left side of her head with one hand. "No, Zhou-Zhou, it's not the sickness, the *vaudou* sickness. . . . It's a migraine . . . you know . . ."

Victoria had periodic migraines. Zhou-Zhou remembered that the last one had been last summer, and she was well aware that migraines could recur at any time, for no apparent reason. Still—

"I'm going to go get Dr. Duvall," Zhou-Zhou said firmly.

By now Victoria was panting—the pain was so intense, it actually hurt for her to breathe deeply—and she was feeling the beginnings of the gnawing nausea that always accompanied a migraine headache. "No," she said faintly. "I . . . I . . . can't explain to you, Zhou-Zhou, but I don't want to see anyone." Half-blinded, she felt the rumpled bedclothes behind her, attempted to smooth them out, then lay down slowly on top of them, cradling her face and head with both hands. Closing her eyes, she whispered, "I can't shriek at you . . . but no . . . doctor . . . no one."

Zhou-Zhou frowned, but she knew exactly what Victoria meant. Madame de Lancie was physically unable to use her usual method—speaking sharply to her—to impress upon Zhou-Zhou that she didn't want to see Dr. Duvall, or anyone else for that matter. Zhou-Zhou knew that if she didn't promise not to let anyone in to see Victoria, Victoria would lock the door behind her and refuse to let even her in.

With a sigh, Zhou-Zhou relented. "All right, *madame*. But I will stay, and I will take care of you. And we're not going anywhere today."

Victoria said nothing; she only turned her face toward the wall.

Cheney . . . my best friend . . . the best friend anyone could ever have . . . and I betrayed her. It seemed so right, then, when Dev was right there, and I knew—I knew! He's not in love with Cheney! He could be—would be—in love with me if only . . . if only . . .

If only you could seduce him into being dishonorable enough? a nasty voice inside her tortured head suggested.

"No," she whispered weakly and closed her eyes, and hot tears flooded down her cheeks again. The pain in her head increased to a burning sensation so vivid she thought that even her skin must be hot. Brushing her trembling fingers against her cheek, she realized that she was indeed hot; she was fevered. But that was not unusual with her migraines. Victoria tasted bitter bile and bitter tears.

It just was . . . different when Shiloh saw us. I suppose—let's face it, Madame de Lancie—you got caught, and then you were ashamed, and all of your excuses . . . that Cheney and Dev weren't meant for each other anyway, that Cheney doesn't really love Dev, that they would be miserable if they were married, that you could make Dev happy. . . . All that looked a little different when you saw it through Shiloh Irons's eyes, didn't it. . . . Iron Eyes, that's him . . . iron in my heart, a big sharp-edged lump of it . . . and screaming flames of fire in my head. . . .

The pain and the fever turned into an insensible fog of delirium, and Victoria welcomed it with all her heart.

★ ★ ★ ★

Precisely at noon Devlin Buchanan slammed the door of his *garçonniere* and hurried down the pathway toward the servants' cottages. He had bathed and was dressed in a fine black morning coat, meticulously pressed gray breeches, crisp white shirt, and perfectly knotted black tie—yet he still felt grimy and bedraggled.

Ten days' journey, and I arrived here only yesterday, he reminded himself stubbornly. *With Grand-mère Journée and Becky Colton until midnight last night . . . up all night . . . no wonder I feel so bleary!*

Grimly Dev put aside all beginnings of thoughts that perhaps the reason he felt so besmirched and dreary had nothing to do with physical strain and lack of sleep. Stubbornly he refused to review the events at the lagoon at dawn. Angrily he vowed not to go over in his mind—again—what he would do, and how he could get away from this place and these problems and these people ... particularly one Shiloh Irons. ...

"Hullo there, Dr. Buchanan." Shiloh fell into step beside him. "Going for a stroll?"

Dev kept walking quickly, but Shiloh's long strides easily overmatched his. Dev glared up at him briefly. "I'm going to attend to Grand-mère Journée, Irons," he growled. "And I certainly don't need your help to do my job."

Shiloh looked positively energized, Dev reflected irritably. His eyes were clear and glinted a brittle marine-blue. His color was high, but not unduly so. Indications of his state of mind were evident to one who knew him; his shoulders were visibly tense, occasionally he clenched his jaw, and there was a certain recklessness in his speech and a noticeable roughness in his stride and his gestures, in contrast to his usual easy, smooth grace.

"I'm coming with you," Shiloh said brusquely. He was carrying his medical bag, and for the first time Dev noticed that it was Cheney's old one. Dev had given her a brand-new one, fully stocked with medicines and implements, when she graduated from medical school. The sight of Shiloh Irons using Cheney's old doctor's bag made Dev feel unaccountably sad. With almost unbearable irritation he swatted away his reflections and murky emotions and tried to walk faster without actually breaking into a run, although it made no difference, as Shiloh easily dogged his steps at any pace.

The two hurried along in an uncomfortable silence. Dev began to wonder if Shiloh was going to actually, physically, watch him every waking moment. But again Dev couldn't, wouldn't contemplate that particular horror right then, and fiercely ordered himself to ignore Shiloh and concentrate on the patient he was going to see. He succeeded in this very well; by the time they reached Grand-mère Journée's cottage, Dev had forgotten about Shiloh and the shattering morning he had had and was weighing in his mind the possible treatments he might employ for Grand-mère Journée if she should awaken today. ... Dev hurried into the old woman's cottage without another glance at Shiloh.

Rebelliously Shiloh sat down on the porch steps and looked around with a jaundiced eye. The truth was that he had been unable to sleep and had decided to come to see about Grand-mère Journée himself. When he had come out of his *garçonniere*, he had seen Dev hurrying along with his medical bag, and before he could stop himself he was alongside of him, taunting him.

"Huh," Shiloh muttered sarcastically to himself, "guess I showed him. Here I sit, a big lump, nothin' to do. . . ."

Feeling in his breeches pocket, Shiloh found his whetstone, a souvenir of his time in Arkansas. His friend Glen Rawlins had found the stone and had carved and polished the sandy, gritty rock with the silvery glitters into a smooth rectangle for a gift to Shiloh. With relief he pulled his Bowie knife out of its sheath at the small of his back and began sharpening the long, gleaming blade. Normally the rhythm, the concentration required to get the blade angled against the stone just right, the somehow pleasing steel-against-stone rasp, had a soothing effect on him.

This morning he scowled down at the knife and pulled it back and forth against the stone with hasty, impatient strokes.

"Ow! Black and blue skies!"

Bright red drops of blood rolled down his thumb and across his palm and plopped down to the wooden step.

"Great," he muttered, sticking his thumb in his mouth. Shiloh had never cut himself before. Normally he was extremely deft and never made a false move with a gun, a knife, a needle, or a scalpel.

A shadow fell across him, and he looked up.

Gowan Ford's single eyebrow lifted sardonically. "Hope you cut your thumb," he rumbled.

With a smacking noise Shiloh pulled his thumb out of his mouth. "I quit sucking my thumb when I was fifteen," he retorted.

Ford settled down on the step just below Shiloh and picked up the knife. It was a wicked-looking blade, fifteen inches long. The single cutting edge was honed to a bright, sleek gleam. The back curved concavely to the point, while the edge curved convexly, with great sharp serrations in the curve. Contemplatively Ford turned it this way and that, and the bright, cheerful morning sun flashed like lightning all the way down its length.

"Knew Jim Bowie," Ford murmured.

"You did?" Shiloh exclaimed.

"Yep. I was just a kid, but I remember him and his two brothers,

Resin and John. They all joined up with Jean LaFitte in 1818 and smuggled slaves into New Orleans for a couple of years. Made a pile of money, all of them. The Bowies went back and forth between here and Natchez up until the Mexican Revolution. Good fighters, the Bowies were. Too bad Jim was killed at the Alamo. Thought about him a lot during the war." Ford pointed the knife toward the whetstone and glanced questioningly up at Shiloh. "You mind?"

"Help yourself," Shiloh grunted. Even in his distraction, he was curious to see how Gowan Ford would sharpen a knife with only one hand. He watched with interest as Ford propped one booted ankle up on his knee, then jammed the whetstone tightly into the top of his boot, just below his knee. Slowly, deliberately, he drew the long silvery blade down the length of the piece of whetstone that stuck out of his boot. Shiloh thought that was a pretty clever way to make do and also reflected that Gowan Ford generally did much better than just making do.

"Uh . . . better watch that last serration," Shiloh told him glumly. "It's sneaky."

"So I see," Ford remarked mildly. Shiloh's thumb still bled freely. "Got a bandage or something for that, Nurse Irons?"

"Yeah, I got it." Shiloh fumbled in his medical bag with his right hand, holding his left thumb awkwardly up in the air, which did no good, as the rich red blood still rolled down his hand. Finally he pulled out a thin strip of linen rolled into a tidy ball and impatiently rolled it around his thumb. Ford, drawing the knife across the whetstone with careful deliberation, watched him with curiosity but said nothing. Shiloh's bandage was about the messiest, lumpiest, sorriest-looking thing he'd ever seen. Ford wondered what was wrong with Shiloh, but, as is the way with quiet men, he said nothing, figuring that a man's business was his own and he'd talk about it if and when he wanted to.

Shiloh was absorbed in his lump of a bandage, irritably poking and pulling on it, and Ford was thinking his own private thoughts, honing contemplatively, so neither of them saw Cheney coming. They heard her footsteps and both looked up, then hurried to their feet. Shiloh tentatively moved down the steps toward her when he saw her face.

"What's wrong, Doc?" he asked. Cheney looked as if she'd been running; she was breathing heavily, her cheeks were flushed, and her strong features were lined with worry.

Rudely she rushed past Shiloh. "Dev's in here? I want Dev."

After she disappeared into the small cabin and almost slammed the door behind her, Shiloh muttered darkly, "Yeah, I noticed."

Ford gave no sign, as he calmly returned to his seat and resumed methodically sharpening Shiloh's knife. After long moments Shiloh threw himself down on the porch step again and growled, "Women!"

"Uh-huh," Ford agreed companionably.

For a long time no one said anything.

Ford drew the knife across the whetstone, a long, slow, careful stroke, then held the knife contemplatively up in front of his eyes. The blade edge looked as fine as a new straight razor. Shiloh, fascinated with Ford's ingenuity, realized that with one hand Ford couldn't check the keenness of the blade in the usual way and stuck out his arm. "Here, give it a look-see," Shiloh said.

Calmly Ford pulled the edge of the blade against the thick golden hair on Shiloh's arm. It cut a few hairs as smooth as a hot shave. "Usually have to check it on my leg," Ford muttered. "Feel like a pure imbecile."

"Good," Shiloh rumbled. "Glad I'm not the only man that goes around feeling like the village idiot all the time."

"Nope," Ford assured him, then looked contemplatively up at La Maison des Chattes Bleues. The lovely house glowed in the benevolent sunshine.

Cheney burst out of the cabin, almost fell over Shiloh as she rushed down the steps, and started to run off. Suddenly she turned and looked at Shiloh accusingly, propping her hands on her hips. "You—Shiloh—come with me," she said imperiously.

"Why? Dr. Buchanan refuse to obey your orders?" Shiloh challenged her.

"Yes, and I can't believe it!" she said with disgust. "Victoria's sick!"

Shiloh's eyes flickered, and he shifted restlessly but didn't rise. "Well? She hasn't got the *vaudou* disease, has she?"

Impatiently Cheney made a sharp cutting gesture with her hands. "Zhou-Zhou says not. She says Victoria has another one of her migraines." Cheney had treated Victoria for migraine before, but it had been almost six months since she'd had one.

"Then you—and especially Mrs. de Lancie—don't need me clomping around," Shiloh muttered. "What's the problem, anyway? You always treated her for migraine before, and besides, there's nothing anybody can do except hold her hand and give her perfumed hankies and all that women stuff!"

"She . . . she won't let me see her," Cheney replied, her voice dropping uncertainly. Slowly she dropped her hands to her sides and began fidgeting with the fine percale material of her gray skirt. She took a tentative step closer to Shiloh and Gowan Ford. "I . . . I . . . don't understand it. She won't let me see her, and Dev won't go to her."

"I'm not going either," Shiloh said brusquely. "Take my word for it, Doc, she doesn't want to see me, especially if she has a migraine."

Cheney's eyes narrowed and began to blaze. Childishly she stamped her foot. "Oh! Men! You're enough to give a woman a migraine!" With that she whirled and almost ran back to the house.

They watched her go, Shiloh with an irascible expression and Ford with ill-concealed relief.

"Women," Ford grunted, both in agreement with Shiloh's earlier comment, and in an observation of his own.

"Uh-huh," Shiloh agreed.

With sudden savagery Ford stabbed Shiloh's knife into the porch step beside him, burying the long curved end fully three inches into the aged cypress. "You think you have a fighting chance with 'em," he muttered as if lecturing himself, "but you never really do. They've always got you outsmarted and outgunned and outmanned."

"Outnumbered, I guess you mean," Shiloh said dryly.

But Ford missed the pun and went on, scowling at the graceful lines of Les Chattes Bleues. "Yeah, that too. And you think they . . . want you . . . around, you know . . . even when you might not be the prettiest thing in the world. . . ."

With a shrewd look at Ford, Shiloh said caustically, "I gotta tell you, bein' considered a pretty man ain't all it's cracked up to be, Ford."

"Wouldn't know," Ford grumbled. " 'Specially now."

"Just take my word for it."

"Yeah," Ford agreed absently, then continued with his odd lecture. "And then, you finally think that maybe they don't really want you, and maybe they don't really care about you all that much—but you think that 'cause you're a man, and they're a woman, they might just . . . kinda . . . maybe . . ."

"Need you?" Shiloh murmured.

"Yeah," Ford said with relief, but then he shook his leonine head

271

helplessly. "Then it turns out they don't, and never have, and never will need you for anything."

Shiloh, now personally absorbed in Ford's ruminations, stared hard at Les Chattes Bleues. On the second-floor gallery, Cheney still stood at Victoria de Lancie's door, talking to Zhou-Zhou, who had stubbornly come outside and closed the door when Cheney knocked. "Women," he muttered, "can take care of themselves."

"Yeah," Ford agreed.

Neither of them spoke for a long time.

Gowan Ford looked around La Maison des Chattes Bleues—the lovely gardens, the neat cottages and outbuildings, the lovely great house, the indigo fields in the distance, the lush border of the sweet bayou. *Home . . . only home I've ever known. But Elyse—I always, somehow, thought Elyse and I—that maybe she'd need me, someday, somehow. . . .* At the thought he grinned with savage amusement. *As if a fine woman like Querida Elyse de Cheyne Buckingham would ever want a one-armed, ugly old grunt like me for anything except to work for her . . . and now I find out she's got piles of gold, and she'll never want nor need for anything, and neither will Les Chattes Bleues. . . . Maybe it's time I thought about making a life for myself . . . by myself . . . somewhere else, away from Elyse. . . .*

"It's time for me to go," Shiloh muttered in an uncanny echo of Ford's thoughts. "I don't even know why I stopped here, anyway. All I was supposed to do was escort the Doc from Charleston, and here I sit like some big stupe. . . . I'm not her nanny!"

"Women," Ford muttered in a whisper as savage as a bear's growl.

"Yeah," Shiloh growled in return.

★   ★   ★   ★

As Shiloh and Gowan Ford sat outside on the porch reflecting on such grim thoughts, inside the cabin Dr. Devlin Buchanan was having a long, somber discussion with himself.

He sat by Grand-mère Journée's bedside, staring down at her tiny, still form, amazed that her heart still beat. Grand-mère Journée was eighty now, and frail and fragile as a hothouse orchid. She had awakened during the night and asked for water, and Luna had wisely moistened a clean cloth and pressed it to her mouth. Thirstily Grand-mère Journée had licked the moisture from her lips, smiled weakly at Luna, and fallen into a deep sleep.

Dev had deliberately awakened Grand-mère Journée when he arrived and observed that she was, indeed, asleep, and no longer wandering in the dangerous unknown land of the comatose. After he had checked her heartbeat, pulse, and respiration, and had given her small sips of some cool water, he allowed her to fall back to sleep. Now he sat by her bedside, watching her with childish wonder, marveling that God had fashioned such an extraordinary invention as the human body. It was nothing short of miraculous that Grand-mère Journée's delicate heart still beat, and today it was beating steadily, though faintly.

But Dr. Buchanan's thoughts didn't linger on these pleasant thoughts for long. With a sigh he looked up and out the single window. It looked out onto a small, immaculate garden, and unconsciously Dev admired the straight, clean rows, the symmetrical spacing of the tiny shoots of green. Though the thought was not fully formed in his mind, he would have much preferred that his life be like that garden: straight, uncomplicated, geometrically precise, with good results an exact mathematical permutation of the effort expended.

"What a mess," he muttered blackly, his eyes unfocused. Obviously he didn't speak of the garden outside. His thoughts, when he wasn't severely disciplining them, spun out into erratic little snatches of conversations, words spoken, and unconnected visions: Cheney's voice, entreating him to go to Victoria . . . Victoria's face . . . her profile in the dawning day . . . Shiloh's hand on his shoulder, heavy and burning, seeming to brand him with the guilt he felt deep inside. . . .

Dev shook his head fiercely, as if he could throw off the confusion that reigned in his mind and heart. "I must go," he said dully, staring at the gleaming wooden floor of the cabin. "I must leave. This is . . . unbearable . . . for everyone. For me, for Victoria, for Cheney . . . and Richard, and Irene . . ." The thought of the Duvalls' pain at his dishonor made Dev physically ill, and he dropped his head hopelessly. "I've got to leave. Cheney won't mind . . . she's not in any hurry to get married . . . I'll stay away from all of them . . . for a long, long time . . . until . . . until . . ."

But he couldn't imagine how long it would take for him to get over how deeply, how richly, how helplessly he loved Victoria Elizabeth Steen de Lancie.

★　★　★　★

At four o'clock that afternoon, Tante Marye and Irene Duvall sat together in the downstairs parlor, sipping steaming tea sweetened with rich honey and liberally diluted with heavy cream. Irene looked tired, but on her it took the form of a certain dewy frailty in her sea-green eyes, a delicate moon-glow pallor of skin, a vulnerability about the lips. Tante Marye smiled as she considered her niece and reflected that even at forty-four, Irene de Cheyne Duvall was quite a lovely woman.

Tante Marye, however, looked worn and pale, and her faded blue eyes were red-rimmed with weariness. Her head thumped slightly, just enough to irritate her, and curtly she reminded herself never again to stay up all night like some idiotic young girl.

But the tea was hot and strong, and honey is a natural energizer, so after one cautiously sipped cup both Tante Marye and Irene felt better. Both of them had slept until two o'clock and had dawdled at their *toilette*. They had only come downstairs at a quarter of four.

"I wonder where everyone is," Irene mused.

"We'll ask Monroe when he comes back in," Tante Marye said complacently. "He knows where everyone is all the time. More tea, Irene?"

"Yes, Tante Marye, please. It is so delicious, and so refreshing. And you do pour so beautifully, *ma tante*," Irene said graciously. "I always observe you, so I can learn to pour as elegantly as you do."

"Nonsense, child, in all things you are *très èlègant*," Tante Marye said curtly, but her lined parchment cheeks grew pink with pleasure as she took Irene's cup and performed all the little silvery rituals of preparing a cup of tea in polite company.

Cheney came stamping into the parlor, glowering, and threw herself down moodily on the divan across from her great-aunt and her mother. "Victoria's sick! No, no, it's not that stupid *vaudou* poison or whatever it is. She has a terrible migraine. And she won't let me see her! She won't let anyone see her, even though no one seems to be the least bit interested in taking care of her . . . even Dev . . . even Shiloh, although she is quite as ill—"

"Cheney," Irene said softly, "calm down, darling."

"*Bon soir*, Cheney," Tante Marye said pointedly. "What a perfectly charming, polite entrance. Do sit up, Cheney, you look as if someone crumpled you up and threw you there!"

"I feel like it," Cheney grumbled, though she did assume a more ladylike position, with her back straight and not touching the divan, her feet neatly crossed at the ankles, and her hands folded in her lap.

She did, however, unconsciously begin to pleat the material of her dress into small folds between her fingers while she stared hungrily at the gleaming silver tea service. "Mmm, Tante Marye, that tea smells marvelous. May I join you?"

"Certainly, child. I will pour." Now satisfied with Cheney's carriage and deportment, Tante Marye prepared her a cup of tea with lots of honey and cream. "Now, exactly how ill is Mrs. de Lancie? Is there anything we might do to make her more comfortable?"

Rising and walking with deliberate ladylike steps to take the proffered cup of tea, Cheney replied, "No, Tante Marye, there's really nothing anyone can do for a migraine. But I do wish she would at least allow me to see her. I would like to sit with her for a while. I've taken care of Victoria before when she had these horrendous headaches, and she always said that I could soothe her even more than Zhou-Zhou."

Cheney returned to her seat and delicately sipped the tea. It was, indeed, marvelous. "Actually, I do understand why she doesn't want Dev—I think," Cheney added almost to herself. "She can't bear any kind of light, or noise. And she usually does—" With a quick guilty glance at Tante Marye she finished lamely. "She's quite nauseated."

Tante Marye nodded slightly with approval at Cheney's ladylike phrases, but Irene looked thoughtful and apprehensive. "But, Cheney, did you say that Dev didn't want to see Mrs. de Lancie? Or that Mrs. de Lancie didn't want to see Dev?"

"Both," Cheney replied with disgust. "Victoria, as I said, doesn't want to see anyone at all, except Zhou-Zhou. And Shiloh doesn't want to see Victoria. And I don't think he particularly wants to see me, either. Which is fine with me. I don't need to see him anyway. Or Gowan Ford, either." Rebelliously she gulped the tea, which scalded the tip of her tongue to immediate deadness and burned all the way down her throat. Tears sprang to her eyes, and defiantly she blinked them back.

"I've never heard such a ridiculous tirade in my life," Tante Marye sniffed.

"Tante Elyse says stupid things, Tante Marye," Cheney said sullenly.

"Elyse never speaks so hurtfully, so cuttingly, of anyone or anything, Cheney," Tante Marye said with sudden gentleness. "What's wrong, child? Did you and Mr. Irons have some sort of argument?"

"And why should I have a tirade if we did?" Cheney retorted.

"You should not," Irene asserted, "ever. And particularly to Tante

Marye. Apologize for your disrespect and harshness, Cheney. Right now."

Irene Duvall hadn't spoken to Cheney Duvall so sternly since she was a small child, and it almost broke Cheney's heart. Suddenly she felt as if she were suffocating, for her throat constricted tightly with unshed tears and shame. But when Tante Marye turned to Irene and murmured quietly, "It's all right, Irene, something has upset Cheney or she wouldn't be so unkind—"

Cheney couldn't stand it anymore. The tears spilled over, and her head drooped like a broken flower, and she cried. Right into her delicate Wedgwood china cup of tea.

Both Tante Marye and Irene hurried to sit close beside her on either side. Irene took the clattering cup of tea from her shaking hands, and Tante Marye smoothed her head just as if she were a small child sobbing with shame—which, indeed, Cheney felt she was. "It's all right, Cheney, darling, oh, don't, don't cry," Tante Marye murmured. "If you cry, I'll cry!"

"I'm so sorry, Tante Marye," Cheney murmured brokenly. "Please forgive me. I didn't realize how hateful I sounded. I love you so much, and I'd never, never purposely be unkind to you."

"I know, dear," she answered calmly. "It's very easy to forgive you, you see, because I know it's true. You would never purposely hurt anyone, for any reason. And I love you dearly, Cheney. Elyse and I love you more than you'll ever know."

"Oh!" Cheney wailed. "I'm so . . . so . . . horrible!" She threw herself into her great-aunt's arms and sobbed against her shoulder. Tante Marye and Irene exchanged small knowing smiles; Cheney had always been subject to these great passionate torrents of emotion. As she had grown older these times had become quite rare and generally tightly controlled when they did occur. Still, Cheney was a deeply emotional, sensitive soul, and sometimes she was overwhelmed with whatever she felt at the time, whether it was regret, sorrow, embarrassment, guilt, shame, or affection.

Tante Elyse made her normal entrance; she wandered in tentatively, as if she weren't sure this place was exactly where she had set out to be. Which was, indeed, the case sometimes, when she was absentminded because of indigo problems or pet problems or Marye problems, and ended up going somewhere she hadn't intended to go. Tante

Elyse ended up on Gowan Ford's porch often because of this peculiar trait.

But now she hurried to the divan where the three women sat and knelt down in front of Cheney. Tante Marye frowned at her, for Elyse had two round delta-dirt prints at the knees of her otherwise spotless white apron, but before she could speak Elyse demanded accusingly, "What's wrong with her?"

"She's upset, but she'll be fine, Elyse," Tante Marye said with exasperation. Cheney still had her face buried in Tante Marye's thin shoulder, but her sobs had subsided to faint hiccups.

"But why is she upset?" Tante Elyse persisted. She rose and seated herself in a nearby chair. "Is it because Shiloh's leaving?"

"What?" Cheney almost shouted, jumping away from Tante Elyse.

"Or is it because Dev's leaving?" Tante Elyse asked earnestly.

"What?" Irene breathed.

"Even Gowan's talking about leaving and wandering off to San Francisco with Shiloh like an old fool," Tante Elyse said wrathfully.

"What?" Tante Marye demanded irritably.

"Nobody is leaving!" Cheney said wildly.

"I should hope not," Irene said with genteel distress.

"But Mrs. de Lancie is," Tante Elyse insisted.

"Elyse, stop listing the persons at Les Chattes Bleues as if we were taking a census!" Marye snapped. "I think you don't even know what you're saying! In the last twenty seconds you've announced that practically everyone at Les Chattes Bleues is making some sort of exodus!"

"No, I didn't," Tante Elyse argued. "I'm not leaving. Although I must say, Marye, that Maxime's insistence that we come to Varennes is sounding better all the time," she finished irritably. "If Gowan can go galloping off to San Francisco, then I can go sailing off to France."

"What is happening here?" Tante Marye whispered, her irritation melting away like a shard of ice in an August sun. "What's wrong with all of us?"

Suddenly Irene's gentle sea-green eyes grew sharp, and with a sudden intake of breath she murmured, "I know. I know exactly what's happening here, and what's wrong with us." She rose quickly and said hurriedly, "Please excuse me, *mes tantes*, Cheney. I must go find Richard." Although she hurried out of the parlor, she still looked as if she glided on a cushion of air.

"Well, there she goes," Elyse said with resignation. "I told you everyone's leaving."

Marye sniffed loudly. "She's going to find Richard, Elyse, and that is hardly the same as Gowan Ford thinking he's going off to Mexico with Mr. Irons."

"San Francisco," Cheney corrected her dully.

"It doesn't matter," Marye said with a grand gesture. "Richard will fix all of this foolishness."

"I hope so," Cheney said in a deadened tone. "But I don't think so."

22

ABOVE ALL, THE SHIELD

Irene hurried upstairs to the master bedroom and found Richard there reading the Bible, as she was certain he would be. He was sitting on the chaise lounge, and she hurried to him. After taking one look at her face, he put his Bible aside and turned so that Irene could sit next to him. "What is it, Irene?" he asked gently. "What's wrong, my love?"

Irene smiled gravely up at him. "Nothing, now that I'm here, close to you. . . ." She wrapped her arms around his waist and clasped him tightly. "I do love you so much, Richard," she murmured. "I'm so grateful to God for giving you to me."

Richard smiled and kissed the top of her head lightly. "God has blessed us mightily, my dear. I thank Him every single day for you. I love you more than my own life, Irene."

"Yes," she whispered, and they sat holding each other, in silence, for a long while.

Finally Irene pulled away slightly, though Richard kept his arm around her. "Richard, I believe that the Lord has given me a message for you," she said, her eyes sparkling.

"Oh yes?" He smiled. "That's wonderful! Please, Irene, tell me. Tell me all of it."

At various times in their marriage, the Lord had spoken to them through Irene; she told Richard that she didn't exactly hear a voice—not in her head, and certainly not in an audible sound—but that she suddenly knew something. Often it was as if the words were written clearly on a page in her mind, and sometimes it was vivid pictures in her mind's eye, like illustrations. When this happened, she knew that although it could not be called a Voice, it was, indeed, a Voice, gently framed so the human mind could take it in. *My sheep hear my Voice, and I know them, and they follow me. . . .*

"First of all, I know that the enemy is here," Irene said softly. "He is going about as a ravening lion, seeking whom he may devour. . . ."

Richard waited quietly, listening closely to each word Irene said.

"He's caused discord and anger and pain and depression and illness here, Richard," she continued quietly. "And he is doubling his efforts, desperate to cause confusion, because his time is growing short."

"Yes?" Richard said alertly. "I've felt that, known that, today. I've been very aware, somehow, that the demonic forces at work here have grown reckless and careless in their attempts to attack us. Does that mean, Irene, that soon we—that I—"

"Soon, Richard, you will see the power of the Almighty God as you've never seen it before," Irene said dreamily. Then she turned to him and smiled triumphantly, brilliantly. "And here is His wonderful, perfect plan. . . ."

★　★　★　★

"I've asked you here for a specific reason," Richard said quietly. "It's not just a social occasion, though I do indeed enjoy and esteem the company of such men as you, Dev, and you, Mr. Ford."

"I heartily return the sentiment, Colonel Duvall," Dev declared.

"Likewise, sir," Ford added.

They were seated comfortably, companionably, in the library. At dinner, only these three, Irene, and Tante Marye had been in attendance. Everyone else seemed to have scattered to the four winds. Tante Marye was distraught—purportedly for the ruination of her dinner seating—but Richard had been so calm and matter-of-fact as he soothed her that she had actually settled down and enjoyed the meal. Irene, likewise, was calm and composed, and when she spoke her lilting voice showed plainly her peace and joy. Dev and Gowan Ford, on the other hand, had been curt and distracted throughout, but they had quickly assented to Richard's suggestion that they adjourn to the library afterward.

Richard rose from the armchair he had settled into and went to stand in front of the sofa beneath the window. Gazing out into the long, graceful oak bower that led to Les Chattes Bleues, mysterious with evening shadows, he smiled slightly. "I want to tell you some things that pertain to Les Chattes Bleues, and to my family, and to each of you, personally." He fell silent and looked thoughtfully out the window for a long time.

Dev and Gowan waited patiently. Their respect for Richard Duvall made both of them certain that whatever he had to say, it was important, and if he stood in silence all night they would wait without saying a word.

Finally Richard turned back to them, his face grave but not saddened, and took his seat. The men were seated closely together, in three armchairs grouped about a reading lamp. Richard searched first Dev's face, then Gowan Ford's, intently, and they bore his scrutiny patiently. Finally he seemed satisfied and began to speak.

"I believe that a great cleansing is going to take place here, at Les Chattes Bleues," he said evenly. "I believe that this land belongs to the Lord God of heaven and earth, for we have repeatedly given it up as an offering to Him. Even the vicomte, before he died, prayed the Lord's protection on this place and on his daughters."

"That's true," Ford agreed stoutly. Dev nodded.

"The Lord has shown me that I am to fight the evil that is here," Richard said matter-of-factly. He waited a few moments for the ominous words to sink in. Dev looked uneasy, and then a certain stubbornness hardened his handsome features, and Richard almost smiled. He had known this would be Dev's first reaction: to protect Richard Duvall by attempting to dissuade him from exposing himself to any kind of danger. Gowan Ford merely watched Richard, the single eye flickering with a burning light, his face set as if it had been fashioned of flawed but unyielding granite.

"The Lord has told me that two men will stand with me," Richard said quietly, "and I know that you are those two men."

A long silence, growing thicker and heavier as each moment passed, seemed to press upon the three men's ears. The odd spell was broken when Dev murmured, "Yes . . . you're right. Of course, you're . . . right, sir. That's why I came . . . that's why I'm here. Why didn't I see it before?"

"Yes," Gowan Ford suddenly agreed. "Of course. If I'd been listening to God as I should—like I try to, and usually do—I would've realized this myself, and I wouldn't have gotten so distracted with other—foolishness."

Richard nodded with certainty. "But neither of you realized this because you—all of us—have been under attack, by—"

"Principalities and powers . . ." Dev breathed with sudden revelation.

"Rulers of the darkness," Gowan Ford muttered.

"Yes," Richard said with relief. "Yes. God has opened your eyes. Now, gentlemen, you must open your hearts, because the Lord has told me"—he smiled gently—"through my blessed wife, who is strong in righteousness and great in wisdom, how we three can fight—and beat—all of the evil principalities, every hellish power, any demon who rules the darkness."

"Thank God," Dev breathed. "I was already feeling . . . inadequate, and . . ."

"Scared?" Ford asked. "Don't be embarrassed, Dr. Buchanan. I'm scared myself, but I learned a long time ago there's no shame in it."

"I was scared, too," Richard admitted honestly. "But since I talked to Irene, I no longer have any fear or doubts. And I know that the Lord will take away your fear and make His strength as tangible, as real, for you as He did for me."

Taking up a heavy old Bible that was on the low table beside his chair, Richard leaned over so that the warm, welcoming amber light fell on the Book. "Wherefore take unto you the whole armor of God, that ye may be able to withstand in the evil day, and having done all, to stand." All three of the men sat up a little straighter in their chairs.

Richard spoke in a voice heavy with emotion, strong and sure: "You, Dev, and you, Mr. Ford, must—literally, though not physically— put on God's armor in order to protect yourself. For I tell you now that the evil day has come, and is waning, and the evil night must fall soon."

"Yes . . . yes . . ." Dev and Gowan Ford murmured in sudden comprehension.

"As do all men who go into battle, we must prepare ourselves. First you must place the helmet of salvation on your head. Dev, Mr. Ford, are you saved? Are you a Christian, saved by the blood of Jesus Christ, the Son of God?"

"Yes, sir!" Dev answered in a deep, ringing voice.

"Yes, sir!" Ford echoed.

"Then you now have the helmet of salvation protecting you," Richard nodded. "God's breastplate is righteousness. Do you, in faith, by Jesus Christ's sacrifice, put on the breastplate of righteousness?"

Both Dev and Ford resounded, "Yes, sir."

"God has ordained that for our protection, and to strengthen us, we must have our loins girt with truth," Richard said sternly. "Do you, in faith, cloaked by the blood of Jesus, put on God's buckler of Truth?"

Both Dev and Gowan Ford mysteriously faltered. Both men dropped their eyes and wouldn't meet Richard Duvall's gaze. This was no meaningless cant, this was no empty ritual. Richard Duvall was asking deadly serious questions that must be considered, and answered honestly, for the protection of their home, their bodies, their peace, and that of their families and friends.

"Sir," Dev said quietly, his dark eyes finally raised to meet Richard's level, unflinching gaze, "I cannot affirm that I'm living in complete and total truth. I am, in fact, living in a lie."

"So am I, Colonel Duvall," Ford agreed hoarsely, "though I honestly didn't realize it until right now."

"This is why we're doing this, right here and right now, gentlemen," Richard said kindly. "For our own protection, for our own strength. So that the loving and saving light of the Lord can bring knowledge of our sins to each of us, because so many times we ourselves are the last to recognize insidious and presumptuous sins. Now, I must ask you, Dev, can you overcome this falsity in your life? Can you repent of your sin and do everything humanly possible to set to rights anyone who has been injured by your sin?"

"Yes, sir, Colonel Duvall, I can; I am suddenly, gladly anxious to do so," Dev answered with a light in his eyes. "And more than that, I *will* do so at my earliest opportunity—after I have prayed and sought the Lord's forgiveness."

"That," Richard said gently, "is the speech of a just man, humble and true, and the Lord honors and loves such men beyond our greatest hope." Wordlessly he turned to Gowan Ford, who was frowning grimly.

"I don't know, Colonel Duvall, about making amends. I'm not even sure I've hurt anyone else besides my own stupid self," Ford muttered. "But, like Dr. Buchanan, I'll sure pray and ask the Lord for forgiveness for my stubbornness and pride, and for ignoring His good advice . . . and I'll be sure and ask Him what I need to do to fix it."

"That's all He wants, has ever wanted," Richard responded sturdily, "and I know that God will bless you mightily for your obedience, Mr. Ford." He looked back and forth at Dev and Gowan and went on, "Now I believe, in faith, that you, Dev, and you, Gowan, will gird yourselves with the Lord's buckler of Truth. And the words both of you have just spoken have affirmed: you both are shod with the preparation of the gospel of peace.

"There are two more important components of God's armor we

must surely cling to, Dev, Mr. Ford," Richard went on steadily. "The Bible tells us that, above all, we must take up the shield of faith. This is our most valuable and powerful defense, you see; with the shield of faith we can cover any other part of our armor that we let falter. If you fear for your salvation, your shield of faith will guard you. If you doubt that you stand in Jesus Christ's righteousness, your shield will always be His righteousness, and you will cling to it forever. If you doubt that you can stand in truth, your shield of faith will be your protection. If you look away from the gospel of peace, your shield will give you peace. Do you understand, Dev?"

"Yes, sir," Dev said quietly. "I understand, and I will take up the shield of faith, now, as you, my brothers in Christ, witness my affirmation."

"And you, Mr. Ford?"

"I take up the shield of faith in the Almighty God," Ford asserted.

Richard smiled. "So much for defense; now for the weapons."

"Yes, sir!" Ford said heartily.

"Our weapon," Richard said, his penetrating gaze never wavering, "is the sword that can never be broken; the blade that will triumph from everlasting to everlasting. It is the Sword of the Spirit, which is the Word of God. With this sword we need never fear; we need not strive; we will fight, and we will win!"

THE CONGREGATION

PART FIVE

OF THE MIGHTY

*God standeth in the
congregation of the mighty,
He judgeth among the gods.*

Psalm 82:1

23

SALT SPIKES OF THE SOUL

"So as soon as Cheney and I agreed that it might be some type of ingested poison, I gave her syrup of ipecac to induce vomiting," Dev explained. "After her stomach was thoroughly emptied, Cheney made a slurry of warm water and activated charcoal. This substance has virtually no side effects; yet it will absorb any substance that has not yet begun entering the intestines."

"Mm-hmm," Richard said, a symbolic assent that signaled to Dev that he was still listening. And he was listening, in a sense; Richard Duvall listened to Dev Buchanan and Cheney the way that all good fathers do when their children speak with animation of their interests, regardless of how incomprehensible the subject may be.

" . . . and so you see that we couldn't possibly treat Grand-mère Journée in the same manner, since she was comatose. Becky was alert and able to physically control taking the medicine and her response to it."

"Uh-huh," Richard murmured.

He and Gowan Ford and Dev had talked for about two hours. When they were finished, they had found that all of the ladies had already retired, and even Monroe was nowhere in the main house. The three men wandered outside together; Gowan Ford said his goodnights and headed for his cottage. Richard, still making small talk with Dev, had asked how it was that Becky Colton was doing so well so quickly, while Grand-mère Journée was progressing but was still gravely ill. Dev had launched into a discussion of the relative treatment of the conscious patient versus the comatose patient, and Richard found himself walking along with Dev to his *garçonniere*.

" . . . so I feel that Grand-mère Journée is over the worst," Dev said as he opened the door and leaned against the doorjamb. "She should improve steadily over the next two weeks, if her heart remains stable."

"Sounds good, Dev," Richard said warmly, extending his hand. "I want you to know that I'm very proud of you. You've grown into a conscientious, dedicated doctor, as well as a courageous and honorable man."

Dev clasped his hand tightly. "Coming from a man such as you, Colonel Duvall, that is perhaps the highest compliment I have ever received."

"It's only the truth, Dev," Richard replied. "And I will pray for you tonight."

"I'm praying for myself, and for everyone else tonight," Dev said fervently. "Good night, and thank you, sir."

"Good night, Dev." Richard turned to go back to the main house as Dev went inside. He had taken several steps before he stopped and turned. *Shiloh's light is on*, he observed, hesitating, wondering whether he should intrude upon Shiloh's privacy. Shiloh had not been at dinner, by choice, Richard assumed. Gowan Ford had told Richard that Shiloh seemed to be planning to leave La Maison des Chattes Bleues almost immediately. After a few moments' uncertainty, Richard decided that he would at least stop and tell Shiloh that he'd missed him at dinner and say good-night.

He knocked lightly on Shiloh's door and was surprised when it immediately was opened. Shiloh stepped back. "How good of you to stop by, Colonel Duvall. Please come in."

The two men settled comfortably in the leather armchairs, and Richard looked around the *garçonniere*. "Nice little place, isn't it?"

"Yes. All of Les Chattes Bleues is a nice place, with nice people," Shiloh agreed politely. "I've certainly enjoyed my visit here, Colonel Duvall."

Richard crossed one booted foot over his knee and searched Shiloh's face. He looked tired, though not unduly so. Richard, however, could feel tension emanating from Shiloh, and a certain restlessness in the way he sat and moved, and the way his eyes roamed the room and went continually to the window.

"Shiloh, we've all enjoyed having you here—much more than I think you realize," Richard said quietly. "Mr. Ford told me that you are thinking about leaving. That you are planning on going to San Francisco."

"Yes, sir."

Richard smiled. "I can understand that, considering what you

288

found out at Shiloh Ironworks." After his visit to see Miss Behring, Shiloh had told Cheney and Richard Duvall of his discovery concerning the clipper ship *Day Dream.* "And I respect your decisions, Shiloh. Your life is your own, and I wouldn't presume to try to dissuade you from a choice that is yours, and yours alone, to make. But I wish you would reconsider leaving for a few days, at least."

"You do?" Shiloh asked with surprise.

"Of course," Richard said simply.

"But . . . but . . . Colonel Duvall," Shiloh stammered, unsure how to express himself clearly to this man he respected so much. He paused, then resolved to begin again and follow a rule that he had found always worked: to tell the truth, plain and simple.

"Colonel Duvall, I've caused some trouble in the last two days, sticking my nose in something that's none of my business. And I guess I . . . hurt some people. Not to mention that though I don't always comprehend exactly what's going on with those voodoo people, I'm not too dense to understand that I'm a definite liability where they're concerned."

Richard regarded him gravely, his gray eyes flickering with an odd light. "These two things you just told me, are these the only reasons you've decided to leave Les Chattes Bleues?"

Since it was very important to Shiloh to be scrupulously honest with Richard Duvall, he considered the question carefully: *Is that why I'm leaving Les Chattes Bleues? Am I really that anxious to ride off tomorrow to go to California to find out about my parents? Am I really all disgusted with this Cheney-Dev-Victoria thing? Or is it something else?*

"Colonel Duvall, I don't know how to answer that question right now," Shiloh finally replied. "I'm just not sure."

"You're confused?" Richard asked quietly.

"Yes, sir, I am, and I don't much like it." Shiloh glowered.

"Neither do I, Shiloh. And the reason I don't like it is because I know why you're confused; I know why I was so depressed and uneasy when we first arrived here, why everyone is so tense, and why people are angry with each other."

"Sir?" Shiloh asked, puzzled.

"You're an intuitive man, Shiloh." Richard grinned humorlessly. "Haven't you noticed that the *vaudou* seem to be getting their way? For one reason or another, everyone is talking about leaving Les Chattes Bleues?"

The realization struck Shiloh with the force and heat of a volcanic wind. "Yes!" he almost shouted. "I mean, no, sir, it didn't occur to me at all before, but now that you've said it I can see it so clearly! How dumb!"

Richard knew what he meant and shook his head forcefully. "No, Shiloh, you are not dumb. All of us have been subject to the enemy's fiery darts of confusion and discord. But I tell you now that I will allow it no longer. In the name of Jesus Christ and by His power, it stops now, here, tonight. So I want you to make your decision about leaving Les Chattes Bleues with a clear mind, without confusion. And I want to be certain that you know that I and my family would like for you to stay."

Shiloh Irons was indeed an intuitive man, and an intelligent one, and he had comprehended all that Richard Duvall had said—and meant—very quickly. "Sir, I would be honored to stay at Les Chattes Bleues. In fact, someone's going to have a chore trying to run me off before I get ready to go," he added stubbornly. Shiloh knew he had been subject to dark powers beyond his control—he had fully realized that on the night of the *vaudou*—but he had no intention of giving them place in his judgment and reason. Instinctively Shiloh knew, deep down, that since he wasn't a Christian he didn't have the means to fight such forces, but he also shrewdly knew that he would have a much better chance sticking close to the winning camp. Recalling a bit of his Bible schooling from the Misses Behring, he reflected wryly, *Even the dogs get the crumbs from the Master's table.*

"Mr. Irons? Colonel Duvall?" Gowan Ford's sturdy knock sounded at the door. Shiloh hurried to open it.

Ford stood in the doorway, his arms crossed, his expression grim. Richard stood up and asked quietly, "Are they here?"

Ford grimaced. "Yes, sir, the *vaudou* are definitely here at Les Chattes Bleues—but not in the way you think. Please come with me, Colonel Duvall. It's trouble."

Richard hurried to the doorway but hesitated as he passed Shiloh. Ford said, "I think you ought to come too, Mr. Irons. This involves you."

Shiloh looked questioningly at Richard Duvall, who nodded affirmation, and the three men hurried to the house. No lights burned in the upper story, where presumably the ladies were already in bed. On the first floor dim lights burned in the dining room.

"Monroe came to get me," Ford told them in a low growl. "He didn't know who else to talk to. But I'm not the man to handle this. You are, Colonel Duvall."

"Did you wake up anyone else, Mr. Ford?" Richard asked.

"No, sir. I'll leave that decision up to you."

Ford led them to the dining room, where an eerie scene met their eyes. A single candelabra was set on the table. Corbett, Adah, and Chloe sat at the table facing the entrance to the room. Luna sat at the far end, alone, watching the children, her face distorted with fury. Behind the children stood Monroe and Molly. All three children sat stiffly, their hands in their laps, their heads bowed. Monroe stood almost at attention; the tension in his body so evident he seemed like a piano string that had been tuned too tightly. Molly's head was bowed; her shoulders shook, although she made no sound. She held a handkerchief, and as the three men came in she wiped both sides of her face with hard, rough strokes.

Richard came into the room and stood across the table from the children. None of them looked up or even moved. Ford and Shiloh stood slightly behind Richard; all three men studied the scene for a few moments.

"Mr. Ford has told me nothing," Richard said calmly. "Monroe? What is the trouble?"

Monroe looked at Richard, and desperation—even a touch of fear—desolated his smooth features. He swallowed hard. "Colonel Duvall, I don't . . . exactly . . . know . . ." He choked slightly, but his gaze never wavered from Richard Duvall's. "*Monsieur*, my . . . children . . ." he tried again.

Luna stood up—a savage, jerky movement—and tossed something onto the table. It slid down to the candelabra, bumped it, and for a few moments the slender candlestick teetered, throwing wavering ghost lights on the averted faces of Corbett, Adah, and Chloe. Chloe did start and look up at the sound, her eyes round with fear, but quickly she ducked her head again.

"That . . . is the trouble, Colonel Duvall," Luna snarled. "That . . . thing."

Richard, Ford, and Shiloh stared down at it. It was a doll, made of wax, about twelve inches tall. The image was crude; it only had a suggestion of eyes, mouth, and nose; but it was clearly a male doll. On its head, stuck into the soft wax, were strands of fine golden hair. It had a strip of rough muslin wrapped around its waist. On its chest, on the left-hand side, was burned a small round hole; stuck into this hole were bits and pieces of cloth, colored a rusty red. It was an alien object, ugly in its crudity, frightening in its barbarity.

Behind Richard, Shiloh moaned, a deep animal sound that he cut off abruptly.

"What . . . what is this?" Richard asked hoarsely. Tearing his gaze away from it in revulsion, he stared at Luna.

Her mouth tightened with anger; her fine sloe eyes flashed darkly. "It's a *vaudou* sorcery doll, Colonel Duvall. With incantations and rites the sorcerer lures the soul of the person the doll represents into the doll itself. Then the sorcerer can control the person whose soul they possess—for good or evil."

"And . . . this doll . . . is . . ." Richard gestured with disdain to the obscenity lying on the table.

"That doll is meant to capture Shiloh Irons' soul," Luna said in a harsh tone. "And it belongs to Chloe."

Every eye in the room bore down on Chloe. She snapped her head up and cried defiantly, "I would never hurt Shiloh! I love him! It's just a . . . charm . . . to make him fall in love with me! I didn't do anything!"

Again Shiloh moaned but with an effort fell silent. His lips were pressed together so hard that the skin around his mouth was white. His eyes flashed dangerously. Though his arms were crossed, his fists were clenched so hard that his knuckles were as sharp and white as bare bones.

Richard Duvall looked grim. "You admit that you made this . . . thing, Chloe?"

"Yes I did!" Chloe said recklessly.

"What kind of . . . rites . . . did you perform to make Mr. Irons fall in love with you?" Richard asked with difficulty. He was so filled with dread and sick revulsion that he could barely talk.

"I got hair from his hairbrush," Chloe answered, her angry defiance turning to sullenness. "And today, when he came into the kitchen to wash out his thumb, he threw that bandage in the trash. So I got it! And if that . . . that . . ." She turned to Luna venomously and could hardly seem to calm herself enough to finish speaking.

"I was in the kitchen and saw Chloe take the bandage," Luna told Richard. "She was acting very peculiar. Sly, I guess—looking around guiltily, but handling that bloody bandage very carefully. And then I knew exactly what she was doing."

"But . . . what . . ." Richard faltered.

"The blood," Luna said with eerie calm. "Marie Laveau used to tell me that if you can get a man's blood, you can own his soul and his body will be yours." She stared down at the doll. "It's the bloody parts of the bandage, you see, cut up and stuck into the doll where his heart is . . . so his heart will bleed . . . for Chloe."

"You . . . you . . . witch!" Chloe spat. "Like it's any of your business—"

"You mind your tongue, girl!" Monroe thundered. "You just keep your foul mouth shut unless Colonel Duvall asks you a question!" He stepped closer to Chloe, and though she didn't turn around, she could feel the heat of his anger at her back and fell silent.

"So tonight I went to Molly as soon as she finished for the evening and went to her cottage," Luna said angrily, her eyes cutting to Chloe with her own venom. "I told Molly what I'd seen, and told her that she'd better see what Chloe was up to."

"My wife —" Monroe began, then stepped closer to Molly. He put a protective arm around her and began again in a stronger voice. "My wife had suspected that Chloe—and Adah and Corbett—were somehow involved in . . . something. But until tonight she didn't know what it was . . . how very, very bad it is. . . ." His voice trailed off, as he seemed to be overcome with grief, and bowed his head. Molly still made no sound, though her shoulders shook violently.

Richard Duvall rubbed his jaw, then dropped his head and shook it regretfully. "All right. I can see that this . . . thing . . . isn't all of the story. Monroe, get chairs for all of us. Let's all sit down and discuss this rationally."

Monroe and Gowan Ford hurried to retrieve the chairs from where they had been lined up along the dining room walls, presumably so the floor could be cleaned. Molly sank into her chair as if she could not hold herself up a moment longer; Monroe sat very close to her and was careful to keep his arm around her, trying to comfort her, although he looked as desolate and hopeless as a man who sees death in the room.

Ford brought three chairs to the other side of the table, across from Monroe and his family, and arranged them. But all three men hesitated before taking their seats.

Richard glared at the wax doll lying face-up underneath the candelabra in the circle of weak light, and his fine nostrils grew white. "I . . . don't want to sit at table with that obscenity," he muttered. "In fact, I refuse to allow it in the room. But—" He turned to search Shiloh's face. "This is your likeness, Shiloh," he said in a low voice. "It's a violation of your peace. What do you want to do with it?"

"Burn it," Shiloh growled. "Now. But I won't touch it."

"No!" Chloe howled. "If you burn it, you'll feel like you're burning, Shiloh!"

Shiloh merely looked at her incredulously, with open disgust.

"Be silent!" Richard ordered sternly. "Chloe, I will listen to you because I want to know—exactly—what you've done. But I will not allow you to spout your evil—yes, evil!—beliefs here. So as your father ordered you, so I am ordering you, in the name of Jesus Christ, to be silent unless I ask you a question."

Chloe cowered, and suddenly her eyes grew clouded and her face pinched with overwhelming fear. Richard stared at her unflinchingly, and Chloe quickly dropped her gaze and whispered, "Yes, sir."

Monroe stood up. "It's my house and my family," he said in a dead tone. "I will burn it." Snatching it up from the table, he almost ran to the door at the back of the room.

Slowly Richard, Gowan, and Shiloh seated themselves. All of them unconsciously folded their hands on the table and stared at the children across from them. The three men looked like stern judges, their faces grim, their eyes flashing, and Corbett, Adah, and Chloe all shrank back in their seats.

Not a word was spoken until Monroe returned, wiping his hands as if they were soiled, and took his seat. "Colonel Duvall," he said, his voice now steady, though grieved, "Corbett will tell you what they have done. Son, you tell them everything. *Everything*." When he addressed Corbett, he looked straight ahead, refusing to look at his son.

Corbett raised his head and stared blankly into space. When he spoke, his voice was strangely detached, as if he were telling a story of people and places that no one there had ever seen. "I met Dédé on my birthday. My eighteenth birthday. I went into town, and I went to Congo Square for the dances. I met her there on Friday night. On Saturday she came to my room and told me that she had only just realized who I was, and that she had to tell me . . . something . . . and that she could advise me, and help me." He hesitated, though his eyes were still blank and unfocused, and his expression was unchanged.

"Go on, Corbett," Richard prompted him, not unkindly.

"She told me that . . . that I . . . that I . . . and Adah, and Chloe . . ." His voice wavered, then dropped inaudibly, and his face seemed to crumple. He glanced guiltily at his father and the crumpled form of his mother. "I . . . can't . . ." he whispered.

"Oh, but you can, boy," Monroe said harshly. "Just like you did all the things you did . . . you just make up your mind and do it. Now."

"Y-yes, sir," Corbett breathed, then stared back into the blackness behind Richard, Shiloh, and Gowan Ford. "Dédé told me that I and my sisters are the vicomte's children. That La Maison des Chattes Bleues should belong to us. And that she could help us get it back."

A stunned silence seemed to stifle everyone in the room. Molly lifted her head for the first time and stared at her children as if they were people she'd never seen before, who had just uttered an obscenity in public. Monroe looked as stunned as if someone had just hit him in the head with a mace.

Richard, Shiloh, and Ford blinked several times; Richard and Shiloh drew in deep breaths, but it seemed as if Gowan Ford had stopped breathing. Far down the table Luna jerked upright in shock, her eyes widened in stark disbelief.

Molly was the first to speak, although if the room had not been so utterly silent, no one could have heard her desperate whisper. "You . . . you . . . my children . . . all of you thought that I . . . ?" She drew in a shuddering breath, then buried her face in her hands. Monroe threw both his arms around her and looked at Corbett, Adah, and Chloe over his wife's head. He stared, his eyes horrified, his face ashen. None of the three children glanced at their parents; Corbett still stared out into space; Adah was bent almost double, her chin pressed against her chest; Chloe's head was still bowed, though her shoulders were defiantly squared.

Luna made an odd snorting sound. "Do you mean to seriously tell me, Corbett, that you actually believed that tripe?"

Chloe's head whipped around. "It's true, Luna! You're just jealous, and you know it! All those times you sneered at us for being mulattos—we're quadroons, and Les Chattes Bleues should belong to us!"

"Chloe, be quiet," Corbett said resignedly. "Just . . . shut up." He dropped his eyes, and his shoulders sagged.

"It's true, Corbett! It is true! Dédé said so, and so did Marie Laveau!" Chloe shrieked hysterically.

"Calm down!" Richard commanded. "Everyone! Calm down."

Adah and Corbett flinched, Chloe lapsed into her former posture of sullen obeisance, Molly tried to sit upright and quiet her sobs, and Luna sat back in her chair with a sarcastic look on her face.

"Now then, I have questions to ask all of you concerning this charge," Richard said quietly. "And believe me, this is a serious, heart-rending charge—against your mother. Molly, is this charge against you true?" he asked gently.

"No!" she wailed and began to sob anew, burying her head against Monroe's shoulder. "Oh no, never . . . the vicomte never . . . I would never . . ."

"It's all right, Molly," Richard murmured regretfully. "Neither I nor your husband, nor, I think, anyone else in this world would think that of you—"

"Except my children!" Molly cried in anguish.

"—so I felt that since this charge was made against you, you must answer it simply and truthfully—which you have done," Richard finished. His features hardened, and he turned to the three children across from him. "Now answer me, Corbett. Did you truly believe Dédé and Marie Laveau when they told you that you are the Vicomte de Cheyne's children?"

Corbett didn't look up. "Yes, sir, I did," he said hopelessly.

"And you, Adah?" Richard asked.

"Y-yes, s-sir," she whispered.

"And you, Chloe?"

"Yes, and I—"

"Be silent," Richard said in a monotone. "Now my second question. Corbett, you have heard your mother deny this charge. Now—whom do you believe? Your mother? Or those . . . women?"

Corbett finally looked at his mother and father, his face crumpled with despair. "I . . . I . . . believe my mother . . . and father."

"Me, too," Adah said in a choked voice.

Chloe stayed silent, her head bowed.

"And you, Chloe?" Richard persisted. "Just exactly whom do you believe? Marie Laveau and Dédé? Or your own parents?"

"I . . . I . . . She . . . told me I was better than that! She told me that I was meant to be a fine lady, like . . . like . . . all you Big Bugs! And that those two women stole Les Chattes Bleues from us!" Chloe screamed. "It's ours, and they—"

"Silence!" Richard thundered and slammed his hand on the table. He leaned over and said carefully, "Child, you are in danger, terrible danger, which you refuse to see. But I tell you now, Chloe, that you had better be quiet and listen and understand what you have done and what is going to happen to you. But if you refuse to be quiet, and calm, and respectful, I will take measures to see that you are removed from Les Chattes Bleues. Now. Tonight."

"Re-removed from Les Chattes Bleues?" Chloe repeated in confusion. "What . . . what do you mean? What does that mean?" she pleaded, turning to Corbett.

Corbett shook his head helplessly. "Chloe, we're in a lot of trouble."

Suddenly Chloe's face was filled with true, helpless fear, and as if in a trance she turned back to stare at first Richard Duvall, then Gowan Ford, then Shiloh. Only then, as suddenly as if she were struck by lightning, did she see and comprehend their disgust. Only then did she see the true loathing in Shiloh Irons' face. Only then did she see the abhorrence in Richard Duvall's eyes. Only then did she see the barely contained fury in Gowan Ford's marred face. She swallowed hard, and tears welled up in her eyes. With a shaking hand she swiped them away and seemed to melt into an awkward lump in her chair.

"I want to tell the rest of it," Corbett said in a faraway voice. "I'm tired . . . so tired . . ."

"Go ahead, Corbett," Richard said.

"Dédé told me that the *vaudou* would help us get Les Chattes Bleues back. She told me that we would have to convince Mrs. Edwards and Mrs. Buckingham to leave, and then Les Chattes Bleues and all its riches would be ours."

"How did she know about—" Shiloh began darkly, but Richard Duvall made a cutting motion with one hand, and he fell silent.

"What riches are these, Corbett?" Richard asked quietly. "You mean the plantation? Even though I can see that you were greatly deceived, surely you didn't think that you and Adah and Chloe could run this plantation by yourselves and make the kind of money that Mrs. Edwards and Mrs. Buckingham and Mr. Ford make?"

"No . . . no . . ." Corbett said wearily. "But we thought they would leave in a hurry . . . and be . . . frightened, and leave everything, you see. So we'd have all the treasures here . . . they have jewels, you know

297

. . . they even have crowns! And . . . and silverware, and fine linens, and horses . . . and I know where Mrs. Buckingham keeps the household money," he said in a strange singsong voice.

"Corbett!" Monroe muttered vengefully, and the boy jumped as though he were suddenly awakened from a trance. "You little fools! What did you do?" he moaned. "For . . . for . . . nothing! What did you three think you would do with fine jewels and crowns! Wear them? Where? And while you were here—all by yourselves, I assume, in this feverish dream—what would you eat? Where . . . what . . ." He stopped and shook his head helplessly. "What have you done?" he finished in a ragged whisper.

"I put salt spikes in the indigo last April when we were planting," Corbett answered in a dull voice.

"Salt spikes!" Ford said angrily. Again Richard Duvall made a quieting gesture and he said nothing more, though he glared at Corbett.

"Yes. Dédé gave them to me. They are salt spikes straight from the salt mine at Avery, and they dissolve at different rates," Corbett said in a low voice. "So the plants didn't all get sick at once. I just dropped them alongside the seeds and pushed them into the ground with my boot. No one saw me."

"Oh, my Lord," Monroe whispered desperately. "Lord, give me strength. Is that all, Corbett?"

"I put the *gris-gris* out," Corbett went on dully. "Dédé made them and told me to put them on everyone's doorstep, and to make the salt cross at the door." With a weary glance at Chloe he went on, "But Chloe picked up the *gris-gris* that Dédé made for Mr. Irons' *garçonniere* and burned it. Dédé laughed when I told her."

Richard shook his head sadly. "Go on, Corbett."

"And Dédé and the *vaudou* came and frightened everyone but us. Me and Adah and Chloe. She told us that she could make people sick, but that we would be protected, because the *vaudou* were helping us."

Now Shiloh and Richard Duvall and Ford exchanged glances. They couldn't—didn't—believe that it was some sort of spell or curse that Dédé had invoked to make the sharecroppers and servants at Les Chattes Bleues sick; they knew that somehow, someone had poisoned them. But Corbett sounded as if he told the truth.

Luna grunted, "Chloe? You have something to say?"

Chloe seemed smaller, younger, than she had before. She looked helpless and vulnerable, huddled forlornly in her chair, all defiance gone. But Richard Duvall eyed her warily; Chloe might be frightened, but she had shown no remorse, no repentance, and once she was over her fear, she would likely be the same rebellious woman-child she had been only a few moments before.

Chloe didn't look up or acknowledge Luna's question in any way. Long moments passed, and no one spoke. Finally Chloe muttered, "It was a potion. Dédé said she had to use a potion, because the bad spirits that everyone had here at Les Chattes Bleues were so strong."

Luna gave Richard a dark glance, and then continued, "A potion, Chloe? And how, exactly, did Dédé give . . . the sick people . . . the potion?"

Again Chloe didn't answer for a long time, staring down at her hands. Restlessly she fidgeted with her apron. "Dédé . . . didn't . . . exactly . . . give it to them. She gave it to me."

"And?" Luna said in an ominous tone, but Chloe appeared not to notice.

"I took the potion—it was just a little bit, you know, of milky-looking stuff in a bottle. Just a little bit. And I . . . just . . . wiped the inside . . . of the . . . of the . . . . cistern dippers with it. Just a little bit every time. Just a little."

"Yes, just a little!" Shiloh growled in a voice so filled with fury that it sounded just like a cougar's roar. "Just a little . . . poison!"

"No!" Chloe screamed, her eyes almost straining out of their sockets. "No! It's a—it was a potion! A *vaudou* potion!"

"No, Chloe," Luna said in a voice now silky with venom, "it was poison. You poisoned people. That is attempted murder. And for that, little Chloe, you can hang!"

Chloe screamed and jumped out of her chair, knocking it sideways. Desperately, as if she were a cornered animal, her wild eyes went first to the front door, then to the back; then she tried to run, stumbling, crying out, toward the back door. Molly jumped up and ran to her and held her. Chloe screamed and flailed out, but Molly held her close and quieted her somewhat. Monroe stared helplessly at them, and then at Richard Duvall.

"Take them home, Monroe," Richard said calmly. "I think we've heard enough. I will consider this matter tonight and pray for wisdom. Tomorrow I will let you know what must be done."

Adah jumped up and hurried to her mother and clasped her about the waist desperately. Monroe stood, then hesitated as Corbett stayed stubbornly seated. "Corbett—"

"Father, may I stay?" Corbett asked hesitantly. "I . . . need . . . to talk to Colonel Duvall . . . if he'll talk to me."

Monroe glanced at Richard Duvall, who nodded, and Monroe said in a low voice, "All right, son. But come straight home when you're finished. Don't . . . don't . . ."

"I won't run, Father," Corbett said wearily. "I have nowhere to go."

After another moment of indecision, Monroe finally went to Molly and the girls and spoke to them in a low tone. Slowly, wearily, almost stumbling, the family left.

Richard Duvall studied Corbett. He was a handsome boy; his face was strong, well-defined, a pleasing mix of his father's even features and his mother's quiet prettiness. Corbett's eyes slid uncomfortably to Luna, then to Shiloh, and then to Gowan Ford. He hesitated, glancing again at Luna.

"Did you need to speak to me alone?" Richard asked.

"No," Shiloh said harshly. "No, Colonel Duvall, I don't think that's a good idea."

"I've got to agree with Mr. Irons," Ford said reluctantly, staring at Corbett. He had known this boy for eighteen years—or thought he knew him—but the reserved, dignified boy he thought he knew was not this hateful child who believed voodoo witches over his own mother and father. . . .

"No . . . it's . . . all right," Corbett finally said resignedly. "I guess I'm kind of embarrassed, but maybe it's good for me." He looked at Richard Duvall gravely and said evenly, "Tonight—just now—I realized what I've done. The . . . evil . . . I've done, Colonel Duvall. And I realized how much I hate what I've done, and I hate . . . myself." He took a deep breath, though his gaze never left Richard's face. "My father and mother are Christians, Colonel Duvall. But I'm not. And I want to be."

"Yes?" Richard asked quietly. "You want to be a Christian, Corbett? Do you understand exactly what that means?"

Corbett frowned. "I . . . think so. At least I know what I want is to . . . to . . . confess my sin, Colonel Duvall. That's why I made myself talk . . . to you instead of my parents. It's . . . this . . . is hard, you know." He swallowed and shifted restlessly in his chair.

"Yes, I do know," Richard replied easily. "But you have already confessed grave sins tonight, Corbett, in front of people who were much harder on you than the Lord Jesus will be. He will forgive you, you know, instantly, without anger, without ever looking back or remembering any of your sins."

"Yes, sir, I . . . think I understand that," Corbett said uneasily. "So . . . now . . . what else do I have to do?"

Richard smiled, a slight, fleeting smile that was gone before Corbett was certain he'd seen it. But Richard's voice held unmistakable warmth when he said, "Well, technically, Corbett, that is all you have to do; confess that you are a sinner, and ask the Lord Jesus to save you from your sin, and come into your heart, and be your Lord. Then He does all the rest."

"What do you mean?" Corbett asked in confusion. "You mean . . . that's it? That's all of it?"

"Yes, as far as Almighty God is concerned," Richard answered. "He sent His son, Jesus, here to die for the sins of the world. When Jesus did that, He took upon himself all of our sins—yours, your sisters', mine —everyone's. All we have to do is ask His forgiveness, and ask to belong to Him. And then, we do— forever."

Corbett's smooth, youthful brow wrinkled. "So . . . so then I'll be a Christian, and I'll be . . . different, because I belong to Jesus . . . and God. But still . . . I'll still . . . have all these things, all these things I did. I'll still have to . . . face them, and pay for them. . . . Is that right?"

"That's right," Richard said steadily. "All of us, while we live on this earth, in these mortal bodies, commit sins. Every sin has a result, and every result of sin is bad, and all of us must live with the results of our sin. The difference—the huge difference—is that when we are one of God's children, He forgives us our sin. Always. And so we never are required to pay His price for our sin, as Jesus did; for that was a grievous price, indeed, and could not be borne by mortal man."

"Yes, I understand," Corbett said, nodding his head forcefully. "Could we pray now? Would you pray for me first, Colonel Duvall? That way I feel like I've got . . . some . . . uh . . ."

"Pull?" Shiloh suggested with a half-smile.

"Yes, sir," Corbett said with relief. "Like a formal introduction."

Richard grinned widely. "That's not necessary, Corbett, because believe me, Almighty God knows you as well as He knows me, and Jesus loves you just as much as He does me. I promise. But I'll be glad to introduce you; in fact, it will be a great pleasure." He bowed his head and prayed simply: "Dearest Lord, here is Corbett, and he wants to come and join You in repentance, in confession of his sins, and enter into Your kingdom. I ask now, Lord, in the mighty and all-powerful name of Jesus, the Lion of Judah, the Sword who will never be broken, that You cleanse this boy of all his dealings with the devil and his demons. I ask, in the name of Jesus, that You deliver him from the forces of Satan that would destroy him. I ask, Lord, in the name of Jesus, for the deliverance, for the cleansing, for the saving of Corbett's very soul."

Corbett still had his head bowed, but he began to speak quietly. "Dear Lord, I'm so sorry for everything I've done. I've done so many bad things, and I know You heard me tonight, so I pray now that I wouldn't even have to say it again to You. Just forgive me, please, Lord Jesus, and help me . . . save me, and help me to . . . love, to love my parents, to love my sisters. Just, please, save me and help me. Because I need You, Lord Jesus, and I . . . love . . . You. Amen."

Corbett looked up at Richard Duvall and smiled with relief. "I feel better," he said quietly. "I sure am tired, but I really do feel better."

Shiloh studied him solemnly, as did Gowan Ford. Richard smiled at him and said, "We'll talk more tomorrow, Corbett. I just want you to know that you've done the right thing, and tonight, and forever, you'll know that no matter what happens you belong to Jesus, and you'll be with Him forever."

Forgotten, half-hidden in the shadows, alone at the end of the table, Luna made a small sound. It was a very small sound, but everyone turned to look at her. Tears were streaming down her face. Gowan Ford's mouth opened in amazement; he had never, ever seen Luna cry, and had never thought he would.

"Colonel Duvall," she asked in a small, breathless voice, "do you suppose we could go through all that one more time? One more time—for me?"

24

THE ROCK AND SHELTER

The next dawn was hazy, hot, and humid. The sun, by eight o'clock in the morning, was a gleeful ball of golden fire that beat down on Les Chattes Bleues with all the boisterous heat of summer, though it was early March.

Devlin Buchanan, M.D., made his morning rounds at Les Chattes Bleues. He visited Grand-mère Journée and admonished her to stay in bed and let Luna wait on her hand and foot, as Luna insisted she would do whether Grand-mère Journée agreed or not.

Dev then hurried to check on Becky Colton, who was sitting up in bed and demanding that her mother bring her lots of cracked ice from the ice house, which her mother was overjoyed to do, and to which Dev gave his amused approval.

After giving Suze Colton some simple instructions for Becky's care, Dev hurried back to his *garçonniere*. He wanted to be alone, to continue to pray and read his Bible and think. He had done this faithfully last night, but he felt that he must seek God even more on this day. He had some hard decisions to make and some difficult actions to take, and he wanted to have a rock-hard certainty of the right course. And Devlin Buchanan reminded himself Who was his Rock, and his Shelter in time of trouble, and that was where he went.

★   ★   ★   ★

Molly came in at dawn to dress Tante Marye and to receive her instructions for the day.

"Molly!" Tante Marye exclaimed. "Whatever is the matter with you?"

"Nothing, *madame*, thank you," she replied dully. Her eyes were swollen almost shut, and her lips trembled. Her uniform—plain black dress, white bib apron—was rumpled.

"I beg to differ," Tante Marye said stiffly. "You, Molly, are in a *state.*" She pronounced the word as if it were a dread disease, but Molly seemed not to notice as she searched wearily in Tante Marye's armoire for suitable undergarments. "I said, Molly, that you are in a *state,*" Tante Marye repeated ominously. "I want you to take the day off. The entire day. Beginning now."

Molly turned and ran shaking fingers across her forehead. "No, *madame,* I can't do that. Who would take care of the house and the guests? What about dinner, and—"

"Do I understand, Molly, that you are questioning my orders?" Tante Marye said. "Really, you must require some time to gather your wits. In fact, take two days off. Today and tomorrow. Do remain silent when I am speaking, Molly. I can run this household perfectly well for two days. Surely you are not suggesting that I am so witless that no one will have food to eat while you are resting; I know my way around a kitchen, and considering the *state* you are in, I shall certainly do better than you at attending to the meals. So that is the end of it. Good morning." She turned her back on Molly, and with weary resignation Molly retreated.

Tante Marye stared out the window toward the distant indigo fields. "Really! Molly is in such a *state*! Something dreadful must have happened last night ... but certainly it was not in the house," Tante Marye told herself. Presumably whatever had happened had affected the outside of La Maison des Chattes Bleues, and Tante Marye's only concern was the inside of La Maison des Chattes Bleues. Stolidly she set about to do all the household chores herself.

Nia Clarkson, after attending to Cheney's morning *toilette,* was just starting to straighten her mistress's bedroom when Tante Marye sailed through the door. She stopped and eyed Nia haughtily. "Hello, Nia. You are such a small, meek slip of a thing that I quite forget that you are on the place."

"Good morning, Mrs. Edwards," Nia replied, a glimmer of a smile playing on her lips. "Yes, ma'am, I am small, but I'm not really very meek. I just don't make as much noise as some people."

"Such as your mother," Tante Marye agreed. "The last time Irene visited, she brought Dally. She was quite an addition to the household staff, I must say; they cowered in terror for days. . . ." Eyeing Nia speculatively, she went on, "I have dismissed Molly for two days. She evidently is fatigued and requires rest. I shall be attending to the cleaning, laundry, and meals myself. Would you do me the service of attending to this room and bringing Cheney's laundry down to the washroom?"

"Yes, ma'am, of course," Nia replied. "But I have a better idea than that."

"Oh? And what might that be?"

"That we do this room, and all of the rest of the house, together, Mrs. Edwards," Nia suggested. "I can do laundry and ironing, and I can cook, too."

Tante Marye eyed her with something that resembled suspicion, but her voice was warm when she answered, "Why, thank you, Nia. Certainly that is beyond your duties here, but I would greatly appreciate your help."

And so a congenial partnership was formed.

★　★　★　★

When Cheney went downstairs, she hungrily helped herself to the breakfast sideboard. No one else was there, and no one else came in, so she ate quickly and went to find somebody. She wandered in the side gardens, in the general direction of Shiloh's *garçonniere*, to find somebody—and she did find one somebody, though it was not exactly the one she was pretending that she wasn't looking for.

"Yoo-hoo! Cheney!" Tante Elyse called from the back of the house. Cheney—with one last furtive glance at Shiloh's *garçonniere*—went to join her.

"I'm on my way to the stables, dear, to see Sock and Stocking. I do so love those horses! They have such wonderful personalities!" Tante Elyse told Cheney as they hurried along at a fast clip.

They found Shiloh in the stables, talking nonsense to the two horses as they munched on some grapes Shiloh had brought them. Tante Elyse kissed the horses and talked baby-talk to them, and they kissed her back.

"You know, Tante Elyse, Mr. Ford's kinda ... uh ... busy this morning," Shiloh drawled. "I figure you're on your way to see him, right?"

"Yes," Tante Elyse answered absently. She was still making kissy noises and cooing to the horses. "Every morning we decide on our chores. Today I was going to see some of the sharecroppers, and I wanted to check on the processing and inventory of two of the drying barns."

"Ford's gonna be calling on most all of the sharecroppers today, ma'am. But I'd like to come with you to see the plant and the drying barns." Shiloh continued lazily, "You wanna ride?"

"Oh! Yes! Can we?" Tante Elyse exclaimed eagerly.

"Sure. You wanna come, Doc?"

"Sure," Cheney replied gamely.

"Okay. Tante Elyse, would you mind riding with me? Sock won't care."

"Ooh, would I mind?" Tante Elyse flirted, looking up at Shiloh through her thick lashes. "Can I hold on to you very tightly?"

"Sure," Shiloh grinned.

"Tante Elyse!" Cheney exclaimed with exasperation.

Innocently Tante Elyse turned to Cheney. "Well, dear, I am an accomplished horsewoman. If you would be thoughtful enough, you would offer to let me ride Stocking. That way you could ride with Shiloh, and you could hug him all day."

"T-Tante Elyse!" Cheney stammered, horrified.

The final disposition of the riders—though Shiloh and Tante Elyse tried hard to rearrange it—was that Tante Elyse would ride with Shiloh, and Cheney would ride Stocking. And so another fairly congenial partnership was formed for the day.

★   ★   ★   ★

Irene Duvall, after a long dawn talk with her husband, went to Victoria de Lancie's room and knocked on the door. Zhou-Zhou answered the door and hesitantly stepped aside; instinctively she knew she shouldn't block Irene's way as she did Cheney's. Irene was much too much of a lady, full of grace and peace, with none of the fire and fight that Cheney Duvall had.

"May I come in, Mrs. de Lancie?" Irene asked politely.

From the darkened room came a thin, weak version of Victoria's cultured voice. "Of course, Mrs. Duvall," she sighed. "Please do."

With a soft rustle of silk Irene went into the room and sat by Victoria's bedside. The shutters were drawn, and the only light in the room was a single candle in the far corner, away from Victoria's bed. She was lying on her back, with one thin arm over her eyes, her hair spread out in a silver fan on the white linen pillowcase.

"Please excuse me, Mrs. Duvall," she said tremulously. "I am quite unable to receive you properly."

Irene took her thin white hand in both of hers and leaned over close to Victoria. "I understand, Mrs. de Lancie," she said soothingly. "I know that you are ill. Cheney has told me of the terrible sufferings you endure with your migraines."

Still Victoria covered her eyes with her forearm and even turned her head slightly away from Irene. "Yes," she whispered, "but I think you know that this migraine is not the real reason I am suffering."

Irene stroked Victoria's hand. It was fevered and moist. "Yes, I do know. I came here, Mrs. de Lancie, to pray for your healing, if you will permit me. And I want you to know that I will also be honored to pray with you for any needs that you have."

"Like forgiveness?" Victoria asked in a muffled voice.

"Of course," Irene replied.

Victoria slowly dropped her arm, clasped both of Irene's hands with hers, and stared at her with sudden hope dawning in her red-rimmed eyes. "I know that God will forgive me," she whispered. "But will you? And your husband? And especially . . . will Cheney?"

Irene smiled sweetly. "Even though I am unsure of the particulars of your transgressions, Mrs. de Lancie, I forgive you now, as you have asked. I believe that my husband will forgive you quite as gladly. As for Cheney—I know that she loves you very much. More, perhaps, than you realize. She will forgive you, Mrs. de Lancie. Cheney has faults, as do we all, but she has a generous and kind heart."

"Oh, Lord!" Victoria cried in anguish and began to weep. "Thank God you have come, Mrs. Duvall! Already I feel lighter in my soul, and the pain in my head is lessening. Will you please pray for me—and with me?"

"Mrs. de Lancie, I can think of nothing else I'd rather do."

★   ★   ★   ★

Richard Duvall and Gowan Ford met at Monroe and Molly's cabin at dawn and spoke to the family.

"I have not made a final decision regarding your crimes, Corbett, Adah, Chloe," Richard said sternly. "I will speak with Mrs. Edwards and Mrs. Buckingham tonight; this is their home, and your criminal acts were directed toward them. They should take part in the final decision regarding your punishment."

Corbett met Richard's gaze unflinchingly and nodded. "Yes, sir." Chloe and Adah stayed seated with their heads bowed.

"Mr. Ford, Mr. Irons, and I have agreed on one course of action that will be taken today," Richard went on. "The three of you will accompany me and Mr. Ford. We will visit each home that has been affected by your actions; Mr. Ford has prepared a list of each sharecropper who has lost part of his crop from the salt spikes. Also we will visit each household where someone was poisoned."

Corbett looked grieved, Adah cowered in her chair, and Chloe visibly flinched.

"Each of you will confess his or her part in these crimes to each person," Richard continued firmly. "Each of you will then ask each affected person for forgiveness."

"Yes, sir," Corbett said quietly. Adah nodded soundlessly.

"No, I won't—" Chloe began faintly, looking up at Richard with a pleading expression.

"Yes, you will, Chloe," Richard said grimly. "You will say the words, whether you mean it or not. I assure you that before this day is over, you will have confessed to each person you have wronged exactly what you did. And you will ask their forgiveness."

Monroe stepped forward. "Yes, sir, she will. All of my children will do this without one word of dissent. But, Colonel Duvall, I have a request to make of you."

"Yes, Monroe?"

"May I come with you?" Monroe asked humbly. "Last night I decided that I would take charge of my household; I also decided that my Lord Jesus Christ would take charge of me." He turned and smiled faintly at Corbett, who smiled back. Turning back to Richard he said in a strong voice, "I must stand with my children, for good or ill."

"I agree wholeheartedly," Richard said with satisfaction. "And I believe, Monroe, that what you have just told me means that you have victory, no matter what happens to you, to your family, or to Les Chattes Bleues. You are in the hands of the Lord Jesus Christ, and by your own admission He holds your house in His hands. You, Monroe, have already won. Now, shall we go?"

The family and guests at Les Chattes Bleues did not all meet again until seven o'clock in the evening. Tante Marye and Nia were busy in the kitchen, preparing dinner and talking about the relative merits of fresh herbs over dried when Irene and Victoria, arm-in-arm, came into the kitchen. They were dressed for dinner; Irene was radiant in a soft sea-green watered silk, complete with elbow-length gloves and diamond bracelet and earrings. Victoria was pale and shaky, but looked ethereally fragile in pastel yellow with heavy gold Etruscan ornaments.

"Irene, Mrs. de Lancie, get out of this kitchen immediately," Tante Marye ordered. "Dinner will be served at eight-thirty in the dining room."

"Mmm, that smells delicious," Irene commented, ignoring Tante Marye's stern injunctions. "Why can't we stay in here, Tante Marye? I can help, and I'm certain Mrs. de Lancie would rather stay here with us than in the house all by herself."

"The guests of La Maison des Chattes Bleues do not congregate in the kitchen as if they were a gaggle of servants," Tante Marye said wrathfully. She still wore her day clothes, a serviceable gray linen with a bib apron, and her gray hair was invisible underneath a white mob cap. Her sleeves were rolled up above the elbow, and her gaunt face was flushed with exertion and the steam rising from the pot she stirred.

"Don't you mean gaggle of geese, Marye?" Tante Elyse said earnestly, popping her head in the door. Riff and Raff peeped around her skirts. "Hullo, everyone." She turned to address someone outside: "Everyone's in here! Marye wants us to come in!"

"Elyse!" Tante Marye exclaimed with disgust, stirring the pot with angry circles. "I forbid you and anyone else to come in! And no, I certainly did not intend to call the guests of Les Chattes Bleues a gaggle of geese!"

Merrily Tante Elyse gathered up her skirts—Raff was jumping up on her, begging to come in—shooed the dogs away, and wandered over to the worktable. Unconcernedly she picked up a carrot from a bowlful of carrots and potatoes, scrutinized it with narrowed eyes, then munched it reflectively. "No, you called them a gaggle of servants," she finally replied mildly.

"No, I didn't—" Tante Marye began, then suddenly, dramatically, pointed her large dripping spoon toward the door. "Stop! Cheney! Mr. Irons! Not only are you not coming into this kitchen, but I want you to escort everyone else back to the house!"

"I believe they would be obliged to enter the room to do that, wouldn't they?" Tante Elyse said guilelessly.

Nia assisted Victoria to the table and brought her an iced pink beverage in a tall, slender glass. "Here, Mrs. de Lancie. It's a fruit punch I made. Maybe it'll make you feel better."

"Mmm, it's delicious, Nia, thank you," Victoria said gratefully. "Quite refreshing."

"Can I have some?" Shiloh asked, making his way through the growing crowd of people to the table. He licked his lips. "Looks so good, and I'm thirsty." He smiled tentatively at Victoria, who looked up at him gratefully. "Please, join me, Shiloh," she said graciously, and Shiloh sat at the crude oak table.

Nia hurried to fix more fruit drinks. Tante Elyse leaned negligently against the worktable, munching noisily and watching Marye and Nia with interest. Irene hovered over Tante Marye's shoulder until her aunt ordered her with exasperation to go make herself useful somewhere else in the kitchen if she was determined to stay against all reason and decorum. Cheney eyed the enormous bowl of carrots and potatoes doubtfully. "Do these require some sort of . . . processing before they can be cooked?"

Shiloh laughed out loud, and soon everyone except Tante Marye joined in. This grand lady turned on Cheney triumphantly. "And that," she crowed, "is a perfect illustration of why I don't want all of you helpless people in my kitchen!"

"I'm not helpless," Gowan Ford announced as he strode confidently into the room, followed by Dev and Richard, who looked around curiously. They very rarely saw kitchens.

"That is true," Tante Marye agreed magnanimously. "And I must also mention that this only emphasizes my point: when a *man* with only one arm is more help in a kitchen than many women." With that final huff she stubbornly turned her back on the now-crowded room.

"Don't worry about that, Miss Cheney," Gowan said politely. "I'll peel these potatoes and carrots."

"This I gotta see," Shiloh murmured.

"Oh, they are to be peeled?" Cheney asked with interest. "Shouldn't they be washed or something?"

Taking a paring knife with a small, flexible blade down from where the knives hung from a ceiling-mounted rack, Gowan Ford muttered darkly, "I know that Marye has scrubbed these things at least three times by now; and I ask you, what good does it do to scrub the skin when you're getting ready to peel it off?"

"That," Tante Elyse said thoughtfully, "is a very interesting question."

Without turning around Marye intoned, "That is a very interesting comment from the person who was just devouring a raw carrot that still had the skin on it."

"Yes, that's true," Tante Elyse agreed complacently.

"Can I do something?" Richard asked Irene, who was standing at the table and staring, perplexed, at a bowl of grapes, cherries, apples, and figs.

"I don't know," Irene said absently. Frowning, she murmured to herself, "Do these need to be . . . processed in some way. . . ?"

A shout of laughter echoed in the room at Irene's unconscious echo of Cheney's previous—dumb—question. Irene looked around, bewildered, and Richard said hastily, "It's nothing, dear. Perhaps Nia can help us, considering we are quite helpless."

"Quite," came Marye's sonorous tone.

"I shall help Mr. Ford peel these potatoes," Dev announced proudly. "Although I must say that even though I am quite good with a knife—and a scalpel—"

"And a whip," Shiloh added mischievously under his breath. He winked at Victoria, and she smiled with undisguised relief and gratitude.

Dev rounded on Shiloh, his face dark, but when he saw Shiloh's amused expression, he suddenly assumed an arrogant, uppity tone. "And a whip, of course. But I doubt that that would be of much help in peeling potatoes."

"Interesting thought," Ford grunted. "If I could just master a whip, that'd be an easy way to do it with one hand. Just whip the skin off of 'em."

"Kinda looks to me like you don't need much improvement on your method," Shiloh said with fascination. Gowan Ford laid a potato down on the table, anchored it—somehow—with the heel of his hand, and nimbly ran the blade of the paring knife in a continuous circular motion against the top of the potato, while turning it with the heel of his hand. "I don't think I could ever learn to do that," Shiloh said with admiration. "And—didn't you tell me you were right-handed, Mr. Ford? And you've taught yourself to do that with your left hand? And fast, too!"

"Yep," Ford said succinctly. The potato was done, and he grabbed another.

Ruefully Shiloh held up his thumb. "Sure, and you're doing better with a knife than I've been doing lately."

Cheney stared at it in surprise. She hadn't noticed that Shiloh's thumb was cut; now, as he held it up, she could see a deep slice across the pad of his thumb, and the lips of the wound were swollen apart. "Shiloh!" she fumed. "That should have taken a stitch or two! Now look at it! And—did you say that you cut yourself?"

"No one else did it this time," Shiloh admitted slyly. "I did it all by myself. With my own trusty Bowie knife."

"Oh! One of the famous knives that Mr. Bowie designed? Can I see it?" Tante Elyse asked, her eyes bright.

Shiloh reached behind his back and brought the startling-looking knife out. Tante Elyse grabbed it and perused it as if it were a new tiara or a new kitten. "Goodness! What a dangerous-looking knife! It's wonderful! Where do you suppose I might get one, Shiloh?"

"Now that's what I would call a dangerous knife," Ford muttered darkly. "One that belonged to Elyse."

"Watch it, ma'am," Shiloh said uneasily as Elyse ran a finger down the knife, perilously close to the edge of the blade. "Take my word for it. That thing will reach out and get you when you're not looking."

"Oh yes, of course," Tante Elyse murmured, smiling. "You cut your thumb . . . and what was that you said today about that starting a whole cartful of trouble yesterday?"

An interested silence fell upon the room. Cheney, Victoria, and the two aunts knew something had happened last night, but they didn't know exactly what. Richard had told Irene the entire story that morning, but the other ladies only had an inkling that something had happened that concerned Monroe and his family.

"Nia," Tante Marye said into the quiet, "would you please go to the kitchen garden and pick some squash blossoms? I believe this broth is about ready."

"Yes, ma'am," Nia said obediently and left the kitchen.

Tante Marye sniffed. "I do not hold with discussing private business in front of the servants."

"Oh, Tante Marye—" Cheney began, but Richard interrupted her gently.

"No, she's right this time, Cheney. We've already been obliged to go to practically everyone on the place and tell them what we know as certainty. But as the matter stands right now, I would prefer that we all know the whole truth, and our conclusions—mine, and Mr. Ford's, and Dev's, and Shiloh's—before we tell all of the servants and sharecroppers the entire story."

"Yes, Father," Cheney agreed quietly. "That does make good sense.

So—what has happened? What happened last night? And what in the world does it have to do with Shiloh cutting his own thumb?" She gave him a disdainful glance, but he winked at her flirtatiously, so she looked away quickly, blushing slightly.

"The . . . story is too complicated to explain all the details now," Richard said with difficulty. "I know you are all very curious, and rightly so. But for now I think all I'll say—all I have time to say, before Nia returns—is that Monroe's children were deeply involved with the events here at Les Chattes Bleues. They were responsible for the sick indigo plants, and for the illness that the sharecroppers and servants have suffered."

A stunned silence greeted this revelation. Gowan Ford, however, kept on peeling potatoes in his unusual way, with renewed ferocity. "Corbett, Adah, and Chloe were partly responsible," he said dourly, "but I still hold Dédé, and Marie Laveau, and the *vaudou* ultimately responsible for everything that has happened here at Les Chattes Bleues."

"That is true, Mr. Ford," Richard agreed quietly. "But it occurs to me that the final responsibility for this entire . . . plot . . . may actually be on someone else's shoulders."

Ford stopped peeling and looked up at Richard, frowning. "What do you mean, Colonel Duvall?"

"I mean that Corbett, Adah, and Chloe never offered us a clue as to why the *vaudou* were so eager to help them," Richard asserted with disgust. "I hardly think it was a noble gesture, intended to help those children . . . and, also, you must take into account that Corbett and the girls knew—know—nothing about the real treasure here at Les Chattes Bleues. The gold."

"That's true," Shiloh said thoughtfully. "But—let me think—that means that maybe Dédé and the *vaudou* do know about it? And that somehow they thought that if Corbett and Adah and that silly little Chloe actually succeeded in running off Mrs. Edwards and Mrs. Buckingham, they could get their filthy hands on it?"

"Those people cannot possibly know about the gold," Marye said flatly, and Elyse nodded her head in agreement. "I tell you that I—and Elyse—have never told a soul about it except for Dev, that one time!"

"I believe you," Ford said vehemently. "If you two ladies hadn't been so very discreet, I would have known about the gold long ago. And, think: if the very people who have lived here all their lives know nothing about that gold, how in the world could those *vaudou* find out about it?"

"I suppose that those men at the mint wondered about it and perhaps gossiped," Dev suggested. "Although I never told them that it belonged to you. It was, after all, in my possession, and they never questioned where I got it."

"Perhaps someone—someone else—suspects that there really is gold here at Les Chattes Bleues," Richard murmured almost to himself. "But perhaps he doesn't actually know where it is, or how much there is. . . . Perhaps this person thought of a way to scare Marye and Elyse so much that they would be obliged to try to leave. . . ."

"And then he could either knock them in the head and steal it in . . . in the bayou, or something . . ." Shiloh said excitedly.

"—or hope that Marye and Elyse would need it for a sudden upheaval such as moving to France—and trust him enough to tell him about it," Ford blustered angrily, his single blue eye lighting with sudden comprehension.

"—and most especially, where it was, so it would be easy to steal!" Dev finished triumphantly.

Shiloh, Richard Duvall, Dev, and Gowan Ford stared at one another with amazement. It appeared that the same idea—the same person—had occurred to each of them at the same time.

"John Law," Richard pronounced in a particularly ominous tone.

"Sir—Mistah Duvall—Sir—" Nia's high, breathy little voice barely cut through the tension in the room.

"Hmm? Yes, Nia?" Richard asked, turning to the door.

Nia stood in the doorway, holding the corners of her apron up. Piled inside her apron were a dozen squash blossoms, delicate golden flutes. Nia's childlike features were distorted with fear, and her mouth worked for a few moments before she could manage to sound the words. "The *vaudou*, sir. They're here."

And then the drums began.

25

VAUDOU VANQISHED

This time there was no hesitation.

This time there was no fear, or doubts.

This time Richard Duvall walked directly into the firelit clearing, his face set, his steps sure, his mind and soul at perfect rest. Devlin Buchanan and Gowan Ford walked alongside of him, their strength and wisdom a comfort and surety to Richard.

Dev looked around with an oddly detached curiosity; he, after all, had never seen a *vaudou* gathering. Though he found the sights, the barbaric music, the smells, the savage chanting to be repugnant, still the clinical portion of his mind registered everything with a peculiar impartiality, as if the scene were of a distant, dark land viewed through a stereopticon.

Gowan Ford looked first for Dédé and immediately saw her dancing at the opposite end of the clearing, roughly where they had found her the last time. Even as the three men walked into the crowd, Dédé looked straight at them as if she sensed their coming. She screamed "Ay-yi-yi!" and threw her head back, making signs and gestures with her hands. Then she pointed dramatically to Richard and Gowan and Dev and screamed, "*Vaudou! Vaudou Magnian!*"

Richard never wavered, never hesitated, never even gave Dédé the slightest bit of notice. The drummers increased the infernal tempo when Dédé screamed; the dancers jumped and undulated even more wildly; the same two cats hissed and yowled; the chant grew louder, more insistent. Still Richard passed through the crowd as if he were merely making his way along a busy city street.

Gowan and Dev followed him closely. Dev looked to his right and saw two women dressed shamelessly in bits of red cloth, jumping up and down in frantic little hops, their arms straight and stiff at their sides, their heads wobbling in a sickening manner. He saw their eyes, turned upward in their heads, so that only white crescents showed beneath their half-closed lids. Suddenly one woman leaped impossibly high, screaming shrilly; then she fell hard to the ground. Dev watched impassively as they passed. The woman began to foam at the mouth, and her eyes were now wide open, though still only the bizarre whites gleamed. Slowly she began undulating exactly like a snake, crawling, slithering, her body writhing impossibly, her hands straight down at her sides. She was crawling—slithering—toward Dev and Gowan Ford. Dev watched her with an odd pity and an odd impassivity. *I hope she doesn't get under my feet,* he reflected. *I should truly hate to tread upon her ... but I would, definitely, before she should so much as touch Richard's boots....*

Gowan Ford looked to their left. A man, tall and slender, stood up and tore the shirt from his body, scratching himself brutally as he did so. He was screaming some chant, mindlessly repeating the same incomprehensible words over and over again, and he wheeled and jerked and turned in frantic circles. Then his scream was suddenly cut off; he turned his face to the sky, opened his mouth wide, and began to howl, a high, animal keening that was not only inhuman but unearthly. Foam covered his lips and ran down his throat to his bare chest, and then thick red blood began running down the sides of his mouth. Gowan Ford shook his head slightly. *Possessed, as he was asking for,* he thought calmly. *And probably bit his own tongue in two. How can they plead to be possessed by this evil ... the demons always rend them and tear at them and mutilate them....* He, too, felt calm, at peace, as if he were in a bell jar that allowed him to witness everything about him but kept him securely and surely shielded from all evil things. Which, of course, he and Dev and Richard Duvall truly were.

Dédé ran, springing lightly on her naked, shapely legs, and came to a rebellious standstill directly in front of Richard Duvall. "You fool! You must leave!" she screamed.

But Richard Duvall never missed a step, and though his stony gray eyes raked Dédé in passing, it was as if she were completely invisible, a pitiful wraith, a scream with no substance. He neatly sidestepped her and continued on his direct line to the table.

The crude table was set up; the tree and the horrific doll were there, propped up on a large box. The two cats, terrified, cowered and screeched in their cages at the ends of the table.

When Richard reached the table, he walked calmly to the center, where the box, the tree, and the doll were. After studying them for a brief moment, he reached out with strong hands and shoved mightily on the heavy box. The tree teetered; the doll swung back and forth from the denuded branches as if it were a hanging man.

Dédé screamed and ran toward them. Dev turned and simply looked her straight in the eyes and said in a low, guttural tone, "Get back, you evil creature. Don't touch us."

Dédé stopped as if he had shoved her; in fact, she stumbled backward as if she had run up against a high wall.

Dev turned back around, placed his hands on the box next to Richard's, and pushed. Ford, with his single strong left hand, joined them. The box squeaked, screamed, then toppled over onto the ground. Dev, Richard, and Ford watched unconcernedly, though the din of screams and curses from the people slowly drawing close to them was truly a scene that only could be drawn by the very demons from hell.

The box burst, and snakes came out, wriggling and crawling all over one another, squirming in a sickening mass. They were sluggish and moved slowly, lifting their heads and flicking their forked tongues stupidly.

The chants and screeches increased; the *vaudou* tightened the circle. Dédé took a tentative half-step closer to Dev and Richard and Gowan, her face twisted and ugly with hate and murderous intent.

Suddenly, gloriously, Richard leaped up onto the table as easily as if he were mounting a great horse.

The *vaudou* stopped moving. The chants died out. The screams stopped. Fear showed on many of the women's faces.

His face was an exquisitely chiseled marble statue, his shoulders broad and sure, his form straight and strong. Richard lifted his right fist to the sky and looked up to the darkened heavens. Then he called out clearly, "In the name of Jesus Christ, the Son of Almighty God! I command all of the evil forces, all of the accursed demons, and Satan himself, who cowers at the Blessed Name: Begone!"

A deafening, jarring, fearful, overwhelming clap of thunder seemed to rend the very air. As a mighty, rushing, triumphant force of wind, it rolled over, through, around, and back again, seeming to run along the very earth.

Silence fell like a stone.

Then the air seemed to boil in agony. The *vaudou* were struck dumb and blind and helpless, and they stumbled against one another, and fell, and called out in mind-numbing fear.

The snakes suddenly came alive; they jumped and seethed in the air as if they had suddenly been thrown into hissing flames of fire. Then, so fast that the human eye could barely follow them, they slithered off, over fallen men, over horrified women, and disappeared into the darkness.

Dédé had fallen unconscious, but now she awoke. She could neither see nor hear, and she knew fear such as she had never known before. Screaming mindlessly, she struggled to her feet and ran off blindly, disappearing into the woods.

All of the *vaudou*, with wrenching, horrible cries of pain and fright, ran here and there, falling, crashing to the earth, crawling, sobbing, seeking the woods. Far below them they heard splashes, and like blind, unthinking sea creatures desperately seeking the muck and slime of their home, they fell down the hill and threw themselves into the sleeping waters of the bayou.

Devlin Buchanan, Gowan Ford, and Richard Duvall stood alone in the clearing. At some point Richard had stepped off the table and now stood between Dev and Ford as the three of them calmly watched the chaos around them. After the desperate cries from the bayou somewhere below them died out and the frenzied splashes stopped, Richard said quietly, "We must burn that image and that tree."

Obediently Dev went to pick up the doll—it seemed a pitiful, childish thing now—and threw it into the fire at one end of the clearing. Ford threw the desolate tree into the other. As one, the flames shot upward; a roar of orange fire curled and leaped toward the sky. Then the fires died down and crackled with a rather warm, comforting sound. Gowan Ford found that he was smiling, and he looked up toward the heavens. Not a cloud was in the sky. The night was clear; the stars, in their milky-white cradle, shone down joyfully. "Praise you, God," he said humbly. "Thank you, God."

Dev was thinking and saying much the same thing as he returned to Richard Duvall's side. Ford started back to the table and hesitated. The cats, which had seemed so menacing and evil before, were now just sleepy half-grown kittens. The white one blinked owlishly as she stared at Gowan Ford with mysterious green eyes; the black one was still and calm and regarded him with unblinking, enigmatic yellow eyes.

Ford rejoined Richard and Dev. "This place—this earth—is cleansed, and clean, and consecrated," he announced. "Thank God."

"Amen," Richard said.

Dev said reverently, "He is the Alpha and the Omega, the beginning and the end; and in Him, and in His peace, and in His righteousness, we shall dwell forever. Amen, and amen."

26

From South to West

The western boundary of Les Chattes Bleues was Bayou du Chêne, as it lazed southward from the mighty Mississippi. Along this stretch of bayou, in one certain secret place, the waters widened into a sluggish pond, and the banks flattened out into a beach of rich black delta dirt instead of noncommittal beige sand. One day the bayou would reclaim this flatland, as sure as the sun rises; the banks behind the beach rose up, wooded and green and strong, and one day the bayou would slowly creep up to this barrier again. But meanwhile Elyse Buckingham often visited this place, and walked barefooted in the cool dirt, and watched the bayou in its eternal course.

"That's where she is, sure enough," Gowan Ford told himself. No one had told him that Elyse was at the Brown Beach, as the two of them had named it, but Gowan just knew she was. Most of the time he just knew where Elyse was, and what she was doing.

He dawdled along, kicking clods of dirt, muttering to himself and glowering at the beetles and grasshoppers that hastened out of the way of his wayward boots. Once he jammed his hand into the pocket of his breeches, and when he looked down at himself, he grinned satirically. "A one-armed fool, stumbling along with his only hand in his pocket, on a fool's errand," he told the sweet morning air. "But for sure I know this is the good Lord's will. And if I have to be a pure fool because He says so, so be it."

He made his way, slowly but inevitably, to Brown Beach. As he climbed the small rise he hesitated at the crown, intending to search up and down the low ground for Elyse.

But she was right below him, her skirt hem dripping, her feet bare. She was humming as she walked with exquisite slowness, her face turned toward the secret dark expanse of water spread out beside her.

A twelve-foot alligator stalked along behind her.

Gowan Ford stopped, his single eye wide, his mind struggling to comprehend the picture. Elyse was strolling along, humming; the alligator was most definitely following her. It was a huge beast, its gait prehistorically clumsy on its stubby land-legs as it waddled along, its tail waving a counterpoint behind it.

But Gowan Ford knew that an alligator could move with murderous speed when it took the notion, even on dry land.

"Elyse!" he yelled hoarsely, and then found his paralyzed legs and started running.

Elyse looked up at him, startled, and froze in her tracks. The alligator kept walking in a straight line toward her.

Gowan Ford's powerful legs pumped; he reached her; in a frantic moment his mind agonized because he couldn't sweep her into his arms, as he desperately wished to do. . . .

But Gowan Ford had always made amends for his lost arm, and he did so now, with great efficiency. He bent at the waist, aimed his shoulder at Elyse's midsection, and rammed into her. When he stood he was still running, Elyse was neatly bent over his shoulder, and his hand steadied her behind her knees. Desperately he ran, not daring to look back to see if the great lizard was running after him.

He reached the top of the rise, in a grove of cypress trees, and stopped, panting and groaning with exertion and fear. Elyse was curiously still—not kicking or beating his back with her fists or screeching at him to put her down, as Ford had expected she would, from the shock if nothing else.

"Gowan? Is this as far as we're going?" came her calm, though slightly muffled, voice.

"Leave it to you to say something that doesn't make any sense!" he raged, thumping her down to the ground. But, as usual, Tante Elyse bounced lightly on her feet.

Smoothing her skirt, she maintained, "I thought it a perfectly reasonable question. To begin with, certainly."

"You . . . you . . . there was an alligator about to eat you alive, Elyse!" Gowan barked. "You . . . you . . . should be scared, woman!"

"But I'm not," she said sweetly. "Besides, you rescued me. And also besides, it was just Sheba, you know. She was just walking along, minding her own business."

"No! No, Elyse! That was an alligator! A twelve-foot alligator!" Ford snarled desperately. "And her name is not Sheba!"

"Oh? Whatever is her name, then?" Elyse asked, wide-eyed.

"Stop it, Elyse!" Ford thundered. "I have a serious question to ask you, and you just stop putting on that silly act with me!"

"But, Gowan—" she began, but, with the impulsiveness of a desperate, doomed man, Ford ignored her and continued on his course.

He threw himself down on one knee and took Elyse's hand in his. "I love you!" he bawled defensively. "I always have, all my life! Will you marry me?"

Elyse looked down at him; her youthful eyes grew moist, her lips grew soft, and her voice sounded as sweet and kind as the first gentle spring breeze. "Oh, Gowan . . ." She fell to her knees and threw her arms around his shoulders. "I thought you'd never, never ask!"

★　★　★　★

"Cheney, thank you for coming here," Dev said with his customary formality. "I would not have been quite so stubbornly insistent on waiting until we were here to talk, but I really must be certain that we can speak in absolute privacy."

Cheney looked around the pleasant, cool shade of the gazebo by the lagoon. It was quiet, with only the sounds of the morning calls of birds. A gentle mist rose from the still waters, curling frothily as it joined the pure air. "It's lovely here, Dev," she said warmly. "As if I would mind coming down here with you!"

The gazebo had three wooden lawn chairs on one side of the pathway through it, and a small bench on the other side. Cheney and Dev sat close together; she watched him curiously, but he stared down at the well-beaten dirt pathway that led to the great oaks of La Maison des Chattes Bleues.

"Cheney, I love you, and your parents, more than my own life," he said simply, raising his eyes to meet hers.

"Yes, of course, Mother and Father and I know that, Dev," Cheney replied, rather puzzled. "And you know that we all love you just as much."

He stared at her, searching her face, looking deep into her eyes, as if he sought an answer to an unspoken question. Cheney waited, with curiosity and a touch of impatience. Normally Dev was much more direct, more decisive.

But Devlin Buchanan was not hesitant with indecision. The simple truth was that when he looked at Cheney, and heard her voice as she spoke of the love she had for him, it was as if it were the first time he had heard her. He suddenly knew that Cheney Duvall did, indeed, love him, and always would; but he also knew, undoubtedly, that she was no more *in* love with him than he was with her. It made him choose his words carefully, so that she could see, as he did, so clearly.

"Cheney, dear, I have made a terrible mistake," he said gently. "For years, I thought that we should—must—marry. I was wrong. But in my arrogance I refused to acknowledge that my long-time plans should go awry"—he smiled awkwardly—"and I refused to let you tell me this, even though I do believe, now, that you have tried, in your own way."

Cheney caught her breath, and her eyes widened with shock. "But . . . but, Dev," she stammered, "are . . . are you saying that you don't want to marry me?"

Dev's eyes creased with sorrow. "Yes, Cheney, I am. I am truly sorry. I would never purposely hurt you, but through my arrogance I have done just that. And it grieves me."

Cheney stared at him, her mind whirling desperately. Dev met her eyes without flinching, though his pain clearly showed.

"I . . . I . . . d-don't know what to say," she murmured almost inaudibly.

"I know," Dev said comfortably. "Let's just sit here for a while. You can gather your thoughts and decide what you need to say to me. . . ."

"Th-thank you, Dev," Cheney said, still confused and distressed.

The sun rose higher, and the first slivers of light touched the edges of the bayou. Golden faerie-lights danced upon the sleeping waters; Cheney stared at them, her eyes enjoying the sight while her mind stumbled along. Dev settled back, crossed one leg over his knee, and slid his arm comfortably along the back of the seat. Occasionally he patted Cheney's shoulders affectionately.

Dev doesn't want to marry me, she kept repeating dully to herself. *He . . . said . . . he's made a mistake . . . a terrible mistake. . . .*

After Cheney's active mind grew weary with this litany, her natural strength and common sense began to take over. *Dev loves me*, she thought, as if it were a sudden revelation. *He's always loved me, and he loves me now just as much as he ever did . . . and I love him, and always will. . . . What's changed? What's the earth-shattering difference here?*

Perhaps my pride has been bruised? Perhaps my heart is not bleeding dismally, but my ego is?

Cheney turned these thoughts—painful as they were—over and

over in her mind, analyzing them, compartmentalizing them, making a decision to let her silly pride go hang, and let her ego go with her pride. She loved Dev, and he loved her, and would do anything—anything!—for her. As she, and her father, and her mother would do for him.

Although to Cheney it seemed only a few moments, Dev sat, patiently waiting, watching Cheney's expressive face as it changed from moment to moment, from thought to thought. *She knows, she sees*, he thought exultantly. *I was ready to take a beating if she chose—I deserve it—but bless her, she knows!*

"Dev, I understand perfectly," Cheney said quietly, turning to him and taking his strong, slender hands in hers. "And you're right! You're absolutely, positively right! Oh, how glad I am that we didn't make a horrid, irrevocable mistake!"

"You don't have to be quite so happy that you don't have to marry me," Dev teased. He knew Cheney well enough to realize that she was ready for lightness.

"I'm going to tell everyone that I refused to marry you," Cheney sniffed. "I shall never admit that you threw me over."

"Fine with me," Dev said with relief. "I deserve worse."

"Yes, you do," Cheney said with a smile. "For not talking to me earlier. Last year, before you left Manhattan, you . . . you . . . ?" Suddenly her face grew somber and she asked, almost as if she asked herself, "Did you know . . . then? Did you . . . realize it then . . . because of . . ."

Dev frowned and again looked his usual stern self. Cheney looked at him accusingly. "Dev, are you in love with . . . someone else?"

"Yes, I am, Cheney," he answered instantly. "I was about to tell you that, because even though I didn't exactly believe that we were . . . meant for each other . . . still, I had asked you to marry me, and I thought . . . until just a few days ago, I thought . . ."

"Dev, I know exactly what you thought," Cheney said impatiently. "I've known you all my life. But what I want to know is, who is this lady that you've fallen in love with, in spite of all your best-laid life plans?"

"I must ask you to forgive me, Cheney," Dev said firmly. "I cannot tell you that, because I haven't spoken to the lady. I don't think I should . . . speak of her in such a private manner until I have."

Cheney laughed with delight. "Oh, Dev! Really, you are entirely too proper and staid and correct for me! How did we ever think we should get married and try to live with each other for the rest of our lives?"

"Because we do truly love each other," Dev said gravely. "And although we are not meant to be husband and wife, Cheney, I will love you with all my heart—forever."

Cheney grew serious, too, though her eyes still sparkled with joy. "And I, too, love you, Dev. Always."

Half an hour later Devlin Buchanan could be seen pounding on the door of the bedroom known as the Amethyst Room on the second-floor gallery of La Maison des Chattes Bleues. The door opened, and Zhou-Zhou stepped outside; then she was hastily yanked back inside as Devlin Buchanan, M.D.—all staidness and properness and correctness aside—hauled her inside the room with him. He did, as his undeniable tendency toward propriety demanded, leave the door open. He did not stay very long, only minutes, perhaps, and he hurried back out onto the gallery. But Victoria de Lancie flew out onto the landing and gave him a joyous, clinging hug. For once Devlin Buchanan, M.D., bore up under such public display very well.

★ ★ ★ ★

Tante Marye sat at the head of the dining room table. On her right sat Richard, Irene, Gowan Ford, and Elyse. On her left sat Shiloh, Cheney, Dev, and Victoria. Tante Marye was very happy with these so-satisfactory seating arrangements since both Dev and Gowan Ford had come to their senses, and now Gowan sat at his rightful place by her sister's side.

The only odd things about this tranquil picture were the hole gaping in the dining room floor, where the black tile was missing; the gleaming, glowing gold bar on the table; and the two kittens—one white, one black—playing underneath the table with Tante Marye's shoe.

"Ouch!" she exclaimed and reached down to shoo the kittens away.

"I can't believe you like cats," Elyse said mournfully. "You never told me!"

"You never asked," Tante Marye answered haughtily.

"I can't believe this thing," Shiloh muttered, his eyes on the heavy glowing rectangle that was the centerpiece of the bare table. "It's really something, isn't it?" He reached out to hold it again—the entire table had passed it around twice already. It was so heavy for its size, and the yellow color was so pure and bright. The stamp of the de Cheyne crest was intricately detailed, finely finished.

"I must say it has a strange beauty," Tante Marye admitted. "Quite apart from its worth, it is a beautiful object."

"God made gold, too." Shiloh shrugged as he replaced the heavy gold bar in the center of the table. "Nothing wrong with admiring it. It's just another one of His decorations, you know."

"That's true," Cheney said, eyeing Shiloh curiously. "But it's odd to hear you say it, Shiloh."

"Why?" he asked guilelessly. "Miss Behring told me that. Miss Tanzen Behring."

"Wise woman," Richard commented, but he was looking at his wife.

"Give me that," Tante Elyse commanded, and Gowan Ford handed her the gold bar. With an effort she lifted it twice, as if to judge the heft of it. "I'd like to take this thing to town and bash John Law over the head with it."

"I'll do it for you," Shiloh volunteered eagerly.

"He would, too," Cheney muttered.

"Aside from head-bashing, what are we going to do about him?" Dev asked Richard.

"We have no proof of his involvement," Richard said with resignation. "Just Corbett's vague recollection that Dédé once mentioned a powerful man, a lawyer, who would see to it that Corbett and his sisters would be awarded full legal recognition of their parentage and their rights to La Maison des Chattes Bleues. So the only proof we have the slightest chance of getting is if Dédé or Marie Laveau should confess and testify against him."

"Those *vaudou* persons will never do that," Tante Marye said with ladylike disdain.

Richard sighed and absently picked up the gold bar, turning it end over end in his hands as if it were a mud brick he had decided to fidget with. Irene and Cheney exchanged amused smiles. "I just don't know," he said thoughtfully. "I don't see how we can ever gather enough evidence to charge him with anything, much less evidence that would convict him."

Victoria cleared her throat delicately. "I have a suggestion, Colonel Duvall. I don't think there is any legal action we can take for the conspiracy here at Les Chattes Bleues. But I happen to know that John

Law is involved in fraud, and I can prove it." She glanced at Dev for affirmation, and he smiled warmly at her and leaned just a tiny bit closer to her.

"Hmm? What?" Richard asked alertly.

"John Law is . . . not John Law," Victoria stated. "That is, he is most certainly not a descendant of the Scottish financier who began the colony of *Nouvelle-Orléans.* That John Law's line ended with his grandson, who died in infancy. I happen to know this because my father's family is distantly related to the Laws. But to be absolutely certain, I wired my father and asked him for confirmation. I received it . . . yesterday . . . or the day before. I forget."

"You've been so ill," Dev said protectively, "and so much has happened."

Cheney rolled her eyes in mock disgust at Shiloh, who grinned in genial agreement. Irene smiled fleetingly as she observed them, and Tante Elyse poked Gowan Ford in the ribs.

"Hunh," he grunted.

"Stop making such disagreeable noises, Gowan," Tante Elyse said with splendid disregard for the cause of such noises. Gowan Ford said nothing, as he had long ago discovered that beginning a discussion of such matters with Elyse generally took a long time to conclude.

"That is indeed fraud," Richard said thoughtfully, unaware of all the little signals buzzing around him. "But I'm not certain that I would wish to publicly destroy a man's reputation—no matter how well-deserved—for revenge."

"I will," Shiloh again magnanimously volunteered. Now Cheney jammed him in the ribs. "Ow!" he scowled. "You sure got some sharp elbows, Doc!"

"Sharp tongue, too," Dev muttered.

"Sharp wit, I say," Cheney pronounced grandly. "Sharper than either one of you two. Two—men. Two—wits. Two's."

"Why are you talking about tutus, Cheney?" Tante Elyse demanded. "I seem to have lost the thread of the conversation."

"Me, too," Richard sighed.

"It's all right, dear," Irene said with a stern glance at Cheney. "They aren't talking about anything sensible anyway."

"Oh, good," Tante Elyse murmured.

Richard Duvall continued the previous—sensible—conversation, even if he only talked, and answered, himself. "I shall go to John Law and have a talk with him. I will tell him what I know about his part in the conspiracy here at Les Chattes Bleues, and I will tell him that I know of his fraudulent claims to his identity."

"Can I go with you?" Shiloh asked, half-joking.

"Yes," Richard said instantly, his eyes alight. "I think Mr. Law would be . . . impressed with your particular powers of persuasion, Shiloh."

"Head-bashing?" Victoria asked coolly.

"No, not that," Richard replied hastily. "But I'll tell Mr. John Law, Esquire, that if he doesn't pack up and leave New Orleans that I shall be obliged to press charges against him. Even if I can't get him convicted in court, his fraud will be exposed."

"So what do I get to do?" Shiloh asked with mock disappointment. "I don't even get to tell him all that stuff?"

"No," Richard said firmly. "It's my decision, Shiloh, and my responsibility. But"—he grinned like a young boy—"you get to tell him that you'll make sure he leaves town. Personally."

"Hey, I can do that," Shiloh said with satisfaction. "I'll be glad to handle that part of it—personally."

"Don't kill him," Cheney said seriously.

"Cheney, you are impudent," Tante Marye put in. "Of course Mr. Irons won't kill him. Will you?" she finished crisply.

"No, ma'am," Shiloh promised.

"See?" Tante Marye said triumphantly to Cheney, who sighed helplessly.

"But what about those *vaudou* persons?" Tante Elyse said glumly. "We have no proof against them, either."

"We have Corbett's testimony," Richard said hesitantly. "But to tell the truth, I don't believe it would do much good. I think that since Corbett actually sabotaged the crop, he would stand trial for that alone. Adah knew about everything; though she was too timid to actually commit any crime, she would most certainly be found guilty along with Corbett. And Chloe . . ." Richard shook his head regretfully.

"She would hang, wouldn't she?" Victoria asked quietly. "After all, she was the one who actually poisoned these people. And some of them were white people."

"Yes," Ford said sorrowfully. "They'd hang her within a month. And I don't think anyone would be interested in her defense—which means that I doubt if anyone would even bother to question Dédé, and certainly not Marie Laveau."

"But those people are nothing but common criminals!" Cheney cried. "And their cult practices are demonic!"

Ford explained patiently, "Yes, Miss Cheney, we know that. But, as we were just discussing, we have absolutely no proof of the actual conspiracy, except the word of a young boy with pitiful delusions of grandeur and a silly love-smitten little girl. And as for the *vaudou* and their infernal worship, you must understand; here in New Orleans, the *vaudou* are dismissed as harmless entertainers, like magicians and sword-swallowers at a fair. Their *gris-gris* and charms and amulets and potions are viewed with amused indulgence by most white people."

"That's wrong!" Cheney insisted. "Even if we hadn't been subjected to—the things we have—from them, people should be more aware of exactly what it is they are countenancing when they think such things are merely harmless parlor tricks."

"That's very true, Cheney." Richard nodded. "But the only way we can fight such evil is to insist upon speaking the truth, even when people scoff at us."

"But, Richard," Tante Elyse said with gentle dismay, "how will we speak the truth about Dédé and the *vaudou*, and demand justice, when it will almost certainly result in Molly and Monroe's children being arrested . . . and in little Chloe being—" She shuddered.

Gowan Ford awkwardly patted her hand. "I do wish the *vaudou* could be arrested and stand a fair trial, but I don't see how that's going to happen. I must say, though, that I think they received a more severe punishment the other night, because they saw just a few moments of God's wrath. If that didn't reform them, then nothing will."

"That's true," Richard said quietly. "I, personally, am satisfied with their punishment." Everyone except Shiloh murmured in agreement.

"But about 'little Chloe,'" Shiloh snorted. "You didn't see her the other night. You didn't see the real Chloe, like I—like we have, Mrs. Buckingham."

Tante Elyse still looked distressed, and Tante Marye glanced at her with an instant of sympathy. Then Tante Marye said frostily, "It may be true that Elyse doesn't understand Chloe, but you may be assured that I do. Even though I haven't known the nature and extent of her sins, I have understood Chloe for a long time." Her faded blue eyes flashed with stubbornness. "The difference now is that Molly and particularly Monroe see her as she really is. I have full confidence that Monroe can control his own household and bring up his children with discipline and love."

"That's a noble, generous sentiment, Mrs. Edwards," Shiloh growled. "Considering she tried to poison half the people on the place. I think that the little minx oughta be shackled to a keeper until she's thirty!"

"Actually she does have a keeper," Tante Elyse ventured. "I think it will work out for all the good. . . ."

"And who's got that thankless job?" Shiloh said belligerently.

"Luna," Tante Elyse replied. "She said that Chloe reminds her of herself at that age . . . although I don't believe Luna ever actually poisoned anyone. And Molly and Monroe have forbidden Chloe to set foot in La Maison des Chattes Bleues . . . although Gowan did warn her not to set foot *off* of Les Chattes Bleues."

"Elyse, talk sense!" Ford growled. "Please," he added begrudgingly.

"Gowan!" she sparkled. "How nice! You said 'please'!"

"You'll civilize him yet, Tante Elyse," Cheney teased.

"I think it will take thirty or forty years," Elyse said slyly. "But I shall try very hard to shorten his initial training period to twenty-five."

Everyone laughed, and Victoria and Dev exchanged warm glances.

Irene smiled gently at them but turned to Richard and prompted him. "Go on, Richard. Tell them of the decisions you and Mr. Ford and *mes tantes* have made regarding Chloe."

"Huh?" he asked, puzzled. "Were we talking about that?"

"Yes, dear."

"Oh yes," he said hastily. "Anyway, she is forbidden to wait upon Marye and Elyse in any way, and Monroe went a step further and told her that it would be at least a year before she even set foot in the house again. So Luna offered to take her under her wing, as it were, and teach her how to make indigo." He grimaced. "It's hard, taxing work, but I believe that Luna will be fair."

"And I have told Chloe that if she so much as sets one little toe off of Les Chattes Bleues land without strict supervision, I'm going to immediately contact the authorities and have her arrested," Ford grunted. "And if the story of certain people at Les Chattes Bleues falling ill should leak out in the confusion—so be it!"

"And how is 'little Chloe' taking all these suggestions?" Shiloh demanded.

Ford grinned his lion's grin. "She's scared."

"That's good," Shiloh stated. "But watch her."

"There are twenty-nine people on this place who watch her every move now," Ford grunted, "and she knows it."

"Speaking of twenty-nine people, how long will all of you be staying?" Tante Elyse asked innocently.

"Elyse!" Marye snapped. "That's quite rude!"

"Why?"

"Because . . . because . . . oh, never mind!"

"All right," Elyse said agreeably.

Ford declared with exasperation, "She doesn't want anyone to leave, you know. Ever. Don't pay any attention to what she says. Ever."

"No, that's not quite true," Elyse stated with certainty.

"What?" Ford demanded. "Which is not quite true, Elyse?"

"That's right," she said with maddening sincerity, "I don't ever want any of you to leave, which is quite true. And I certainly want you to stay for our wedding, which is to be next Sunday."

Cries of "Certainly!" "How wonderful!" "Congratulations, Ford!" and feminine giggles and teasing rang out happily in the dining room. The men shook hands all around; Richard Duvall called for a toast to the bride and groom; the ladies all gathered around Tante Elyse to kiss her and tease her. She blushed like a young girl!

After Tante Marye had served lemonade all around, and they had toasted the happy couple, they settled back down at the dining table.

"No one answered my question," Tante Elyse persisted.

"Elyse, you didn't ask anyone a question," Ford mumbled.

Grandly ignoring him she continued, "Will everyone please promise to stay for our wedding, at least?"

"Of course, Irene and I would love to," Richard promised.

Tante Elyse turned to stare threateningly at Dev. "You can't leave, Dev. Not now. Not since you and Mrs. de Lancie have fallen so desperately in love, and she is staying."

"Tante Elyse!" Dev growled, his coloring a deep pink. "I . . . we . . . haven't made any sort of . . . plans, and certainly not a formal announcement . . . or pronouncement . . ."

Cheney laughed richly. "Oh, Dev, how typical! Do you really believe that all of us here don't know what's going on with you and Victoria? I mean, you've gone to everyone at this table and apologized to them for deciding not to bully me into marrying you!" Hastily she added, "Except for Shiloh, that is." She was teasing Shiloh and glanced at him mischievously—but Cheney was startled to see that Shiloh looked nonplussed.

"No, I did in fact owe him an apology and an explanation concerning my relationship with you, Cheney," Dev said stiffly. "And I duly made them to him."

"Duly?" Cheney repeated rather stupidly. "Duly?"

"Is that a word?" Tante Elyse wondered.

Cheney frowned, the "I-want" lines between her eyebrows deep and determined. "And what, exactly, kind of explanation did you owe him—about me—and you—and things—Dev?"

"I don't like it when people talk about me like I'm not in the room when I'm here," Shiloh said decisively.

"No one's talking about you! We're talking about me!" Cheney snapped.

"Yes, Cheney, are you going to stay here for my wedding?" Tante Elyse said out of the heavens, as it were, with utter disregard for the entire course of the conversation.

"H-huh?" Cheney stuttered.

"Ladies never say huh, Cheney," Tante Marye said primly. "They politely ask their conversational partner to repeat the question."

Cheney deflated, her high temper dissolving in the air of suppressed amusement in the room. With a quick glance at everyone around the table, and an exaggerated air of delicate distress, she rested her head on her hand and murmured, "Yes, Tante Marye. Would one— any one—of my conversational partners please repeat the question?"

Tante Elyse giggled, and then everyone smiled at Cheney's antics. With sparkling eyes she looked up and said, "Yes, Tante Elyse, I would love to stay for your wedding. Especially since I don't know where to go when I leave here." Unintentionally Cheney shot a tentative glance at Shiloh, but he merely smiled.

Richard and Irene looked at each other; Victoria and Dev exchanged guilty glances. Finally, after a long awkward pause, Irene sighed and said, "Mrs. de Lancie? Have you mentioned to Cheney that you had so kindly considered a possible position for her at your hospital?"

Cheney's mouth dropped, and she turned to look at Victoria accusingly. "Your hospital? What hospital?"

Victoria, who was looking particularly animated already, actually blushed. Cheney was further astounded; she had never seen Victoria Elizabeth Steen de Lancie blush. It made her look ten years younger; in fact, the bloom of Victoria's delicate skin, the sparkle in her cornflower-blue eyes, the animation in her gestures, were quite unlike any Victoria Cheney had ever seen before.

No, that's not exactly true, Cheney thought fleetingly. *She's still the same Victoria . . . only before she was . . . guarded, artificial—always in public. Now she's more open, more . . . free. Strange, considering that she is now bound to someone . . . Dev . . . forever.*

But the thoughts passed as Victoria answered, "Cheney, I had . . . considered . . . this possibility before, when you said that you would like to work in a small hospital, especially when you said that if you could find a position where you would be accepted and given at least the same chance as any other physician." She kept glancing worriedly at Dev, who stroked his mustache nervously.

"Victoria," Cheney repeated slowly, "what . . . hospital?"

"It's not really my hospital, you know," Victoria hedged. Blushing deeply again, she dropped her head and murmured, "Oh! This is so very awkward!"

"I know, Victoria," Dev said sympathetically. "But go ahead. Cheney's . . . fine, you know."

"What!" Cheney almost shouted. "I do declare, you two are made for each other! What in the world is so embarrassing, may I ask?"

"Not embarrassing," Dev corrected her meticulously. "Awkward. Because of me—of us—that is, of Victoria and . . . me . . . and you . . ."

"I almost wish Tante Elyse were telling this," Cheney muttered, which made everyone laugh, including Tante Elyse.

Victoria took a deep breath, then leaned over so she could look directly at Cheney. "I do so love you, Cheney dear. And I had checked into a possible position for you at a hospital where my father is on the Board of Directors, and they are willing—no, even eager—to offer you a staff position. But at the time I was considering going with you, you see . . . and now it might seem that I'm trying to . . . um . . . get you out of the picture, I suppose."

Cheney smiled warmly at her and reached all the way across Dev to hold out her hand to Victoria. "No one in this room—especially me—would think that of you, Victoria. I promise you that I wish you and Dev the best, with all my heart. All of us here feel the same way."

Victoria held on to Cheney's hand tightly, and for a fleeting moment Dev laid his hand on theirs and squeezed lightly. Then he sat up stiff and erect and proper in his chair, and Victoria returned to her ladylike posture. "Well, then," she continued calmly, "if you are interested, Cheney, I can put you in touch with this hospital, and you can consider it."

"That's fine, Victoria. But—where—is—this—wonderful—hospital?" she emphasized irritably.

"Oh yes." Victoria smiled. "It's in San Francisco, California."

Cheney's head swiveled stiffly, slowly around to stare at Shiloh accusingly. His eyes were alight, his mouth turned up in a delighted grin. With mock fear he leaned back and threw both hands up in an "I surrender" gesture. "Huh-uh, Doc. Don't even look at me like that! I didn't say a word to anyone but you and your father!"

"You stomped around here for two days telling everyone you were going to San Francisco!" Cheney fumed.

"What?" Victoria exclaimed in genuine surprise. "Cheney, I had no idea! Honestly!"

"I didn't know Irons was going to San Francisco," Dev said helpfully.

"Neither did I," Tante Elyse offered.

"Oh yes, you most certainly did," Tante Marye argued. "We sat right here in this dining room and talked about Mr. Irons and Gowan going to Mexico."

"No, it was in the parlor," Tante Elyse declared. "Where we talked about it, that is. Not where Mr. Irons and Cheney are going."

"I'm not going to Mexico!" Cheney blustered.

"Neither is Gowan," Tante Elyse reminded him sweetly, but he was laughing too hard to take much notice of her.

"It's San Francisco," Shiloh reminded Cheney sincerely. "We're going to San Francisco. You and me, I mean. Not me and Mr. Ford."

"Stop!" Cheney shouted. When all the noise and laughter died down, she turned to her mother and father. "Did you know, Father? Did you realize, Mother?"

"Of course, dear." Irene smiled.

"Did I know what?" Richard asked in bewilderment.

Irene patted his hand. "I'll explain later, dear."

"So you wouldn't disapprove, Colonel Duvall? Miss Irene?" Shiloh asked casually, though his expression as he watched them was quite intent.

"Nia is quite a sufficient chaperone," Irene told him quietly. "And by now Richard and I are quite accustomed to the thought of you and Cheney working together, which, obviously, often means traveling together."

"Yes, I do agree with that," Richard said with sudden comprehension.

"And I must admit I do feel much better about Cheney traveling with an escort," Irene admitted. "It's completely acceptable when she is chaperoned."

"I completely agree with that," Richard said with relief.

"I also agree," Tante Marye said imperiously, as if that put the final seal of approval on the arrangement. Which, in a way, it did.

Shiloh turned to Cheney and grinned delightedly, which automatically made Cheney smile back. "You know, since I was such a dismal bodyguard here, Doc, and got into so much trouble, I was kinda hoping that you'd escort me to San Francisco. And Nia is a good chaperone for me."

Cheney laughed. "An adequate chaperone for you, Shiloh Irons, does not exist. But I'll be happy to escort you to San Francisco and try to keep a watch out for you. Little Nia is turning out to be a quite capable nurse, but I don't think she can keep you under control."

"Maybe not," Shiloh murmured with satisfaction, "but you sure can. So thanks, Doc."

"Shiloh," she said, her eyes shining, "it is my pleasure. Always."